THE SHIRT ON HIS BACK

*The new 'Benjamin January' novel
from the best-selling author*

Abishag Shaw is seeking vengeance for his brother's murder and Benjamin January is seeking money after his bank crashes. Far beyond the frontier, in the depths of the Rocky Mountains, both are to be found at the great Rendezvous of the Mountain Men: a month-long orgy of cheap booze, shooting-matches, tall tales and cut-throat trading. But at the rendezvous, the discovery of a corpse opens the door to hints of a greater plot, of madness and wholesale murder...

*The Benjamin January Series
from Barbara Hambly*

**DEAD AND BURIED
THE SHIRT ON HIS BACK**

THE SHIRT ON HIS BACK

A Benjamin January Novel

Barbara Hambly

Severn House Large Print
London & New York

This first large print edition published 2012
in Great Britain and the USA by
SEVERN HOUSE PUBLISHERS LTD of
9-15 High Street, Sutton, Surrey, SM1 1DF.
First world regular print edition published 2011 by
Severn House Publishers Ltd., London and New York.

British Library Cataloguing in Publication Data

Hambly, Barbara.
   The shirt on his back. -- (The Benjamin January series)
   1. January, Benjamin (Fictitious character)--Fiction.
   2. Private investigators--Fiction. 3. Free African
   Americans--Fiction. 4. Murder--Investigation--Rocky
   Mountains--Fiction. 5. Rocky Mountains--Social
   conditions--19th century--Fiction. 6. Detective and
   mystery stories. 7. Large type books.
   I. Title II. Series
   813.6-dc23

   ISBN-13: 978-0-7278-9890-6

Severn House Publishers support The Forest Stewardship Council
[FSC], the leading international forest certification organisation. All
our titles that are printed on Greenpeace-approved FSC-certified paper
carry the FSC logo.

MIX
Paper from
responsible sources
FSC® C018575

Printed and bound in Great Britain by the
MPG Books Group, Bodmin, Cornwall.

For Victoria

PROLOGUE

March, 1837

The third time that day that Benjamin January walked over to the Bank of Louisiana and found its doors locked, he had to admit the truth.

It wasn't going to reopen.

The money was gone.

Admittedly, there hadn't been much money in the account. Early the previous summer he'd taken most of it and paid off everything he and Rose still owed on the big ramshackle old house on Rue Esplanade, and *thank God*, he thought, *I had the wits to do that...*

Even then, there'd been rumors that the smaller banks, the wildcat banks, the private banks all over the twenty-six states were closing. Months before the election last Fall the President's refusal to re-charter the Bank of the United States had begun to pull down businesses along with the banks, and at meetings of the Faubourg Tremé Free Colored Militia and Burial Society – or less formal get-togethers with his friends after playing all night for the white folks at some Mardi Gras ball – January had frequently asked: what the hell did the Democrats think was going to happen, when they knocked the foundations out from under the only source of stable credit in the country?

Not that it was any of January's business, or that of his friends either. As descendants of Africans, at one remove or another – though January's mother loftily avoided the subject – not one of them could vote. And in New Orleans, by virtue of its position as Queen of the Mississippi Valley trade, the illusion of prosperity had hung on longer than elsewhere.

Still, standing in the sharp spring sunlight of Rue Royale before the shut doors of that gray granite building, January felt the waves of rage pass over him like the wind-driven crescents of rain on the green face of a bayou in hurricane season.

Rage at the outgoing President – a fine warrior when the country had needed a warrior and a hopelessly bigoted old blockhead with a planter's contempt for such things as banks.

Rage at the whites who saw only the war hero and not the consequences of letting land-grabbers and shoestring speculators run the country for their own profit.

Rage at the laws of the land, that wouldn't let him – or anyone whose father or grandparents or great-grandparents back to Adam had hailed from Africa – have the slightest voice in the government of the country in which they'd been born, regardless of the fact that he, Benjamin January, was a free man and a property owner ... Artisans like his brother-in-law Paul Corbier, merchants like Fortune Gérard who sat on community boards, his fellow musicians and the surgeon who'd taught him his trade of medicine, and all those others who made up his life, were free men too, had been *born* free men and had fought a British invading force in order to stay that way...

And rage at himself – the deepest anger of all as he turned his steps back along Rue Royale toward home. For not taking every silver dime out of the bank and putting it...

Where?

Ay, there's the rub, reflected January grimly. There were thieves aplenty in New Orleans, and if you were keeping more than a few dollars cached in your attic rafters, or under the floorboards of your bedroom, word of it soon got out. And if you didn't happen to be rich enough that there were servants around your house at all times, that money was eventually going to turn up gone.

He wasn't the only man standing in Rue Royale looking at the closed-up doors of the Bank of Louisiana that spring afternoon. As he turned away, Crowdie Passebon caught his eye – the well-respected perfumer and the center of the libré community in the old French Town. Like most of January's friends and neighbors, Passebon was the descendant of those French and Spanish whites who'd had the decency to free the children their slave women had borne them. January knew Crowdie had a great deal more money than he did in the Bank, but nevertheless the perfumer crossed to him and asked, 'Are you all right, Ben?'

'I'll *be* all right.' Many people January knew – including most of his fellow musicians – didn't even have the slim resources of a house.

Petronius Braeden – a German dentist with offices on Rue St Louis – was haranguing a knot of other white men outside the bank doors, cursing the new President: *hell, the man has only been in office a week, and see what he done to the country already? We need Old Hickory back...*

As if it wasn't 'Old Hickory' who'd precipitated the whole mess and left it for his successor to clean up.

January walked on, shaking his head and wondering what the hell he and his beautiful Rose were going to do.

It had been a bad winter. Tightening credit and the plunge in the value of banks' paper money meant that fewer white French Creoles – and far fewer Americans – had given large entertainments, even at Christmas and Twelfth Night. January, whose skill on the piano usually guaranteed him work every night of the week from first frost 'til Easter, had found himself many nights at home. The same spiral of rising prices and fewer loans had prompted many of the well-off white gentlemen who had sent their daughters 'from the shady side of the street' to board and be educated at the school that Rose operated in the big Spanish house, to write Rose letters deeply regretting that Germaine or Sabine or Alice would not be returning to the school this winter, and *we wish you all the best of luck...*

And we're surely going to need it.

10

Other well-off families – both white and *gens de couleur libré* – had decided that Mama or Aunt Unmarriageable would be perfectly able to take over teaching the children the mysteries of the piano, rather than hiring Benjamin January to do so at fifty cents a lesson. The last of them had broken this news to January the previous week.

Since early summer, January had been hiding part of what earnings he did make here and there about the house – in the rafters, under the floor-boards ... But summer was the starving-time for musicians, the time when you lived off the proceeds of last year's Mardi Gras. The little money he'd made from lessons, January had fallen into the habit of spending on groceries, so as not to touch the slender reserve in the bank.

In the God-damned locked-doors Lucifer-strike-you-all-with-lightning Bank of Louisiana, thank you very much.

Rose was sitting on the front gallery when he climbed the steps. She'd been quiet since the first time he'd walked to the bank that morning, for the week's grocery money. Sunday would be Palm Sunday, and once Easter was done, the planters who came into town for the winter, and the wealthier American businessmen, would begin leaving New Orleans. Subscription balls ordinarily continued up until April or May, but John Davis, who owned the Orleans Ballroom, had told January that this year he was closing down early. With the Bank of Louisiana out of business, January guessed that the American Opera House – where he was supposed to play

11

next week – would follow suit.

Rose met his eyes, reading in them what he'd found – yet again that day – on Rue Royale.

In her quiet, well-bred voice, she said, 'Well, damn,' put her spectacles back on and held up the letter that had been lying in her lap. 'Would you like the good news first, or the bad news?'

'I'd like this first.' January took the letter from her hand, dropped it to the rough-made little table at her side, stood her on her feet and kissed her: slender, gawky, with a sprinkle of freckles over the bridge of her nose and the gray-hazel eyes so often found among the free colored. Though she stood as tall as many men, against his six-foot-three bulk she felt delicate, like a sapling birch. 'You're here sitting on the gallery of our house. No bad news can erase that; no good news can better it.'

She sighed and put her head briefly against his shoulder. He felt her bones relax into his arms.

'I take it that letter is from Jules Gardinier informing us that he's taking Cosette out of the school and sending her to live with her grand-mother?'

She leaned back, looked up into his face in mock wonderment: 'You must have second sight! And here Cosette was the only one of our pupils left to us—'

'And her father owns stock in the Bank of Louisiana.' January grinned crookedly. 'Which is going to be converted into a livery stable as soon as they can get up enough money to buy hay. What's the good news?'

Rose was silent for a moment, as if thinking

12

how to phrase an awkward question. Then she propped her spectacles more firmly on to the bridge of her nose, took a deep breath, looked up into his face again and said, 'We have two dollars and fifty cents in the house. And we're going to have a child.'

An hour later, with the street gone quiet in the dinner hour, they were still on the gallery talking. The two dollars and fifty cents was in hard coin, not the now-worthless notes from the Bank of Louisiana – or the various other banks in the town – in which January had been paid over the winter: 'They'll make good kindling,' said Rose in a comforting tone.

'That's not funny.'

'Nothing is,' replied Rose. 'Not today. Benjamin, I've spoken to your sister Olympe. If this—' She hesitated, then went on with some difficulty. 'If this isn't a good time for us to have a child—'

January cut her off firmly. 'It is.' Olympe was a voodoo-ienne, versed in the termination of unaffordable pregnancies among the poorer blacks of the town. He added, 'My mother won't let her grandchild starve.'

Rose mimed exaggerated surprise. 'Whatever gives you that idea?'

'Hmmn.' Since January and Rose had refused his mother's advice about investing their little money in slaves – *you can feed them dirt cheap and make a dollar a day renting them out to the logging companies* – that astute businesswoman had repeatedly asserted that it was none of her

13

business if her son and his wife starved together. January was fairly certain that this stricture would be expanded to include Baby Rose. Besides, the last he'd heard, his mother's money had been in the Bank of Louisiana, too.

'Something will turn up,' said Rose.

'Hmmn.'

He closed his eyes, wondering, as he had wondered all the way home, what the hell they were going to do. *Holy Mary, Mother of God ... Please have something turn up.*

When he opened his eyes, Lieutenant Abishag Shaw of the New Orleans City Guards was standing on the gallery.

'Lieutenant.' January got quickly to his feet, held out his hand, even as Shaw removed his greasy old excuse for a hat and bowed to Rose: 'M'am.'

As Shaw turned toward him, January thought that the man did not look well. It occurred to him to wonder if Shaw, too, had been among the unfortunates who'd discovered that morning that they'd lost everything they owned. Framed in his long, thin, light-brown hair, the Kentuckian's face had a strained tiredness to it, beyond what keeping the peace in New Orleans through Mardi Gras usually did to him. There was a slump to the raw-boned shoulders under the scarecrow coat and a distant look in his gray eyes, a reflection of bitterest pain. January had seen his friend take physical punishment that would have killed another man, but this was different, and he was moved to ask – as Crowdie Passebon had earlier asked him – 'Are you all

14

right?' He remembered to add, 'Sir,' even though his mother wouldn't have permitted Shaw into her house.

Shaw nodded – as if he weren't quite sure of the affirmative – and said, 'Maestro, I have a proposition for you.'

'I'll take it.'

The long mouth dipped a little at one corner: 'Don't you want to hear what it is?'

'Doesn't matter,' said January. 'If it's money, I'm your man.'

ONE

June 29, 1837

They crossed the ford mid-morning and came up out of the cottonwoods where the valley of the Green River spread out into a meadow of summer grass: it was their eighty-second day out from Independence. Abishag Shaw rode point on a hammer-headed gelding the color of old cheese, with a dozen half-breed French camp-setters in his wake. A line of mules laden with shot, trap springs, coffee, liquor, trade-vermillion and checked black-and-yellow cotton shirts from Lowell, Massachusetts at two thousand percent markup; fourteen remounts in various stages of homicidal orneriness; Hannibal Sefton sweating his way through his fifteenth case of the jitters since leaving the settlements; and January riding drag eating everyone's dust. Mountains rose west, east and north beyond a scumble of foothills: pinewoods, ravens, bare granite and a high, distant glimmer of snow. A few miles upriver the first camps could be glimpsed: makeshift mountaineers' shelters or handsome markees where the traders had set up shop. Westward from the river, Indian lodges grouped, hundreds of them gathered into a dozen

17

little villages, and horse herds browsed the buffalo grass under the charge of brown, naked children. Dogs' barks, sharp as gunshots, sounded in thin air blue with campfire smoke.

'That's it.' Shaw drew rein on the rise, spit tobacco into the long grass that edged the trail. 'Man what done it, he's someplace here.'

Shots rang out: men hunting in the hills on the other side of the river. Closer gunfire as they drew nearer the first of the shelters, men shooting at playing cards tacked to cottonwoods in the bottomland that lined the water. January knew the breed. He'd seen them, ferociously bearded with their long hair braided Indian-fashion, shirts faded colorless or glaring-new and rigid with starch, swaggering along Bourbon and Girod Streets with their long Pennsylvania rifles on their backs, visitors to the world he knew.

Now he was the visitor. They clustered around to greet the pack-train, holding out tin cups of liquor in welcome. On the trail from Independence January had mostly gotten over his surprise that white men would extend such hospitality to a black one – the rules changed, the farther you got beyond the frontier. It was a dubious honor at best: it was hands down the worst liquor January had ever tasted.

The trappers roared at the expression on his face, and one of them shouted good-naturedly, 'Now you had a gen–u–*ine* Green River Cocktail, pilgrim! Waugh! Welcome to the rendezvous!'

Shaw leaned from the saddle, greeting the men, but January wasn't fooled by his affability.

18

He saw the Lieutenant's pale eyes scan the bearded faces, seeking the man he'd come twenty-five hundred miles to kill.

The pack-train moved on along the river. Gil Wallach, of Ivy and Wallach Trading, had arrived before them, a small outfit – according to Shaw, on one of the three occasions between New Orleans and the South Pass that he'd spoken more than half a dozen words at a time – backed by men who'd once made up the Rocky Mountain Fur Company, before that organization had succumbed to the murderous business practices of the rival American Fur Company. A dozen of these smaller traders were camped along the river, between the military-looking establishments of the AFC and its rival, the British Hudson's Bay Company, peddling watered liquor to trappers in faded blanket coats and dickering fiercely over the price of beaver pelts. Just above the line where the ground sloped down to the bottomlands, a thin path had already been beaten into the grass, forming a sort of main street of the camp.

Mentally, January noted it all. Tents of canvas bleached by years of weather; cruder shelters, ranging from a few deer hides, to huts of pine and cottonwood boughs skilfully lashed with rawhide. Here and there a tipi, where a trapper had an Indian wife. When he'd gotten on the steamboat for Independence, Rose had handed him an empty notebook and told him to bring it back full.

'The only way I can keep from hating you for being able to go, when I can't,' she'd said softly, 'is to know you'll bring this back.' She was a scientist. January knew it was agony to her, to be left behind, to be shut out of the wonders of a world unglimpsed because she was a woman, and with child.

Four months now he'd been making notes for her: animals, birds, plants, rocks. On the nights when he'd felt he would go insane with longing for her, it had been a little – a very little – like touching her hand. Like Shakespeare's comic lovers, whispering devotion to one another through a crack in a wall.

In the dappled shade of the cottonwoods on the river side of the trail, traders had hung scale beams to weigh the furs: the men of business in neat black broadcloth to mark their status, or gayer hues if they were Mexicans up from Taos. Most were clean-shaven, as befit representatives of all that was best in nineteenth-century civiliz-ation. Most wore boots.

At six dollars a pound, the furs they weighed represented the whole of a man's work for a year.

June was ending. Some men had been here for weeks – others would still be coming in. For the trappers, it was more than just the only chance they'd have to sell their furs, or resupply themselves with gunpowder and fish hooks, lead and salt and sharpening stones. For many, it was the only occasion they'd have to talk to anyone in the language of the land they'd left behind, or to see faces beyond the narrow circle of partners and camp-setters; the only chance to hear news of the world beyond the mountains, to talk to

20

anyone of events beyond the doings of animals, the chance of foul weather, the clues and guesswork about which tribes might be nearby – and were they friendly?

It was also the only occasion for the next eleven months that they'd be around enough white men to be able to get drunk in safety, and despite the quality of the liquor, most of them seemed to be taking fullest advantage of this facet of the situation.

He'll be at the rendezvous, Tom Shaw had said, of the man who had killed his brother.

'He'll be at the rendezvous.' And as he'd said it, Abishag Shaw's brother – five years the elder, Shaw had mentioned on the steamboat, breaking a silence of nearly forty-eight hours on that occasion and then returning to it at once – had laid on the table between them in the firelit blockhouse of Fort Ivy a human scalp, the long hair a few shades fairer than Shaw's own.

Shaw had looked aside. 'Why'n't you bury that thing with him?'

Tom Shaw had taken his surviving brother's hand in his own, picked up their brother's scalp and laid it in Shaw's palm. ''Cause I know you, Abe,' he said. ''Cause I heard you go on about a thousand goddam times about law an' justice an' the principles of the goddam Constitution. An' I tell you this: if'fn any single one of the men that wrote your Constitution had had his brother murdered the way Johnny was murdered – scalped so's we'd think it was the Blackfeet, *an'* worse – an' left up the gulch for the wolves, he'd

21

go after the men that did it, an' screw all justice an' law. I wish you'd seen him when they brought him in.'

Shaw stroked the dried skin, the fair straight locks that he'd touched times without number in life. 'I wish I had.' His chill gray eyes seemed to see nothing, and there was no expression in his light-timbred voice.

On the steamboat – deck-passage, which in January's case meant the narrow stern-deck just inboard of the wheel – Shaw had informed his two companions only that his younger brother Johnny had been murdered at Fort Ivy, a fur-trade station some six weeks beyond the frontier. Their older brother Tom was 'bour-geois' – the head man – of the fort; he pronounc-ed it 'bashaw'. 'If it was Indians,' he had said quietly, 'Tom wouldn't'a called it murder.'

After a long silence, with the firelight devils chasing one another across the log walls of the fort's little office, January asked the bourgeois, 'How is it you're sure where this man will be?'

The oldest brother's face had tightened in the flickering gloom. He was much shorter than Abishag Shaw's six-feet-two, and darker; his body reminded January of something that had been braided out of leather.

'Frank Boden was the fort clerk.' Tom Shaw's voice was an eerie duplicate of Abishag's, but thinner, like steel wire. 'Johnny told me he'd found a half-wrote letter in Boden's desk, to a man named Hepplewhite, that spoke of creatin' some kind of trouble at the rendezvous this sum-mer. Bad trouble, Johnny said. Killin' bad. I

22

didn't believe him.' A bead of fatwood popped in the coals, and the tiny red explosion of it glinted in the back of his dark eyes.

'When I got back from Laramie a week later, Johnny was dead. Blackfoot, the engagés said.' Tom cast a glance back at the door in the partition that separated the lower floor of the Fort Ivy blockhouse in two: his office where they sat, with its sleeping loft, and the store, where Clopard and LeBel – the oldest and the youngest of the half-breed ruffians who hunted meat, prepared hides and looked after the stock – were bedded down in their blankets. 'They said Boden got so spooked at the way Johnny was cut up that he left the next day. Goin' back to the settlements, he said. Then a week later it thawed, an' one of 'em found Johnny's scalp, stuck into the hollow of a dead tree a couple yards from where his body had been. No Blackfoot would leave a scalp that way. I knew then Johnny'd been right.'

Shaw had said nothing through this. Had only sat looking into the fire, his brother's scalp in his hand.

'You kill him, Abe.' Tom's voice was cold and as matter-of-fact before witnesses as if there were no law against the killing of a man one merely suspected had done you a wrong. 'You find him, and you kill him. You was the best of us. Best killer on the mountain, Daddy said—'

'I never was.'

'You was 'til you lost your nerve.'

Shaw said nothing, his narrow gargoyle face like something cut from rock.

23

'He'll know me if I come to the rendezvous. He'll know there wasn't but one reason I'd leave this post. But he'll think, seein' you, only as how I called you to take Johnny's place on account of him bein' killed by the Blackfoot. You kill him, an' you bring me his scalp, for me to nail to that wall.'

Something in those words made Shaw glance across at his brother, straight thin lashes catching a glint of gold. Someone in the family, thought January, had nailed scalps to the wall of whatever cabin it was in the mountains of Kentucky where they'd grown up. 'An' this Hepplewhite feller?' Shaw spoke cautiously, as if he feared a trap. 'This killin' trouble Johnny read of—'

'What the hell is that to me?' Tom Shaw took Johnny's scalp out of his brother's hand, sat back in his chair, the only chair in a room that was furnished primarily with benches of hewn logs, stroking the long fair hair. 'You been on the flatlands too long, brother. You know better'n that. They's a million square miles of mountain out there, Abe, an' only this *one* chance to find him in that *one* place. You can kill anythin' with one shot. I seen you do it. So don't you breathe one single word that'll scare him off. That ain't our business.'

The elder brother's eyes burned like those of a man in slow fever. It was as if January, and Hannibal sleeping curled up in the corner by the dying fire, had ceased to exist. 'You owe me, Abe,' he said. 'Hadn't been for you runnin' the way you did—'

'I walked away. I never ran.'

24

'A man that turns his back on his family is runnin',' retorted Tom. 'Hadn't been for that, Johnny an' me, we'd never have had to go down to New Orleans the way we did, sellin' hogs so's there'd be money at home. You owe our blood, an' you owe Johnny, an' you owe me. You tellin' me you'll run away again?'

Shaw sighed. 'No,' he said softly. 'No, I won't run away.'

The pack-train passed the camp of the American Fur Company, a big store-markee with its sides up, and another – sides down – with a makeshift bar on trestles across the front and a gray-coated man with the blue eyes of a defrocked angel pouring drinks. Trappers and engagés clustered along the bar and around the half-dozen Mexican girls who lounged on rough-built benches along the front of the tent.

'Hey, Veinte-y-Cinco!' yelled Clopard, who had ridden with the train from Fort Ivy, 'you wait right there 'til we get set! I got a little somethin' for you!'

The skinny whore gave him a dazzling, gap-toothed grin, 'Hey, *minino*, I remember how little it is—'

At the female voice Hannibal looked up, roused from his nightmare of barely-suppressed panic, and murmured, *'Malo me Galatea petit, lascivia puella...'* a classical allusion that January hoped wasn't going to spell trouble.

The American Fur Company was making a good showing: in addition to a separate liquor tent, they had what amounted to a full-scale dry-

25

goods store set up and half a dozen canvas shelters – watched over by engagés – to store the furs that their trappers under contract had brought in already. These were not traded for by weight, but simply handed over by the mountaineers in exchange for their pay, as if the land they trapped through was the AFC's private farm, and they, laborers in the vineyard. January couldn't help wondering if the Mexican girls were also on the Company payroll.

A quarter mile further upriver, Shaw drew rein before a small store-tent and a couple of deer-hide shelters, which marked the camp of Gil Wallach, a former-mountaineer turned trader. The little black-haired bantam came from around the store's counter and held out his hand to Shaw as he dismounted: 'Tom wrote me you'd be heading up the train, Abe. I surely am sorry about Johnny.'

Shaw made a motion with his hand, as if to brush the name away like a cobweb. 'Ty Farrell in the camp? Tom had a message for him.'

Wallach tilted his head a little, as if he smelled trouble even in this simple request. Ty had been a clerk at Fort Ivy. *He'll know Boden*, Tom had said, in the firelit office that first night at the fort. *They shared the room above this one, up 'til last Fall. He knows him, better'n any man at this fort: how he moves, how he talks, what he'd look like if he shaved off his beard ... An' he hates him. He won't go cryin' it around, like the engagés will, if they learn you're on Boden's trail.*

Like everyone else, Wallach would have heard that Johnny Shaw had been killed by the Black-

26

foot. Like everyone else, he seemed to accept that naturally the middle brother would leave his position as a Lieutenant of the New Orleans City Guards, to take up his junior's responsibility of getting the supply-train up to the Green River. But Wallach had been a trapper, thought January. *He can smell blood in the wind.*

'Ty's camped about halfway to Hudson's Bay.' Meaning, January assumed, not the actual arctic bay, but the handsome agglomeration of tents that he could see another half-mile up the trail on the far side of Horse Creek, ringed with the tipis of its Indian allies. The British Hudson's Bay Company had established the fur trade with the Indians long before the Americans had pushed their way to the north, and ruled the trade from the Yellowstone to the Pacific.

'He's fightin' shy of me,' Wallach continued wryly. 'Seein' as how he took an' sold all his plews to that snake Titus that's runnin' the AFC camp here this year, without a word about the salary we paid him or the money he owes us. He may take some lookin' for.'

Shaw said, 'Consarn,' in a mild voice and commenced unloading the mules.

The Ivy and Wallach markee had been pitched next to one of those great granite boulders that littered the riverbank, to discourage canvas-slitters in a country where theft from one's enemies was a virtue among the tribes. January helped haul the stores inside, and he saw that two sides of the tent were further fortified with stacked packsaddles. Hannibal, a little shakily, carried his and January's saddlebags down to an open

27

spot in the cottonwoods just below the store, where a shelter could be set up behind a screening thicket of rabbitbush.

The fiddler had attached himself to the expedition rather than endure alone the black depressions and attacks of unreasoning panic that still plagued him, though his last dose of opium had been the previous November, and had made himself useful as a sort of valet to his companions. For his part, January was grateful he'd done so of his own accord. After a winter of walking the French Town 'til dawn to keep his friend from throwing himself into the river, he still – at Easter – hadn't been entirely certain that he would return from a six-month journey to find Hannibal still alive.

'That a fiddle I see in your friend's pack, pilgrim?' A red-bearded trapper loafed over from his own nearby camp to help with the unloading. *Dieu*, it's been years since I heard fiddle music! You tell your friend from every man in this camp, he's got only to put his hat down outside Mick Seaholly's –' he waved toward the AFC camp with its various accommodations – 'an' he'll have a stack of trade-plews higher'n his knee inside an afternoon. Name's Prideaux,' he added, offering his hand as soon as he and January had set down their respective bales of shirts and trade-beads inside the markee. 'Robespierre-Republique Prideaux.'

'Ben January.'

'Not up here before, I think?'

'First time,' said January, liking the man's friendliness. They returned to the mules, pulling

28

buffalo-hide apishamores from the animals' backs and stacking them in the back of the tent.

'Clerk?' Prideaux took in at a glance January's obviously store-bought clothing: calico shirt, coarse wool trousers, battered corduroy roundabout. With a sly grin, the mountaineer added, 'Or you care to try your hand at huntin'?'

'If ever I lose my faith in humankind,' returned January solemnly, 'and wish to put a period to my existence, I'll do so by taking an oath to eat only what I can shoot,' and Prideaux crowed with laughter.

'Never say die, hoss! You come out with me tomorrow mornin' – what kind of rifle you got? A Barnett? Them's first-class guns ... I'll have you shootin' the pips outta playin' cards at three hundred yards by sundown, see if I don't! Waugh! Why, sure as there's meat runnin', I once shot a bobcat as it leaped out of a tree straight behind me, on a pitch-dark night, aimin' only by the sound of its cry—'

'Maestro—' Shaw appeared around the corner of the tent, quiet as the smallpox in his weathered scarecrow clothing, his long Kentucky rifle in his hand. There was another on his back – Mary and Martha, he had named them – and a knife at his belt; he looked as if he had been a part of this world for years. 'Looks like I need to go out an' hunt Ty Farrell, as he ain't like to come around here anytime soon.'

'Check for him at Seaholly's, hoss,' advised Prideaux cheerfully. 'I hear Edwin Titus – that sourpuss Controller the Company's put in charge this year – hired him on to the AFC for a hundred-fifty a year, plus *seven-fifty a pound* for his plews! Waugh! For that kinda wampum, he's gonna be plowin' through them girls like a bull buffalo through the prickly pears. I never did see a child go for the female of the species like Ty, 'ceptin' for a sergeant of the marines I knowed down on the Purgatoire...'

'I'll keep the store,' offered January.

'Obliged.' Shaw looked as if he might have said something else – asked Prideaux, perhaps, after Mr Hepplewhite, or queried for rumors about the unspecified trouble that Johnny had thought serious enough to risk his life pursuing. But January guessed how word of anything would fly from man to man in a camp where there was nothing really much to do but trade, get drunk, copulate and talk. Even the relatively short journey from Fort Ivy to the Green River had brought home to him how vast was this land beyond the frontier, how endless these mountains and how right Tom Shaw had been: *only this* one *chance to find him in that* one *place*.

He'd also learned that trappers, engagés, and traders – whose survival depended on observing the tiniest details of their surroundings – would gossip about *anything*.

Only in silence lay any hope of success. Silence, and Ty Farrell's willingness to play Judas.

You can kill anythin' with one shot. I seen you do it...

January had, too.

Shaw nodded his thanks, then set off down the trail afoot, in quest of his prey.

TWO

The goods in the tent hadn't even been completely arranged – traps hung from the frame
Clopard knocked together from cottonwood
poles, twisted brown plugs of 'Missouri manufactured' set out on a blanket-draped trestle-
table, skeins of trade-beads dangling temptingly
from the inner frame of the markee – when
others besides Robespierre-Republique Prideaux
came to shop. Ivy and Wallach employed about
six trappers full-time and some fifty engagés,
who for a hundred dollars a year ranged the
streams and rivers of the wilderness that stretched from the Missouri to the Pacific hunting
beaver. This wage was paid in credit, and they
spent this – and more besides – in the company
tent. But the rendezvous camp also included
independents, who had had enough money to
outfit themselves and sold their skins to one
company or another by the pound. These were
the men who came to see what Gil Wallach was
offering, and what he wanted for his wares.

And, they came to talk. Inside that first hour,
January discovered that the thing the trappers
wanted most to do at rendezvous – besides get
blue-blind drunk and roger their brains out at
Mick Seaholly's liquor tent in the AFC camp –

31

was to talk. To tell tall stories. To trumpet their pristinely uninformed opinions about what President Van Buren ('It is Van Buren, ain't it, now?') should be doing to fix things back in the States. To brag of their exploits in the mountains, in the deserts, on roaring rivers in flood or of how they'd triumphed over a whole encampment of Crow Indians in the competitive swallowing of raw buffalo entrails, waugh!

(*Waugh indeed*, reflected January...)

To hear their own voices – and the voices of others like themselves – after eleven months of hunting prey that would flee at the sound of an indrawn breath and leave them hungry or at least beaver-less that day.

Fortunately, it was one of January's greatest pleasures to hear people who knew what they were talking about talk about their work. Inside that first hour at the store tent, he heard endless comparisons of the relative merits of French and British gunpowder, discussions of the proper ways of dealing with Mexican authorities if you happened to find yourself a little farther south than you'd counted on, discourses on how to locate water in the arid stretches that lay between the western mountains, or where the beaver could still be found as thick and populous as they'd been ten years ago. ('Say, Prideaux, is it true that Cree squaw of Clem Groot's showed Groot where there's a secret valley where the beaver's the size of baby bears? You should see the pelts Groot brought in...')

Indians came as well. As a child, January had played with the children of the local Houmas

32

and Natchez bands, who occasionally camped on his master's land, but even then he'd known that they were only the broken remnant of the people they once had been. Since crossing the frontier, he had found himself in the world of the Indians, where the tribes and nations were still strong. Shaw's little party had travelled from Independence along the Platte with a trading caravan bound for Santa Fe, for protection against the Pawnee, who still held sway on those endless grasslands, and here at the rendezvous a dozen tribes and peoples were represented: Crows and Snakes keeping company mostly with the trappers who worked for the AFC, Flatheads and Nez Perce camped around the Hudson's Bay tents, alliances mirroring the ancestral enmities of the plains. There were Shoshone and Mandan, Sioux and Omaha. There was even a bunch of Delaware Indians, who had fled the ruin of their people on the east coast two generations ago, to take up a sort of vassalage with the Company as scouts – 'I'll take you down there tomorrow, hoss, they got a squaw does nuthin' but sew moccasins, an' she can fix you up a new pair for fifty cents in twenty minutes...'

January had filled pages of Rose's notebook with jottings of their characteristic designs of war shirts or tipis, and with unsifted gossip about this tribe or that. Despite the fact that it was, as January well knew, completely illegal for white men to sell liquor to any Indian, when the tall Crow in their beaded deerskin shirts came with their packs of close-folded beaver skins, Gil Wallach shared several tin cups of watered-down forty-rod with them before negotiations began as to price. When they came into the store tent later – with the variously-colored 'plew' sticks that represented credit for pelts – January was given to understand that a water bottle filled with liquor was to be quietly set out behind the tent for them as part of the deal.

Other traders weren't so discreet. As the afternoon progressed, tribesmen in all degrees of serious inebriation came and went along the path or across the green open meadow to the west: shouting-drunk, singing-drunk, howling-drunk, weeping-drunk, men who had little experience with the raw alcohol doled out by the traders, and none whatsoever in how and when to stop.

One man staggered out of the trees, naked except for his moccasins, and began a reeling dance with his arms spread to the sky; Hannibal emerged from the tent beside January, asked, 'I never got like that, did I?'

'Every night. Rose didn't want to hurt your feelings by telling you so.'

'Tell me that again if you ever see me head for the liquor tent.' The fiddler had gotten over the sweating jitters, but still looked like many miles of bad road.

'I promise.'

The squaws came, too, to admire the beads and, even more loudly, to admire the trappers who had skins to purchase them with. Beautiful, many of them, with their long black braids and doe eyes. Though he had not the slightest intention of being unfaithful to Rose, the sound of female voices after months of hearing nothing but masculine basses made January's loins ache.

It didn't help matters that every man at Fort Ivy, and every engagé on the trail across the mountains to the rendezvous, had at one time or another informed him that most of the women of the tribes hadn't the slightest objection to a friendly roll on a blanket with a trapper who'd provide the vermillion, beads, mirrors, or knives that constituted wealth among the peoples of the plains and the mountains. It was a way of adding to her own and the family's wealth, and in addition, a way of obtaining the white men's luck and magic to pass along to their husbands. A number of the mountaineers who came by did so with Indian 'wives', purchased from their fathers for a couple of horses or a good-quality rifle, sometimes for the few weeks of the rendezvous and sometimes for years.

'If you don't fancy supportin' the girl's whole family with gifts, there's always Seaholly's girls,' added a wiry little trapper named Carson, on one of the extremely numerous occasions that afternoon when the subject of coition was brought up. 'They're mostly pretty clean, though myself, I'd wear protection if I was to venture there.'

'If you was to venture there,' rumbled a huge mountaineer whose black beard seemed to start just beneath his eyes, 'you'd *need* protection, Kit, 'cause Singing Grass'd scalp you.' And he laid on the counter two blue-and-yellow-striped plew-sticks for a checked shirt: Ivy and Wallach plews, universally pegged at a beaver skin apiece. It was the first time January had seen the

35

man that day, and he thought: *he must have been at the fort during the winter...*

Carson grinned. 'Singin' Grass bein' my wife,' he explained to January. 'It true you got a feller here with a fiddle?'

January glanced across the tent at Hannibal, who made a small shake of his head: 'Twisted my hand in a pack rope on the way up here,' said the fiddler. 'it may be weeks before I can play again.' He turned almost immediately and left the tent, lest well-meaning questions and sympathy – January guessed – uncover the fact that he had done no such thing.

It had been a long and difficult winter.

Following a murderous binge in November – which coincided with and immediately followed the wedding of the son who wasn't aware that Hannibal was alive – Hannibal had once more sworn off the liquor and laudanum on which he'd existed for decades, with the result that he'd lost an entire winter's income to illness and a depression of spirits so violent that he had found himself unable to make music at all. January had not been surprised – he'd known other men who had broken free of the opium habit – and had patiently sat by his friend, played endless games of all-night chess, made sure he ate – when he *could* eat – and walked with him through the streets of the French Town in the small hours of the morning ... 'What the hell good does it do me to get my life back, if it costs me the only thing that matters to me?' the fiddler had cried, on the occasion that January had tracked him down on the wharves at four o'clock one morning after a Mardi Gras ball.

By Easter, Hannibal had begun to revive a little, and even practice again, in the shack behind Kate the Gouger's bathhouse where he was living by then. When Hannibal had announced that he was accompanying January and Shaw to the mountains, January had suggested that he bring his fiddle with him, guessing that at some point in the months they would be away, he would heal enough to want it. Still, he had the sense, when he looked at his friend, of seeing a tiny pile of desiccated moth-wings heaped in the midst of the endless prairie, waiting for the next wind to rise and scatter them all away.

Then his sadness for his friend – and his uneasy fears about what he would do if Hannibal didn't find his way back to the music that was his life – were swept aside by the sound of a woman's screams.

There had been, more or less, an intermittent punctuation of female shrieks all afternoon. Years of playing piano in New Orleans had given January the ability to identify in their sound the outrage, anger and drunken curses he knew from the levee and the Swamp: pissed-off whores cursing their customers or each other, or a girl squealing with excitement when two men came to blows over her charms.

This was different, and he knew it instantly.

This was rape.

'Stay here,' he ordered Clopard and ducked out through the back of the tent at a run.

It was a good bet that nobody else in the camp

37

was going to take the slightest notice.

There were three of them, in the brush close by the waterside. A yellow-bearded man was holding the girl while another, smaller and dark, cut her deerskin dress off her with a knife. A third, burly as a red bull, stood back laughing; he was the one January caught by the back of the shirt and threw at the knife wielder, before turning to Yellow-Beard – he only heard them splash as they hit the river. Yellow-Beard ducked his first punch – 'Waugh, Sambo, wait your turn!' – but when January came at him he pushed the girl aside and whipped out his knife. January scooped up the limb of a deadfall tree as Yellow-Beard lunged at him, rammed its broken end at that broken-nosed, blond-bearded face.

The trapper cursed and staggered back, then came on again, murder in his red face. January had his own knife out already, though he had never used it as a weapon – in New Orleans, or anywhere he'd been in the United States, he wasn't even permitted to carry it – and in any case he saw the original dark-haired knife-wielder pelting up dripping from the river at him, to stab him from behind. January ducked, sidestepped and was aware of a fourth man emerging from the trees behind him, to throw himself into the fray. January had a glimpse of long black hair, a black beard that seemed to start just below the eyes and shoulders the size of a cotton bale: the man who'd joked with the trapper Carson about Carson's Indian wife. The huge newcomer caught Yellow-Beard by the hair, slashed with a knife of his own—

38

Then Yellow-Beard and the dark little rapist were dashing away across the rocks to the river, splashing in its shallows in their fervor to escape.

Cheering in the trees behind him told January that the fight had, in fact, attracted an audience. He turned, took note of the volunteer rescuer at his side – a human grizzly nearly his own six-foot-three-inch height, with a prognathous jaw and the small, brown, glittering eyes of an animal – then faced the crowd of a dozen trappers, all whooping and waving and shouting, 'You sure showed 'em, Manitou!' and, 'Good fightin', nigger!'

'I catched her for you!' yelled somebody, and sure enough, two of the camp-setters hauled the half-naked girl to the fore, struggling despairingly in their grip. 'You won her, fair and square, nigger!'

The big black-haired trapper Manitou turned to regard January with those cold brown eyes, and January said, 'Let her go.' He walked toward the crowd, held out his hand. The girl looked about fifteen, and he could see the bruises her attackers had left on her face. 'If I won her, I say let her go.'

'She gonna get away!' protested someone.

Someone else yelled, 'Watch it!'

Three Indians appeared from the brush at the water's edge. Someone in the crowd called out, 'Oh, hell, now you gotta pay for her,' but the voice sounded unnaturally loud in the sudden hush. Knives whispered in the crowd. Rifle barrels came down ready for firing.

The smallest of the Indians stepped forward, a stocky, heavily pockmarked man in his thirties, a skinning knife in his hand. The other two – bare-chested as he was, and wearing feathered caps of a kind January hadn't seen before – moved off to both sides, rifles held ready to answer fire.

January said, louder, 'I said let the girl go.' The girl cried out something, and the man holding her cursed. The trapper Manitou crossed the distance between himself and the other mountaineers, wrenched the girl free and shoved her in the direction of the Indian men.

'God damn your hairy arse, Manitou, the nigger won her fair an' square—'

The girl stumbled in the sandy soil of the riverside. January reached down to help her to her feet, and when the two Indian rifles leveled on him he opened his hands to show them empty as she fled from him to them.

Without a word Manitou turned away, as if none of this concerned him any longer, and shoved his way off through the crowd.

January turned back to the four Indians. 'Are you all right?' he asked the girl, who stared at him with uncomprehending eyes.

The pockmarked man snapped, 'She is well, white man.'

Robbie Prideaux moved up out of the crowd to January's side, his rifle pointed; Carson and another man put themselves on his other side. 'Well, here's damp powder, an' no fire to dry it,' Prideaux murmured. 'The runty one with the pockmarks is Iron Heart. He's chief of the Omahas. You watch out for him, hoss.'

40

Iron Heart put the girl behind him. The two other Indians flanked her, and slowly, in silence, the four of them backed away to the river's shallows, then waded in them away upstream.

'That was good fightin', though,' added the trapper approvingly. 'You's busy right then, hoss, but you shoulda seen Jed Blankenship's face when old Manitou come to your colors. Waugh! I thought he'd piss himself—'

Hannibal slipped through the dispersing crowd of trappers. *'Salve, amicus meus?'*

January thrust his knife back into its sheathe. 'I'll know that as soon as I know how many friends my opponents have.'

'Oh, hell, pilgrim, you don't need to worry about Jed Blankenship.' Prideaux, who'd waded out to the shallows where the burly red-haired man lay face down, paused calf-deep in the purling water. 'Not unless you mind him struttin' all over the camp sayin' as how he had you licked flat an' beggin' for mercy 'fore Manitou came roarin' up—'

'He can strut and flap to his heart's content if that's what pleases him.'

'Everybody in the mountains knows Jed's all cackle an' no egg to speak of. 'Sides,' added Prideaux as he knelt to turn over the red-haired trapper in the shallows, 'I don't think there's a man in the camp who'd ask why anyone in his right mind would run away from Manitou.' Ribbons of blood, bright around the body, dispersed themselves to nothingness in the water.

'An' Blezy Picard – that's Jed's l'il friend – he won't even remember what happened, when he

41

sobers up. Well, don't that just suck eggs,' Prideaux added in a tone of mild regret as January and Hannibal approached to help him carry the dead man up from the riverbank. 'What a way to go, eh? Ty here got himself through clawin' by a grizzly bear, gettin' shot an' chased by the Blackfeet, an' being clapped by that whore last year at Fort Ivy, an' how does he die? In a damn fight over a damn Injun girl 'cause he's too damn drunk to get out of the way of Blezy Picard's damn knife.'

'Ty?' said January, straightening up. 'Ty Farrell?'

'Oh, yeah,' said Prideaux. 'That's him. You know him?'

January sighed. 'Not exactly.'

THREE

A bishag Shaw said, 'Well, consarn,' and stood for a time with his long arms folded, chewing on both his tobacco and the news of his informant's death.

'Wallach wouldn't know Boden by sight?'

Shaw cast a glance up through the cottonwoods toward the store tent. The little trader had taken over at the counter while January led Shaw down to the river's edge, allegedly to have a look at the scene of the fight. 'Wallach works mainly out of St Louis. I doubt he seen Boden more'n two–three times, an' those most likely in the post store where the light ain't good. Even Clopard an' LeBel knew him bearded, an' I'm guessin' his beard was the first thing to go. Boden kept apart from most of the men in the fort, Tom says.'

'That's a strange disposition to have,' remarked January, 'for a man who takes a job at a trading post.' He recalled the muddy palisaded yard – eighty feet by sixty – and the cramped quarters that were snowbound five months of the year.

Shaw spit at a squirrel on the trunk of a cottonwood half a dozen paces away: the animal jeered at him but didn't bother to dodge. For a man who could kill anything with one rifle-shot, Abishag Shaw couldn't hit a barn door with spit. 'An' I'd say your disposition for helpin' your fellow man an' goin' to confession regular is a strange one to have for what we're doin' here, Maestro. But yeah, I'd say it's strange. Johnny did, too. Else he wouldn't have been pokin' his fool nose around Boden's desk.'

'He write to you about it?'

Shaw shook his head. 'Johnny couldn't hardly write his name. But Tom said, Johnny asked about him, months before he found that letter. *He's too smart for what he's doin'*, Johnny said. *An' he's stayed out here too long.* Tom told him it wasn't none of his affair.'

January leaned his shoulder against the tree, looking out over the river – low in the thin gold light of afternoon, exposing a long strand of rock and driftwood – and seeing instead the cramped

43

blockhouse of Fort Ivy. Each night the stock was herded into the gray wooden palisade, and the ground, the walls, the air smelled of their dung. Through the six months of winter the snow would lie deep around the walls. No travelers, no news: nothing to do but play cards and drink and talk about women and beat off. Even sharing a two-room slave-cabin with twenty other people in his childhood, with a drunken and unpredictable master thrown in, January and the other slave children had at least been able to seek the cypress woods, the bayou, the batture along the river with its fascinating mazes of dead wood and flotsam ... and to do so at any season of the year.

On the plains beyond the frontier, even in the summer, you stood the chance of being murdered and scalped if you went too far from the walls.

As Johnny Shaw had been.

Though he had never met the young man, he knew exactly why Johnny had asked himself: *what was Frank Boden doing there?*

'Boden hated it, Tom said,' Shaw went on in his light, scratchy voice. 'Wouldn't drink. Wouldn't play cards. Hated it – an' hated every soul in the place. Farrell shared that loft above the store with him. From the start they was always pushin' at each other: Boden would go silent, Farrell would talk louder an' dirtier. Once Farrell pissed on his books. Yet Boden stayed.'

They'd searched that low-raftered ten-by-ten-foot room – January, Shaw, Hannibal and Tom – the morning after their arrival at Fort Ivy and

44

had found nothing. Tom had said that he'd searched it himself three times before they came, for any sign of the half-written letter that Johnny had found, or any clue or hint as to the 'trouble' he and his correspondent Hepplewhite had been plotting that might help in tracking Boden down. There were few enough places to look. The walls were bare log with the bark still on them, the rafters open to view from below. A puncheon floor – split logs – provided no loose boards or convenient carpets to cache things under. If Boden had had anything he didn't want Ty Farrell to know about he'd taken it away with him when he left.

And what did you carry, January wondered, *when you left your world behind*? Books? Letters? A Bible? The only things he'd taken from his years in Paris had been a gold thimble and a single gold earring in a camel-bone box, that had belonged to the wife who had died there. If Farrell had pissed on his room-mate's books, Boden had probably hidden whatever else was dear to him.

With odd, clear suddenness he remembered his hatred of 'Mos, the eleven-year-old son of the other slave family with whom his parents and younger sister had shared that single cabin-half. The older boy had bullied him, stolen his food, broken or traded away to others anything January treasured, given him 'Indian burns' and challenged him to do things that had nearly killed him. January could still hear his high-pitched nasal voice, still smell the peculiar individual scent of his flesh. He hadn't thought

45

of 'Mos in decades. Yet he knew he would recognize him even now, however the years had changed him, bearded or clean, hair black or gray...

Ty Farrell would have known the man he'd lived with and hated, if no other had.

But he remembered, too, weeping with Kitta and the others, when 'Mos had been sold away.

After a long time he asked, 'Didn't Tom think it was odd? That Boden stayed on in a place he hated?'

'Tom figured it wasn't none of his business.' Movement downstream: the Mexican trader whose pitch lay downstream of the AFC had led his mules to the water to drink, his rawhide jacket a cinnabar flicker in the dappled shade. Despite the placidity of the river, January could see how far up the banks lay the debris of recent rises: whole trees uprooted, boulders of granite rolled loose from the stony bed, matted tangles of torn-off shrubs. On the plains he'd learned how quickly water could rise, and he didn't grudge the walk of fifty yards through the cottonwoods he'd have to take the next morning to bathe.

Shaw sighed and scratched his long hair with broken fingernails. 'Tom's got about as much imagination as a steamboat. They's plenty men in the East, gentlemen like Boden, that has to stay beyond the frontier. Tom didn't think much of it.'

You owe me ... Had the oldest of the brothers spent sleepless nights, wondering how things could have been different had he paid more

46

attention to his inquisitive junior's words? Had his thoughts of vengeance fed on that possibility, or sponged it from his mind?

'What about the trappers?' They walked back up toward the markee again. Out in the meadow in the long slant of the afternoon light, a bunch of Robbie Prideaux's friends had organized a shooting match, a common pastime to judge by the shots January had been hearing all afternoon. 'There's no way of knowing whether Clopard and LeBel can keep their mouths shut if they get drunk, but there are trappers that must have known Boden. They'd be more observant, even if he's done something to change how he looks.'

'More observant,' agreed Shaw. 'Less like to go shootin' off their mouths, if'fn word gets out as to how Johnny Shaw's brother is askin' questions about Frank Boden?' He spit again at a pocket mouse at the foot of the boulder behind the store tent, missing it by feet. 'Like Tom said, I get one shot at the man. I purely don't want to have to go trackin' him through the mountains.'

It was on the tip of January's tongue to ask, *Would you?* but he held back from the question, as he would have held back from grabbing a man's broken arm. In the four years he had known Abishag Shaw in New Orleans, he had never heard the Lieutenant speak of any family, save once, when he had mentioned a sister who had died. *Hadn't been for you runnin' the way you did*, Tom had said. What had happened because Shaw had walked away?

It was clear to him now that Tom and Johnny had been the only family Shaw had.

47

Will you give up your beliefs about law and vengeance, so as not to lose the single person of your own blood that you have left?

Follow a man into endless and deadly wilderness, rather than go back to your only kin and say, 'I couldn't? I wouldn't?'

January recalled swearing once that nothing would ever induce him to return to New Orleans. He had learned since then what it was to need your own blood, your own kin, as a drowning man needs air. To need to know that you weren't utterly alone.

'That feller who helped you out in your fight, Manitou Wildman—' They ducked beneath the line of dangling traps as they came into the store tent. 'He was at the fort last winter.'

'I thought he might have been. He had credit-sticks – plews? Or are plews the skins?'

'Plews. An' yes – they call the sticks same as they call the skins, just so's everythin's clear an' understandable.'

'He had plews from the fort.'

'He's one I need to talk to. Clem Groot – the Dutchman – an' his partner Goshen Clarke was camped near there, too. Trouble is,' Shaw added more quietly as Wallach gave them a salute and headed off up the path for the Hudson's Bay Camp, 'we got no way of knowin' that they wasn't part of whatever Boden is mixed up in. That goes for the engagés, too.'

'What *could* he be mixed up in?' January waved out across the counter at the rolling meadows, the distant clusters of white tipis, the long string of shelters and campfires upstream and

48

down. 'What trouble, what *evil*, could a man be here to do?'

'Other'n murder, without proof, a feller he thinks *might* be the one who killed his brother, you mean?' Shaw perched on a bale of shirts. 'That I don't know. They's money in furs, Maestro, more'n you or I'll ever see. The American Fur Company's already crushed out two big outfits that they felt was takin' their Indian trade away from 'em, an' God knows how many little ones like Ivy an' Wallach, an' not just by gettin' their trappers to desert 'em with all their season's furs, neither. You talk to Tom Fitzpatrick sometime, 'bout how the AFC works. They got agents livin' regular with the Crow villages – hell, Jim Beckwith's a *chief* of the Crows these days – an' the Crows or any other tribe is just as happy to scalp a white man they catches on their huntin' lands ... an' the Flatheads is just as tickled to return the compliment on anyone who ain't a friend of *their* friends, the Hudson's Bay Company.'

A trapper named Bridger – older than most and recognized through the length and breadth of the mountains as being as wise as the Angel Gabriel, for which reason he was generally called Gabe in spite of the fact that his name was actually Jim – came to the counter to ask the prices of salt and tobacco.

When Bridger had gone, Shaw went on, 'The Hudson's Bay men been tryin' for years to spread east into the Rockies. At Seaholly's this afternoon they was sayin' as how that Controller the AFC sent out – that snake-eye Titus – has his

49

orders to do what he can to cripple 'em. An' in a place where there ain't no law,' he concluded quietly, *'Do what you can* takes on a whole new meanin'.'

A couple of Shoshone came to the counter next, joking in their own tongue and smelling faintly of cheap whiskey, offering winter fox and wolf as well as beaver in trade. Even the Indians allied with the enemies of the AFC, January was aware, knew themselves to be outnumbered and outgunned, and therefore kept the peace, not only with the whites, but with one another. On the plains they were constantly at war, tribe against tribe, and in the course of the afternoon January had learned that their tribal politics were inextricably tied up with keeping on the good side of the trading companies. Without guns and powder, each tribe knew its enemies would wipe it out.

Even so, looking out across the meadows in the clear gold crystal of the evening light, January resolved to steer well clear of the pock-marked Iron Heart and his Omahas.

Campfires were being built up. Men he'd been introduced to by Prideaux or Wallach in the course of the long afternoon greeted him as they went past. Others he already knew by sight: Edwin Titus, the AFC Financial Controller Shaw had spoken of, frock-coated and prim, with eyes like chilled blue glass; red-haired Tom Fitzpatrick, whose company the AFC had crushed two years before and who now worked for them; fair-haired little Kit Carson. Engagés – camp-setters – many of them very young. These were

50

often the sons of Indian women themselves from an earlier generation of mountaineers, hired cheap to go out with the trappers, to pitch camps, mind horses, flesh and stretch the skins when the trappers brought them back to the brigade camps deep in the wilderness, hunt meat while the trappers sought more valuable prey.

'Could Boden be passing himself as an engagé?' January asked.

'He could.' Shaw stood and stretched his back with an audible popping of bones. 'Or a trader; or a clerk with the AFC, if this Hepplewhite he was writin' to is of their Congregation...'

The sun had slipped behind the low western peaks. Shadow began to fill the little tent. Shaw started gathering up the tobacco and knives, the vermillion and beads, from the blanket-draped trestles and stowing them in a lockbox, while January untied the rolled-up side of the tent. 'He could be a clerk with Hudson's Bay, or even – if he's real clever – that fool preacher that was standin' outside Seaholly's shoutin' about how the whole passel of us was bound for perdition an' brimstone. Or he could be passin' himself as a gentleman come to the rendezvous for the huntin'. They got a Scottish nobleman that's stayin' with the AFC – *with* his private gun-loader an' horse-minder an' his personal artist to memorialize the trip for when he goes back home.'

'That's a lot of money for a disguise.'

'It is to you an' me. But we got no idea who Boden's workin' for, nor how many are in it with him. AFC's got their own store-bought Con-

51

gressmen – one of whom ran for President last year – so a murderer'd be picked up for small change. Good thing I seen this Sir William Stewart in New Orleans over the winter or I might shoot him from behind a tree just on the suspicion.' A trace of bitterness flickered across Shaw's gargoyle face – a trace of self-contempt. 'Pretty much the only thing Boden *can't* be passin' hisself off as is a trapper.'

'Do we know he *didn't* do any trapping? You said yourself Tom didn't know anything about him—'

'Nor did he.' Shaw nodded at Robbie Prideaux and half a dozen mountaineer friends gathered around his little campfire a dozen yards on the other side of the path, ferocious-looking in blanket coats and bristling beards. 'But I'm guessin' he could no more pass hisself off as a trapper than I could get up at a Mardi Gras ball an' pass myself for a musician, just from talkin' to you. First time somebody handed me a bassoon I'd be a dead beaver.' He cracked his knuckles. 'Truth is, Maestro, we're trackin' an animal that we don't know what its prints look like. Where's Sefton got to?'

'He went off to explore the camp.'

Shaw grunted and answered January's thought rather than his words. 'If'fn he stays sober in this place, we'll know he has truly drunk his last drink.'

Out on the meadow, two more trappers approached Robbie Prideaux's fire, lugging between them an appalling mess of the entrails of what looked like an elk, heaped up on the

52

animal's skin between them, and were greeted with cheers. January had heard of this particular contest and groaned. 'I'd hoped that was just a tall tale.'

Shaw grinned. 'Hell, Maestro, you think anyone could make up a story like that?'

The point of the contest – usually involving buffalo intestines, further to the east in that animal's range – was for one mountaineer to start at one end of the some eighteen feet of entrails, with his opponent at the other end, and to see which man could swallow the most, raw and whole. Judging from the whoops, shouted comments, cheers and slurps which followed, the only lubricant involved – other than the general texture of the guts themselves – was large quantities of AFC liquor.

January shook his head in amazement. 'Do they clean them first?' he asked. 'Rose is going to want to know.'

'Depends on how they feels 'bout bein' called a sissy.'

Shaw struck flint with the back of his knife, lit the candle in the lantern, a warm ball of gold in the cindery blueness which he hung to the corner of the markee. The air was cooling rapidly: in New Orleans it would be like a slow oven until the small hours of the morning.

Rose ... He pushed the thought aside.

'Sounds like your brother Johnny would have made as good a policeman as yourself.'

'He was sharp.' Shaw's flat voice held the first trace of sadness January had heard in it, in all these weeks. The first trace of human grief. 'He was a good hunter. But he had no hardness to him. He was kind. But if brains was gunpowder,' the Kentuckian added, shaking his head, 'Johnny couldn't'a blown his nose. He probably walked straight up an' asked Boden: *"Who's this Hepplewhite an' what kind of trouble you talkin' about in your letter...?"* He didn't think evil of no one. It wasn't in him.'

Words floated up on the wind from Seaholly's: '—hollowness of the world – sinful fornication – writhing in eternal flame—' It definitely sounded like there was a preacher in camp.

'Sometimes I think it's 'cause he left the mountain so young,' said Shaw. 'He was only twelve when he come downriver with me an' Tom that last time, us all thinkin' it was just for the summer an' we'd sell them hogs an' puke our guts out on Bourbon Street an' then head back to our mama an' our wives an' find 'em as we'd left 'em ... The mountain was like this,' he added, looking out into the growing blue of the twilight. 'No law; no reason not to kill a man who put your back up, 'ceptin' fear of what his friends'd do to you, or to your kin. There was bad blood all over the mountain, from the Tories sellin' weapons to the Indians durin' the war.'

From the direction of the liquor tent came the sudden spatter of gunfire, whores' shrieks and a man's voice raised in a howl of pain. *'Damn it, am I killed? Am I killed...?'*

'Couldn't hardly have a weddin' or a dance, 'thout somebody gettin' killed from ambush. If your kin called on you to go burn somebody's barn or kill their stock – or maybe shoot some-

54

body 'cause maybe his brother might of killed your cousin – you went. You didn't ask. I was awful old 'fore I even saw a sheriff, much less knew what one was. We grew up lookin' after our own.'

He shrugged his bony shoulders as if trying to shift some unseen weight. 'Johnny had a good soul.'

The last streaks of gold and yellow dimmed above the western ranges, the sun gone but light still saturating the evening sky. *Looking after our own...*

January prayed that his sister Olympe, the voodoo-ienne, and their youngest sister, the beautiful Dominique – not much older than Johnny Shaw had been – were looking after Rose. It was fever season in New Orleans. With the quick-falling tropical dusk, mosquitoes would rise in whining clouds from the gutters and drive everyone from the galleries into the stuffy dark of the house. *Please God, don't let Rose be taken with the fever...*

He wouldn't know until November, whether she was living or dead.

There was nothing he could do but pray, and trust.

'I was twenty-five years old,' he said after a time, 'before I saw a mountain. The first year I was in France, some of the medical students at the Hotel Dieu asked me along on a trip to Switzerland with them. I'd seen pictures, but I almost couldn't imagine what they'd be like.'

'Somebody in New Orleans,' sighed Shaw, 'gotta put up a hill or somethin', so's the child-

55

ren growin' up in that town knows what the word means. I do miss 'em,' he added. 'For all what it was like, keepin' a watch on your back when you went anywheres, or hearin' hooves in the dark outside your house an' havin' to go for your gun just in case – I miss the mountains. The stillness there ain't like the still you get in the bayous. Johnny missed 'em bad. He wasn't but twelve when we come downriver in '29. Tom never was much hand for writin', but after they left New Orleans an' came out here, I'd think of 'em, in mountain country. An' I woulda bet money,' he concluded resignedly, *'if'fn* I coulda found a taker, that 'fore full dark Sefton would get hisself hooked up with some filly—'

'Well, no takers from anyone who knows him,' agreed January, following the direction of Shaw's gaze. Hannibal came walking back from the direction of the Indian camps, his spidery silhouette against the lavender dusk trailed by a smaller, plumper and more curvaceous figure in a deerskin dress.

'Pleased to meet you, m'am,' said Shaw, and he and January removed their hats.

'She only speaks French,' explained Hannibal.

'And this is—?' January prompted.

The fiddler gave them a happy smile. 'Gentlemen, permit me to introduce to you my wife.'

FOUR

Her name was Morning Star. Her father had been
– and her brothers were – warriors of the
Ogallala Sioux, and the entire family visited the
Ivy and Wallach camp that night for dinner and
the ceremonious giving of presents. 'Didn't
nobody *tell* you when you marries a squaw you
marries the whole tribe?' demanded Shaw,
yanking Hannibal aside at one point during the
feast of elk ribs, stew, and cornbread. And, when
Hannibal shook his head, 'Well, that vermillion
we just give 'em is comin' out of your wage.'

Hannibal didn't get wages – or indeed any
payment at all – from the Ivy and Wallach Trading Company. 'All right,' he agreed. 'I won't do
it again.'

Morning Star and her sisters put up a lodge
behind the Ivy and Wallach markee, Morning
Star took over the cooking of the feast from the
camp-setter Jorge (which was just as well, in
January's opinion), Robbie Prideaux and his
friends invited themselves over with all the rest
of the elk (sans entrails – January wanted to ask
who had won the contest, but didn't dare lest he
be given more details than he wished to hear),
and after supper Hannibal, to impress his new
in-laws, played the violin. Mozart and O'Caro-

57

lan, jigs and shanties and sentimental ballads. Some of the men got up in the firelight and danced, with the Taos girls who – hearing the music – walked up from Seaholly's in their jingling *poblana* finery, or with each other in the time-honored frontier fashion, the 'lady' scrupulously marked with a red bandanna knotted around a hairy wrist. As the music flowed out like a shining rainbow over the meadows, January saw them gather in the darkness beyond the light of the fire, as Prideaux had predicted: traders and engagés from the Hudson's Bay camp, independent trappers and representatives from half a dozen Indian tribes. Most who came hauled along contributions to the feast: grouse, pronghorns, a bighorn sheep...

Most also brought liquor, and Hannibal smiled and shook his head; to the first of them, his new brother-in-law Chased By Bears, he explained, 'The Sun spoke to me in a dream and told me that if I tasted firewater again, he would take my music away from me forever.' Everyone seemed to accept this except yellow-bearded Jed Blankenship, who was stupendously drunk himself and was finally removed by Prideaux and Shaw for a non-consensual bath in the river. Manitou Wildman, also drunk, burst into bitter tears when Hannibal played 'Für Elise' and retired to the meadows to howl at the moon.

Had they planned it, January reflected later, they could have found no better way of meeting two-thirds of the camp and bringing the Ivy and Wallach store into the mainstream of gossip for the remainder of the rendezvous.

The bride herself was a little pocket-Venus, about twenty-two years old, with a round face, twinkling black eyes, and – like most Indian ladies – a repertoire of jokes that would put a preacher into seizure at forty paces. She was a better cook than Jorge (the same could also have been said of Robbie Prideaux's dog) and murderously efficient at moccasin repair, no small boon given the quickness with which the soft leather footwear wore through. Before the end of the wedding festivities, she had bargained for Robbie Prideaux's elk hide and the skin of the bighorn sheep that had been the contribution of Sir William Stewart – second son of the Laird of Grandtully and guest of the AFC – to the celebration; January came back from his morning bath in the river to find her fleshing and stretching them outside the lodge. 'Why should you trade good beads to that woman with the Delawares who sews moccasins,' she asked, 'when I can make you better ones for nothing? But you also should have a wife, Winter Moon,' she added gravely.

'I do,' replied January. 'But she is back in the city of the white men on the Great River, being unable to come with us on account of being with child.' Even speaking her name filled him with longing and with joy.

'Rose.' Morning Star gave him her beautiful smile. 'Sun Mouse told me.' Sun Mouse was her name for Hannibal – one which had been almost immediately picked up by every whore in the camp as well. 'I meant, a wife for the rendezvous. I have two sisters—'

59

'Tall Chief forbade more than one of our party to have a wife.' The twin concepts of being faithful to a spouse a thousand miles away, should one possess such a thing, or of avoiding a massive dose of the clap by steering clear of Mick Seaholly's girls, were so alien to almost everyone at the rendezvous that January didn't waste his breath explaining them. Instead he spun Morning Star an elaborate tale of the shooting contest by which it was determined which of them would be permitted to marry, and how Sun Mouse had bested both himself and Tall Chief – Shaw – by putting sand in their powder.

The Indian girl laughed with delight – January had known from childhood that the myth of the stoic, silent Indian was exactly that, a myth – and said, 'To speak the truth, Winter Moon, I would have been happy with any of the three of you, though of course I will be a very good wife to Sun Mouse and never look at other men.' She winked at him. 'But I do have two sisters, should Tall Chief ever change his mind.'

Given the number of knives, awls and blankets, and the amount of trade-vermillion the Sioux had walked off with last night, January didn't think this at all likely, but he thanked her nevertheless. Even taking into account the cost of the lambskin condoms stocked in a discreet box at the back of the Ivy and Wallach tent – of which they had sold precisely one, to a trader named Sharpless from Missouri who had never been at the rendezvous before – and adding in the price Mick Seaholly charged for liquor, retail appeared to be more cost-effective in this area than wholesale.

Hannibal emerged from the lodge shortly after that, greeted January sleepily in passing and went down to the river to bathe. When he returned, bringing a can of water to heat for shaving, he listened to January's account of his conversation with Shaw the previous evening and nodded. *'You speak like an ancient and most quiet watchman.* It sounds as if the best we can do, given the circumstances, is turn ourselves into spies: find the men in camp that no one knows and no one can vouch for. Surely not so difficult—'

'It will be if Boden's in league with men who'll vouch that he's someone else,' pointed out January. 'If Hepplewhite, for instance, is working for the Hudson's Bay Company, or the AFC—'

'Too true. *Secreta tagatur.*' The fiddler lifted the can of hot water from the fire – even in his worst days in New Orleans, January had never known his friend to be less than fastidious. 'I suppose the first thing we ought to do is get on the good side of the trappers who were at Forty Ivy last winter: Manitou Wildman, Clemantius Groot, and Goshen Clarke.'

'Wildman's supposed to have a camp in the hill about three miles up Horse Creek.' January dug in his pockets for his own razor. 'Prideaux will know where to locate Groot and Clarke.'

They found Robespierre Prideaux making bullets preparatory to going hunting as soon as his various friends either wakened in their blankets – their bodies strewed in the vicinity of

61

the fire like battle dead – or staggered back from Seaholly's. 'In the mountains they are wise as wolves and savage as owls,' said the mountaineer, shaking his head over them. 'But thunder my dogs, in camp they are as sorry a parcel of tosspots as ever caused a mother to sink down into her grave with grief.'

When January brought up the subject – casually, he thought – of Clarke and Groot, Prideaux's blue eyes narrowed sharply, and his voice sank to a conspiratorial hush: 'What have you heard, pilgrim?'

January suppressed the urge to hastily disavow having heard anything, looked around him and whispered in turn, 'What have *you* heard?'

The mountaineer showed signs of a cautious rejoinder, and for an instant January thought the conversation would degenerate into mutually unintelligible hints, but after long thought, Prideaux seemed to conclude that attending Hannibal's wedding had made him part of the Ivy and Wallach family. 'Rumor is, hoss, that Beauty Clarke was seen buyin' five shirts – *five!* – up at the HBC camp. An' Clem Groot – I heard this for truth – bought *ten* trap-springs from that Mex trader Morales down the other side of the Company. An' that can only mean they're gettin' ready to pull foot.'

Dammit, thought January. He recalled Shaw's remark yesterday about not wanting to track his quarry through a million square miles of mountains, with or without hostile Indians...

But the mountaineer's conspiratorial tone urged him to frown, as if putting pieces together, and counter with, 'Already?' It was a reasonable question: generally the rendezvous would last through July. In summer furs weren't worth taking.

'Listen to me, hoss,' Prideaux whispered, though it was quite clear the Last Trump wouldn't have waked any of the sleepers around them. 'You throw in with me – and swear to speak to no one else of this –' he glanced across at Hannibal, who raised his left hand in avowal and crossed his heart with his right – 'an' when they leave the camp, you an' me, we'll be right on their trail. You ain't thinkin' of goin' for a trapper, are you, Sun Mouse?'

Hannibal shook his head. 'I'd never be back in time to open with the Opera in New Orleans,' he said. 'But you go on ahead, Benjamin—'

'Once they're in the high country,' continued Prideaux, 'we'll show ourselves to 'em, an' they'll have to cut us in. Think of it! You seen them skins they was sellin' day 'fore yesterday to John McLeod at the HBC! Waugh! Beaver as big as bears, an' with fur as thick as bears! Beaver like ain't been seen in this country for ten years, since it's got so trapped over!'

January snapped his fingers like a man enlightened. 'They've got a secret valley!'

'Hell, yes!' cried Prideaux, utterly forgetting the need for secrecy. None of his companions stirred.

Inwardly, January sighed. Through all of yesterday's gossipy conversations across the counter of the store, the rumor of a Secret Beaver Valley had come and gone: an elusive

63

Cloud Cuckooland where every stream swarmed with beaver, as all streams in this country had – the oldest trappers agreed – before the Company and the HBC and the now-defunct Rocky Mountain Company had sent in brigades in an attempt to run one another out of business by scooping all the furs for themselves.

'Stands to reason they'll be sneakin' out of camp any night now.' Prideaux sank his voice to a whisper again and glanced around as if he expected black-cloaked conspirators to be crouched behind every prairie-dog hill. 'We gotta watch 'em, hoss. The Dutchman's sly as they come, an' that Cree wife of his knows this valley like I know the back of my hand. But when we catch 'em, we'll tell 'em there's plenty for the two of us an' them, too – steal my horse if I ever seen two men trap seven packs in one season, like they did! We'll be rich!'

'Wonderful,' sighed January as he and Hannibal made off across the meadow in the direction Prideaux pointed out to them ('But not a word we guessed, now!'). 'Secret valley or not, with half the camp breathing down their necks they're *not* going to appreciate company—'

So indeed it proved. After nearly tripping over Jed Blankenship – who had chosen to clean his rifle sitting on a slight rise of the ground that overlooked the Dutchman's camp – January and Hannibal were greeted by Clemantius Groot's wife Fingers Woman, with the news that no, she had no idea where her husband and his partner were ... The Dutchman's three camp-setters all shook their heads. Nor any idea when they'd be back. As they left the little cluster of shelters around Fingers Woman's tipi, January could not but notice, some three-quarters of a mile away, among the thin timber on the hills that rose beyond Horse Creek, another couple of watchers, loafing on the creek bank with spyglasses...

'What about Wildman?' Hannibal shaded his eyes to scan the rough country west along the creek. Clouds had begun to build above the mountains to the north; the wind that rippled the prairie grass smelled of thunder. The Dutchman's camp, set in the meadow nearly a mile from the river, was one of the furthest removed from the main rendezvous, and standing in the midst of that endless openness, January was conscious of just how defenseless he was. South and north, the valley floor was dotted with the white clusters of tipis that marked the Indian villages: Shoshone, Sioux, Cree, Snake, Flathead...

And Omaha.

'Let's find out first,' he said, 'if Iron Heart and his men completely understand my intentions toward that girl yesterday. I don't have my rifle with me, and I'd rather not discover suddenly that I should.'

'He may be at Seaholly's. Manitou, I mean, not Iron Heart.'

'And if he's not,' said January, 'since, as far as I know, Wildman doesn't have a secret beaver valley, he probably will be later.'

Mick Seaholly's tent – the farthest north of the AFC encampment – was a fair-sized markee, with a trestle bar built across the long side that stood open to the path and an assortment of tree trunks on the ground before it for the accommodation of customers who wanted to have a seat while drinking. Two ash-filled pits announced the further amenities of campfires after dark, and across the trestle, January could see where rough tables had been constructed by nailing together slats from dismantled packing-crates, to accommodate games of monte, poker, and vingt-et-un, which Americans referred to as blackjack. At any time of the day or night the makeshift saloon was a center of activity: in front of it, on the other side of the trail, a well-trampled half-acre or so of the meadow served as a site for shooting contests and wrestling matches, while behind it, six rough shelters – barely more than sheets of canvas tacked over ridge poles – served the Taos girls as cribs.

Seaholly, looking as usual like a debauched seraph, greeted them with a friendly query about what their poison might be and – much to January's surprise – admitted his willingness to provide Hannibal with what was called fizz pop: vinegar and sugar mixed with water to which a small quantity of soda was added, to provide 'kick'. 'You're not the only man in the mountains who's taken the pledge,' the barkeep said, regarding Hannibal with his strange blue eyes. 'And you are welcome to as much of that revolting potion as you can drink, if you'll grace my establishment with your fiddle of an evening. Yourself, sir?' he added, turning to January, exactly as if there were drinking establishments anywhere in the length and breadth of the United

States that would permit a black man to stand at the same counter as white ones.

'A champagne cocktail,' said January gravely, and Seaholly gave him a devil's grin and the usual glass of watered-down forty-rod that everyone else got for the cost of a beaver pelt. There were traders who had better liquor – Charro Morales, just down the path from the AFC, supposedly had the finest in the camp, if anyone wanted to pay three plews a shot for it – but nobody had cheaper.

'*Tu patulae recubans sub tegmine fagi Silvestram tenui Musam meditaris avena*,' declared Hannibal, raising his glass. 'You have a deal, sir. Perhaps you might assist us with a quest?'

Seaholly allowed that Wildman, Groot, and Clarke had all been in his establishment earlier in the day and were likely to return: 'Though if you – or Mr Wallach – have specific business to transact with Manitou I'd suggest a different venue. He comes here for a single purpose, when he comes, and pursues it single-mindedly, and I do not refer –' he glanced down the bar at the whores Veinte-y-Cinco and La Princessa – 'to the pleasures of congenial company. On the occasions when Wildman comes in to make a night of it, it's best to catch him early.'

A shooting contest was forming up on the other side of the path, and while Hannibal improved his acquaintance with the two ladies at the end of the bar, January crossed to observe. 'Steal my mule, hoss, you can't just stand there!' protested Robbie Prideaux, and he offered January the loan of his own piece, a very

67

handsome Lancaster. January had not been a bad shot before – given that no black man in the United States was permitted to own firearms – and had practiced every evening on the trail, and he felt that he didn't acquit himself badly. He felt, moreover, that he deserved extra points for not shooting Jed Blankenship, when that gentleman trumpeted, 'Not bad shootin' for a nigger! Where'd you learn which end of the gun the bullet comes outta, boy?'

'My daddy was Daniel Boone,' January replied blandly. 'You never heard how he was kidnapped by the Barbary Pirates, and rescued an African princess, before he got away by killing ten of the Sultan's guards and building himself a raft of their dead bodies? The only reason my shooting isn't better,' he added modestly – because in fact he'd been outshot by all the trappers and most of the engagés at a hundred yards and considered himself lucky to have seen the playing-card target at two hundred and fifty – 'is that I was twelve years old before she sent me to America to learn from him, and he was old then, and his sight was failing. But I'm here to learn.'

A number of the trappers had to cover their mouths to hide huge grins, but Jed – a fair-haired Missourian with an ingratiating manner when he was sober – looked like he believed every word.

'The man's an excrescence,' muttered Sir William Stewart, when Blankenship made off across the path with his slender winnings – from bets on the other contestants as well as on himself – to *do them gals a FAVOR!*, as he loudly put it. 'I can think of few civilized societies in which he'd be able to prosper as he does here. But I can only assume that the Laws of Nature will eventually deal with him as he deserves: as, indeed, they deal with every man in this land.' The Scotsman studied January's face for a moment, a slight frown pulling at his dark brows, while January – in company with two or three of the trappers – examined the new Manton rifle Stewart had been trying out.

'Orleans Ballroom,' said January, interpreting his glance.

The tall man's face broke into a smile. 'Good heavens, the piano player! What on earth are you doing up here?'

'Trying to keep my house,' said January, and Stewart grimaced.

'It is bleak down there, isn't it? I thought to make a go of it as a cotton broker, but it's hardly the year to try to start any business, is it?' Camp rumor had it that the tall, commanding Scotsman was the heir to a title, a castle and considerable property in his homeland, but despite his blood horses, private loaders and pack-train of civilized amenities like brandied peaches and foie gras, Stewart was an unpretentious man who had won the respect of the trappers by his businesslike attitude and his willingness to do his share of the work on the trail.

'See here – January, isn't it?'

'You can make it Ben – Your Lordship.'

'Not "My Lordship" just yet, thank God; Bill will do. The Company's holding a feast in Jim Bridger's honor tomorrow night, and I meant to

69

ask Sefton if he'd favor us – do you play anything besides piano? You must—'

'You didn't bring one?'

Stewart smote his forehead theatrically,
making all the long fringes of his white buckskin
jacket flutter. 'Dash it, I *knew* I was forgetting
something!'

'I'm sure if you ask around the camp, someone
will have one,' said January comfortingly. 'Or, if
that isn't the case, I'm fair on the guitar.'

'Excellent! One of the Taos traders usually has
one. Or perhaps that fellow Wynne from Philadelphia ... Heaven knows he has every other sort
of useless thing for sale. Could I induce you and
Sefton to come down and play for us? Bring the
lovely Mrs Sefton as well. I know the chief of
her village has been asked, and – damn it!' he
added and, turning, strode across the path to
where Jed Blankenship, far from approaching La
Princessa or Irish Mary (Veinte-y-Cinco having
disappeared with another customer), had gone
over to Pia, Veinte-y-Cinco's thirteen-year-old
daughter, who ran errands for Seaholly's and
worked behind the bar. The yellow-bearded trapper had the girl by the arm, and Pia was pulling
back, not fear in her face but a child's disgust at
adult stupidity.

'For God's sake, Blankenship—' Seaholly
came around the bar as January, Stewart and
several other men crossed the path. Blankenship
– who'd had several drinks already – turned to
Seaholly, thrust toward him a handful of credit-
plews of various companies at the rendezvous
and snarled, 'Waugh! You want a cut of *every*

piece of commodity in this camp?'

The Reverend William Grey – at his usual stand next to the liquor tent – waved his Bible and thundered, 'Generation of serpents! You are as fed horses in the morning, neighing after whoredoms and strong drink! Woe unto you!'

More expeditiously, the trapper Kit Carson seized Blankenship by one shoulder, whirled him around and knocked him sprawling. As he lay on the ground, Moccasin Woman – the gentle, gray-haired woman of the small tribe of the Company's Delaware scouts – stepped out of the crowd and kicked him.

'As I said,' declared Stewart contentedly, 'the Laws of Nature will take their course. It's what I love about this land, January. The very lack of human law brings out what is essential in Man – what each man is in his heart. And it's comforting to find that so much of it is good.'

January opened his mouth to ask whether the Good lay in the fact that men would object to injury to a child – the girl Blankenship had tried to rape two days ago on the river bank had been barely two years older than Pia, and no one besides himself and Manitou had interfered – or injury to a girl who was more or less white. But his job, he reminded himself, was to befriend as many potential informants as possible – and to put himself in a position to receive whatever gossip was going – not to have any opinions of his own.

So he only shook his head, sighed and asked, 'Where's Blezy Picard when we need him?'

71

FIVE

The clouds gathering over the Gros Ventre mountains to the north swept down the valley that night, unleashing a torrent of wind and a succession of short-lived cloudbursts that rattled on the skins of Morning Star's lodge like the hoof-beats of a passing stampede. The bags of pemmican, the bullet pouches and powder horns that hung from the lodge poles swayed gently in the glow of the embers, and the poles themselves creaked as they rocked, as if the lodge itself were a living thing, dreaming of flight. January was twice wakened by lightning, huge blue-white explosions that shone through the semi-translucent skins: when he went outside, wind flowed down around him, and he could hear the river roaring in spate, all the cottonwoods stirred to a rushing tumult nearly as loud. Another bolt flashed almost overhead, and by it he had a startling vision of a river of cloud pouring past above him, close enough, it seemed, that he could reach up and put his hands in it, before purple-black darkness slammed down again.

Rose would love this, he thought as he groped his way back into the tent again, found his blankets by the tiny whisper of the fire. Rose reveled in lightning and storms. *How can I note this in that little book? Why can't I fold up the night, the air, the lightning and the soft creak of the lodge poles into a little packet to store in my pocket, to unfold for her when I come home?*

If I come home.

If she's alive when I get there...

From beneath the bundled jacket under his head he drew his blue-beaded rosary with its cheap steel cross, counted the beads with grim concentration. *Hail Mary, full of grace, the Lord is with thee...*

Let her be there when I return. Don't let me lose everything twice...

In the morning Robbie Prideaux and his dog Tuck joined them at their breakfast fire in front of the lodge, with the news that, on the strength of a rumor that Clem Groot and Goshen 'Beauty' Clarke were going to sneak out of the camp under cover of the storm, half the trappers and camp-setters in the valley had stationed themselves in the woods and the hills on both sides of the river, with the result that at least twenty men were now stranded on the far side of the Green, waiting for the torrent to go down.

Morning Star cried in triumph, *'Bien, alors!* We will make a fortune, Sun Mouse!' – for she, Clopard, and one of her sisters had spent the previous day fashioning a canoe. 'Nevertheless,' she added, scooping into her wooden mortar another handful of dried elk meat to pound up, 'they are lucky, those across the river, to survive the night. The Blackfeet are camped up the draws there –' she nodded across the green-brown flood, toward the hills that loomed be-

73

yond – 'and they watch for those who are so foolish as to hunt alone.'

All the way across the plains January had heard about the Blackfeet, a powerful tribe engaged in permanent war with almost every other Indian nation west of the frontier. In general the Blackfeet refused to have dealings with either the American trading companies or the British, acquiring guns and powder through raiding and theft more than by trade, feared by all and watching the slow encroachment upon their territory with angry eyes.

'My mother's brother Owl was killed by Blackfeet,' added Morning Star quietly. 'They chopped through his back on both sides of his spine and pulled his ribs out, so that his lungs collapsed. This was after they drove splinters of fatwood – resin pine – under his skin all over his body, then threw him on the fire. It took him two days to die.' Her small hands stilled on the stone pestle, and her brows pulled together over her aquiline nose. 'Owl was a strong man. They still sing songs about him. I'm glad they keep to their own side of the river, mostly—'

'*Mostly*?' Hannibal's eyebrows raised a whole ladder of startled little wrinkles up to his hairline. 'Did I hear you utter the fatal word *mostly*, o dove of the rocky places?'

She made a gesture at him, as if shooing flies, but January saw her smile.

'Chased By Bears, and Faces The Wind – my other brother – tell me they've seen signs of Blackfeet on this side of the river, but those aren't the ones they're worried about.' She

74

shrugged. 'In the villages they say that there is another band in the mountains north of here, and no one knows who they are. Faces The Wind says there are at least twice as many of them as there are of the Blackfeet; eighty lodges, he thinks. Chased By Bears thinks they may be Crow, who have quarreled with the Company's Crow and won't come into the camp on account of it. But Moccasin Woman says no, they are Flatheads ... But if they are Flatheads, why are they not camped with the traders of Hudson's Bay? But there are a lot of them,' she concluded and resumed her steady pounding. 'And they take great care not to be seen.'

'Any chance they'll attack the camp?' asked January, after a moment's mental computation of how many warriors generally slept in one lodge – anywhere from five to nine, as a general rule. He did not much like the number he came up with.

Gil Wallach, sopping up cornbread and stew on the other side of the fire, shook his head. 'Indians may have rifles, but they've seldom got the powder and ball to sustain an attack,' he said. 'It's why they fight the way they do. They need that ammunition for hunting. And, even if the Crow wanted to come down on us for some reason, there's enough other tribes that want to preserve us – as a source of powder, ball, vermillion, steel knives, an' what-have-you – that they'd be mightily pissed at the Crows for upsettin' the apple cart.'

'There's the Law of Nature for Captain Stewart,' mused Hannibal. 'Either simple acquisitiveness for the fruits of decadent Civilization ... or the fact that the neighbors may be watching.'

'Which don't say anythin',' put in Shaw softly, 'about smaller groups – either them or the Blackfeet – comin' into the camp, when they think nobody's lookin', an' pickin' off a few here an' there.'

'And on the subject of the fruits of decadent Civilization...' Hannibal nodded toward the footpath that led toward the main trail as Edwin Titus, Controller of the AFC camp, appeared around the screen of scrubby rabbitbrush that bordered the Ivy and Wallach pitch.

Titus was a big man, bland-faced, frock-coated, and despite a tidy Quaker beard and the pomade he wore on his hair there was nothing in him of the weakness that trappers usually saw in citified Easterners. The trappers loved to boast of how their farts and sneezes could send lesser mortals like Mexicans and niggers ('Present company excepted, Ben...') fleeing in terror, but they walked quietly around Titus. There was a deadly quality even to his geniality – he'd lost no time in offering January a job with the Company the previous afternoon, the moment Gil Wallach was out of hearing: a hundred and twenty dollars a year, to clerk at their St Louis offices – and at the AFC store tent, effective immediately. 'You know Ivy and Wallach aren't going to last the year,' he'd said with his wide, impersonal smile. January guessed this to be true – the AFC was mercilessly undercutting the prices of every independent trader in the camp. 'They're losing money in that little fort of

76

theirs—'

'I didn't know that, sir.' *And YOU wouldn't know it either, unless you had someone IN that fort sending you reports...*

Unless, of course, you're simply making that up.

Titus had shrugged. 'It's not something they'd tell a man they'd just hired. But if you think your loyalty now is going to mean there'll be work for you when you get back to the settlements, you may find yourself left standing.'

Later January had learned that Shaw, too, had been approached – 'Only, he offered me a fifty-dollar bonus if I'd bring some skins with me when I come. An' he sort of implied that he took my refusin' in bad part.'

Bad part or not, Titus was all smiles today. Possibly – January learned later – because he'd just hired the small trader Pete Sharpless's clerk away from him, leaving the Missourian to do all his camp-work himself. Titus complimented Hannibal on his marriage, said he much looked forward to hearing the two musicians play at the banquet in Bridger's honor that evening (just as if Jim 'Gabe' Bridger, now a Company employee, had not come very close to being scalped by Indian allies of the AFC while he was still leading brigades for the now-defunct Rocky Mountain outfit), and invited Gil Wallach and Abishag Shaw to the festivities as well.

'He planning to poison you?' asked Hannibal interestedly, when the Controller had taken his leave, and Wallach laughed.

'He'd do it if he could figure out a way not to

77

kill half his allies in the process,' the little ex-trapper said. 'No, I rode with Old Gabe in '32, up in the Beaverhead Mountains. I'm guessing he's asked all his old compadres to this fandango tonight. And I'm guessing, too, Titus invited every trader in the camp, up to and includin' John McLeod of Hudson's Bay – though it'll choke him on Captain Stewart's foie gras, to look down on us all sittin' there drinkin' his liquor.' And he grinned to himself at the thought as he got to his feet and headed up the path to open the store.

'Be that all as it may,' remarked Shaw quietly, uncoiling his tall height to follow, 'it'll give us a chance to look over the camp an' see who it *couldn't* be.'

'It would help,' said January that evening as they set out on foot down the trampled pathway toward the AFC camp, 'if your brother were just a little more observant – or if Boden had something convenient like a deformed ear or a broken nose or a mole on his chin. Or one blue eye and one brown eye, like the villains in novels. Because *medium height, medium build, brown hair and beard, brown eyes, straight nose* could be a description of Hannibal ten years ago. Or Jim Bridger. Or the pilot of the steamboat we took up the Missouri – how old is Boden?'

''Bout thirty-five. Tom's age. Old for the mountains.'

Killin' bad, Johnny had told his brother. But having seen, in the past three days, what the camp considered not much worth bothering about – including Blezy Picard accidentally murdering Ty Farrell, Jed and Blezy attempting to rape an Indian girl, and three of the Mexican trader Byron de la Vega's engagés driving a grizzly bear from the woods through the Hudson's Bay camp for a joke – January guessed that whatever it was, it involved more than just shooting someone from behind a tree.

And in fact, no man in the camp would be discomposed by being shot at from behind a tree, anyway. Earlier that afternoon, one of Robbie Prideaux's friends had shot his hat off just to see him jump, which he hadn't.

'I'm guessin',' went on Shaw after a time, 'that Boden's either passin' as a trader hisself, or clerkin' for the Company or for McLeod of Hudson's Bay – dependin' on what him an' this Hepplewhite between 'em had planned. *Hepplewhite* sounds good an' British anyhow ... but so does *Shaw*. An' for all what Tom says about shootin' him dead first chance I get, I can't turn my back on it, that he's got at least one partner in this an' maybe more. Maybe lots more.' He spoke softly, though behind them, Wallach and Hannibal were joking in French with Morning Star and her sisters, Sioux girls tall and slim as willow trees with feathers braided in their straight, midnight hair.

'Tom give me a page of Boden's handwritin'. Beyond that, if'fn you come up with any good way of tellin' for sure who it is, Maestro, I surely hope you'll share it. Last thing anybody needs around here is somebody killin' an innocent man they *think* is the one they's after, only it turns out

79

later he ain't. I had that up to my hairline in Kentucky.'

Five or six of the AFC's spare shelters had been set up on the bare space of the contest ground opposite the liquor tent, far enough back that the AFC camp-setters could turn aside any uninvited drinkers who might mix up one tent for another in their befuddlement. Cressets of burning wood blazed around it, and three camp-fires formed an island of brightness just outside. January could see as they neared that candle lanterns hung from the tent frames within.

And if I had a Gilbert Stuart portrait of Frank Boden rolled up in my pocket, he reflected dourly, *I wouldn't be able to make out his face in there, no matter what he currently looks like.*

Voices hailed Gil Wallach: John McLeod – the jovial chief of the Hudson's Bay camp, who was, unusually for a trader, bearded like a holly bush – crossed the path, resplendent in a long-tailed violet coat the like of which hadn't been seen in public since Jefferson was President. There was a deal of rough good-natured pushing, jokes about what they'd been up to, exclamations of 'Waugh!' and 'Waugh yourself, Yank!' in Mc-Leod's rich Scots voice. Like Sir William, Mc-Leod had seen service in His Majesty's forces, and his presence in the camp was a reminder that Britain's king still claimed ownership of these lands.

Other men emerged from the dimly-glowing golden box that was Seaholly's tent: Flatheads who had been trading partners of the HBC for generations, wearing blue British sailors' jackets

80

with brass buttons that winked in the firelight, and the handful of Mexican traders in black-laced coats of yellow and red. Independent trappers, too, including Goshen 'Beauty' Clarke – goldenly handsome as his nickname attested – and his partner Clem Groot, the squat Dutchman, chuckling over last night's ruse and the dumb coons who'd spent the night out in the rain on their account.

To newcomer Charro Morales's admonition that the dumb coons in question were damn lucky they hadn't encountered the Blackfeet, rose a dozen protestations of how many Blackfeet each of the various independents could take on single-handedly: *Waugh!*

Ribs and haunches of elk and mountain sheep dripped over the coals of the three fires, along with skewers of *appolos*, that delicacy of fat meat spitted alternately with lean. Since coming to the frontier, January had been almost constantly hungry, the result – he had noted for Rose's sake – of a diet that consisted almost entirely of lean meat. In addition to these viands, the AFC cooks had turned out pots of stew, rice, and cornbread, enlivened with the more exotic fare Sir William Stewart had packed along: pickles, sugar, strawberry jam and Stilton cheese, brandied peaches and potted French pâte, as well as port and cognac. Someone had clearly paid Charro Morales's prices for liquor also, because the whiskey that was going around among the commonality – while barely up to the worst New Orleans standards – was still better than anything on offer at Seaholly's, and when

Hannibal entered the orange-lit murk of the tent with his fiddle, there was a general shout of joy. 'We gonna see some *prancin'*!'

Around the entrance, the Crows who worked for the AFC were already gorging themselves on the meat and passing around tin cups of Company liquor. Wallach muttered, 'Titus better watch how much of that stuff's goin' out, if he don't want there to be trouble.' Red Arm, the chief of the Crows, sat inside, between Titus and Sir William at the back of the tent, and glared derisively at McLeod's companion, the Flathead chief Kills At Night.

Among the independent trappers the talk was all of beaver and trade and the damn settlers comin' over the passes like damn idiots, and whether Montreal traps were or were not superior to the St Louis design, and how soon do you think the government's going to kick the damn British out of the Columbia country and let us take what it's our right to take? In between this, January would occasionally whisper to Gil Wallach to identify this man or that. ('That's Byron de La Vega, that was at Pierre's Hole in '32 when they had that fight with the Blackfoot ... That feller? Wiegand – been clerkin' for the Company forever. You know that shirt I got, with the quill embroidery on the front? His squaw quilled that for me ... No, I never seen that coon before but I hear tell his name's Wynne an' he can't shoot for sour owl shit...') The noise outside the tent, where the Indian allies of the two fur-trade companies had begun to howl and dance, was even worse.

Speeches were made about the election of the new President (toasts to Van Buren and to Old Hickory); challenges issued – Americans against British – to wrestling matches, horse races, competitions in shooting and knife throwing and swallowing elk guts: *Waugh*! The guest of honor, Company trapper Jim 'Gabe' Bridger, was ceremoniously presented with a suit of medieval armor that Stewart had hauled up the mountain for him, to whoops of approval from all present; Chief Red Arm was given several Company medals and a very handsome beaver hat worth ten dollars in St Louis.

Sir William made his way over to the Ivy and Wallach party, carrying a guitar and followed by a young man in a buckskin coat bearing what looked like a sketchbook. January creased his brow in an expression of vexation: 'What, *nobody* in the camp had a piano?'

'Not a one,' grieved His Lordship, stroking his black mustaches. 'What this world is coming to I can't think. This belongs to Mick Seaholly, of all people – you'd scarcely think the man would be a practitioner of the musical arts. And speaking of the arts,' he added as January bent an ear to test the sound of the guitar's strings behind the ever-increasing clamor in the tent, 'might I introduce my friend Mr Miller? Mr Miller is a painter I asked to accompany me this year, since this may well be my last visit. In New Orleans I had word that my brother is ill, and I – I regret to say – am the heir of Grandtully Castle.'

'I wish him a full recovery, then,' said January, 'and long life.'

'Not as heartily as I do.' Stewart sighed and looked around him at the candlelit gloom. 'I fear that when I'm finally able to come back, it'll all be gone. Settlers—' He shook his head. 'Not to speak of missionaries like that repellent chap Grey ... I'm sure Parliament will give your government an argument about it, and I'm equally sure that argument will come to exactly nothing. I've been in this country long enough to know that when Americans start to move into land, it's going to be theirs, no matter who has prior claim on it.'

Across the firelit Breughelesque confusion, men's voices rose in anger. Stewart turned his head sharply: John McLeod was shaking his fists almost in Edwin Titus's face. 'Lord, they'll be at it in a minute, look how red old Mac's turning. Could I get you and Sefton to give me a little Meyerbeer, before the storm breaks? Something from *Robert le Diable*, maybe?'

'It'll be our pleasure.'

Hannibal had barely got halfway through the ballet of the mad ghosts of the dancing nuns, however, when the storm did break. McLeod surged to his feet shouting, 'And that's your way, then? To hell with what your government promises, to other nations or to the Indians themselves, so long as your bloody Company gets its profits—'

In the corner, January could see young Mr Miller sketching frantically: waving arms, men lining up behind their chiefs, Indians looking in at the door...

'And I suppose the trustees of the Hudson's

Bay Company are in the trade to improve the lot of the heathen by their sterling example?' Titus said.

'As you've improved the lot of the Crows, by paying them with liquor to murder those who stand in the Company's way?'

'You've been listening to your Flathead friends.' Titus, coolly sober – January wondered if he, like Hannibal, had quietly paid one of the clerks to fill his cup with brown spruce-water instead of liquor – glanced scornfully at the Flathead chief Kills At Night. 'I never met an Indian yet who didn't claim that Americans had done him wrong. Yet they keep clamoring around the gates of the Company forts, begging to be wronged again, I presume. I only stated the obvious: that America's right to the Oregon Country has been demonstrated, over and over again, in the sight of history—'

'Don't you give me your bilge water about history!'

'Don't want to bring up who's lost two wars on this continent?' The Controller raised his sparse snuff-colored brows. 'Well, I can understand that.'

McLeod – usually the most equable of men – lost his temper then and lunged at Titus. Kills At Night, who'd been following the discussion closely, was on his feet in the same moment, and if the Flathead chief had been a little less fuddled with Stewart's cognac, and a little quicker at pulling his knife free of its sheathe, he would have been killed. Shaw, sitting close to them, had both hands over Kills's knife-wrist, pinning the weapon and at the same time blocking the line of fire of three trappers who'd brought their rifles up at the first movement of attack; January was among the men who launched himself to drag McLeod back from strangling Titus. The noise within the shelter was nothing to the sudden wave of howling and shouts from outside, where ten or a dozen of McLeod's Flatheads sprang to their feet and the Company's Crows sprang to theirs.

Stewart shouted, 'Damn it!' as both groups of warriors flung themselves at one another in the darkness, and he caught up his rifle – nobody at the banquet was more than twelve inches from a loaded weapon – and leaped over a log bench and outside into the fray. Others tried to follow, and January, Shaw, and the glum-faced newcomer Warren Wynne formed a rank at the edge of the firelight: the last thing anyone needed, January thought, was for trappers intoxicated on expensive port and cognac to charge into twice their number of Indians drunk on Company firewater.

For a moment it was touch-and-go: he could hear McLeod shouting outside, and also Jim Beckwith, the Company trapper who was also a chief among the Crows (and who was probably responsible for a great deal of the alcohol being circulated outside). But he was watching Titus, and though it wasn't easy to distinguish expressions in the glow of firelight, the Company comptroller didn't stand like a man who was ready to charge into a fight.

He was hanging back, watching and listening

to see how things would develop.

It was at this point that the Reverend William Grey came storming into the tent, like Moses descending from Sinai to discover the Israelites disgracing themselves around the Golden Calf.

'*Strong drink is a mocker*, saith the Lord!' Grey lifted his gaunt fact to Heaven. '*Partake not of strong drink*, saith the Lord, *lest ye die*! Publican!' the minister thundered, one long finger stabbing at Titus. 'Whoremaster! Is this how you keep them your slaves, then? Poisoning the bodies and the minds of God's children with your evil swill?'

'That's coming it a bit strong,' muttered Stewart, 'for a man who refused to stay in the Oregon country because he said the Nez Perce were devils incapable of salvation—'

'Evil is he who destroyeth the body, but more evil still, he who casteth the soul down into Hell, as you have cast these souls into hell with the liquid devil, rum!'

'That ain't rum,' pointed out Jim Bridger, standing behind January's shoulder. 'Tastes like whiskey to me – the part of it that don't taste like bear piss.'

'How do you know what bear piss tastes like, Bridger?'

Titus snapped, 'Somebody get him out of here.'

'The Lord shall have his revenge!' Grey shouted as three of the Company engagés closed in around him. 'Touch not the servant of the Lord! His servant cometh, even now, to break the chains of Satan – to break the chains that *you*

87

have forged...' He managed to get a hand free and point at Titus again, who was probably – behind the impenetrable gloom of the tent – red with wrath. 'And to bring you and your hell-begotten Company to the justice of the Department of Indian Affairs!'

At this sudden descent from the Biblical to the governmental, Titus held up his hand. 'What?' The Controller's voice was deadly quiet.

Grey smiled in triumph – perhaps at having gotten Edwin Titus's attention – and shook his arms free of the grip of his captors. 'The Department of Indian Affairs,' he answered smugly, in a conversational tone. 'There's an Indian Agent on his way up the mountain, to verify the charges that I sent to Congress last year, that the American Fur Company was selling liquor to the tribes.'

There was nonplussed silence. The Missouri trader Sharpless said, in a voice of honest surprise, 'It's agin the law to sell liquor to an Injun?'

Titus spoke no word, and his thick-boned face revealed nothing, but the set of his shoulders, the tilt of his head, were like the clash of a drawn weapon.

'And don't think you can bribe your way out of this one.' Grey displayed stained teeth in the flickering shadows. 'Or convince the agent that every Company man needs to carry forty gallons of raw spirits with him for personal medicinal purposes. Asa Goodpastor is a man of my own Church, a righteous man, unshakeable in holiness. A man who cares for the souls of the heathen, and who despises as much as I do the filth of liquor and all those who spread it. Woe unto you, children of Belial!' His tone, which had been creeping back into evangelical thunder, pealed forth again like a warning bell. 'Get thee behind me, Satan! For the footsteps of the Lord resound in the hills, and his righteous vengeance advances apace!'

In a quiet voice, Titus repeated, 'Get him out of here. Before I kill him myself.'

SIX

Whether any of this had anything to do with the trouble being brewed between Frank Boden and the mysterious Mr Hepplewhite, January wasn't certain, but the evening had at least been instructive.

It was unfortunately to become more so.

'*Could* an Indian Agent actually close down the Company?' inquired Hannibal, on the way back up the trail to camp.

'By hisself?' Shaw spoke without taking his attention from the formless darkness of the land to their left. Though the smell of that many humans was generally enough to keep bears from getting too close, it was by no means an uncommon thing to find them prowling at this time of night, drawn by the smell of camp garbage. Last night January had nearly walked into one when he'd gone down to the river to piss. 'Not hardly. But he can sure shut down their operations for a year, while they sort things out with that gang of licensed thieves in Washington. If so be the British raise a stink...'

'Which you know they're gonna,' put in Wallach gloomily. 'Or businessmen in their pay. Money bein' as bad as it is right now, a year can make a difference. Things ain't like they was, even a year ago.'

No, thought January, his mind catching the echo of words he'd been hearing, not only at the rendezvous, but all the way up the trail from Fort Ivy.

It'll all be gone, Sir William had said, looking around him at the candlelit gloom of the banquet tent: the mountaineers with their Indian braids and porcupine-quill moccasins, the dark eyes of the Indians gleaming with Company whiskey, the spit of venison dripping over the fire. It was the true reason His Lordship had brought his own private artist out from the East: to capture not what he was leaving, but what was leaving the world, evaporating like smoke on the wind of time.

Yet, looking out over the vast stillness of the valley, the pale blurs of the tipis under starlight, the gleam of coyote eyes flashing suddenly in the grass, January thought: *it's gone already, if rich sportsmen have begun to come up here to hunt with the savages and pretend they're savage themselves.*

A member of His Majesty's Sixth Dragoon Guards, Sir William had fought at Waterloo. The regret January had heard in his voice, when he spoke of going back to the duties of his family, was genuine. But there were two other gentleman hunters in the camp: Germans who had come in quest of excitement and the right to say: *I've chased buffalo on the Plains ... I've seen the wild Indians...*

And behind the gentleman hunters – and the missionaries like Grey – emigrants were already on the road, following the mountaineers' trails to the western country in search of unexhausted land that hadn't been divided up between uncles and cousins of prior generations. In search of a new start after the bankruptcies sweeping the East. He remembered New Orleans when it had been a walled city. The cane fields had come right up to within a block of Canal Street. On cricket-haunted summer nights he'd hunted rabbits and fished in Bayou St. John, where wooden American houses now stood.

An owl hooted in the darkness – it was only an hour short of dawn. After Grey's departure the feast had gone on for hours, Hannibal fiddling like an elf drunk on starlight, and the men had danced out of sheer high spirits as well as Company booze. Jim Bridger had put on the armor Stewart had given him – cuirass, greaves, and helmet of old Spanish plate, *suitable*, Stewart said, *for a Knight of the Plains* – and this had led into mock battles and demonstrations of how the stuff could or couldn't protect a man in combat. Stewart had sat back and beamed, almost – but not quite, January told himself, because he liked His Lordship – like a father contemplating his children playing with a particularly successful Christmas gift. To judge by the noise behind them now, there were trappers who were at it yet.

The scents of last night's storm still whispered in the air: wet forests, quenched grass, damp earth far out among the streams on the meadow. *New Orleans*, thought January, *will be a sewer now: reeking, crawling and hot as the hinges of Hell.*

Fever season.

Blessed Mary ever-Virgin, uphold Rose in your hand...

His wife in Paris, his beautiful Ayasha, had died in the fever summer of 1832 ... *Five years ago, only five...*

He had come home from working in the plague hospital and found her dead.

It was not only law that did not reach to this achingly beautiful place. It was word of those you had left behind.

It would be September before he knew if Rose was still alive. Before he knew if the child she carried would ever be born. *Not even that*, he realized. *The letter that will be waiting for me in Independence will have been written weeks before. I won't know – I won't KNOW – until I walk each step along the brick banquette of Rue Esplanade up from the levee, until I run up each step of the gallery...*

'Maestro?'

He turned, aware that Shaw had spoken to him, and said, 'I'm sorry...'

'She'll be all right,' said Shaw, with surprising

gentleness in his voice.

Behind them, in French, Morning Star asked Hannibal, 'What will you bet me, Sun Mouse, against this sour God-man who threatened Cold Face at the feast getting himself down the mountain alive?'

'Would Cold Face kill him?' asked Hannibal, turning to Wallach. 'Or have him killed?' Cold Face being, of course, Edwin Titus. Morning Star's sisters – who seemed to have found boyfriends at the feast, because they'd been nowhere to be found when it was decided to return to camp – had a far less flattering name for him.

'If that child thought he could foist the blame on the Hudson's Bay Company somehow,' said Wallach, 'you bet your second-best fiddlestrings he would, pilgrim. Grey's been McLeod's guest up at the Hudson's Bay camp for weeks. The man's got nuthin' but holiness to sell, an' he'd have starved on that in *this* camp. He'll do what McLeod tells him to. And sure as the Brits are trying to make trouble for the AFC, the AFC's got its men in Congress just climbin' the backs of their chairs, lookin' for a reason to push Van Buren into startin' a war with Britain so as to give us a good excuse to send troops into Oregon.'

He pointed upriver into the darkness, toward the faint gleam of snow that even at this season whitened the highest tips of the Gros Ventres. 'Five miles upstream of here, you'll find what's left of Fort Bonneville. Everybody said Bill Bonneville was a blame fool, to try to build a tradin' post in a valley that's snowed in six months of the year ... especially since Bonneville was only on leave from the US Army for a year. Myself, I couldn't help thinkin' how it's a blame stupid place for a tradin' post, but a damn smart one if you wanted to put a garrison up here. If the Brits send troops down, they'll have to come this way.'

A dog barked – in Iron Heart's camp, January calculated, the farthest from the river and from any other Indian camp. He'd seen neither the pockmarked Omaha chief nor any of his men at the feast. Other than the most necessary trading, none of them had come into the camp since the day January had fought Blankenship for the Omaha girl.

'So it ain't the liquor that's the issue,' said Shaw after a time, returning to Hannibal's question. 'It ain't even the Indians, but the land. It always comes back to the land.'

'Well, if we don't take it,' pointed out Wallach, 'either the Brits – or God help us, the Russkis down from Alaska – will. Same as all that hooraw about sellin' whiskey to the tribes. You don't hear the redskins objectin' to it, do you? We're not here to found a church; we're here to do business. If the tribes see what happens when they get theirselves liquored up, an' they don't like it, then why do they keep askin' for liquor? Why don't they all just sign the pledge and put us all out of business?'

Hannibal sighed. 'Why indeed? *That we should, with joy, pleasure, revel and applause, transform ourselves into beasts...*'

'Titus was right,' said the little trader. 'If the
94

government—'

Shaw yelled, 'Down!' and dropped. In the same instant that January heard a sort of soft *vrrrtt* in the air near his face, and Wallach – who was standing nearest him – shoved him down into a shallow depression in the ground off the track. Lying flat on the dark earth January could see men silhouetted against the sky, and Wallach brought his rifle up and fired. At the same time another shot cracked – Shaw's, January guessed – and he brought up his own rifle as a man sprang down into the hollowed ground, too close to aim at...

January swung the rifle butt, smelled the other man's sweat; the blow hit and glanced off as other shapes rose out of the grass all around them. Someone seized him from behind, a bare arm like iron around his neck; a hand gripped his hair. He pulled his knife and cut at the arm, even as the corner of his vision caught the glint of a knife and he felt the blade cut his forehead – his own knife ripped muscle and the choking hold loosened. January surged to his knees, twisting like a harpooned whale, and dragged his attacker over his shoulder with his own greater strength and smote the ground with him as with a blanket.

Then he grabbed for the rifle he'd dropped at some point – he didn't even remember when or how – scooped it up, swung around...

And the Indians were gone, as if they'd never been.

Movement. He crouched, swung the rifle in that direction...

'Maestro?'

'Here.'

Footfalls pounded along the track from the camp, louder than any Indian would make. Prideaux's voice yelled, 'You all right there?'

'Sefton?' called Shaw, and Hannibal's voice replied:

'I'm perfectly safe hiding behind my wife here.'

'Gnaye,' said Morning Star – *fool*!

'You still got your hair on?' Shaw's tall form stood lanky against the stars.

January straightened up. Beside him, Wallach said shakily, 'Let me check.'

January felt the knife-slash on his forehead, the ribbon of blood dribbling down his cheek. 'More or less,' he said. 'Pretty close to less.'

With Prideaux were two of his trapper friends and the engagés Clopard and LeBel. Now that the fighting was over, January felt slightly weak in the knees.

'Any idea who it was?' Prideaux asked, and Wallach retorted:

'You know, I think it was the Chinese, but I ain't all that sure.'

'If'fn it was the Chinese,' remarked Shaw, 'they's hittin' us awfully close to the camp.'

Maybe, thought January as the group walked back toward the Ivy and Wallach shelters. But the ambush had been laid precisely between the AFC camp and that of Ivy and Wallach – at the greatest distance from either, and where the cottonwoods came up closest to the path.

A guard was set, for what remained of the night.

SEVEN

Prideaux, Shaw, Morning Star and January went out to the place at first light – January with four more of Hannibal's inexpert stitches in his head and a three-inch strip shaved out of his hair with Shaw's skinning knife. They found evidence of an ambush carefully planned. Four men had lain in wait among the cottonwoods, just at the point where the bottomlands came closest to the path. Three more had lain flat in the deep grass of one of the meadow's several small streams, a few yards west of the trail. 'Laid here for over an hour, looks like,' said Prideaux, kneeling beside a few scuff marks and flattened blades that were perfectly incomprehensible to January. 'Which means me and Dalrain – you remember Gordy Dalrain from yesterday, hoss? – musta walked right betwixt 'em, 'cause we hadn't hardly sat down an' stirred up our fire, 'fore we heard your hoo-rah.'

'This is Flathead work.' Morning Star stood up from where she'd knelt some ten yards west of the trail, came back with beaded knife-sheathe in her hand.

'What'd we do to get on the Flatheads' wrong side?' protested January, and Prideaux replied promptly:

'Had some decent piece of plunder on you, maybe. Hell, they mighta been after Sefton's fiddle. That thing's *hellacious* medicine.'

'That is fool talk,' replied the Indian woman. 'Seven Flatheads, killing and scalping white traders at a rendezvous? English Chief would have *their* scalps. And Kills At Night too, for driving the white traders away so there will be no gunpowder or liquor for anyone.'

'Coulda been drunk.'

'What, all seven of 'em?' Shaw turned the sheath over in his bony fingers. 'Layin' there so quiet in the dark? That sound like drunks to you, Maestro?'

'That's a handsome piece of work.' January took the beaded leather from him, studied the band of stylized birds on it, green on white. 'How often does it happen that an Indian would just drop a piece of gear? Particularly a sheathe like this that goes on a belt.'

'How often does it happen that an Indian'll take pains to stick the blame for his killin' on another tribe?' countered Shaw thoughtfully. 'The point of killin' is to count coup for your own glory, not somebody else.' He knelt and made his way back toward the river in a sort of duck walk – crouching, stooping, long body bent almost double – with Prideaux and Morning Star scouting the ground on either side. 'Delaware moccasins,' he added, and Morning Star mimed a woman smitten by Buddhist Enlightenment.

'And the woman who makes moccasins for the whole of the camp is one of the Delawares! Perhaps there is some connection?'

Shaw grinned up at her, then returned his attention to the damp ground.

Inquiry up and down the river – and along Horse Creek where the camp had thrown out a sort of suburb for a few hundred yards – unearthed no evidence of other ambuscades in the night, and January got a great deal of good-natured backslapping from the mountaineers, who regarded the near scalping as a sort of initiation rite. 'By God, pilgrim,' said little Kit Carson, grinning, 'now you can for sure tell your grandchildren you seen the elephant an' heard the lion roar.'

'I'd just as soon have missed it.' January grinned back and drank down the liquor that Mick Seaholly poured out for him on the house – a ritual he knew well enough required the purchase of a round for everyone present. The stitched and scabbing cut on his forehead still ached like the devil, and he hoped he'd live to see his child, let alone his grandchildren...

'Never say that, hoss,' protested AFC agent Beckwith, a wiry little man, resplendent in beaded Crow finery, and one of the very few men of African descent January had seen among the mountaineers. 'Bastards didn't hurt you, did they? To perdition with 'em then, I say! Waugh! You wear your scars with *pride*...' Which led directly – as conversations with Beckwith frequently did – into accounts of Beckwith's glorious adventures in the mountains: single-handed fights with Blackfeet, weaponless triumphs over grizzly bears, long treks naked and wounded in the snow with two broken legs and a whole tribe

99

of Blackfeet in pursuit...

And yet, reflected January, for all his boasting, Jim Beckwith had been a trapper for many years and was a warrior respected among the Crows. His chieftainship among them had been hard earned, considering how easily the man could have spent his life chopping some white man's cotton in Missouri.

January left Seaholly's and made his way back to the tipi shared by Clem Groot, Beauty Clarke and Fingers Woman, who were still chuckling over leading half the camp on a wild goose chase in the rain. He brought a bottle of trade whiskey, and Fingers Woman immediately put a grouse on to roast – Indians spent so much of their time hungry that any visitor was instantly fed – and the tale of January's adventures led naturally into the time Clem nearly got his hair lifted by the Assiniboin, and from there to the fight they'd had with the Crows in the Absaroka Country in the Fall of '34. At last January judged the time right to ask, 'They ever find out who it was, scalped Johnny Shaw at Fort Ivy last winter?'

The partners shook their heads. With very little nudging from January, the two independents gave an account of events which closely paralleled that related by Tom Shaw back at the fort: in midwinter Tom had gone down to Fort Laramie, a journey of about a week at that season, for supplies, and a few days after his departure Johnny Shaw's body had been found about a quarter-mile from the fort, mutilated and scalped.

'I said I'd head down to Laramie, tell Tom,'

100

said Groot, handing January a chunk of grouse from the stewpot. 'Boden – the fort clerk – said he'd go. It'd snowed the week before, so they packed Johnny's body in it real good, to keep him 'til Tom got back. Beauty an' me left Ivy a few days after that, so we never did hear no more about it, but I guess Tom musta wrote Abe to come take the supply-train. It true Abe's in the City Guards at New Orleans?'

January let the conversation run on a little – about Johnny's relations with the various tribes that came to trade at the fort, and the time Fingers Woman had taken four horses and his boots off him playing the Hand Game – and then mentioned that Tom Shaw had had no warning when he'd returned to the fort: Frank Boden had not made it to Fort Laramie. This elicited some exclamations, and some cursing at the Blackfeet, but no remarks concerning: *gosh, I saw a feller here at the camp I woulda SWORE was Boden...*

'Manitou Wildman was at the fort at the same time, wasn't he?'

'He was,' agreed Clarke, and with a careful finger fluffed the long, golden ends of his mustache. 'But I doubt you'll get Manitou to say a word about any Indian, no matter what tribe.'

'Has he gone that much into the tribes?' There were, January knew, trappers who became virtually Indians themselves, though he'd noticed they were just as ready to trap streams bare and kill members of other tribes as were any of the Company hunters.

The Dutchman shook his head. 'Nah, the red-skins think he's as strange as we do. Well,

101

you've seen him – or you ain't seen him, more like. He's one of those fellows who's best left alone. Hell –' he grinned whitely in a tangle of sandy beard – 'ain't we all?'

January was still considering what excuse would be most plausible for him to ride up to Manitou's solitary camp in the hills above Horse Creek and start a conversation, when the chance to get better acquainted with the man was more or less dropped into his lap.

When he returned to the camp and made his way to Seaholly's, he found – in addition to an improvised jousting match in progress involving Jim Bridger's new armor – that Hannibal had set up a table outside the liquor tent and announced himself ready to take on all comers at chess, at a dollar a game. He had immediately – the trappers gleefully informed January – gutted and skinned Sir William Stewart and stretched his plew to dry, to the Scotsman's utter delight. There were four trappers lined up to be initiated into the mysteries of this new pastime ('That's better'n I've had all week,' commented Veinte-y-Cinco) and Pia had undertaken to keep the challengers supplied from the bar and Hannibal provided with spruce water and fizz pop, in-between running a faro bank at the next table. 'I hope he's giving her a cut,' murmured January to the girl's mother.

Veinte-y-Cinco winked at him and went back to stand behind Hannibal's bench. Having a wife back at the camp, reflected January, bemused, didn't seem to have reduced his friend's attraction for women in the slightest. Even the gray-

haired, motherly Moccasin Woman of the Delawares – whose baptized name was Ann Bryan,
though Hannibal was the only one who ever
remembered it – would flirt with him when she
came past. Young Mr Miller was perched nearby
on a pack saddle, sketchbook on his knee,
capturing the group around the chess game,
though January noticed he had tactfully trans-
formed Veinte-y-Cinco into an Indian squaw.

'There's the man!' From the direction of the
scuffed and trampled pitch of last night's
banqueting tent, a voice called out, and half a
dozen mountaineers and camp-setters came over
to surround January at the bar.

'Just the child we been lookin' for, waugh!'

'Let us all buy you a drink, Ben.'

'Whoa!' January held up his hands. 'I may be
a pilgrim here, but I'm learning to smell war
smoke in the wind! Let *me* buy *you* a drink—'

'See, Ben,' said Kit Carson, when they were all
gathered around one of Seaholly's makeshift
trestles, 'you're not only the biggest damn nigger in this camp, you're the biggest damn nigger
anybody here's ever *seen*.'

Which was probably true – January stood six
feet three inches and was built on what English
novelists liked to call 'Herculean lines' – but he
replied promptly, 'That's 'cause you haven't
spent enough time in New Orleans,' which got a
general laugh.

'Fact is,' coaxed Bridger, removing his helmet
to wipe his brow, 'a couple of us was wonderin'
how you'd shape against Manitou Wildman.'

He stepped back and motioned up the big,

103

silent trapper. January looked the man up and down, and said, ''Bout the same as Pia over there'd shape against a grizzly bear. I'm a pilgrim,' he added, against the general chorus of protest. 'I may stand a little taller, but I'm no wrestler. What fighting I've done was boxing, and I can't afford to get my eye gouged out or my thumb broken. I'm gonna need that thumb if I'm to get work this winter playin' the piano.'

'You play the *pi'anna*, Ben?' Stares of disbelief from those who hadn't been party to last night's interchange with Stewart. Like most white men, they assumed that anyone his size would have spent his life picking cotton.

'For the best whorehouse in New Orleans.' This happened to be true, though January's brief stint at the Countess Mazzini's quim emporium the previous Fall hadn't been his usual venue. But it got a better reaction, he reflected, than if he'd said he played regularly for the New Orleans Opera House. Young Mr Miller, he reflected, wasn't the only one to alter details to make a better tale.

In a slow bass rumble, like a man struggling to remember what human speech sounded like, Wildman said, 'I can box.'

It was like hearing that Kit Carson could dance the minuet.

''Sides,' added a young New England trapper named Boaz Frye, 'Manitou's a fair fighter, long as you don't get him mad.'

'Yes, and I've heard that same thing about grizzly bears.'

'If that's all that's bothering you, *amicus meus*

104

–' Hannibal appeared at his elbow and accepted another tin cup from Veinte-y-Cinco – 'why, there isn't a man in this camp who hasn't killed a grizzly with his bare hands. Just ask them. Waugh,' he added politely and slugged back the contents of the cup.

January's eyes met Manitou's, but found no expression in them that was readily decipherable. Manitou only stood, his head a little down, like a bull buffalo startled by something he'd heard and making up his mind whether to charge or not. And yet, January knew, from his own days of studying 'the sweet science' – as boxing was called – with an English professional in Paris, that there was no quicker means to open a door to conversation with a man than a clean, hard fight with no ill feelings involved. *You can't lie on the stage*, they'd said at Colonel Rory's boxing salon.

Dancers he'd known said the same thing of their own 'sweet science'.

'Come on, Ben,' urged Jed Blankenship, and he slapped January's arm familiarly. 'We already got money on you.' He'd spilled his last two or three drinks down his buckskin shirt-front, and his breath would have killed trees at thirty paces. 'You ain't scared of him, are you?'

'Are you?' January countered.

Jed grinned slyly. 'You just gotta know how to handle him, is all.'

'Good,' said January. 'I'll fight him if you'll do it first.'

Blankenship blenched visibly under his tan, and everyone cheered.

105

'Suits me,' Manitou rumbled.

Blankenship's dark-blue eyes darted from side to side like a man contemplating physical flight, and Prideaux whooped, 'Jed today,' over the yelling, 'and Ben tomorrow. Wouldn't want to take Manitou's edge off,' he added with a wink.

There was very little danger of that. Men were already shoving Blankenship across the path toward the dusty contest-ground, and Pia was collecting plews and recording bets with the businesslike briskness of long practice. January – detained by the crowd at the bar – didn't even make it to the front of the mob that surrounded the fighters before the combat was over. One moment he was struggling to get through the wall of backs, and the next, it seemed, everyone was jostling their way back to the bar and Manitou was putting his new checkered shirt back on, with Jed sprawled before him unconscious – and suspiciously unbruised – in the dust.

January knelt beside him and saw his eyelids move.

He was faking a knockout.

'Did you think he wouldn't?' inquired Veinte-y-Cinco as plews and plew-sticks changed hands before the bar. There wasn't a lot of exchange, since nobody had bet on Jed to win. All the wagers had concerned how long it would take Wildman to knock Jed out, and one or two optimists on Wildman killing his opponent – and, January heard later, eating him as well. 'Hell, Jed bet *himself* to lose.'

'He found a *taker*?' asked Hannibal incredulously.

'Goshen Clarke. The man'll bet on anything.' Veinte-y-Cinco shook her head, counted out red-and-yellow markers from the AFC, blue-and-reds from the Brits, reds from Morales and Company (not that the Mexican trader *had* a Company) just down the path, Pete Sharpless's red-white-and-blues, and blue-and-yellows from Gil Wallach ... 'He gets the Dutchman – well, the Dutchman's squaw, really – to keep his money for him, so he'll have enough to buy powder and ball. It's the only reason their whole outfit hasn't gone into debt to the AFC years ago.'

It was true, January reflected, that every time he'd passed a horse race or a shooting match, if the Beauty wasn't a participant, he was deep in conversation with whoever was keeping track of the wagers. If Clarke wasn't playing poker on some crony's blanket, or at little Pia's faro table, he could be found in one of the Indian camps playing the Hand Game – which consisted of chanting and switching a carved fox-bone from fist to fist in rhythm until the gambler tried to guess which fist it was in. It reminded January of a game he played with his little nephew Chou-Chou, only these men played it drunk for 'Made Beaver' at six dollars a plew.

'Jed was saying it's 'cause he wanted tomorrow's fight to be fair.' Pia cocked a bright dark eye, like a squirrel's, up at the adults. She was a little thing, skinny like her mother, and ordinarily clothed in a mix of men's cast-offs and women's, her long black braids making her look like an Indian child. 'But I don't think that's what Mr January meant, was it, when he said Jed

107

had to fight first?'

'That's what he's saying?' January felt the tips of his ears get hot with anger, that he hadn't thought of that when he'd come back with his stipulation. *Of course it sounded like I didn't want to fight* ... 'That I said he had to fight first because I thought he'd soften Manitou up?'

And Shaw, who'd left Clopard on guard over the store and ambled down too late to catch any of the proceedings, repeated Veinte-y-Cinco's earlier question: 'Did you think he wouldn't?'

Pia added wisely, 'Nobody believes him. But he's got seventy-five dollars on you tomorrow, Mr J.'

'Almost makes me want to lie down the way he did.'

'An' what odds are they offerin',' inquired Shaw, leaning his bony elbows behind him on the bar, 'that that teetotal Indian Agent of Grey's, that's on his way up here, is gonna turn up dead 'fore he makes the camp?'

His eyes met Veinte-y-Cinco's, asking what she had heard, and she leaned her own elbows, like him, on the bar at their backs. 'Slim ones, pilgrim,' she said. 'Slim ones.'

EIGHT

The boxing match with Manitou Wildman – set for noon of the following day – almost didn't take place after all. Sufficient sums were involved that the gamblers were insisting on an hour when no chance ray of sunlight would take either fighter in the eyes. But an hour before the sun reached zenith, Veinte-y-Cinco came breathless and shaking into the Ivy and Wallach store tent with the news that Edwin Titus had been seen a few minutes before taking Pia into his quarters. *'Take a walk*, Mick tells me.' The woman turned her head, as if she could see back to the AFC camp. *'Take a walk*, just like that. *Come back in an hour*, he says—'

Shaw said, very quietly, 'Jesus,' slung one rifle on his back and picked up the other. 'You watch the place,' he ordered Jorge on his way to the horse line. Silently, January fetched his own weapon and followed. John McLeod, who'd been at the back of the tent talking to Gil Wallach about mules, whistled to a couple of the Canadian trappers; Prideaux and his camp mates joined the group as they were saddling up. January hoisted Veinte-y-Cinco on to the rump of his horse behind him, and close to thirty men rode downriver to the AFC camp.

'Titus, he never comes around for none of us girls,' Veinte-y-Cinco whispered, clinging to January's waist. 'He says we got the pox—'

January guessed this to be true, something which made faithfulness to Rose less difficult, notwithstanding the protective sheaths on sale at the store. The corollary to that fact – that, as a child, Pia was probably the only female in the AFC camp who wouldn't be poxed – had already crossed his mind.

And while Titus was not exactly Mick Seaholly's boss, without the Controller's financing – and his protection on the road – the saloon keeper would never have been able to get his liquor and his girls up to the Green River from Taos. Certainly, he would not be able to do so in future years.

And, anyway, it was known throughout the camp that Mick Seaholly would sell his own sister for the price of a Long-Nine cigar.

Unlike the Indian women, the Taos girls had nothing to offer the mountaineers in the way of camp-keeping, moccasin-making and the endless ancillary work of preparing beaver skins for the market. Their chief value lay in that they were cheaper than buying an Indian bride, and you didn't have to be constantly giving presents to their families.

They had no families.

Only Seaholly.

And, in Veinte-y-Cinco's case, Pia.

Through his back, January was aware of the woman's trembling. Without Seaholly's protection, it wouldn't be long before a woman on her

110

own would find herself selling her body for pemmican – to those who simply didn't drag her down to the cottonwoods for free. January knew women in New Orleans who'd have greeted the situation with a shrug ... or a demand for a cut of the proceeds.

The posse found Edwin Titus outside his tent, faced off against Hannibal Sefton ... and Manitou Wildman. Seaholly, slouched nearby, would clearly have dealt with the fiddler had Wildman not been looming silently at his elbow. 'You heard the girl, Sefton,' Titus was saying impatiently. 'She's perfectly willing—'

'She's perfectly dosed to the hairline with opium—'

'Are you suggesting that I held her nose and poured it down her throat? I could have you up for libel.'

'In what court?' retorted Hannibal. 'If there's no law against raping a drugged child, there's certainly not any statute against my saying so.'

'You have to go back to New Orleans sometime, Sefton. And when you do, you'll find—' He turned his head as Shaw, January and McLeod dismounted and strode toward the tent; January saw his thin mouth twist with anger. Then at once it smoothed as Veinte-y-Cinco ran forward—

'Pia! Corazon!'

Seaholly grabbed the woman by her arm. She wrenched at his grip, and Titus laid a hand on her shoulder: 'Señora Vasquez, thank Heaven you have come!'

While Veinte-y-Cinco stared at him, startled

speechless at this turnabout – *didn't she think that's what he'd say if she showed up with armed force?* – McLeod almost spat the words, 'Damn it, Titus, I knew you Yanks were scoundrels—'

'Scoundrels?' Titus's head jerked back in melodramatic shock. Then, his face changing, 'Good God, man!' he thundered. 'I find the poor child staggering about the camp – ill, I assumed, for surely no man here is so debased as to deliberately give liquor to a girl of her years – and you *dare* to suggest—?'

Hannibal, looking as if he'd just heard the Serpent of Eden claim that Eve had pinned him down and spooned applesauce down his throat, slipped past Titus and thrust the tent flap aside. In the shadows January could see Pia lying among the buffalo robes on the Comptroller's cot, her long black hair unbraided over her shoulders in a silky cloak, her shift loose and drawn up to her thighs. She was giggling, but when Veinte-y-Cinco ran into the tent she held out her arms, sighed: 'Mama!'

'They say no good deed goes unpunished,' proclaimed Titus, in tones of bitterest reproach. 'Had I not brought the child here, God knows who would have found her. Yet, instead of thanks, I am accused of ... Good God, McLeod, will you listen to yourself? Get the little tramp out of here, Madame,' he added as Veinte-y-Cinco supported her stumbling daughter past him and into the open. 'For that matter, I should like to know where *you* were, when someone was feeding that poor child liquor.'

He glanced significantly from the woman to

112

Seaholly, put on an aggrieved expression – just as if he were not splitting Veinte-y-Cinco's income with the publican in exchange for food – and shook his sleek sandy head.

Drawn by the commotion like a cow to the pasture fence, the Reverend Grey chipped in: 'What kind of a mother do you call yourself, woman? The fruit falleth not far from the tree! Bring up a child in the way she will go—'

'I suddenly have considerably greater insight,' stated Titus, glaring at the men around him in disgust, 'as to why the priest and the Levite rode by the stricken traveler on the other side of the road. Gentlemen, good day to you all.'

He retreated into the tent.

The men looked uneasily at one another, and then at Veinte-y-Cinco and the sleepy, giggling Pia, like men who fear they may have made fools of themselves. Edwin Titus was, after all, a respected trader – and it was Edwin Titus who held their rather considerable debts for the liquor they'd consumed so far. Moreover, for many of them, it was Edwin Titus who could set the prices they still had to pay for the trap springs and gunpowder that they'd need for the year's trapping. Compared to Titus's frock-coated respectability, Veinte-y-Cinco, with her dark hair tumbled loose on her skinny shoulders and her grimy satin vest cut low over sagging breasts, looked like exactly what she was: a Mexican whore.

'Lo, how the Lord looketh on the hearts of the unrighteous—' Grey went on, his alliance with McLeod evidently taking second place to new

113

material for a sermon. *'Her house is the way to Hell, going down to the chambers of death...'*

'I don't know what kind of a mother you call yourself,' remarked Hannibal quietly as they turned away, 'but that's not liquor she was given. That was opium – and I'm not sure where else you'd get that in the camp, except in Edwin Titus's tent.' He walked back to his chess table, packed it up and walked off up the trail to the Ivy and Wallach pitch.

For all his expressed grief at the foul mistrust he'd seen demonstrated that forenoon, Mick Seaholly made no move to shift the venue of the boxing match. When January returned to the liquor tent an hour later, he estimated that three-quarters of the men in the camp – and three-quarters of the Indians in the valley – were on hand to watch.

Deadfall trees had been hauled from the river bank to make a rough border around the square that Sir William paced off, the precise size of a London boxing-stage. While the Scots nobleman was cutting the scratch lines for the combatants with his knife in the dirt, January was offered so many drinks that if he'd accepted them all he'd have had trouble identifying Wildman at ten paces.

'Keep a few.' Hannibal stepped aside to let Mr Miller edge to the fore with his ever-present sketchbook. 'If you get cut again we can use it to cleanse the wound.'

'My teachers recommended spirits of wine to cleanse wounds,' returned January, stripping off his shirt, 'not snake venom mixed with river water. Which way did you bet?'

'Benjamin!' The fiddler clasped a hand to his breast. 'You wound me. You cut me to the heart. *Detrahit amicitiae maiestatem suam, qui illam parat ad bonos casus.* This is a boxing match, not an eye-gouging contest.' He fished into the dripping gourd that Prideaux was holding for him and wound strips of wet rawhide around January's hands, tucking the ends in tight.

'And if you think anyone is going to lodge a protest with the Rules Committee and proclaim me the winner if Manitou fouls me, I suggest you check the contents of that fizz pop you've been drinking.'

Men came streaming across from Seaholly's, where final bets were being laid. Charro Morales brought in his horse to the edge of the crowd for a better view and whooped, 'Free liquor tonight, if Wildman wins!' which set up a roaring cheer; the two German noblemen who, like Stewart, had come to the rendezvous for adventure and hunting, attempted to better their viewpoint by purchasing Jim Bridger's front-row spot and were unceremoniously shoved to the farthest rear.

On the other side of the boxing-stage men were shouting Wildman's name. The spectators parted, to let January through, and January's eyes widened with shock. Yesterday's bout had been so quick that he had not only missed seeing Wildman's style of combat, but also by the time he'd reached the front of the crowd, Manitou had already been putting on his shirt.

Now, for the first time, January got a look at that scarred torso. He'd helped the Army surgeons with the wounded after the Battle of Chalmette, and since he'd been in the rendez-vous camp he'd seen a surgeon's textbook of scars: tomahawk, skinning knife, bear claw, broken branches ... the wicked Xs that told of snake-bite poison far from other help. As a child, he'd seen what a five-tongued whip with iron tied into its ends would leave of an 'uppity' slave's back.

He'd never seen scars like Wildman's. Ever. Anywhere.

He couldn't even imagine what had made them or how the man had survived whatever it was.

And that ripped and mended hide covered muscle like hammered iron.

Manitou had hacked off most of his long black hair for the fight – something he hadn't bothered to do when facing off against Blankenship – as well as much of his beard, both operations obviously performed with a bowie knife and no mirror. He was clearly not a man who craved the glance of the Taos ladies. Beneath the unbroken line of brow, those clear brown eyes had a curious focus to them, distant, like a man striving to remember something long forgotten. January hoped it was the rules of the ring.

'Gentlemen,' declaimed Stewart, in a voice that could have been heard in St Louis, 'to your scratch. The fight will proceed by London rules: holding and throwing are allowable, but no gouging, no biting, no strangling, no foul blows. A man upon his knees is considered down; the

116

round is concluded with a man down; thirty seconds to rest before returning to the scratch. Is this clear?'

January said, 'Yes, sir,' and Wildman grunted.

'No crowding the contestants. No man to enter the stage except the fighters and their seconds. Understood?'

Incoherent yelling from all sides to get on with it. Men pressed up to the edges of the stage, with more standing on the tree trunks to get a head over those in front of them. A third ring of men on horses crowded behind them. Dust fogged the air. *Rose will never forgive me if I get my nose broken in the cause of getting friendly with a witness...*

Mountaineers and camp-setters passed the word to their Sioux and Flathead friends that this was fighting as it was done in the country of the English King across the sea – there wasn't an Indian alive who didn't relish a good fight. On the mountains at the north end of the valley, thunder grumbled distantly, and wind blew chilly across January's naked back, bearing the smell of coming storm.

Shaking hands with his opponent was like grasping the paw of an animal.

'Gentlemen,' called Stewart, 'begin!'

Wildman had a stance that wouldn't have been out of place in Gentleman Jackson's boxing salon in London and a punch that a grizzly would have envied. And he was – somewhat to January's surprise – a clean fighter: trained, calculating, scientific, with a precise sense of distance. January hadn't had a formal match

117

since he'd left Paris and had almost forgotten how much he'd enjoyed the sport.

They circled, watching each other for an opening – the trapper was huge, and January guessed he'd be fast. He knew already that he was going to lose, simply because his opponent would outlast him. Aside from being ten years younger, Wildman was someone who really *could* drag himself for eight days through the wilderness with two broken legs and Indians on his trail, and when all was said and done, for all his size, January was a forty-three-year-old piano-player.

And yet – as he had never been able to explain, either to Rose or to the wife of his Paris days, the beautiful Ayasha – there was great pleasure in fighting a man who fought so well.

He knocked Manitou down twice, and was himself downed, his opponent standing back, like a polite bear, to let Shaw and Hannibal get him on his feet and back to the scratch. They waded in again, hard straight punishing blows and the salt taste of blood on his mouth. He felt his stamina flagging, and sparred for wind and distance, but Manitou crowded him, forced him back toward the ring of spectators, who fell away before them. They grappled, clinched, broke apart – *if I can get him down again...*

They circled, and January squinted against the westering sun—

And saw clearly the bright bar of light that speared into Manitou's eyes.

Squaw wearing a mirror ... He reacted even as he thought this, saw his opponent flinch. His fist

118

connected with jawbone, a blow that came all the way through his back heel from the earth—

Manitou's face changed. He'd been fighting a well-trained beast. Now he suddenly faced the wild one.

The trapper bellowed something – January didn't hear what – and threw himself in, disregarding January's blows and attempts to block, caught him by the throat and hurled him aside as if he'd been a child, then kept on going into the audience. Someone screamed, 'Get him off me! Get him—!' and January struck the ground, tucking his head and curling his body to avoid being trampled. Spectators surged over him, to stop the enraged man. January was kicked, stepped on – at least four men tripped over him and a horse's hoof nicked his shoulder – and when he sat up he couldn't see anything but a surging struggle enveloped in dust, nor hear beyond a thunderous howl of rage.

Shaw and Hannibal thrashed free of the crowd, dashed to his side. 'What the hell happened?' January gasped. 'It looked like sunlight caught some squaw's mirror and threw it in his eyes—'

'That's what happened, all right,' returned Shaw grimly, and helped him to sit. 'Only it was Jed Blankenship holdin' the mirror.'

Of course it would be. So much for the possibility of getting Manitou to talk to him – or even, now, of going out to that isolated campsite with a friendly bottle some evening. Wearily, January said, 'God damn Jed Blankenship.' A dozen yards away, men were hanging on to Wildman as if to a roped bull, and Blankenship, wisely, was nowhere to be seen. 'That goddamned seventy-five dollars – and now Manitou's going to think I was in on it.'

'I'd say there's that possibility.' Shaw got him to his feet. January tried to turn his head, winced at the pang in his muscles. 'Such bein' the case, it may be best you make yourself scarce 'til he cools down ... Which, Tom tells me, can take years.'

'God damn Jed Blankenship.'

Manitou's voice rose above the din, a bull roar of insane rage, as they walked away up the path for the camp.

Shaw stationed himself outside Morning Star's lodge and spent the remainder of the afternoon explaining over and over to what sounded to January like two-thirds of the camp: 'No, we didn't have nuthin' to do with it ... Hell, no, we didn't bet on him! Friend or no friend, we ain't crazy! Ask anybody in the camp...' Morning Star anointed January's bruises with a poultice of sagebrush and mullein and brought him cold water from the river to soak his knuckles. A little later, Gil Wallach brought the news that such had been the confusion over who'd won and who'd lost that Mick Seaholly had disbarred Jed Blankenship from the AFC liquor tent and all its various amenities. 'And God help slow mares,' the trader added with a grin.

Veinte-y-Cinco was already at the camp, watching over a flushed and fretful Pia. The girl had a massive opium-headache and no very clear idea of what had happened to her: 'I remember talking to Titus, but he wasn't there before. I was just talkin' to a couple of his boys, outside Sea-holly's—'

'Anyone buy you a drink, honey?'

The girl moved one thin shoulder, with an adolescent's impatience: *what a stupid question.* 'No. You know you told Mr Seaholly you'd kill him if he sold me liquor. We were drinking coffee, is all.'

January had tasted camp coffee. It could have been doctored with gunpowder, let alone laudanum, without altering the taste. 'It could have been anyone,' he said softly, when the girl had fallen asleep among the buffalo robes. 'Anyone Titus paid off.'

Veinte-y-Cinco cursed, quietly and without any real hope in her voice, then sat for a time with her chin on her drawn-up knees, gazing into the swept stones of the lodge fire-pit. 'But he's right,' she said after a time. 'That filth-eating— Titus is right. What kind of mother am I, that I can't even keep my child from harm? I brought her up here—'

'And she'd have been safer back in Taos by herself?' Hannibal and Morning Star ducked through the entry hole into the tent, carrying wood for that night's fire.

'I don't know—' The woman looked aside, in grief that had long ago exhausted its lifetime allotment of tears. 'I don't know what to do.' She made a move to rise. 'I got to get back. Can she sleep here tonight?'

'You both can,' said Morning Star. It was her lodge, after all.

'It's coming on to rain,' added Hannibal. *'Numquam imprudentibus imber obfuit...'*

'Hoss!' yelled Prideaux's voice from outside. 'Hoss, you got to come! You got to – where'd he go? Hoss!' The red-haired trapper thrust his head through the entry hole. 'Hoss, this is it! It's startin' to rain, an' I just heard from that kid Poco – that camp-setter of Blankenship's – that Beauty an' the Dutchman sneaked around whilst everyone was at the fight an' bought up everythin' they'll need for a year's trappin'! Salt, whetstones, lead ... They're headin' out tonight, with the rain to cover their tracks—'

January rolled his eyes. 'Weren't they supposed to be heading out three nights ago? When everyone went out and skulked around in the rain—'

'But tonight is really it!' Prideaux was so excited he could barely get the words out. 'I went out an' had a look at their camp an' that squaw of the Dutchman's is *takin' down her dryin' racks*!'

'When my mama started takin' in her dryin' racks from the yard,' remarked Shaw, ducking into the tent at Prideaux's heels, 'it generally meant there was rain comin' in, not that she was gettin' ready to light outta there in secret.'

'But this's their *secret beaver valley*!' insisted Prideaux, as if the Kentuckian had somehow missed the critical importance of that fact. 'You just wait 'til this child follows those boys to their secret valley, an' comes back next rendezvous with beaver skins big as buffalo hides! Wee–augh! How's your neck, hoss?' he asked in a

122

more normal tone.

'After today I won't fear hangin'.'

'Well,' remarked Hannibal to Veinte-y-Cinco, when Prideaux finally left – on the run – to gather up what plunder he'd need to pursue Clarke and Groot into the hills, and the first spatters of rain rattled on the lodge skins, 'you might as well make yourself comfortable, m'am; it's not like there's going to be anything happening at Seaholly's with half the camp out in the woods. Come, *amicus meus*,' he added, turning to January as Morning Star knelt to kindle the fire, 'let's have some stories. Tell us about the strangest person you ever met...'

January woke to voices. The river's roar, to which he'd fallen asleep last night, thundered unabated, but the light that came through the semi-translucent lodge-skins told him that the sun was up and shining. He felt as if he'd fallen down a flight of stairs and broken his neck. On the other side of the fire, Veinte-y-Cinco and her daughter slept close together, a tangle of soft limbs and dark hair under a five-point trade-blanket. A short distance away, Hannibal was a knot of draped bones. Outside the tent he heard Shaw ask someone in French: 'An' no sign around the body?'

If he's speaking French, he'll be talking to Morning Star...

'None that could be read, says Chased By Bears. Only that his throat was cut.'

Goodpastor. The Indian Agent.

Or Blankenship...

Trouble at the rendezvous. Bad trouble, killing trouble...

Morning Star's voice went on: 'He was no one from the camp. An old man, his hair was white and his face shaven like the traders. Chased By Bears and Little Fish –' that was Morning Star's cousin – 'say they found no trace of horses near the place. But the old man had built a shelter and a fire before he was killed—'

'He dressed like a trader?'

January rolled silently to his feet, found his pants and his boots, and ducked through the door of the lodge, blinking in the morning sunlight. The whole world glittered with last night's rain.

'No, Tall Chief,' said the Sioux girl to Shaw, worriedly. 'He is not dressed at all. He lies in his shelter naked, his throat cut, wearing nothing but...' She held up her hands, searching for the word. 'Wearing nothing but white man's perfume on his hair and black gloves on his hands. And my brother is afraid – all the tribes are afraid – that this is the man the government has sent to cause trouble with Cold Face about the traders' liquor, and that the next ones to come here will be the Army, saying that we are to blame.'

NINE

They woke Hannibal, poured coffee down him –
he was no easier to rouse now than he'd been
when he was drinking himself unconscious six
nights a week – and left him in charge of the
store. Then they rode north along the river,
swung west where Horse Creek purled along the
feet of timbered hills. North of the creek the
drier valley stretched away in miles of bunch
grass, to where William Bonneville had tried to
establish a fort a few years ago – a silly place to
try to set up a trading station, as Wallach had
pointed out. But if the British ever did make a
serious attempt to take and hold these disputed,
fur-rich lands, this would indeed be a very good
place to stop them.

They crossed the creek, the water high and
freezing cold. On the south side the hills rose
under a thin cover of lodgepole pine, last year's
yellow needles wet underfoot. Shaw dismounted
and led his horse, stopping to examine the
droppings of horses and mules (January couldn't
tell the difference, but his companion evidently
could). 'Looks like Groot an' Clarke,' the Kentuckian surmised. 'Rain washed out most of the
sign.'

Ahead, January could hear the hoarse calls of

ravens. Wind passed through the pines; like the deep rushing of the trees in the bayou swamps of his earliest childhood, before he'd known New Orleans or Paris. A world of silence, and of beasts: cruel Bouki the Fox, wise old Mbumba the serpent rainbow, silly M'am Perdix and her chicks and wily, nimble Compair Lapin the rabbit ... who, even now, paused on his errands in a patch of sunlight between the pines and sat up, watching the two men pass with the young woman in her deerskin dress.

Then the ravens called again, harshly, squabbling over the tastiest bits of a dead man's flesh.

The black birds flew up cursing when the three companions came into the little clearing, just below the crown of the ridge. The brush all around rustled with an explosion of fleeing foxes. The ants and the flies ignored the interlopers, as ants and flies will.

In a rough shelter of branches against the huge roots of a deadfall pine, the dead man lay on a bed of more boughs, raised a little off the ground on stones. In front of it a fire pit had been dug, protected from the rain. January knelt and held his hand over the ashes. They were still mildly warm.

As Morning Star had reported, the dead man wore nothing but a pair of black kid gloves, and his throat had been cut almost to the neck bone, severing carotids, jugulars and windpipe. A few feet in front of the shelter – and the pine needles were scuffed up everywhere in the small clearing – even the rain had not completely washed

126

the blood out of the ground. Flies roared above it in clouds.

January said, 'Jesus.' It was obvious – even through the predation of the ravens and foxes – that, prior to having his throat cut, the old man had been viciously beaten.

'Well,' observed Shaw drily, 'this for sure ain't Indian work.'

'No.' January knelt beside the pine-bough bed as Shaw moved about the clearing, examining the bindings on the shelter, the stones around the fire. 'And nobody tried to make it look like Indian work.'

'Lets out Boden, don't it?'

When January repeated this observation to Morning Star in French, the young woman replied, 'Will your Great Chief in the East know this? Or the men in the camp, when they hear that a white grandfather has been killed? Or will they say only, *"It cannot have been one of us who did this thing, so it must have been the Blackfeet ... but since there are no Blackfeet to lay hands on, let us go kill some Sioux instead?"*'

January said nothing, but felt the dead man's wrists, which were just beginning to stiffen, and – rather gingerly – the muscles of his neck. Just above the bed, bark had been scraped away from the pine, and on the pale wood beneath someone had cut a cross with a knife.

'When did your cousin find him?'

'The sun was two hands above the mountains.' She had walked a little distance away – as angry as Shaw, in her own way – and now came back, steadied by the request for specifics. 'Little Fish

127

saw the ravens and thought it might have been a bear's kill, from which he could take the horns. He said his first thought was to drag the man deeper into the hills and bury him in a coulee. But, he said, bears would dig him out again, and with men all over these hills looking for the Beauty and the Dutchman, someone would find him. Then, of course, they would say: *see how the Indians tried to hide the body?*'

'They would at that,' Shaw murmured, coming back to the shelter. 'Scalped or not scalped ... Your brothers followin' us?'

'Little Fish is.'

'Send him to your camp,' said Shaw. 'Get a couple horses with a litter – not a travois, but a horse litter, like you'd carry someone real sick in – an' a couple braves. It'd be best if all was to see you an' your family bringin' this man in with honor. Then they'll pay attention to the fact that he weren't scalped nor tortured, no matter what else was done to him. Bring a couple of robes, too, to cover him decent.'

Morning Star whistled, and for a moment January thought that another squaw had trailed them as well; then realized that Morning Star's cousin was a *winkte*, a man who had chosen the dress and duties of a woman ... and who was permitted to do so, something he wouldn't have been in any city in the United States except maybe New Orleans. Little Fish listened to his cousin's instruction and was turning to go when January said, 'Ask him, did he move anything? Touch anything?'

'Nothing,' she reported, when the question was

128

conveyed and answered. Little Fish – tall and thin in contrast to his cousin's neat smallness – explained: 'My cousin realized he needed his older brother's advice, so he left things as he found them.'

'Your cousin is a wise man,' said January.

'He says,' she added, 'that the branches of the shelter were wet on their undersides when he was first here, as well as above, though they have dried now. It rained three times in the night, stopping between times.'

Shaw knelt and moved the cut wood that had been laid close to the fire: 'Damp on the underside. Cut with a tommyhawk,' he added, turning the end of one of the short aspen-branches in his bony fingers.

'Well, that narrows it down.' Every trapper in the camp carried an Indian belt-ax. January turned back to Morning Star. 'How close are we to Manitou Wildman's camp?'

'About half as far as it is back to the river.'

A mile, give or take...

'Would your cousin be safe in fetching him?'

Morning Star gave the matter some thought, then asked Little Fish something. The *winkte* made a sign with his hand, replied.

'My cousin says, he does not know. He has spoken to Crazy Bear at the camps, but he says – and he is right – that sometimes this is safe to do, and sometimes not. I will go,' she added. 'Even when his worst spirit is in him, Crazy Bear will not lift his hand against a woman – unlike the husbands among my people,' she finished pointedly. 'And his camp is close enough that he may well have heard what passed here last night.'

The two cousins departed in opposite directions, and Shaw stood for a time, still fingering the cut end of the branch. 'Think he'll come?'

'It'll tell us something if he doesn't. But that shelter doesn't look like the work of an amateur.' January knelt again beside the dead man, carefully worked one of the gloves from the stiffening hand. 'If this man ever did manual labor, it was decades ago. No calluses...' He ran a gentle finger over the soft palm, the unswollen knuckles. The fore and middle fingers were stained with ink – many weeks old – and marked with older and deeper stains: yellow, brown, faded red. The pale body was in keeping with the hands, slender but flabby, certainly not the body of a mountaineer. 'You think he's our Indian Agent?'

'If he is, his party'll be in the camp when we get back.' Shaw bent his long body around, to examine more closely the inside of the shelter. 'An' if they ain't, we can at least have a word with the Reverend Grey about his friend Goodpastor – what you make of this, Maestro?' He touched the scratched cross, and January shook his head.

'That after beating an old man with his fists, breaking three ribs, breaking his knee –' January lightly touched the swollen joint – 'cutting his throat and stripping him naked, the killer decided his victim needed the blessing of God to send him on his way? It's good to know such piety still exists in the world.'

'Well, the Reverend Grey'll purely bear witness to that.' Shaw's thumb brushed the dead man's smooth chin, where traces of blood had been carefully wiped away. 'The old man coulda cut that cross hisself, when he made the shelter. If he made the shelter. Would a man bruise up like that if'fn he got his throat cut right on top of a poundin'?'

'I've seen it,' said January slowly. 'Not with a throat-cutting, nor with a man this old, nor someone who's lain outdoors naked on a rainy night. But bruises will form for a short time after death. His killer must have hated him,' he went on, contemplating the old man's white hair and silvery side-whiskers, 'to hammer him like that before he killed him. Or been drunk,' he added. 'Or insane with rage, to do this to a stranger.'

'It does, indeed, bear the marks of some of the family sentiment I seen.' Shaw had, January reflected, been a City Guard in New Orleans for eight years. 'Any bruises on the feller's back or shoulders? Long bruises, like from a stick or a whip?'

January turned the body over, revealing no bruises ... but a deep and bloody puncture just beneath the left shoulder-blade, where a knife had been driven into the old man's heart.

January said, 'Jesus Christ,' and laid him back down again. It was like handling a scarecrow. The old man couldn't have weighed a hundred and twenty pounds.

'Look at where he's bruised,' said Shaw softly. 'He's bruised where you're bruised, Maestro – 'ceptin' Manitou was fightin' you by London

131

Boxing Rules an' so didn't kick you in the stones nor break your knee like this killer done. But the rest of it's same as you: jaw, belly, ribs, all in the front. I'd paste Methuselah hisself that way, if the old man were to come at me with a gun an' I had none. But with a knee broke, an' ribs too, there was no need to stab him in the back nor cut his throat. That says hate to me ... or panic.'

Or madness.

Shaw returned to the fire pit and stirred carefully through the ashes with the tip of his knife. 'Panic, too, not to scalp an' mutilate him, with all the Indians in the world a couple miles away to put the blame on. Might as well leave a sign tacked to his chest sayin': *A White Man Done This*. You think any of our friends down the camp would panic if they killed a man?'

'Only if they found out too late that he actually knew the way to Clarke and Groot's secret beaver valley.'

Keeping together, Shaw and January worked their way around the outer perimeter of the clearing, Shaw checking the ground for sign and January checking the woods in all directions for Blackfeet – not, he reflected, that he'd be able to see them coming until he got an arrow in the back. The needles seemed to be scratched about by animals larger than foxes, but because of last night's rain it was impossible to tell who had passed that way, or when. 'Is reading sign something they teach white boys in Kentucky?' asked January softly, when Shaw straightened up.

'It is if the family's gettin' half their food out of the woods.' He moved from tree to tree

132

craning his skinny neck to look at the trunks, as if seeking some further mark. 'Then, too, my uncle Naboth was kidnapped by the Shawnee as a child, raised among 'em for a year an' a half – family never could teach him to sit in a chair after that, my daddy said. He taught us ... Johnny was wild to be kidnapped by Indians, too,' he added with a half grin. 'Even if he had to travel clear to the Nebraska Territory to arrange it. Tom—'

He turned, bringing his rifle up before January was even aware that there'd been movement in the trees.

It was Morning Star.

'Crazy Bear is gone from his camp,' she said. 'His blankets are there, and his food also. Last night's fire was burned out; even the ashes are cold.'

'He could be down at the camp.'

'We'd'a passed him.' Shaw glanced back through the trees, to where ravens were regathering around the corpse. 'Damn birds,' he added, and the three companions returned to the body's side. 'But I would be most curious as to who-all else has turned up at the camp today, an' what they have to say about what our friend here was doin' out in the woods all by hisself. What you got to say about his glove, Maestro? An' them stains on his hands?'

'I think the yellow ones are acid,' said January. 'Gomez – the man I studied surgery with before I went to Paris – had some like it. The others I don't know. The glove's expensive – a dollar a pair at someplace like Au Cheval de la Lune in

133

New Orleans. But it's old; you see where it was mended, and how the dye's worn off on the finger edge and thumb where reins would go?'

With great care he removed the other glove from the left hand.

'Somebody missed somethin',' remarked Shaw as the sun through the lodgepole pines gleamed softly on the gold of a wedding band.

'Shall we take that off him?'

Shaw sighed. 'If'fn we don't, somebody back at the camp is bound to, the minute we turns our backs.'

January grinned. 'You been a policeman too long, sir.'

TEN

'Five dollars says Beauty Clarke done it,' offered Jed Blankenship. 'This pilgrim cut his trail last night—'

'Don't be a dolt, Blankenship,' sighed Jim Bridger. 'Does this old buzzard look savvy enough to cut Beauty Clarke's trail?'

The knot of trappers holding a shooting contest near the mouth of Horse Creek had been the first to sight the little party of Sioux as they'd crossed the stream with their burden. By the time they'd reached the Ivy and Wallach camp, the knot had grown to a procession, with Robbie Prideaux running ahead to alert Hannibal, so that a fly could be rigged under the trees near the store tent and trestles set up to receive the robe-draped litter. The Reverend Grey had been sent for – he was found, as usual, preaching a temperance sermon outside Seaholly's – and gazed in horror at the face of the man on the bier. January had laid a folded bandanna from his pocket over the worst of the damage done by foxes and birds. Grey lifted it momentarily and laid it hastily down again.

'No,' he whispered, his usual sanctimonious-ness completely shattered by pity and shock. 'No, this isn't Asa Goodpastor. I've never seen this poor man before in my life.' He looked as if he wanted to do something like close the corpse's eyes, but of course that wasn't possible.

By this time most of the camp was arriving at a run. Booze, whores, five-card monte and shooting matches were one thing, but a wanderer in the woods who *hadn't* been killed by Indians was a nine days' wonder and trumped any amount of Mick Seaholly's liquor.

'Fitz, get some of your boys to get these people out of here,' snapped Edwin Titus in disgust. He and the Company's senior trapper, Tom Fitz-patrick, had been two of the quickest arrivals.

'Rather'n do that,' suggested Shaw, 'whyn't we get 'em in a line and file 'em past the body for a viewin'? That way we'll hear right away, if'fn anybody knows him.'

'Good God, man, why would anyone in the camp know him?'

'He sure didn't come up to the mountains for his health.'

135

'If he did,' remarked Hannibal, 'he should sue his doctor.'

'It is *asqueroso*,' cried Charro Morales. 'Disgusting. Can you not let the poor old man rest in peace?'

'Anybody new come into the camp today?' asked Shaw as Tom Fitzpatrick and Jim Bridger moved off into the gathering crowd to get the men into a rough line. Looks were exchanged, heads shaken.

Mick Seaholly pushed his way into the growing crowd around the bier, caught Shaw's elbow: 'We've got a spare markee down at the AFC camp and more room than this. I'll give you two hundred dollars to move him down there.' January opened his mouth to protest and saw Shaw glance sidelong at Titus – who, to his credit, looked totally revolted at the suggestion.

But then, he'd managed to convey a near approximation of total revulsion yesterday when accused of attempting to drug and rape a thirteen-year-old girl.

'Or let me set up a bar in your store and I'll split the proceeds fifty percent.' Seaholly gestured behind him to a couple of the AFC campsetters just coming up with kegs and tin cups, clearly prepared for anything.

Shaw bowed to the inevitable. 'Fine with me, but you gotta ask Gil Wallach. Looks like the only way we're gonna make money this summer.'

'*Asqueroso*,' muttered Morales, but went off to get a barrel of his own liquor in case Seaholly ran out.

For the remainder of the day, January and Hannibal took turns standing by the unknown man's bier, watching the faces of those who passed. Whichever of them wasn't on duty at the bier side, sat on a packsaddle by the line and told the story three hundred and fifty times: they'd found the body in a clearing on the other side of Horse Creek, by the signs he'd been killed sometime in the night, always making sure to exclaim that it sure hadn't been done by Indians.

'Looks a bit old for the game, doesn't he?' remarked Sir William Stewart as he emerged from the fly. 'Wonder where he's left his razors?' By the way he spoke in passing to Edwin Titus, it was clear to January that he believed his host's version of what Pia had been doing in Titus's tent.

And why not? Even as a child, January had been aware that white gentlemen believed white gentlemen; and that the face a white gentleman showed his white gentlemen friends frequently concealed horrors done in the privacy of what he considered his exclusive domain.

He replied, 'I wondered that myself, sir.'

'Not to speak of his valet.' Stewart blew a line of cigar smoke and glanced down the row of waiting men with speculation in his dark eyes. 'Since there are at least two other trade caravans due to arrive in the camp – and since it's clear our Senex Incognito isn't going to keep – I wondered if you'd like me to get Mr Miller to take a likeness of him?'

'I think that's a brilliant idea, sir, if Mr Miller would be willing,' said January. 'Thank you.'

137

So Mr Miller was summoned – actually, he was only a few yards down the line, waiting his turn – and made sketches of the old man as he lay, and of what he had probably looked like in life, while men walked past exclaiming: 'What the Sam Hill—?' and 'Where in blazes did he drop from?' and 'He ain't been scalped...' (*Good*, thought January, *you go repeat that around the camp if you please...*)

And everybody went to the store tent next door and bought liquor at three dollars a pint. Even allowing for a fifty-percent split with Seaholly, it was definitely the best profits Ivy and Wallach had made all summer.

January was taking his shift beside the body when he heard the buzz of voices outside suddenly rise. Past the line of men, he saw three Indians approaching on foot. Beaded belts, naked to the waist...

Iron Heart and his Omahas.

Hannibal got up immediately and went to them, realizing – January guessed – the obvious fact that it was better to risk a few grumbles from the whites in the line about Indians getting in for a look ahead of them, than to risk combat in the line itself if they waited among whites for any length of time. The trappers by and large got along well with the Indians of whatever tribe they dealt with, though many of the AFC men sided with the Crow in saying that you couldn't trust a Flathead as far as you could throw a piano ... But enough men were visiting Seaholly's end of the store tent *before* they got in line that it was best to nip trouble in the bud.

But Iron Heart only looked down at the ruined face and said, in his Mission Indian English, 'It was a white man who did this.'

'Your people heard nothing?' asked January. 'Saw nothing? The man did not fall from the sky. He must have left a camp in the woods, horses, probably at least one other man. Your hunters have seen no sign of this? Camped as you are above Horse Creek, you might see what others might not.'

'We have seen nothing.' The pockmarked face was expressionless. 'The only sign we have found has been of the Blackfoot, and of hunters – we think perhaps Crow or Flathead – on the other side of the river to the north. If this grandfather were killed by a white man, it does not mean that he who stole his horses and killed his companions was the same white man who killed him. There may be more dead men in the gullies than one, Winter Moon. And more than that,' he added quietly, 'before the camp here breaks.'

'Will you tell me if you find anything?'

'And why should I do that?' Iron Heart looked coldly up into his face. 'Why should it concern me if every white man in this camp dies and lies rotting on the ground, as my people lay among our tents and rotted along the banks of the Platte when the white man's fever came through our homeland? You destroy what you touch, white man, including one another. One day you will destroy the land itself.'

He turned and walked from the square shade of the stretched cover, back upriver toward their distant camp.

139

'Hard point to dispute,' murmured Shaw, who had materialized as quietly as a shadow at the rear of the fly. 'Though, mind you, I didn't care for that business about how maybe there's a couple more deaders up the gullies. You think some of your in-laws might be prevailed on, Sefton, to go have a look 'fore night comes on? I think between keepin' things orderly here, an' makin' sure Seaholly ain't left for ten seconds by hisself in the store tent – Clopard's in there with him now – I think we're here 'til mornin' at least.'

'Do we bury our friend come morning?' January had been using a pine bough to switch away the flies that swarmed around the old man's face, but knew that by morning, in the July heat of the high mountain valley, the maggots that had been laid before the corpse had been discovered would start to hatch. There were other unpleasant symptoms of mortality as well, and the ants no one could do anything about.

Night would bring complications of its own.

'I'd say we gotta. Though I would like to keep him around as long as we can today, as there's folk we ain't heard from yet. None of you's seen Manitou Wildman, have you?'

Hannibal shook his head. 'Nor the Beauty and Groot, though they'll be halfway to their secret ... Ah.' He stopped, as if recalling Jed Blankenship's initial accusation, and why it would have been the first thing anyone in the camp thought of. 'Hem. Yes.'

'You boys see what you can put together, of who went out playin' Leatherstocking in the woods last night, an' of them, who's back in camp now. Get Prideaux an' Veinte-y-Cinco to help. They knows everybody in the camp.'

Shaw slouched his hands in his pockets, spit into the thickets of huckleberry that the camp-setters had hacked back in order to set up the fly. Liquor wasn't the only white man's vice too dangerous to indulge away from the protection of the camp; January smiled a little to himself, at the quickness with which Shaw had sought out 'Missouri manufactured' – as it was called – on his return. 'I don't think it was our friend Boden that did for the old boy – since he didn't try to blame it on the Indians. But hanged if I can see how one feller headin' for the rendezvous alive an' disappearing, an' another feller appearin' at the rendezvous dead out of nowhere, can't have somethin' to do with each other somehow. I better go ask that pusillanimous skunk Titus if'fn one of his AFC boys don't know how to put together a coffin. If Grey shows up again...'

'*Madre de Dios*,' cried a young man's voice from the front of the fly, hoarse with shock.

January, Shaw, and Hannibal all swung around, just as Blankenship pushed his way through the crowd to seize the arm of the youth who had gasped the words – one of his camp-setters, January saw ... What was his name? Poco. A half-breed boy from Santa Fe, small and wiry—

'He has come after me,' whispered Poco, and crossed himself. 'I never thought that it was true, that if you rob the dead they would come to you, demanding their own back.'

141

—small and wiry and wearing a handsome pair of black wool trousers that would have fit the dead man perfectly.

ELEVEN

'That's horseshit,' said Blankenship. 'I robbed more dead men than I got friends livin''—'

We few, we happy few,' quoted Hannibal irreverently.

'—an' not a one of 'em ever come around askin' for his plunder back.'

But Poco was already unbuttoning the trousers. He stepped out of them and held them out to Shaw: 'I am truly sorry. It is not that I wished to rob the dead, but they were so much better than my own.'

'Hannibal,' said Shaw, 'you go mind the store.'

Poco's story was a simple one. He had waited until his master left the camp the previous night – shortly before the onset of the rain – and made his way across Horse Creek alone, aided by a dark-lantern for which he'd traded what remained of his tobacco ration, for the moon, on those rare occasions when the clouds parted, was but two days past new. 'My cousin works for Señor Groot,' he explained. 'He told me that day, that if I wanted work with his party I should meet them at Rotten Draw, that runs into Horse Creek from the hills, when it was fully dark—'

'An' you didn't think to tell me this?' Blankenship, who had refused to be turned out of the fly, smote the boy with his wolfskin hat. 'I ought to—'

'I feared it might be a trick, Señor,' explained the young man ingenuously. 'Ramón is clever, and it would be like him, to tell me this, hoping that I would then tell you and draw you from the true trail.'

Blankenship's eyes narrowed with suspicion at this tale, but he let the matter pass.

The brush along Rotten Draw – 'If it was Rotten Draw where I found myself, Señor, for it was dark and raining like the Great Flood' – was thick, and Poco became thoroughly lost. 'When the rain stopped I heard shots – not in the camp, but closer, in the woods above the creek it sounded like.'

'How many shots?'

'Two, Señor Shaw. Also, for a time I thought that I was being followed. But it began again to rain, and with the darkness of the clouds, I could not be sure. It might only have been some other, to whom Ramón let "slip out" this story about Rotten Draw, but it might also have been the Blackfoot. I dared not call out. I slipped and rolled down the draw, and tore my trousers. So I went to ground, like a fox, under some bushes, and waited until there was enough light to see.'

At daybreak – for the young man had drifted off to sleep once the rain had ceased for good – Poco had climbed back out of the draw and made his way to the top of the ridge and back toward the camp. 'I was cold and very hungry,

143

and frightened too, because of the Blackfeet. When I smelled smoke I thought that it was the camp of Oso Loco – Señor Manitou – which I knew to be somewhere along the creek. But I found instead a shelter made of boughs, with a dead fire before it, and a dead man lying on the ground.'

'On the ground?' repeated January.

'*Sí*, Señor. The shelter was at one side of a clearing, and the man lay on his face. His feet were pointing toward the shelter – perhaps three feet distant – and his arms lay at his sides like this.' Poco demonstrated, holding his arms curved away from his sides so that his hands were about a foot from each hip. 'He had been stabbed in the back. His shirt was all soaked with blood, and when I turned him over I saw that his throat had been cut, and the breast of his shirt was also red with blood—'

The youth looked aside, suddenly white around the mouth.

'So he's wearin' a shirt?'

'*Sí*, Señor Shaw. A new shirt...' Poco's eyes narrowed as he tried to call back the scene. 'Just an ordinary checkered shirt, like Señor Enero's –' he nodded toward January – 'or Señor Prideaux's...'

The men gathered before the fly, standing or hunkered, or sitting on chunks of firewood on the still-wet ground, looked at each other. Checkered shirts from Lowell, Massachusetts were among the most common in the camp. Prideaux's, which he'd loyally bought from Ivy and Wallach a few days previously, was – like

144

January's – yellow-and-black, brand new and stiff with starch. Others represented had been worn hard and faded colorless with weather and wind.

'Big shirt or small shirt?' asked January, and Poco frowned again.

'To tell the truth, Señor, I cannot remember. Only the blood.' He shivered, drawing his long, thin, bare brown legs together under his own dangling shirt tails.

'Boots?'

'No, Señor. Nothing. His leg had been broken, and someone had tied two straight sticks on it. I— May the Mother of God forgive me, I untied them and threw them away. I could see that the poor old man had no need of his trousers anymore, and ... and they are very fine trousers, Señor. And my own had never been very good, even when they were whole. And I thought, perhaps the old man had a son, to whom he would willingly have given his trousers, if he had found him cold and naked in the wilderness. By the Mother of God –' Poco crossed himself once more – 'truly I meant no harm.'

'You leave him where he laid?' asked Shaw, and Poco nodded miserably.

'I had no means to bury him, Señor. And, in truth, I could not rid my mind of the Blackfeet, and what they do to those they capture. I told myself, the dead are the dead; he has no more use even of his poor body, much less of the garments which clothed it.' Guilt and wretchedness filled the young man's brown eyes. 'Had he been still living, I would have—'

145

''Course you would.' Rising, Shaw laid a hand on Poco's shoulder. 'Any man here would.'

Looking across at Blankenship, January did not feel prepared to lay money on that assertion.

And Pia, who had slipped into the fly between the men, piped up, 'Was there anything in his pockets?'

'What there was, I have left there.' Poco gestured toward the black trousers, which Shaw still held in one hand. 'All of it. For in truth, no good can come of taking from the dead.'

Shaw dug in the trouser pockets and brought out a sizeable chunk of vermillion – the flame-colored dyestuff from China, which all the traders dealt in, still wrapped in its paper – a thick packet of banknotes and a very handsome silver watch.

Gil Wallach said kindly, 'Here, Poco—' and tossed him a pair of new wool pants. 'I'll put these on our dead friend's tab.'

It was near dark when the liquor ran out. By that time, everyone in the camp had been through the fly at least twice, the exceptions being Manitou Wildman, everyone connected with Goshen Clarke and Clemantius Groot's party, and the young New England trapper Boaz Frye. Bridger and Fitzpatrick of the AFC volunteered to comb through the rough country south of Horse Creek for any others who, like Poco and Blankenship, had thought to follow the two independents to their secret beaver valley, while Kit Carson returned to Wildman's camp. Through the tail end of the long afternoon, a fair-sized troop of

146

would-be Beauty-trackers made their way back to the rendezvous, cursing their elusive quarry and agog to hear what had happened in their vicinity, unbeknownst.

Most of these claimed to have heard two shots, shortly after the rain had ceased for the first time, at which point the moon, what there was of it, was coming to zenith. Some had assumed these shots to be Blackfoot. Others thought they were Clarke and Groot trying to discourage followers. Most agreed that the shots had been slightly less than a minute apart.

During these testimonies, conducted alternately by Shaw and January at the rear of the fly, Hannibal assisted Mick Seaholly and Charro Morales in pouring drinks. Thus, by the time even the Mexican trader's more expensive barrel was exhausted, and the AFC publican took his empty kegs and his customers back down to their regular venue, Hannibal had a list of about a hundred theories as to who might have committed the murder, propounded to him across the bar.

'I like the one that claims it was Generalissimo Santa Anna,' he mused, studying his notes by the light of the campfire that had been built in front of the fly. 'Is he in Washington these days?'

'They let him go home.' January shook his head, bemused. 'Considering the Americans he massacred at the Alamo, I'm still astonished that Sam Houston's soldiers didn't kill him on the spot when they caught him...'

'I'd have held their coats for them.' During Hannibal's visit to Mexico two winters ago, the

147

dictator's negligence had very nearly gotten him hanged.

January adjusted a trade blanket over the side of the fly, knotted it into place with strips of rawhide – the ubiquitous fasteners of everything beyond the frontier – and held the corner of another blanket for Morning Star and Veinte-y-Cinco to do the same. 'How many were with Blankenship, that it was Groot or Clarke or both?'

'About a dozen.' Hannibal edged aside on the flat rock on which he sat, to let Pia arrange supper over the fire: green sticks laden with skewered meat. 'There's the usual accusations that it was either the Blackfeet, that band of Crows – only, Tom Fitzpatrick said he'd heard it was Flatheads that are lurking – in the hills to the north, or Iron Heart's Omahas—'

'In spite of the fact that our friend there still got his hair on.' Shaw came into the circle of the firelight, from closing up the store.

Hannibal tapped the side of his nose and looked crafty. 'They're sly. One vote apiece for the Sioux, Red Arm's Crows here in the camp, the Hudson's Bay Flatheads – this isn't counting those who believe that the group lurking in the north *are* Flatheads, working for Hudson's Bay. Votes also for the Company's Delaware scouts, the Snakes, the Crees, the Assiniboin, and the Nez Perces, with no more argument for motive other than that they are Indians.'

'*Cabrons*.' Veinte-y-Cinco knelt to set a Dutch oven of cornbread on the coals. 'Like any Indian's gonna kill a man and leave that much

148

vermillion in his pocket.' She settled on the rock next to Hannibal, took a comb from her skirt pocket and proceeded to comb out her long hair.

'*Homini praeposuit veritatem.*' Hannibal turned the pages over, thin hands a little shaky in the firelight. Other than occasional bouts with the symptoms of withdrawal from long-term opiate consumption, the fiddler had held up surprisingly well. But the journey, January was well aware, had been hard on him: his friend was not one of those specimens of American hardihood so beloved of temperance-tract writers, who had only to be thrown on his own into the company of red-blooded mountaineers in the embrace of Nature, to abandon all thought of evil habits and be restored to complete health. Though his consumption had gone into abeyance, January could still hear it whisper in the rasping of Hannibal's breath; could see it sometimes, when the fiddler put his hand to his side in pain when he didn't think anyone was looking.

'We also have accusations against Sir William Stewart – you can't trust these aristocrats, you know; ten for Edwin Titus, assuming that the victim actually *is* the missing Asa Goodpastor – although I think Warren Wynne would accuse Titus of anything at this point, since the AFC has pretty much bankrupted him this summer. Three for the Reverend Grey, also assuming that the victim is Goodpastor, who knew some terrible secret about the Reverend; one for John McLeod; one for the secret long-lost husband of Irish Mary –' he named the youngest and

149

prettiest of the Taos girls, who was in fact no more Irish than the rest of them – 'and, of course, twenty-five votes for Manitou Wildman. Gordy Dalrain swears the dead man is actually Aaron Burr—'

'*Aaron Burr*?' January – who had settled on the opposite side of the blaze to count out the stranger's banknotes – almost dropped them into the fire.

'—who faked his death last year in New York with the express purpose of returning to the West for another try at setting up his Empire. According to Gordy, Burr was pursued by government agents who ran him to earth here and killed him—'

'And then erected a comfortable shelter out of the rain and left a fire to warm his corpse?'

The fiddler shrugged. 'I don't suppose we could prove it *isn't* Burr.' He poured himself tea from the tin camp-kettle that Morning Star had hung on a green-stick tripod above the fire, grimaced at the taste. Among his young wife's many accomplishments, tea-making was signally lacking. 'The fire, of course, was to destroy all record of Burr's nefarious plots, plus any proof of his identity. And how much money did our third Vice President have there in his pocket when he was killed?'

'Five thousand dollars, always supposing the Bank of New York, the Bank of Pennsylvania, the Germantown and Lancaster Citizens' Bank, Wesley's Private Bank of Manhattan, the Ohio and Albany Commercial Bank, and about ten other such establishments are still in business.

We can discount the two thousand here from the Bank of Louisiana—'

'Proving conclusively that it was Burr.' Hannibal shook his head. 'So many secret papers in his pockets, they didn't need the banknotes to start the fire. It explains why they stripped him, too, of course. There's coffee here, too, *amicus meus*—'

Veinte-y-Cinco rose, and Shaw set aside the saddle-worn black trousers, the plain German silver watch that he'd been studying, and walked her down the path to Seaholly's, with the matter-of-fact obligingness of a man walking any woman to her work after dark. When he returned he was accompanied by Kit Carson and Jim Bridger, who accepted the invitation to stay and dine.

'I think I got 'em all,' said Bridger, tearing – with perfect politeness – the elk meat from the rib he held. 'All but that child Frye – he come in? No? An' not even a footprint at Wildman's camp.'

'No sign of any other camp?'

'Plenty sign.' Carson tugged a corner of his light-brown mustache, vexed. 'Hell, we had half the rendezvous stampedin' across those hills lookin' for Beauty and the Dutchman. The rain washed out pretty much everythin' but droppings. Didn't see nothing clustered together, like you'd have if anyone had put down for any length of time.'

'How far'd you go?'

'Maybe four miles back along the creek, 'bout two miles over the ridge.'

151

'Cross the river?'

Carson shook his head. 'I was huntin' for Wildman, not our friend's camp.' He nodded toward the gaily-striped blanket walls of the makeshift morgue. 'Damnedest thing I ever saw,' he added – which, January reflected, coming from Carson, was saying a great deal. 'Old buffer's got to have a camp someplace, and folks looking for him – 'less they're all of 'em croaked. They would be, if they were across the river and ran into the Blackfeet. You folks need help keepin' our friend from havin' dinner guests tonight?'

'It'd be a help, yes, thank you,' said Shaw. 'I 'preciate it.'

Curious, January reflected, that Senex Incognito, as Stewart had dubbed him, was almost universally referred to as 'our friend,' though in life he might easily have been plotting trouble – *killin' bad* – serious enough, perhaps, to endanger every man in the camp. Death – and the savage manner of his death – had brought out the ready friendliness of the trappers, the willingness to speak of him as a friend and to sit up all night to keep vermin from eating his corpse.

Already, January could hear furtive rustlings in the brush of the bottomlands below the camp. He hoped the only things drawn to the smell of the corpse would be foxes and coyote.

If it's a bear, he thought, *he can have him...*

'That boy Poco was right, though,' went on Shaw after a time. 'The old man got no more need of his body now than he has of those britches Poco borrowed. Still, it's a lonesome business, watchin' alone.'

So they split the watches, two and two, through the night in the time-honored way: Shaw and Prideaux, January and Jim Bridger, Hannibal and Kit Carson, LeBel and Clopard. At one point on January's vigil something quite large snuffled at the other side of the blanket wall, but evidently the scents of men and fire were enough to convince it – or them – to stay away. Certainly, the conversation with Jim Bridger – about beaver and bears and navigation in the wilderness, about white and Indian medicine, about slavery and Andrew Jackson and the kind of men who chose to leave the United States and live in the mountains in solitude and constant danger – was worth every foot of the long journey up the Platte, an attempted scalping and longing for Rose...

The old man – dressed in his own black trousers and a new calico shirt that Gil Wallach had donated from the company's store, and moccasins that Morning Star had spent the night embroidering – was laid to rest in the morning, in a coffin gouged from a hollowed log and with a makeshift cross set up above his grave at the foot of the hills west of the main camp. Aside from a near murder occasioned by the Reverend Grey's sudden assertion that the deceased was, in fact, the Indian Agent Asa Goodpastor after all – and his sworn oath that he was going to write immediately to Congress accusing Edwin Titus of the crime – the obsequies went well. Over a hundred men escorted the old man to his grave, and January saw in more than one bearded face genuine sympathy and pity for this aged man – whoever he was – who'd met his death alone and by violence, as any of them might meet theirs tomorrow ... or even later on today...

As Veinte-y-Cinco had put it, as she'd made coffee in front of the lodge early that morning, 'Poor old *abuelo*. What would bring him all the way out here to die?'

TWELVE

Even before the procession left camp, Edwin Titus dispatched Tom Fitzpatrick with ten men, to ride post-haste down the river and meet and escort the missing Indian Agent to the rendezvous if he was delayed, or to find him if he was lost. Bets were taken at Seaholly's – according to Pia they ran five to two in favor of the deceased actually being Goodpastor – and Hannibal played a Mozart requiem, after which every man in the camp, with the exception of January and Shaw, repaired to Seaholly's for the wake.

'Bridger tell you last night 'bout the winter of ... musta been '31 or '32?' said Shaw, in response to January's question as to his opinion on the matter. They crossed Horse Creek at the same spot they had the previous morning – deadfall pine athwart the stream bed marked the best ford – and climbed the ridge beyond; the stream was much lower than it had been yesterday, but just as cold.

'Was that the winter Bridger was working for Rocky Mountain Fur?'

'It was – 'fore the AFC strangled 'em out of business.' Shaw leaned forward in the saddle as the horses scrambled up the trail. He kept one rifle in hand and the other scabbarded on the saddle, and had added a US Army pistol to his armory and a second bowie-knife stuck in his moccasin top – an uncomfortable reminder of the fact that whoever had murdered either Johnny Shaw, or poor old Senex Incognito or both, they weren't the only killers abroad in these high, empty-seeming lands.

'RMF brigades would go into a territory, and AFC had orders to follow 'em in an' trap the streams bare 'fore Bridger an' his men – Tom Fitzpatrick was one of 'em, then, too – could get enough plews to make back what their company was payin' 'em,' went on Shaw. 'They did this for a month or two, then Bridger got fed up with it – an' fedder up of the AFC tellin' the local tribes that if they did business with the RMF, they could forget AFC goods forever. Finally, Bridger turns around an' heads straight into Blackfoot country, knowin' the AFC boys would *have* to follow an' knowin' what'd happen to 'em when they did. Bridger an' his boys was in danger too, but they was in smaller groups, they was the first ones in, an' Bridger figured they had a better chance. An' he was right. Bridger an' his men got through pretty clear. AFC lost some men, some of who died pretty badly. Bridger knowed that would happen. That's the kind of fightin' we're lookin' at. The men we're dealin' with.'

January was silent. He now had a pretty good idea of what the pelts stacked in the AFC storage tents would bring when Titus got them to St Louis, and what the Company paid the trappers for them, even *before* the trappers were docked Company prices for liquor and powder and salt. Britain and the US were fighting over profits well equivalent to a silver lode.

'So, would Titus egg on a pack of Crows to kill an Indian Agent that was like to get questions asked in Congress about sellin' liquor?' Shaw shrugged and swung down from his horse as they neared the clearing where the old man had lain. 'Beats hell outta me. Would Congress *believe* it's the kind of thing the AFC would do an' start an investigation? I would. Well, consarn,' he added, scanning the ground around the clearing and its shelter. 'I knew this would happen whilst we was keepin' an eye on the viewin' of the corpse.'

'Every man in the camp hiked up here to have a look at the shelter?'

The Kentuckian straightened up and surveyed the clearing around him. Even so inexpert a tracker as January could tell that the place had been well and truly visited. 'If I'd been the Blackfeet,' sighed Shaw, 'I'd'a just put up an ambush here by the trail. Coulda picked off every man in the camp that way.'

'Except you and me and our deceased friend,

156

now in his honored grave.' January took the reins of Shaw's horse as Shaw began slowly circling the clearing afoot, more often crouched than straight, examining the ground, the trees, the scrubby thickets of huckleberry around the bases of the pines. January glanced at him every few seconds, but his attention remained on the woods around them: on the chittering of squirrels and the hidden rustle of foxes in the juniper thickets; on the voices of larks, the squabbling of jaybirds. Sounds that would cease, he knew, if someone were coming behind them.

In just such a fashion, he reflected, were Hannibal, and Veinte-y-Cinco, and Pia, pursuing their own investigations at Seaholly's, listening for gossip, words, chance remarks ... Anything out of place.

Out of place like an old man's naked body – like a pair of expensive black kid gloves.

Shaw said, with a note of satisfaction in his voice, 'An' here we are.'

January followed his gaze and saw the bright orangey-yellow scar of a fresh bullet-mark high on a scraggy-barked fir.

Branches didn't even start on the trunk until some twenty-five feet from the ground. January set his own rifle and one of Shaw's where he could grasp them in seconds, leaned on the tree and gave his hand for his companion's moccasined foot.

'Looks to have been a wild shot.' Shaw prized the bullet loose with his knife, dropped lightly off January's shoulders with the deformed wad of lead in his hand. 'Pistol,' he added, and held it

157

up for January to see. 'Fifty caliber. Johnny's was a fifty, an' it wasn't on his body.'

He pocketed the bullet, resumed his search of the trees while January went back to watching for danger. After a time he asked, 'Was there a reason Johnny didn't stay with you in New Orleans, and came west with Tom? Other than wanting to be kidnapped by the Indians like Uncle Naboth?'

'He hated bugs,' replied Shaw simply – as good a reason as January had ever heard for staying out of New Orleans. 'An' he missed the mountains. He was only twelve,' the Kentuckian went on quietly, 'when the three of us come to New Orleans. I'd been down the river twice before. But it was Tom's first trip, an' Johnny's, an' him wild to come an' see the elephant an' hear the lion roar. Probably saved his life, an' Tom's too, when the fever come through at home. I don't think Tom ever got over it.' His hand brushed the bark of another tree, and he added, 'No second ball, far as I can see. Since Mr Incognito didn't have it in his hide, there's a chance Wildman took it, which might account for him not bein' at his camp.'

'Wouldn't account for his horses being gone.' January nudged his own mount along after Shaw as Shaw made his way from the clearing upslope to the top of the ridge. 'And I didn't see any birds circling when we were coming up toward the hills.'

Our mama an' OUR wives, Shaw had said, when he'd spoken of his brother: it was the first time January had ever heard his friend mention

158

that he might have once been married. *When the fever came through at home...*

Tom wasn't the only one, who never got over it.

'Don't smell any smoke,' remarked Shaw. 'You?'

January shook his head. 'Did Tom meet Gil Wallach in New Orleans?'

'Gil Wallach was still trappin' back in '29. But the Chouteau Brothers, that just about runs the fur business outta St Louis, come down to New Orleans pretty regular, an' Tom hooked up with them on the business side – Tom was always the businessman, of the three of us.' He knelt, probing at a tangle of hemlock. 'He clerked a spell at Laramie, but it wasn't long 'fore he was the bourgeois of a post. Johnny went with him.'

And you didn't, thought January. *You stayed alone, in New Orleans...*

'An' about,' Shaw added, straightening up, 'goddam time.'

In one hand he held a straight stick some two and a half feet long, cut on both ends with a fresh knife-gash and trimmed of branches. Under its rough bark was snagged a single long, white thread.

'The splint?' January reined in close to see. 'That Poco found on the dead man's leg?'

'One of 'em. I ain't seen anythin' resemblin' a rag hereabouts. That shelter's tied together with rawhide strips—'

'Now we just need to find someone in the camp who carries those in his pockets.' Every trapper, camp-setter and Indian from the Rio Grande to the Columbia generally had strips of

159

rawhide about his person, for the thousand uses of the camp and the hunt: tying carcasses to saddles, or float-sticks to mark traps, repairing moccasins or rigging makeshift hobbles...

'Well, who we wouldn't find with 'em might be our friend with the banknotes an' that German silver pocket-watch. I don't reckon there's much Mrs Sefton would miss when it comes to viewin' the scene of a disappearin', but let's go have a look at what there is to see.'

Manitou's solitary camp, as Shaw had guessed, was still deserted when they reached it. The big man's traps, wrapped in oilskin, hung from the branches of an alder tree; other limbs sported parfleches of pemmican and the remains of a couple of rabbits, now torn at by birds and buzzing with insect life. A bear had certainly come through at some point. A shelter of boughs very similar to the one in the clearing had been rigged over a couple of trade blankets, but January guessed that Manitou slept under the sky when it wasn't actually raining. Besides the blankets, the shelter held a tin cup and a camp kettle, a half-constructed pair of moccasins, a bullet mold, a bar of lead, a small sack of spare powder and, of course, six or eight thin strips of rawhide tucked in a corner. Horse droppings on the edge of the camp had been rained on, but (said Shaw) had been fresh when that had occurred.

'One of the Indian villages?' suggested January, and turned in the saddle to look down toward the valley to the north. 'If he had one of those bullets in him—'

'We'd'a heard. Mrs Sefton picks up all every-kind of gossip from those sisters of hers – 'ceptin from Iron Heart's Omahas, an' so far as I know, they'd scalp any white man that came among 'em.' Shaw straightened up from examining the cold ashes in the fire pit and shoved his sorry hat back on his head to scratch. 'If the old man shot Wildman bad enough to put him down, why ain't he here? An' if he shot him *not* bad enough to put him down, why didn't he take an' dump the body out in the hills where he wouldn't be found? An' if it wasn't Wildman at all that made that shelter an' was on the receivin' end of those bullets, where is he?'

'Maybe he didn't dump the body because he didn't want to risk meeting the Blackfeet?' surmised January. 'Or any of the seventy-five parties of trappers who were out running around hereabouts looking for Clarke and the Dutchman? And if he took the shot in his head – a glancing blow that didn't kill him – the concussion might not have manifested until later. He could have come back to his camp, saddled up his horses—'

'I seen that happen,' agreed Shaw. 'Feller down to Tchapitoulas Street held me an' two of my men off for fifteen minutes with a shotgun after bein' cracked over the head by Fat Mary with a slung shot, an' didn't remember a thing about— *Watch it!*'

He flung himself sideways and down even as he shouted the warning, rolled behind Manitou's shelter as his rifle came up ready. January dived

161

in the other direction behind the nearest juniper bush, his own weapon swinging to point at Morning Star as the young woman emerged from the woods, her small hands held in the air.

'Behold a mighty warrior,' she said, without so much as a smile.

January stepped from cover, gun lowered but ready to come up again in an instant. After a moment Shaw emerged from a hemlock thicket a considerable distance from where he'd gone to ground.

'Well,' said January, going to pick up the reins of the startled horses, 'think how foolish we'd have felt if you'd *been* a mighty warrior, and we'd only shrugged and said: *That noise is only Hannibal's clever and beautiful wife...*'

'The wife of Sun Mouse is clever and beautiful,' agreed Morning Star, helping herself to two parfleches of Manitou's pemmican, which she slung over her shoulders. 'And her eyesight is good enough for her to find the tracks of white men who passed along the other side of these hills going west the night before last in the rain ... and who this morning passed the same way, going east. When they traveled west on the night of the rain, all of them – trappers and camp-setters and one Cree woman – wore moccasins. Now this morning, traveling east, one of them wears boots.'

THIRTEEN

The trail swung south through the broken jumble of gullies and hills: five men, a woman – Shaw pointed out where she'd squatted to urinate – and twice that many beasts. As Morning Star had observed, one of the men was definitely wearing boots.

'That'll be the Beauty,' remarked Shaw after a mile or two. 'He gets Fingers Woman to rawhide his moccasin soles, like they do in Mexico. I ain't yet seen that track.'

'Staying off their horses until they get clear of the valley.' January shaded his eyes to squint east, where a long, dry draw led toward the distant river. 'Cute.' As much to keep their own dust down, as to better read the ground-sign, Shaw, January, and Morning Star were afoot as well.

'This far south of the camps, white company might not be all they're lookin' to fight shy of.'

Again and again the trail disappeared, eradicated by the dragging of blankets, the use of old stream beds or rocks: the Dutchman had been in the mountains a long time and knew all the tricks. 'I'm beginning to feel we're not wanted,' said January.

'They really got a secret valley, where beaver's

163

plentiful?' Shaw asked Morning Star in his painful French, coming back down what had turned out to be a false trail back toward camp.

'If you had a lovely lady,' replied the young woman, 'and hid her away in a secret place, would you thank one who spoke of that place to a stranger? The whole of this land was once a secret,' she went on gravely. 'Every valley had a stream where the beaver were plentiful and big. Now those streams run silent. And the Beauty and the Dutchman don't want to keep their valley a secret out of respect for the beaver or care for the spirits of the valley: it is only that they do not wish to share their furs with another man. When the beaver are all gone – not a single one of them left – what will you do then? What next will you want?'

She broke away from them and walked on ahead, leading her spotted Nez Perce horse, and her short, slightly bowed legs outdistanced even the men's long stride in her anger. For a time January had nothing to say. They were far beyond sight of the camps here, alone in a world of larks, buffalo grass and yellow-brown sagebrush on the hill slopes above. The stillness was enormous. The world as it had been, thought January, before the Americans came ... Americans wanting beaver skins to sell for hats so they could make money. Americans wanting slaves brought in from Africa so they could grow cotton to sell to make money. Americans wanting land that the Sioux and Shoshone and Cherokee had since time immemorial lived on as hunters and as farmers ... not so that they could farm themselves, but so they could sell it to other whites for farms, so that they – the sellers – could make money.

He'd been poor too long to have turned down a partnership in the American Fur Company had someone offered it to him ... or a hundred acres of Arkansas land baldly stolen from the Cherokee, for that matter. But last night Bridger – who had been all over these mountains – had said that it wasn't just one stream or one valley or one area that was trapped out: it was all of them. Stacks of pelts were piling up behind the AFC tents, and in the enclosure of the Hudson's Bay Company, by the thousands.

Hats for New York. Hats for London. Hats for the world ... which might go out of fashion tomorrow. For each hat, a beaver struggling frantically against a steel trap underwater until it drowned.

What next will you want?

Here among the hills the windless heat was oppressive. Away to their left the crest of the ridge made a sharp yellow division against the sky. Closer and ahead, a startling, perfectly cone-shaped hill stood apart from the rougher terrain all around, like the ruined pyramids he had encountered in Mexico: 'Could we see them from up there?'

'Climbin' it'd just lose us time.' Shaw pushed his hat back, shaded his eyes. 'They's headed east, so they gotta be makin' for the ford where the river oxbows. That many horses, loaded for a year's trappin', they ain't gonna swim 'em.' Ahead, Morning Star had apparently come to this conclusion herself, and she mounted to ride down the draw to the ford: a dark, straight little figure against the immense prairie sky. Anger still radiated from the set of her back, the angle of her head, but as they came nearer, January saw sadness in her face as well.

Did she understand, January wondered, that as long as her people saw the white men as a tribe like themselves – a potential ally against their particular tribal enemies – they were doomed? Did the Crows understand that as long as they thought they could get the American Fur Company to side with them against the Flatheads, they were doomed? *Do ANY of them understand that even the whites who are their friends don't see them as Crow or Blackfeet or Flathead or Sioux, but only as Indians? Savages to be brushed aside because their rights to their land are less important than the Americans' right to make money?*

Morning Star delighted him – friendly, clever, bustling, efficient and without the slightest intention of remaining married to Hannibal past the rendezvous' end. Her aim was quite frankly to accumulate as much vermillion and gunpowder as she could with her services as housekeeper and tent-setter and animal-skinner and cook. Yet what would become of her in the long years ahead?

It was as absurd to follow his thoughts into that darkness, as it was to torment himself wondering about Rose: was she well? Was she alive? Would she die in childbed before he ever saw her again? *There's nothing you can do about it here, now,*

166

today...

It marks you, he thought, watching Shaw's pale thin figure move slowly along the side of the draw. *It changes you, to come home one evening and find the person you most love in the world dead* – as his beautiful Ayasha in Paris had lain dead of the cholera, across the bed in the room they shared. *It marks you forever.* As if this had happened yesterday instead of five years ago, he still recalled that sickened shock: *wait, no, there's been some mistake ... She and I were going to be together for the rest of our lives...*

Go back to our mama an' our wives, Shaw had said.

Had Ayasha not died he would not have returned to New Orleans. Would not have met his beautiful Rose...

Yet sometimes, waking in the hour before first light, *even with Rose beside him whom he loved with the whole of his heart* ... with everything in him he wanted Ayasha back, and the life that they'd lost together. The life he sometimes still felt he was supposed to have had.

He turned his head, sweeping the landscape with his eyes, and there on the pyramid hill, behind them now, a man was standing, watching them from its top.

They rested among the cottonwoods by the river. 'What you want to do, Maestro?'

January broke off a chunk of pemmican from the parfleche his companion had tossed him and considered the sun, halfway from noon to the westward crags. 'How far is it back to camp?'

167

'If we go straight on up the river, 'bout six miles. If we cross over, we can catch our friend back there, see who he is.'

'You're the one who's paying me,' said January. 'I'm just here to follow orders. Madame –' he turned toward Morning Star – 'you wouldn't happen to know which side of the river the Blackfeet are on, would you?'

'I've not seen their tracks on this side today.' In addition to what she'd taken from Manitou's camp, she'd brought her own rawhide satchel of that mix of dried, shredded meat and rendered fat that seemed to be the standard trail rations of every hunter in the mountains. 'There are forty lodges of Blackfeet, my brothers tell me, led by Silent Wolf, a man of caution and good counsel who has little interest in this secret beaver valley ... I think this man you saw behind us on the butte must be one of the trappers, who held to the Beauty's trail through the night.'

'Makin' it either Boaz Frye or Manitou hisself.' Shaw licked pemmican grease from his fingers, then wiped his hands down the front of his shirt. 'They both bein' unaccounted for as of last night. Or one of the Dutchman's men. Or someone that's followed *us* from the camp—'

'Who might be working for Edwin Titus,' finished January. 'Or John McLeod. Or whoever it was who tried to lift our hair the other evening. I agree. We need to see who it is.'

Accordingly, after an hour's rest, the three hunters crossed the ford, January uneasily conscious that this course of action would put their return to the first of the rendezvous camps far

168

after sunset. If there were something like three hundred Blackfeet on this side of the Green, it wasn't anywhere he wanted to be come nightfall.

The moment they were in the trees on the eastern bank, January dropped off his horse and shed his corduroy jacket and wide-brimmed slouch hat. With equal speed, Shaw cut saplings with his knife and made a sort of legless scarecrow, which he then lashed upright to the saddle of January's sturdy liver-bay gelding. It wouldn't have fooled a blind grandmother at a hundred paces ... but the Green was considerably wider than a hundred paces broad at this point, and the man or men behind them would be either among the cottonwoods on the west bank – in which case all they'd be able to see was that there were riders on all three horses – or further back in the hills, in which case ditto. January stretched out under a clump of the huckleberry bushes, rifle at his side, as his companions – and his makeshift double – rode on.

And waited.

Sunlight flashed on the water like flakes of fire. Four deer emerged from the trees upstream, trotted hesitantly to the bank to drink. January wondered what he'd do if the tracker turned out to be Manitou. He guessed the big mountaineer had little concern about anybody's secret beaver valley, but if Manitou had indeed killed the old man in the woods, he'd be well aware that trackers had come investigating the clearing and his camp.

But if Wildman had killed the stranger – and taken a pistol ball in the process – why bother to

169

hide? These mountains belonged jointly to the United States and Britain, and neither nation had anything resembling a lawman on-site (and in fact wouldn't have been permitted by the other to do so). Had Abishag Shaw walked up to Edwin Titus and shot him in the open, the only repercussion he would have had to face would have been from Titus's friends (if he had any), the Company (a serious consideration), or such champions of civilization as Sir William Stewart, who would probably have been distressed, but couldn't have legally done anything except shoot Shaw in return.

Wind brought the smell of dust and drying grass down the draw and across the water; the leaves of the cottonwood flickered and sighed. He'd described them for Rose in his notebook, examined the papery bark with the English magnifying lens she'd sent with him (accompanied by threats of murder in the night if anything happened to it).

Shadows lengthened, the stillness a balm on the heart. At this hour the streets of New Orleans would be clattering with carts, the air jagged with the voices of jostling drunks. Here, the silence was almost magical.

Then a man emerged from the cottonwoods on the far side of the water, leading a mule and a horse. Not Manitou. *One less thing to worry about.* A mountaineer – even at the distance, across the flashing water, January could see that. Dark beard, dark braids. Wiry build. A wool jacket of the kind sold by the AFC, the indigo dye new and glaring against the softer hues of sagebrush and cottonwood. He carried a rifle, but scabbarded it and led his animals quickly to the ford, bending now and then to study the ground.

The river was still fairly high, and in the cottonwoods on January's side of the water, the little party had again taken care to obliterate their tracks. The ford was rocky, treacherous underfoot. The mule balked, and the newcomer – after some truly choice epithets in the nasal yap of New England – led the animals across. January let them get breast deep, with the man's hands fully occupied with bridle reins and equine hysterics, then stood up and in two bounds reached a flat rock beside the river, his rifle aimed for business.

'I don't mean you harm,' said January immediately, as the man made a move to grab his own weapon and dodge behind the mule.

The man squinted across the glare of the water. 'You're holdin' that thing kinda strangely for a friend.'

January lowered the barrel, but kept his finger on the trigger. 'You're following us a little quietly for a man with good intentions.'

The trapper laughed. January recognized him from around the camp, very young behind his tangle of black beard, twenty or twenty-one at most. 'Like the preacher said when he came out of the widow's house at midnight,' said the young man, 'I realize this looks a little strange. Ben, ain't it? I had four pelts of Made Beaver on you against Manitou, day before yesterday. Wasn't that a sorry to-do? Bo Frye.'

'I thought you might be.' January signed for him to come on. Frye turned his attention back to coaxing the mule up out of the water.

'I'd offer you my hand,' added Frye genially as he reached the bank. 'But if you really doubt my good intentions, you'd be a fool to take it.'

January shifted the rifle to his left hand and held out his right.

'And here I thought I was the only one to hang on to the Beauty's trail,' lamented the young man. 'Tell you what, though, January. I'll go in with you and your friends – that's Shaw with you, ain't it? And the fiddler's squaw? Once the Beauty gets up into the mountains, he'll quit hiding his tracks, and then we can double back to camp, gear up good and follow 'em straight— What is it?' he added, seeing the direction of January's gaze. 'What you lookin' at?'

'Your fancy waistcoat.'

Frye's face colored above the dark beard, and he looked aside.

'Where'd you get something like that out here?' January went on. 'And whose throat did you cut to take it off him?' He extended a finger, to the remains of the crusted blood still visible on the puckered and water-ruined black silk.

The young man's flush deepened. 'Like that preacher said,' he repeated, opening his coat further so that January could see the garment, 'it's not how it looks.'

'I know it's not,' said January. 'We came on the same man, dead on the ridge by Horse Creek.'

172

FOURTEEN

'You know who it was?' asked Frye, after he'd fired a shot – the signal for Shaw's return – and with a professional's swiftness reloaded his piece before removing the waistcoat for closer inspection.

'Not the tiniest hint.'

'I figured he had to been a friend of that Englishman Stewart's. That's good silk, a dollar an ell. My ma was a dressmaker,' he added, as if this unmanly piece of knowledge needed explanation.

'So was my first wife.' January turned the creased and water-faded fabric in his fingers, examined the edges of the knife hole that had been ripped in the back. 'Anything in his pockets?'

'Just this.' Frye held out a silver locket and, when January pressed open the delicate catch, added a trifle wistfully, 'She's right pretty.'

She was indeed. The miniature within had been painted on ivory, by an artist not quite skilled enough to convey the girl's youth. Sixteen? Seventeen? Her mouth was a childlike rosebud, but her light-brown hair was dressed high: January recalled the style as being all the rage in Paris about ten years ago. So she was, at least, old enough to be 'out'. Under a watch glass in the locket's lid, a curl of hair that same light-brown color had been carefully preserved.

Frye brought up his rifle at the sound of horses coming down to the bottomlands, then lowered it as Shaw called out, 'Yo, Maestro?'

'All clear, Lieutenant.' The use of Shaw's title was a signal. Had somebody been holding a gun to his head, January would have called out, *All clear, Captain*, and Shaw would have taken whatever steps he deemed necessary from there. He held out the vest and the locket as Shaw dropped from the saddle.

'Well, Lordy Lordy...'

'It's funny,' mused Frye. 'My granny always said, if you went around stealing things from the dead, they'd find a way to make sure you got caught for it. Hell, I've took heaps of plunder from Injuns, and if God's keeping count of the horses and saddle tack I took off dead Comanche and Mexicans, well, I can only hope Granny'll be praying for me when my account gets tallied. But you know, I sure did feel queer, pullin' the weskit off that old man.'

But you did it anyway. January reflected that if you'd happened to have been soaked by the rain, a silk under-layer between your new red calico shirt and your new blue wool coat would have been extraordinarily welcome. Even if you did have to rinse blood out of it before you put it on.

'When did you find him?'

'Just before sunup. You could see colors.'

'How was he layin'?' asked Shaw.

'On his back.'

174

'On the ground?'

'Well, yeah. His feet was pointing toward that deadfall tree, maybe two–three feet between his toes and the fire pit.'

'Barefoot?'

Frye nodded. 'He had splints on his left leg, like as if he'd broke it. Somebody'd tore the hem of his shirt to tie 'em on with. Black gloves – a real gentleman, I thought, which is why I thought he mighta been one of Stewart's friends. The fire'd burned out, but somebody'd put wood by it for him. I thought he'd broke his leg fallin' off a horse, and they'd put up a little shelter for him and gone back to the camp for a litter. I sure wouldn't want to try to pack a wounded man down out of these mountains and back to the settlements.'

January thought about the steep trails beyond Fort Laramie, the gullies – climb down, climb up – and the crossing of the Platte, the Sandy, the Popo Agie and a thousand swollen creeks in-between.

'It wasn't Indians, though, was it?'

January shook his head. 'I don't think so, no.'

'Poor old buzzard. I'm sorry I robbed him, now.'

'If'fn you hadn't,' remarked Shaw, 'Indians might've, an' this locket'd be halfway to the Columbia.' He turned it over in his long fingers. ''Sides, we know the Beauty got to him 'fore you did – we been trackin' him by his boots – which means the odds is good that he got his coat an' his hat as well.'

'Do you know?' said January suddenly. 'I

175

think our friend was in mourning.'

'If you're goin' by the color,' returned Shaw, 'it'd mean Edwin Titus an' half the traders in the camp just lost their whole families.'

'Titus's coat-buttons are steel.' January held up the weskit again. 'Look at these. They're covered in the same silk, so they'll be black like the rest of the garment. It's bombazine silk, too, that doesn't catch light. Mourning is mostly what it's worn for. And expensive as it is, it's an old vest. Nobody does this kind of lacing on the back anymore, or has lapels cut in a triple notch this way—'

'Oh dearie dear,' squeaked Frye, with upflung hands, 'don't *tell* me I must get rid of all my old weskits before I go back to the States! Don't grieve a body so!'

January grinned and made a move as if to push the young trapper out of the shelter of the cottonwoods and into the river. 'Don't *you* tell *me* your ma never cut out a gentleman's vest. And look at how the silk's worn along the edge of the collar. He's got to have bought this ten years ago. Now look at the way his young lady is dressed. Those sleeves are just about ten years out of date – so's her hair. My sister would throw herself in the river before she'd wear a wired topknot like that. Doesn't it look to you,' he went on, 'like our young lady died about ten years ago, which is when her – father, shall we say? – outfitted himself all in black – rather expensively – and has remained so ever since?'

'Hair's what folks mostly take, goin' into mournin'.' Shaw rubbed his thumb at the silky

176

glitter of stubble on his jaw. 'An' that locket's plain enough to go with a funeral rig ... not that some of them ladies in New Orleans don't put on as much of a dog biddin' their Dear Departed *adios* as they would goin' to the Opera. I am most curious,' he added, 'as to what we'll find in the coat.'

January glanced at the angle of the sun. It stood only a few hand-breadths above the western mountains: every sagebrush, every boulder, that lay beyond the cottonwoods seemed edged in shadow, and coolness rose from the river. 'You're for going after Clarke and Groot, then?'

'I *am* goin' after 'em,' said Shaw gently, 'yes. I need to find out who our friend really is, an' I need to find out what he might be carryin' in his pockets, if anythin' – an' most of all what he was doin' out here. If'fn you go back to the camp, Maestro – an' I reckon if you follow the river you can make it there not more'n an hour after dark – get Prideaux an' Stewart, an' see if you can find our friend's camp, or any sign of where Manitou Wildman mighta got to ... I don't know when I'll be back.'

'Well, hell.' January reflected that it was probably too much to hope for that Shaw had simply forgotten about the Blackfeet. 'Since Rose has probably already spent that three hundred dollars you left with her, I guess I'm with you. Frye?'

'Thunderation, no man's gonna say Bo Frye ever backed off a clear trail. I'm your huckleberry, Shaw. Besides, I want in on that secret valley. They'll have to take me with 'em, or have me trumpetin' to the congregation which way

177

they went.'

Morning Star listened in silence as January reiterated in French all that had been said.

All she replied was, 'They'll camp in Small Bear coulee.' Her moving hands translated the words to Frye as she spoke. 'It is the closest place between here and the mountains where they can water their animals, and there is no other they can reach by dark.'

'You figure they know someone's still after 'em?' Frye's question was answered within a quarter-hour, when the hoof prints divided after another section where the trail had been obliterated with blankets. Half went east, the other half continued north.

'That'll be the Beauty goin' east,' surmised Shaw, when both sets of continuing tracks had been located – some hundred feet apart – and the pursuers reunited briefly to reconnoiter. 'It's one horse an' a passel of mules, so my guess is, that's the Dutchman with the camp-setters an' Fingers Woman turnin' north. There a stream in Small Bear coulee, m'am?' And, when she nodded: 'Then they can follow the stream to each other, an' head into the hills along its bed. You folks want to take the main party, in case our boys split what they found on the old man? I'll come on down the stream to meet you, if'fn I catch Clarke.'

'And what if someone catches you?' asked January.

Shaw grinned and swung into the yellow gelding's saddle. 'Then you'll hear me hollerin'.'

* * *

The sun went behind the mountains, and suddenly the whole of the valley lay in lavender shadow. Frye and Morning Star made patient casts forward and backward through the bunch grass across the hill slope toward the coulee, whenever the trail disappeared. Wind rustled drily in the silent world, broken now and then by the strange tweet-pop of grouse. Like a gray-brown mirage, a line of antelope flowed higher up the slope, heading, like themselves, for the water in the coulee. A peaceful scene, marred only by the inescapable recollection that if Small Bear coulee was the closest place between the ford and the deeper mountains where horses could be watered, there was a certain likelihood that this was where the Blackfeet would camp also. The result of that would not be good.

To hell with wondering if I'll come home to find Rose dead, reflected January grimly. *Let's just worry about ME coming home in the first place.* In New Orleans you might have to keep looking over your shoulder to make sure you weren't about to be kidnapped by slavers and sent to the cotton-growing territories, but at least you didn't have to worry about being tortured to death.

Unless, of course, you encountered one of those truly crazy *blankittes* who thought it was perfectly all right to torture blacks if doing so eased their own inner demons. January had met those, too.

And if Rose was here, where she and he both longed for her to be, he knew he'd be insane with worry for her safety.

179

He knew this world of tribes and beaver and silence and birds would enthrall her. She wouldn't rest, he thought, until she'd talked Jim Bridger into taking her north to the valley of the Yellowstone – Blackfeet or no Blackfeet – to see the hidden mysteries at the heart of the continent of which the trapper had spoken to him last night. Strange geothermal vents, smoking mud-pits, geysers spouting steaming water thirty feet into the air. Waterfalls like walls of lace, hot springs and a mountain of glass and yellow rock, seen only by the Blackfeet, the grizzlies, the wolves.

The coulee dropped away before them, filled with shadow. He smelled water below, but no scent of smoke. The Dutchman would be making a cold camp. Frye and Morning Star moved off in opposite directions along the crest, leaving January just far enough down the slope himself that he wouldn't be skylined, to hold the horses and watch for Blackfeet. He saw no dust in the air, but that didn't mean they weren't ahead of them, somewhere in the creek bed among the thin trees and shadows. No sound.

As the last light faded the young mountaineer climbed back up to him: 'Don't see a damn thing.' And, when Morning Star melted out of the darkness a few moments later, he asked – combining English with the signs universal to the tribes of the Plains: 'What you think about us cuttin' straight down to the creek, so we'll at least have it ourselves if they ain't there?'

Morning Star answered, small brown hands seeming to pluck ideas from the thin moonlight.

'They'll be upstream or down, not opposite where they entered the coulee. They must go up it tomorrow, to meet the Beauty, but there will be more water further down.'

It would be pitch dark in the woods, and having left camp when they had, January hadn't thought to bring a lantern. Not that he'd be fool enough to use one on this side of the river. They descended, cautiously, keeping as close to the edge of the trees – and the flicker of moonlight – as they could.

The wind eased. In its wake, the stillness gritted with the sudden, faint taste of smoke.

And with knife-gash suddenness, a man's scream of agony ripped the night.

FIFTEEN

Frye gasped, 'Fuck me...'

The second scream was worse, like the bellowing of an animal trapped in burning barn.

The Blackfeet.

Shaw.

For a few moments January felt as if he couldn't breathe.

'Downstream.' Morning Star's voice was barely more than the siffle of the wind. Her small hand touched January's elbow in the darkness, guiding him up the coulee and away.

January pulled his arm free. 'We have to get

him.'

'You think he will be in any state to run, should you do so?'

You'll hear me hollerin'...

'I won't leave him.'

Her face was no more than a blur in the shadow as she tilted her head. 'Will you die then, and tell his ghost all about your friendship?'

She was absolutely right, and January felt sick with shock. *Dear God, silence him! Dear God, let him die.*

He knew damn well that Abishag Shaw was too tough to die anytime soon. And the Blackfeet too skilled.

'The least I can do is shoot him from cover.'

'Hell, pilgrim,' said Frye, when January told the young trapper in English what he planned to do, 'I seen you shoot.' He puffed his chest a little in an attempt to sound like Jim Bridger. It would have been laughable if January hadn't heard in his voice how terrified he was. 'No man's gonna say Bo Frye left a feller to be gutted an' minced by the Blackfeet. Waugh! Damn it,' he added, looking around sharply, and when January followed his gaze he saw that Morning Star was gone. 'Where'd that squaw get to? You don't think she guided us here a-purpose—?'

'She's a Sioux.' January didn't feel at all certain, now that she was gone, of his own words. 'And she's my partner's wife. Her uncle was killed by the Blackfeet.'

Frye made a little noise in his throat – 'Huh...' – but it was impossible now to see his face. Only a pallid dapple of moonlight leaked through the boughs overhead; the gulch below was like a lake of indigo and cool. They tied the horses (*what if a wolf comes along*?) and Frye led the way straight down toward the stream, where there was also a little silvery light. 'Got to watch for the camp dogs,' Frye murmured. 'Billy LeBleaux down on the Purgatoire snuck into a 'Rapahoe camp to get back his rifle an' knife when they got stolen, an' ran into the dogs. Raised such a ruckus he had to spend the next three days hidin' up in a rock crevice, while the savages looked for him. It's gonna be a long shot.'

Moonlight cold on water. Night wind in trees. Smells of pine and wet rock. Something dark on the far side of the stream rose on its hind legs to half again January's six-foot-three-inch height, snuffing the air. *Dear GOD*—! He guessed the bears he'd seen near the camp had been black bears, scarcely taller than a man.

He followed Frye's shadow back a few feet into the deeper concealment of the trees. 'I would have sworn Shaw would keep clear of them,' he breathed. 'Or at least that he'd get off a shot—'

'Don't you think it, pilgrim. Five years ago Tom Fitzpatrick walked smack into a Gros Ventre village that he was tryin' to avoid one night, came within a huckleberry of gettin' a prairie haircut.' Further down the coulee came another scream, and behind it, bodiless in the darkness, a single, guttural voice lifted in a chant. Frye's voice shook with the effort to sound nonchalant. 'Happens to the best.'

Firelight glimmered through the trees. The smell of horses, the reek of camp. With the next scream came the howling of the camp dogs. Frye touched January's arm, and they hopped from boulder to boulder across the creek. From there they worked their way up the side of the draw, never losing sight of the orange glimmer of the flames.

'All right, hoss,' whispered Frye. 'Here's how it is.' His hands worked swiftly as he spoke, drawing the ball from his rifle, adding powder to throw the ball an extra distance. 'I only get one shot. That's all I can do, and all I'd expect of any man in the like position—'

'I understand.'

'You ever kicked a hornet's nest? You'll wish you was safe home rollin' on one in a minute. The second I shoot, you go straight up-slope and back up the coulee. There's rocks about a half-mile behind us, with crevices big enough that a man can get in under 'em. You pull in whatever brush you can find in front of you and you lay still, and if a rattlesnake's in there and bites you, you're still ahead of the game.' The fear was gone from the young man's voice and, curiously, January realized he felt none either, only a kind of chilly calm.

He recalled being scared, marching with the Faubourg Tremé Free Colored Militia down to Chalmette Plantation behind Andrew Jackson, twenty years old and thinking about what he'd seen bullets do to human flesh. But once crouched behind those cotton-bale redoubts, straining his eyes through the fog and hearing the British

184

drums, there had been only this sense of cold, and of time standing still.

'If one of 'em tackles you in the woods, use your knife instead of your gun if you can. I'll head down to the stream and try to get to the horses 'fore they do. I'll circle back for you. If I don't come, don't you *move* from where you're layin' until night comes again. They'll stop everything 'til they gets us or we gets back to the camp. Understand?'

'All right.' His mouth was so dry he could barely speak.

'And don't you shoot. You won't be able to hit him, you can't reload in time and you may need that shot later.'

'All right.' But January knew he'd try, if he could get close enough.

Men's voices raised in feral howling as Frye and January edged downslope.

Across the creek he could see horses grazing, bulky shadow and the round glint of eyes. Through the trees, the dim white triangles of the lodges, strung out along the creek bed just above where the waterside bushes got thick. Forty lodges, Morning Star had said. Well over two hundred warriors. Small fires laid gauzy drifts of smoke over the water. They followed the creek for another three-quarters of a mile before coming to where the big fire was. The men were gathered around it, naked shoulders jostling pale skin hunting-shirts, all gilded with the firelight: beating drums, or with the butts of their rifles on the ground. Where the warriors clustered thickest, between the tipis and over their heads

185

January could just see the ends of the lodgepole frame to which they'd lashed their victim, and a single bleeding hand.

He brought up his rifle. *Shaw*, he thought, *I did my best...*

The men moved, and January saw what they were doing – driving splinters of wood under the bound man's skin, among a bleeding horror of gashes and burns. An impossible shot at the distance, with the men moving back and forth, the firelight wavering—

And the bound man wasn't Abishag Shaw.

It was Manitou Wildman.

There had been no mistaking the heavy power of the frame, the cropped-off black hair hanging down where his head lolled back, the harsh strong bones of the face under that bestial beard. The first rush of relief made January feel almost faint, and then, in the next moment, the horrible choice: *I would shoot, and take the consequences, for Shaw who saved my life...*

Will I take those same consequences for a man I barely know?

No man's gonna say Bo Frye left a feller to be gutted an' minced by Blackfeet...

Even a relative stranger, as Shaw was to Frye. Boaz Frye, January thought, would know that some day he might easily be the one bound by firelight in a Blackfoot camp, in hell already and looking at worse...

Are you really going to get yourself killed – and possibly, killed THAT WAY – to shorten Manitou Wildman's agony?

January didn't hear the camp guard's approach,

186

but Frye touched his shoulder, and the two men drew back further into the trees. Willing himself to be willing, January followed him, moccasins sliding in the pine straw, seeking another vantage point for a shot. Like his companion, he'd double-shotted his gun – crammed in as much powder as it could take without, he hoped, having the lock blow up in his face – to speed the bullet over an impossible distance. But at that distance it was anybody's guess if he could aim. Moonlight touched the sleek dark hair of a warrior passing between the trees on the hill slope below, made a ghostly ravel of the down on an eagle feather. Frye led him up on to an outcrop of rocks, but still could get no clear view of the camp, and all the while the screaming went on like a soul in hell. 'Them splinters is fatwood,' Frye whispered. 'Resin pine. Burns like lucifer matches. They lights 'em...'

Dear God—

January remembered the smack of the man's fist on his jaw, the animal glint of those brown eyes and the trained, clean, careful way Wildman had moved.

Remembered how the big man had pulled that Omaha girl from the men who'd held her, not knowing then that he wouldn't have to fight January for her immediately thereafter and maybe others as well, but half-throwing her to her own people, with a *let the girl go*...

A second scout came into the moonlight below, much too near the rocks. Frye and January drew further upslope. The firelight leaped up among the tipis; Wildman's screams passed

187

beyond human, beyond animal even.

The moon's angle changed above the draw. January saw the pale pattern of elk teeth on smoky buckskin, moving on this side of the creek now. When Frye touched January's arm again to signal a further retreat, January could feel the young man's hand shaking, as were his own. Hating himself, he followed, keeping to the border zone of darkness among the trees, as high up the side of the little canyon as they could until they were well clear of the vicinity of the Blackfoot camp. Only then did the mountaineer whisper, 'I'm sorry, hoss. We couldn't—'

'It's all right.'

But it wasn't.

They hid among the boulders Frye had told him about, far up the draw. Shared pemmican, which January was almost too sick with shock to want until he'd tasted some and realized he was famished and his head was pounding. When the wind backed a little they could still hear the screaming. It didn't stop until past moonset.

Not long after first light January heard the harsh scuffle of movement in the trees below them. He put his head over the rocks and saw the Blackfeet moving out. Warriors rode ahead, long dark hair hanging down their backs; women walked with bundles among the horses that drew the lodgepole travois. Dogs and children, silent alike, ghosts between the trees. Medicine bundles – feathers and bones twirling – on the end of travois poles and spears. Rifles held upright and ready.

When the last of the village was well out of

sight, January and his companion slipped from cover, almost ran downstream—

—and swung around, rifles at ready, at movement in the green dawn shadows on the other side of the creek.

'You tolerable, Maestro?'

January let out his breath in a sigh. 'Just.'

Shaw came to the creek's edge as Frye and January waded across. 'Glad to see that warn't you they was settin' fire to.' Together the three climbed the few yards up to where Goshen 'Beauty' Clarke waited with his horse and his laden mules, nearly hidden among the trees. 'An' twice as glad to see you had the good sense not to try an' put that poor bastard out'n his pain.' Clarke had on his wolfskin hood, beneath which his long golden braids flowed down almost to his waist. On his feet he wore a pair of well-cut, and much-scuffed, black boots.

'You were bug-struck loco to even think about tryin', Shaw,' snapped the Beauty. 'Waugh! You near as dammit got us killed.'

'But I didn't,' pointed out Shaw mildly.

'I told you it couldn't have been Clem or any of the boys,' Clarke added grouchily. 'They's all camped in the next draw over. You didn't see *them* riskin' their tripes checkin' to see if that was *me*.'

'Well, don't mean they didn't,' replied Shaw. 'I 'spects they'll meet us at the campsite, if'n the Dutchman wants to see if they left your new boots behind.'

'Naw.' The Beauty shrugged. 'They didn't fit him. The coat doesn't fit him, neither, but he

189

wanted somethin' out of it, an' he wouldn't listen to reason.'

'You tell my partner how you come by those boots, Clarke,' said Shaw. 'I found it right interestin'.'

As did January, when the trapper related in an undervoice – because Shaw and Frye were still listening for the slightest signs of trouble back down the trail that the Blackfeet had taken – the events of three nights ago. 'We thought at first that little speck of a fire mighta been somebody who'd been hurt,' explained Clarke. 'Or somebody who'd camped up, not realizin' how close he was to the rendezvous, like Robbie Prideaux, that time he made his confession to one of his camp-setters an' they both laid down in a blizzard, thinkin' they was dyin' fifteen feet from the gate of Fort Laramie one night. But there's this old man, layin' in a shelter under a deadfall, with his hands folded on his breast an' his throat cut from ear to ear. Stabbed in the back, too, though that didn't keep Clem from takin' his coat. We figured he was that Indian agent Titus was workin' himself up to a stroke over – no lookout of ours even if we *hadn't* been tryin' to ease on out of the camp, quiet like. There's one thing I got no patience with, it's Indian agents, pokin' around causin' trouble...'

'What time was this?'

'First light.'

'Any sign of a horse nearby?'

'We didn't see any, but we didn't look. The rain had slowed us down, an' we knew we still had a couple of those sneaky bastards on our

190

tails, that's too dumb to find their own beaver.' He glared pointedly at Boaz Frye.

'His clothes wet or dry?'

'Damp,' said Clarke. 'Like he'd got under shelter pretty quick after gettin' wet.'

'You have trouble getting his boots off? Was that why you hauled him out of the shelter?'

'The left boot, yeah. His leg was splinted up, and his foot was swole – Clem had to hold on to his shoulders while I pulled at it. The old guy was dead,' he added defensively. 'It's not like it hurt him or nuthin'.'

January reflected that Jed Blankenship would have just cut off the swollen leg and removed the foot the easy way.

'Swelled a little or swelled a lot?'

The mountaineer thought about it for a moment, his hand stroking the stock of his rifle, which had been decorated with an elaborate design of brass nail-heads. 'A little, I'd say. I mean, we got his boot off him—'

Shaw raised a hand. All stopped, and on the morning air, above the animal smells of the empty campsite before them, January smelled fresh smoke. Instinctively, the four men spread out, moving in silence from tree to tree among the cut-down brush, the dung and detritus that littered the edges of the creek where the tipis had been set last night. Further ahead among the cottonwoods, January saw a flash of movement and raised his gun. Beside a small fire two gourd bowls lay, and a tin cup of water. Shaw stepped out of the trees, flanking the clearing. After a moment, from the rocks nearer the creek, a

191

man's hat was raised up on a rifle – a reasonable precaution against trigger-happy intruders.

And the next minute, Manitou Wildman – dressed, unruffled and quite clearly in perfectly good health – stood up from among the rocks.

SIXTEEN

The words, 'Are you all right?' came out of January's mouth even as he thought: *that's the stupidest question I've ever heard.*

Wildman blinked at him, like a man thrust suddenly into light from darkness. 'I'm well.'

Shaw lowered his rifle. 'You didn't look so peart last night.'

The trapper shook his head. His short-cropped hair, January noticed, was clean, new-washed, still wet, and under his tan he was ghastly pale. His slow, mumbling voice had a hoarse note to it, as if indeed his throat had been lacerated by screams. 'Nothing happened last night.'

'Here? This very spot? The Blackfeet?'

'The Blackfeet are my friends,' said Wildman. 'Silent Wolf is my brother.'

'Now, there's been times I wanted to stick splinters under my brother's hide an' light 'em,' said Shaw, 'but I don't recall as I ever actually done it—'

'Nothing happened last night,' repeated Wildman.

192

Shaw, January and young Mr Frye exchanged looks – *are we crazy?*

The big trapper seated himself cross-legged by the fire again, picked up one of the gourds and sipped at the broth within. 'What are you doing here?' he asked, in a voice that sounded more normal. 'It's miles from camp.'

'What are *you* doin' here?' returned Shaw.

'Came to see my brothers.' Manitou nodded in the direction of the stream, where two horses and a mule were hobbled – Manitou's horses, January saw at a glance. Like himself, the mountaineer was a big man and paid extra for the biggest horses in the strings brought up from Missouri and New Mexico. 'Silent Wolf knows it'd be madness to attack his enemies where the white men are in strength,' Manitou went on. 'But it's madness not to know what's going on. Sit.' He motioned to the ground by the fire. 'There's more stew here than I can eat.'

After a moment's hesitation – and another glance traded – the four trackers complied. In the mountains, you didn't turn down stew, and after tracking from sunrise to darkness yesterday January would have eaten raw buffalo with the hair on. Shaw said, 'There was a man killed outside the camp three nights ago, a stranger—'

'I didn't do it,' said Wildman quickly. 'I never saw the old man.' And then, *'Three* nights?'

'How'd you know he was old?'

Hesitation. Then, 'One of the camp-setters told me.'

January opened his mouth to ask: *when? You haven't been in camp since then—* and Shaw

193

elbowed him very gently in the back.

'He tell you the body was nekkid when we found him? We been trackin' down bits an' pieces of his plunder, tryin' to find out who he was an' what he was doin' out there. McLeod an' that preacher Grey been claiming he was this Indian Agent Goodpastor, that seems to have got hisself lost.'

Manitou's heavy brow sank even lower over his eyes. 'No,' he said in his slow voice. 'No, I didn't know ghouls had looted his body.' His glance swept over Frye's waistcoat, and Clarke's boots, and spots of angry color began to spread like wounds over the dark, taut skin of his cheekbones.

'Now, just a goddam minute—' Clarke began, and Shaw held up his hand.

'That's by the way,' he said. 'An' the old man was buried decent at the camp. Grey prayed over him, for what good that's like to do – an' for a fact, he sure don't care now who's wearin' his boots. This camp-setter you talked to wouldn'ta had some idea who the old boy mighta been, would he?'

Manitou looked aside. 'No.' He stood, his sudden movement reminding January of the grizzly he'd seen on the other side of the creek last night, huge and far too close in the moonlight, and went to pick up his saddle from the rocks where it lay. 'Maybe it was old Goodpastor.'

'If'fn it was, he parked his camp an' his horses under a rock someplace. Care to come with us, whilst we takes tea with the Dutchman an' sees if old Mr Incognito was carryin' callin' cards in

194

his coat pocket?' Shaw collected bridle and apishamore, and followed.

'No,' Manitou said. 'I been from my camp too long. Three days, you said?' He shook his head, his heavy brow creasing, like a drunkard trying to reckon the days of a binge. 'Winter Moon,' he added, 'you need one of these girls –' he slapped the shoulder of the taller of his two horses, a heavy-boned buckskin – ''til you get back to the camp? If Beauty'll lend you a bridle off one of the mules...'

'I appreciate the offer,' said January. 'Thank you. We owe you some pemmican, by the way—'

'Surprised a bear hadn't got it. You're welcome to it.'

'You stayin' at the camp awhile?' asked Shaw more softly – perhaps to exclude, January thought, Beauty Clarke and Boaz Frye, who had gone to check loads and cinches on Clarke's mules. 'For a fact I been wantin' to speak with you 'bout what happened down at Fort Ivy this winter, when Johnny Shaw was killed.'

Manitou paused in the act of laying down the apishamore on his other horse, a cinder-gray mare, and regarded Shaw with those deep-shadowed brown eyes. 'That'd be your brother.'

'It would.'

'You look like him.'

'I been told.'

'I wasn't in the fort when it happened.' When Wildman swung the saddle into place January noticed the catch in his movements, and the way he favored his left arm. Where the worn elk-hide

195

hunting-shirt fell away from Wildman's throat, he saw clotted wounds. In places blood leaked through to stain the pale-gold hide. 'I was camped about a mile off, in the woods.'

'Why?' asked Shaw. 'From all Tom an' Beauty both say, it was snowin' billy-bejeezus an' cold as brass underwear.'

'Too many people. People—' Manitou readjusted the apishamore under the saddle, cinched the whole arrangement tight. 'I ain't fit to be around people. Never have been. Guess you know that,' he added, with a sudden shy grin that made his face look suddenly human again. 'I get mad ... Better I keep my distance. You think it was Frank that did it? Tom's clerk?'

'It's who I'm up here lookin' for.' Shaw folded his long arms. 'Though I'd appreciate you kept that one silent as the grave. Why'd you think it might be him?'

'Man don't leave a fort in the middle of winter like that, 'less he's flushed out. One mornin' – before first light, durin' a break between storms, but more bad weather comin' in, you could smell it – I saw him pass 'bout a half-mile from my camp. I only knew him by that townsman's coat he wore: old, black wool with a fur collar. Heard later he'd said he got spooked, the boy bein' killed by Blackfeet like that. But I never saw no sign of Blackfeet. So I figured it was probably him. Hard luck on Tom. I know he was crazy 'bout that boy. Yourself too, I guess.'

Shaw nodded, without speaking.

'Why'd you think he's comin' here?'

'Johnny found letters of his, that sounded like

196

there was gonna be some kind of trouble here at the rendezvous. *Bad trouble*, he said. *Killin' trouble*. Then this old buffer shows up dead, that seems to just fallen outta the sky. The name Hepplewhite mean anythin' to you?'

'Just the feller who made the furniture.' Manitou took the empty stew-gourd Shaw held out to him, knotted it in one of the saddle latigos, then swung himself up as lightly as a schoolgirl. 'If Frank's come into this country,' he went on, looking down at Shaw, 'likely your vengeance'll look after itself. Frank's a clerk. Got a clerk's hands. Can't see him lastin'. You come here, you lay yourself in the hand of God. He don't have far to look if he's after you.'

He leaned from the saddle to rub the buckskin mare's face gently with his knuckles as January readjusted the borrowed bridle around her head. 'Look after that lady for me, Winter Moon. Anybody beat the crap outta Blankenship for that trick with the mirror?'

'I heard Robbie Prideaux beat the crap out of him for something,' replied January. 'It could have been anything, given the number of things people have against that man.'

Wildman made a growly sniff, as close as he ever got, January suspected, to laughter. 'Could have, at that. He's another one the country'll get sooner or later. It was a good fight,' he added. 'Been a long time since I followed ring rules. I enjoyed it. You think twice about vengeance, Shaw.' He glanced back at Shaw beneath the heavy shelf of his brow. 'It never ends well.'

'Nor does it,' returned Shaw quietly. 'Yet I

197

can't turn from my brother, nor my brother's blood. An' there is no law here that'll touch the man who did it.'

'Nor bring your brother back.' Wildman sat for a time, looking down into Shaw's pale eyes. 'Guess you're right at that. We do what we gotta. I see this Frank feller around the camp, I'll let you know.' He touched his heels to the horse, started to move away.

'He may not be callin' himself Boden up here.'

Manitou reined in sharply: 'Boden?'

'That's his name,' said Shaw. 'Frank Boden.'

The trapper was silent for a moment; for the first time January saw the animal watchfulness disappear from his eyes, leaving them, for an instant, blank. Shocked, as if thought had been arrested midstream, leaving him uncertain which direction to go. But this was only for an instant. Then Wildman shook his head, said in a strange voice, 'I didn't know.'

He reined away into the woods without another word.

'I ain't no ghoul.' Clarke came back from his mules, looking after Wildman as the big trapper disappeared into the shadows of the trees.

''Course you ain't.'

'He should damn well talk about goddam ghouls! God Hisself couldn't keep track of how many hides an' horses that child's had off the Flatheads – *and* I didn't notice that deer-hide shirt he was wearin' was part of his plunder back at the camp. An' I know for a fact them leggins he's got on was took off some poor Crow up on the Bighorn—'

198

'It's a fact ever'body gets what they can, where they can,' replied Shaw soothingly. 'An' like I said, Mr Incognito don't care who's wearin' his boots now. You comin', Maestro?'

'Yes, just coming.' January went to kick out the campfire, then stooped to examine the ashes. From the charred earth, he picked a fragment of wood. With the back of his knife – the earth was scorching hot – he dug out two or three more, as if playing jackstraws. Clarke and Frye had already started off up the steep northern slope of the coulee. Shaw waited, still as a scarecrow on his yellow gelding, watching and listening all around him as January scooped up his rifle and followed. He said nothing as January stowed the half-burned splinters inside his watch case, the only hard metal container he had which didn't already hold either powder or lucifers, but the tilt of his eyebrows told January that the policeman had guessed what he'd found.

What it meant, of course, was an entirely different matter.

Given the fact that the Blackfeet – whatever their relationship with Wildman – would certainly carry to its conclusion the operations they'd begun on Wildman last night on a couple of lone whites who *weren't* their brothers, Shaw slipped on ahead on foot to scout the rim of the coulee before anyone else came out of its cover. About two miles lay between Small Bear and the next coulee – Dry Grass or Rotten Cow, depending on who you talked to, said Clarke – open ground in which it would have been almost impossible to evade Blackfoot warriors. The sun stood halfway between the eastern mountains and mid-heaven, and from one hill slope January could see across the glittering green sheet of the river the beginnings of the rendezvous camp, like a scattering of little villages beyond the rim of the cottonwoods.

'Clem's gonna scalp me,' muttered Clarke. 'Lettin' myself get caught like a damn pork-eater—'

'He won't,' promised Frye jauntily. He seemed to have put completely behind him the enigma of Manitou Wildman's visit with the Blackfeet. ''Cause I'll be headin' out with you – it's just me, I don't have a partner or nuthin' – an' when we get to your valley I'll trap just where you say, an' keep outta your way—'

'Yeah, an' the other way he won't is if him and me scalp *you* – *an'* them,' he added, with a truculent glance over his shoulder at January and Shaw.

'You'd still have to catch Wildman,' pointed out January, 'and shut *his* mouth, too. You really think you're up to that?'

'What the hell you know, nigger?' muttered Clarke, but in a tone that told January he had him, there.

January glanced back to make some remark to Shaw and almost jumped in surprise: Morning Star rode at Shaw's side, leading January's big liver-bay from the camp and Bo Frye's mule and his rat-tailed paint. He reined back to join them. 'You know anything about Manitou Wildman and the Blackfeet, m'am?' he asked.

'I know he is their brother.'

200

'And is that a reason for them to torture him – and then turn him loose? Those were healing herbs he was drinking. My sister's a shaman –' *well, a voodooienne, anyway* – 'and I know the smell. But a bowl of poppy and willow bark isn't sufficient reason for pretending they didn't lay a hand on him. At least, it isn't for me.'

'Crazy Bear is a strange man.'

Clarke and Frye swung around in their saddles, 'What the *hell*—?'

'Where'd she come from?'

'Dropped down outta the sky,' returned Shaw mildly. 'Horses an' all. Beauty, you know Mornin' Star?'

'Yeah, Sefton's squaw.'

Frye asked a rapid question in sign, which January guessed concerned the Blackfeet, because Morning Star smiled and pointed up Small Bear Coulee. She added – doubling her quick-moving hands with French for his benefit – 'I have seen nothing of the other tribe, nor of the Indian Agent that Broken Hand was sent out to find. Nor have I seen any trace of the dead man's camp,' she added, 'which I think strangest of all...'

She lifted her head sharply, and at the same moment January heard it: the frenzied whinnying of horses in the draw ahead. January's eyes went instantly to the morning sky: buzzards and ravens circling. Clarke whispered, 'Jesus—'

And whipped up his horse.

Shaw and January followed at a canter, over the rim and down into Dry Grass Coulee. Dry Grass was shallower than Small Bear, and there

201

was less timber. From the high ground, January saw the Dutchman's camp at once. A cold camp, and a dry one, since there was no stream here in summer. Through the trees he discerned packs and blankets on the ground, and crumpled things that could only be bodies. Something gray moved among them; he heard the quarrelsome snarls of wolves.

No wonder the tied horses were terrified.

The smell hit him then, foul in the clean mountain air, and prickled the hair on his head. He shouted, 'Stop!' and saw already that the Beauty had drawn rein, smelling it also and uncertain—

'Christ Jesus,' whispered Clarke, when Shaw and January came up to him. 'What the hell happened? It smells like a fucken plague hospital down there.'

Even at a distance of two hundred yards, it was very clear that everyone in the camp had died purging and puking.

Morning Star rode past them, crossed the bottom of the coulee and put her spotted Nez Perce horse up the opposite slope to circle the camp. While they were waiting for her, Bo Frye came up with the mule string, pale with shock under his tan.

Curious, thought January, that this young man didn't find anything odd in playing tag with Blackfeet eleven months out of the year, with death by torture a daily possibility, yet his voice trembled at the thought of disease.

Maybe because once the First Horseman took you, your knife or your rifle or your wits would do nothing to slither you out of his cold white grip.

'You don't think it's the cholera, do you?' Frye whispered.

'I'll know better when we're close.' He brought up his rifle and shot at one of the wolves. The buzzards flapped skyward with a dark whoosh; the wolves backed away snarling, then flickered out of sight into the brush. Clarke kept whispering, *'Christ Jesus, Christ Jesus...'* as if the words were a kind of lifeline, to keep him from being swept away by the fact that the people he'd been closest to for the past five years of his life all lay before him, dead.

And had died – January could see – very badly indeed.

SEVENTEEN

Clemantius Groot – clothed in a handsome black frock-coat – lay on his blankets, which were stiff with vomit. Beside him Fingers Woman was curled up, as if she'd died clutching her belly, her face pressed to his shoulder. Frye's whisper was edged with panic: 'My grandpa died like that. Yellow fever, in Boston in '93...'

'The vomit's the wrong color.' January had worked plague wards, both in Paris and New Orleans. This was bad – four men and a woman, crumpled and twisted where they had fallen, two with faces and bellies torn open by the wolves.

But nothing to what he had seen. 'And yellow fever doesn't kill in a night.' He dismounted, his borrowed mare fidgeting her feet and thrashing her head at the smell of death.

'But the cholera does, don't it?'

'Yes.' He was a little surprised at how detached his voice sounded, though, oddly, it seemed to steady the frightened young man beside him. 'Cholera can kill in a night.'

Or a day. He had made love to his beautiful Ayasha, early one hot morning in the cholera summer in Paris, kissed her – not an instant of that day had left his memory, nor would it, he knew, until he died, his love for Rose notwithstanding ... He had walked down the twisty stairs of that old tall house on the Rue de l'Aube and along those gray medieval streets where moss grew between the cobbles, to the plague hospital where he was working...

He could even remember the song the two children at the corner had been singing as they bounced their ball against the wall.

'Dans la forêt lointaine
On entend le coucou
Du haut de son grand chêne
Il répond au hibou:
"Coucou, coucou..."'

And she'd been dead, when he'd come back to the room about half an hour before the setting of the sun.

He shook himself. If he let it, the thought would devour him. It had paralyzed him for months after that day – which still felt exactly as if it were yesterday. *Even if it was yesterday, today is today ... And today we have five people dead in a coulee in the middle of the Oregon Territory and no way of knowing whether the contagion has already spread like wildfire over the rendezvous camp...*

He took a breath and said, 'The stools are wrong.'

'You can tell what they died of from lookin' at their *crap*?' Goshen Clarke grimaced, oddly revolted – particularly for a man who engaged in the competition-swallowing of raw buffalo-guts.

'For some diseases, yes. Cholera's one of them.'

Among the bodies, cups and kettles lay, two of them that had been set down still upright containing a little water. Thirst could mean fever...

Standing at the edge of the camp, holding the horses, Shaw's face had a cold stillness to it. He'd been in and out of the plague wards, too – January had seen him there. And had gone into more than one small house in New Orleans, or those small rooms behind shops and groceries and livery stables – only to see the whole family, father, mother, children dead. As his own family had died, leaving only Johnny and Tom.

'Could it be somethin' they et?' Frye tagged at January's heels like a child as he went from body to body; as he knelt to feel faces and hands, though he knew if they'd made camp sometime before dark they'd be cool and only beginning to stiffen. 'Woman that lived behind us on Water Street bought something in the market she

205

thought was juneberries and made a pie of it for her family. All seven of 'em died, and for a couple days the whole neighborhood thought that it might be some sickness from down the wharves.'

'It could be.' January raised the eyelid of one of the engagés, but saw nothing unusual in the dilated pupils, the glazed whites. 'Though I can't see Fingers Woman baking a pie.' He straightened up, then walked the whole of the camp again, observing everything, touching as little as he could.

Morning Star, ever practical, had already taken the thirst-crazed horses further down the draw, to where someone had dug in the sand of the creek bed yesterday evening. The hole was now filled with water from the sunken stream. Clarke stood as close as he dared get to his partner and his partner's Indian wife – perhaps ten feet – staring at them as if he still didn't believe what he was seeing.

It's got to be a mistake...

January knew exactly how he felt.

It's got to be a mistake. I was supposed to be with these friends a lot longer.

And in his mind he heard Iron Heart, the pockmarked leader of what was left of the Omaha village ... *Rotting on the ground, as my people lay among our tents and rotted...*

And Shaw's soft, creaky voice saying: *Tom never got over it...*

One person, a family, a village. The shock was the same, almost physical, like an anchor-chain parting. The stunned mind asking: *what happens*

206

now? What do I do for the rest of the day? The rest of my life...?

He didn't like Beauty Clarke, but that didn't matter.

He said, 'We need to warn the camp.'

'Holy Mother of God.' Frye's eyes showed a rim of white all around the blue of the iris. 'You mean this coulda broke out in the camp whilst we was up here?'

'You want to do that?' asked January. 'You can go straight down the coulee and across the river. You can probably make it by dark. We'll take care of these folks here and follow on—'

He glanced questioningly at Shaw.

'Why'n't you go with him, Maestro? If there ain't panic in the camp, don't start it. Ask around quiet, an' I mean *quiet*, if there's sickness ... But go first to Titus, an' Stewart, an' McLeod. Get 'em together an' tell 'em what we found here, 'fore anythin' else. All right?'

'All right.' January looked down at young Mr Frye at his side. 'That sit with you, Frye? To avoid panic in the camp, people doing stupid things?'

'All right.' The young man sounded a little better, for having someone to tell him how to handle this.

Shaw turned back to Clarke, gestured to Groot's body on its blankets. 'With your permission?'

Clarke looked away. 'Go ahead. I doubt he'll care.' January wondered if he was remembering Manitou's words about ghouls.

Shaw knelt, felt in all the coat's pockets. Nar-

row-cut, January identified the garment auto-
matically; it barely fit the Dutchman's stocky
shoulders. Dried blood still crusted around the
knife hole in the back. Swallow-tailed, with the
same old-fashioned lapels as the black waistcoat
and the same covered black buttons: *he has to
have been in mourning*. From the pocket, Shaw
brought out three envelopes.

One contained a ticket for the steam packet
Charlotte out of Hamburg and fifty pounds in
Bank of England notes. The other two contained
letters in what January thought was German,
until he tried to read it. He blinked, words seeming to make sense and then eluding him...

'What's it say, Maestro?'

He shook his head. 'It's some kind of High
German dialect. Hannibal will know.' He turned
the sheets over. Both were signed: *Franz*.

The envelopes were addressed to Klaus
Bodenschatz, on der Pfarrgasse, in Ingolstadt.

And among the unfamiliar verbiage on the last
page of one, January recognized the name
Hepplewhite. He put the nail of his thumb
beneath it, held the page for Shaw to see.

Shaw's glance lifted from the paper and for a
moment met his, like frost on steel. 'Hell to pay.'

Cholera was the first thing Gil Wallach thought
of, too. 'You're sure?' he asked as he and January walked down to the tents of the AFC through
the darkness. And, when January reassured him:
'It's not the smallpox, is it?'

'Absolutely not.'

The little trader wiped his face nervously. 'I

tell you, Ben, I was down in the Nebraska Territory when the smallpox went through the tribes there, and it's nothing you want to see. Nothing. There wasn't enough living to bury the dead. And the coyotes, and the birds ... I never want to see nuthin' like that again.'

'It's not the smallpox,' repeated January. 'Or yellow fever – and I've never heard of yellow fever up on high ground like this.'

'What can we do?' The man sounded scared – as well he might, January reflected. They were fifteen hundred miles from the United States, and surrounded by tribes who outnumbered them and who might easily convince themselves to take advantage of the white men in their time of weakness.

'First thing we can do,' said January, 'is find out what we're talking about.'

As they approached the AFC camp Robbie Prideaux hailed them from the group gathered in front of Seaholly's, engaged in the old trapper contest of seeing who could put out a candle with a rifle ball: 'C'mon, pilgrim, you can't say you seen the elephant 'til you tried this!'

January waved good-naturedly, but shook his head. The minute they'd entered the camp, he'd dispatched Bo Frye to the Hudson's Bay compound, with instructions to bring McLeod down to the AFC tents and to tell no one but McLeod the reason. The last thing they needed, January was well aware, was panic and finger pointing. That done, he'd lingered only long enough to fetch Gil Wallach and hand the two German letters over to Hannibal. He knew, to within a few degrees of certainty, that most of the other traders would be at Seaholly's.

This indeed proved to be the case. While Wallach quietly gathered up Sharpless, Morales, Wynne and a few of the other traders, January went to the crowd of trappers around the candle, signed to Bridger and Stewart and – when he'd actually fired off a shot that did put out the flame – Kit Carson: 'We need to talk.'

'You find that feller's camp?' asked Bridger as the three gathered around January.

'Not exactly. Titus in?'

'He's gone up to McLeod's – looks like here he's comin' now.' A clatter of hooves and a jingling of bridle bits as the horses emerged from the darkness; January could see in the Controller's face that he knew. Titus signaled to Seaholly to leave the bar to Pia and preceded them all into his big markee.

'What happened?' he asked January. 'What exactly did you find? It true what Frye says, that the Dutchman and his whole outfit are dead?'

'Except for Clarke, yes. It didn't look like the cholera, and it didn't look like yellow fever – I'm a surgeon, I know the signs – but they purged and puked themselves out, and died in the night. They were still warm this morning.'

Silence. The traders bunched in the small tent murmured among themselves, eyes glimmering in the shadowy lantern-glow.

'My question is,' went on January, 'if anyone else in the camp is down sick?' He looked at the men, in their dark town-coats and beaver hats. Sooner or later, these men saw every trapper, every Indian, every engagé in the camp.

And heard every breath of gossip.

Their voices clucked a little like the river stones: *Jim Hutchenson? ... Nah, that's just a hangover ... Fleuron was pukin' pretty bad t'other day ... Well, he's in with Irish Mary now, so I guess he's feelin' better ... What about the savages? ... I ain't heard no death songs...*

'You didn't just leave 'em laying out there, did you?' asked the Missourian Pete Sharpless uneasily, and Wallach retorted:

'What, bring 'em back to spread the sickness here in the camp?'

'Shaw and the Beauty are out there, burying them,' said January. 'They should be back—'

'And what about you?' demanded Morales. 'I don't want to sound cold, señor, but who's to say you're not spreadin' that sickness to every man in this tent?'

Taken aback, January said, 'I've got no reason to think I am—'

Though the tent wasn't a large one, it was surprising how much space the traders – including Gil Wallach – could put between themselves and January without actually backing out the door.

'An' *they* had no reason to think they'd picked it up, until they died.' The Mexican trader looked around at the others. 'I'd vote, first off, that we quarantine Ben and Frye until we know what this thing is.'

'Makes sense,' agreed Wynne.

'Shaw and the Beauty, too, when they get back to camp.'

211

Wallach opened his mouth to protest, but closed it. Bridger asked, 'And how do we keep the Indians from coming in quiet and killing *them*, the minute they hear there might be a white man's sickness there? That smallpox outbreak in Nebraska in '32 has some of 'em pretty spooked.'

'Don't tell 'em.'

'How they gonna know?'

'They're gonna know, boyo,' pointed out Seaholly, exasperated, 'because some Granny Poke-Nose trapper'll see the quarantine camp, ask somebody why he can't go into it, come to me and get himself fogbound and then proceed to go airing his yap to every man in the camp, including the local representatives of the Ten Lost Tribes—'

'Not if you put 'em on that island in the river behind my place,' said Morales. 'It's half a mile to the next camp downstream, and it stands high enough that even cloudbursts don't cover it. I'll keep a watch, to see no man crosses over to it. Those who ask, I'll tell that you have the heat-stroke, or got your head cracked, and must have rest.'

'That sit with you, January?' Titus turned to him.

In the faces of the men around him, January could see that he had little choice. 'Fair enough. But send me word of whatever you find out. I trained in the biggest hospital in Paris—'

'They let niggers be doctors in France?' Sharpless was genuinely startled.

'There's no law against a black man being a

212

doctor in the United States, you ass,' snapped McLeod. 'Lord God—'

'We'll send you word,' Bridger promised. 'Kit,' he added to Carson, 'why'n't you and me ride out tonight and meet Shaw and Clarke – Dry Grass, you said? There's just a few too many Blackfeet wandering around the hills, and the thought of them catchin' the plague from scalpin' the burial party somehow isn't enough to console me for their loss.'

January said quietly, 'Thank you.'

After that it was only a question of making their way in secret among the cottonwoods and wading out – breast deep in the fast-flowing black water – to the island, which January guessed would be easier still to attain in a day or two, barring another storm on the mountains. Wallach went to fetch January's 'plunder' from Morning Star's lodge; Titus donated a small tent for shelter, and Seaholly even contributed a few bottles of whiskey that January wouldn't have touched on a bet. Frye protested – he had assumed when he left the camp a few days before that he was going to find himself a partner in a miraculous secret beaver valley – but was told to shut up. 'Less you say, the better,' McLeod informed him grimly. 'In fact, come to that, if Ben has to be free to give advice on matters medical, that means that you, Frye, are the one who got a crack on the head—'

'God damn it, Mac!'

'—and is being looked after here by January,' approved Stewart. 'I like it. It's got –' he made a gesture reminiscent of young Mr Miller framing

213

a scene to sketch – 'symmetry.'

'It's got horse hockey,' retorted Frye, uncomforted.

The shelter was set up on the backside of the island's ridge, where a fire would not be seen from the camp, and Titus supervised the driving of a ring of stakes about twenty feet in all directions from the shelter. 'Any man comes across, I'll send a man with him, to make sure he doesn't get closer to you than ten feet,' promised the Controller. 'It's nothing personal, I hope you understand, Ben...'

'I understand.' *And I understand you're pretty pleased to rob Gil Wallach of two clerks without having to hire them yourself...*

'We'll see you're provided for. Hell,' the big man added, 'I'll even send one of my clerks up to Wallach's to help out, him bein' short-handed...'

January kept his thoughts to himself as Morales and Sharpless – both newcomers to the trade – exclaimed at the generosity of this gesture and Bridger and Carson exchanged trenchant glances.

By this time the lemon-rind moon stood high overhead. Here on the rear of the island, the noise from Seaholly's – fifty yards upstream and about that distance back from the water's edge – was softened by the intervening cottonwoods, and the smell of the camp's waste dumps mitigated by the river breeze. January debated whether to point out that establishing the shelter on this side of the island not only hid their fire from the curious in camp, but also exposed it to whatever tribes might be wandering around on the east side of the river, but decided to keep quiet about this. This campsite would give Morning Star and Hannibal a much better chance of coming and going unseen.

Only a few of the *ad hoc* Committee of Public Health still lingered when Wallach returned to the island shortly after midnight, carrying January's blankets, clothes and shaving gear and followed by Hannibal and Pia with a pot of Veinte-y-Cinco's stew. 'Don't cross the stakes,' said January – for the benefit of Titus and the ever-inquisitive Morales – and added in Latin, 'I need to have someone who can come and go in the camp.'

In the same language, the fiddler replied, 'That's not all you need,' and taking a camp kettle, picked his way over the moonlit rocks to fetch water. He took his time about it, only returning when the defenders of the camp's health had all sworn each other to secrecy again and started back toward the AFC camp. Wallach, January noticed, kept Pia under his wing and firmly away from Titus, who ignored the child as if she were a pane of glass.

'You let me know if there's anything I can get you,' called Morales over his shoulder. 'I have a couple books up at the tent, if you're inclined that way: an almanac and *Robinson Crusoe*.'

The offer being put off until the morrow, the trader quickened his steps to catch up with the others and disappeared into the trees.

'And left the world to darkness and to me.' Hannibal stepped out of the shadows and

215

through the staked circle. January gestured him into the shelter – he didn't quite trust Edwin Titus's motives – and followed him inside.

'Where's Shaw?'

January shook his head. 'He stayed behind with the Beauty and Morning Star, to bury the Dutchman.' Quickly, he outlined what they'd found in Dry Grass Coulee. 'It never occurred to me they'd quarantine us. It should have.' He slapped at a mosquito. 'New Orleans is such a pest hole, I've gotten used to thinking that everyone's in the same danger of whatever disease is around.'

'You think Titus is behind this somehow?'

'I think he's glad Gil's out two clerks. Beyond that?' He shook his head. 'Whatever this is, it's bad. It strikes hard and swiftly—'

'Rather like the Blackfeet,' said Hannibal grimly. He held up the two folded letters. 'I've got them translated,' he added. 'And what they say isn't good.'

EIGHTEEN

'The letter dated April of 1834 begins: *I have found the monster.*' Hannibal drew himself closer to the fire that burned on the open side of the shelter, for even in early July, the mountain nights were chill. 'It's in the Bavarian dialect, and that bears about the same relation to German

216

as Portuguese does to Spanish. I'll have some of that,' he added as January poured himself some of the coffee Frye had made. Frye settled for a half cup of Seaholly's contribution to the plague tent. After the day he'd had, he said, he needed a drink, and January couldn't argue with him there.

'I have found the monster.' For an instant, January saw in his mind the image of the doomed Baron Frankenstein, chasing the creature he had made across the Arctic ice into the darkness of eternity. He was from Ingolstadt, too.

'Franz Bodenschatz is, obviously, Frank Boden.' Hannibal angled the faded letter toward the low orange light of the flames. 'He describes Fort Ivy, and the enmity between the AFC and its rivals, pretty accurately. He calls Tom Shaw a dullard and Johnny a *schwammerl* – a simpleton – and describes how he, Bodenschatz, came up there from New Orleans, through St Louis. I assume this is the reason his father had the letter with him—'

'His father?'

'The letter starts out: *Honored Father*. At one point he says—' Hannibal turned the creased, discolored sheets ninety degrees; obviously there was little paper available at Fort Ivy, and what there was, January guessed, had begun its life as the flyleaves of Franz Bodenschatz's books. *'Thank you for the news of Katerina. I am sorry that even after your efforts, she seems incapable of understanding why I do as I must. What is wrong with these women? How can her heart be so hardened as to forget what Escher*

217

did? I fear I misjudged her, seeing in her facile pity for – something-or-other, some kind of bird, I think – *and kittens the illusion of true capacity of the heart. When I have returned from America – when I have destroyed the Thing which martyred our Beautiful One – I will naturally pursue the honorable course and return to her. Yet how can True Love exist, knowing as I do now the shallowness of her selfish heart?'*

He folded the letter. 'And how's Katerina Bodenschatz going to have True Love for a husband who runs off to America on a mission of vengeance, leaving her with two children, one of them a babe in arms at the time of Franz's departure, which as of April of 1834 had been – he mentions it somewhere in here – nearly seven years previously?'

'The Thing which martyred our Beautiful One.' From his pocket January took the locket, and he opened it in the firelight. The childish face of the girl within smiled out at them, and a bead of pine resin, popping in the fire, threw up a trail of yellow sparks and gave the illusion for a moment that she was about to speak. 'Escher, I presume.'

Hannibal unfolded the other sheet. *'Honored Father,'* he read. *'All stands now in readiness. We have found an ally at last, whose heart bleeds as ours does, with wounds no balm can heal; an ally unshaken in the righteousness of our cause.'*

'Or who says he is, anyway.' January spooned stew on to the tin plates that had come along with it: cornmeal, grouse, an assortment of

218

Mexican spices. 'A man on a mission of revenge is one of the easiest to enlist to whatever cause you please, because he isn't thinking straight.'

'Hepplewhite seems to have convinced Franz, at all events,' murmured Hannibal. *'He can bring us unseen into the camp where Escher will be, and from there the trap will be easy to lay. No need even for bait, for the man's own disgusting habits will cause him to throw himself upon the trap spring, like the beaver who follow the stink of one another's* – I'm not sure of the word here, but you know what they bait beaver traps with – *to their watery ruin* ... Nice turn of phrase there, isn't it?'

He rubbed his eyes – it was now, January calculated, well past two in the morning, and the fiddler had been deciphering faded handwriting by firelight since just after dark.

'What's the date on this one?'

'This past September. Sa–sa, sa–sa, advice about having the garden and greenhouses looked to, instructions for the trip from Ingolstadt to Hamburg – evidently Papa doesn't get about much – and thence to New York on the *Char-lotte*, to get a steam packet to New Orleans. Who to see in Independence – he's apparently coming the same way we did – which trader will get him to Fort Laramie, and a list of things he needs to bring. The journey is a difficult one, he says – *there*'s the understatement of the year! – good boots, medical kit, tea, coffee, trade goods from St Louis in case the train he's traveling with runs into the Pawnee ... *'In case,'* ha! Here we are.'

He turned over the last page. *'In exchange for*

219

this, Hepplewhite will conceal us and our effects, and see to our safe return from the frontier. I hesitated to make this bargain with him, and yet, what sort of men are these, that we need to concern ourselves with their fates? I have been among them for two years now and can attest that they are brutes, little better than Escher himself. They have long since surrendered their humanity to drink, violence and the shallow pleasures of copulation ... Clearly a man who has never properly copulated. *The whole congregation of them, did you pass their souls through a hundred distillations and the finest filters you possess, would not yield sufficient paste to polish one of our precious Mina's little shoe-buckles. The world will be cleaner for their absence.'*

Hannibal raised his eyes from the letter, a whole ladder of parallel wrinkles repeating the lift of his brows. Only the sound of the river, gurgling over its stones, broke the silence of the night, *drink, violence and the shallow pleasures of copulation* at Seaholly's having given way at last to the peace of the mountains, the stillness that had existed since the great ranges were formed.

'He thinks he's some punkins, don't he?' Frye wrapped his arms around his knees. 'Brutes and beasts, are we? Waugh! Bet he still puts *his* pants on one leg at a time. Is Mina the little gal whose picture's in the locket?'

'I think so,' said January softly.

'And she'd be this feller Boden's sister? If he's callin' her "our Mina" an' his poor old Dad's the

220

one that's carryin' her picture? Sounds like this Escher he talks of killed her ... You said the old man was in mournin'. That's a dirty shame.'

'It sounds like it,' agreed Hannibal. 'And it also sounds like Franz has made a deal with Hepplewhite, whoever *he* is, to kill most – if not all – of the people here at the rendezvous, if this Escher is among them.'

'Kin he *do* that?' Frye looked out of the shelter, at the darkness beyond the fire. All the way up the trail, the camp-setters – and Shaw – had warned them never to get too close to a fire, lest the gold light make of them a target for lurking Indians. 'We got some tough hombres here...'

'And two of the toughest,' pointed out January, 'went out just after dark looking for Shaw, who I'd back against almost anyone in camp – and none of the three of them have returned.'

Gil Wallach had taken Morning Star's canoe that had brought himself, Pia and Hannibal to the island; it made January deeply uneasy to see the fiddler wade out into the river, his clothes in a bundle on his head. Completely aside from the cold of the snow-melt river, travel in the wilderness had made January aware of just how swiftly the water could rise from a thunderstorm on the mountains miles away. Nor had he forgotten the ambush on the night of the banquet.

'I'll pass like a frightened rabbit through the bottomland without even pausing to dress,' Hannibal had reassured him, 'and scamper down the trail in front of the AFC camp. I assure you I scream very, very loudly when set upon. Some-

221

one will have to notice.'

January kept to himself the reflection that any ambushers might well originate from the AFC camp, and took comfort – as he watched his friend reach the shore and vanish into the black shadows of the bottomlands – in the thought that the targets of the earlier assault had probably been himself and Shaw. Hannibal was fairly worthless to anyone, though the thought of vengeful Sioux braves lining up for the privilege of assassinating him to win the hand of Morning Star kept him smiling all the way back to the shelter.

All any Sioux brave had to do to win Morning Star's hand was lay in a stock of trade-beads and wait 'til the end of the rendezvous.

Lying in his blankets a little distance from the dying fire, January listened to the yipping of the coyotes, the mutter of the river around the island's flanks, as the images of Shaw, and Clarke and the crumpled, wolf-eaten bodies in Dry Grass Coulee merged into the image of Victor Frankenstein, wrapped in furs, running across the towering bergs of Arctic ice in pursuit of the thing he had created, the monster that owed him its very existence.

I have found the monster...

And left the world you knew behind...

Or is that me I'm seeing? he wondered in his dream. Bundled up in beaver fur, chasing Death Himself, with Rose and his sisters – and his nieces and nephews whom he cherished, and the music that was the golden heart of all his joy – all left behind him, thousands of miles behind, in

New Orleans...

When I've avenged Ayasha's death, I can go home...

But he knew that, before he returned, they would all be dead.

Rose, no, I'm coming back...

'Winter Moon?'

He jerked awake, groped for his knife which had been under the spare blanket rolled beneath his head—

Morning Star, seated cross-legged a yard away by the embers of the fire pit, held it out to him.

Bo Frye snored on.

Behind the Sioux woman, morning was a monochrome of misty lavender and the dense black-green of the pines. January guessed he had slept less than two hours. The air was the cold breath of God, and his eyeballs had the batter-fried sensation they did during most of Mardi Gras.

'Where's Shaw?'

Morning Star shook her head. 'We finished the burying; he sent me ahead to scout.' Her voice was scarcely more than the waking-up clamor of every lark in the mountains. 'Twice we heard what he thought were movements among the trees up the coulee. I found nothing, but the moon was low, and it was very dark among the trees. On that second time Blanket Chief and Shoots His Enemy's Hand –' January recognized two of the numerous names the Indians gave to Bridger and Carson – 'came riding from the river. I stayed out of sight and followed them back to where I had left Tall Chief and Beauty by

223

the graves of the others, but they were gone, and the ground was rank with the smell of sickness, and of blood. Blanket Chief and Shoots His Enemy's Hand searched the woods. It was only on account of the wolves that they found the body of Beauty, torn nearly to pieces – and scalped.'

'And Shaw?'

'I found no sign of him. Nor did they. All the horses were gone also. When the moon went in I came back here. Sun Mouse told me that Cold Face and the others had put you here, to keep the sickness out of the camp. Are you sick?'

'No.' January pulled his shirt on. 'And it's best you don't linger. Morales will be awake soon and he's keeping an eye on us.' January glanced in the direction of the merchant's small camp, though this was hidden by the island's rise. 'Others, too, and they may send someone to check on us. I can't risk you being seen here. The men are scared, and it'll be worse when Bridger brings back word that the Beauty, and maybe Shaw too, took sick just from burying the dead. The camp'll quarantine a white man. I don't know what they'd do to one of your people.'

Obediently, Morning Star got to her feet and retreated to the line of stakes. January followed so that they stood about ten feet apart.

'What should I do, Winter Moon?'

'First, don't let anyone know you were one of the burying party. I'll make sure Frye keeps his mouth shut. Would your brothers, or others of your family, be willing to cross the river to hunt

224

for Tall Chief?'

'I have already spoken to my brothers, and they have gone.' Morning Star gestured toward the hills across the river – shadowy still, though the sky was filled with new light. 'Chased By Bears said – and it is true – that this sickness seems worse even than the smallpox. Why should we care, he asked, if the whites all perish of it together? I said that Tall Chief is his brother now, and at least we must learn what became of him. But more, I think, he will not do.'

'Nor should he,' said January. 'Yet thank him for whatever he is willing to do to find the source of the evil that I think is walking some-where in this valley. I don't know whether the evil that surrounded the old man by Horse Creek is a brother to the sickness spirit or not. Yet each time I look, I see that the tracks of the one lie close to the tracks of the other. And now I can't look for the tracks of either.'

He stood for a moment in thought, arms folded against the sharp chill, and passed all that had happened the previous day, and the day before, through his mind: the long, patient tracking of Groot and Clarke over the hills south of the camp; the bizarre and horrifying rituals glimpsed through the trees in the Blackfoot village – and the still-more-bizarre conversation with Wild-man by the ashes of the Blackfoot fire the following morning; Fingers Woman curled up beside her husband on the reeking blankets, her head pillowed on the shoulder of the black velvet coat.

In his pocket – shut safely in his watch case –

were four long splinters of burned fatwood that he'd taken from the Blackfoot fire. Their pointed ends were tipped with dried blood. What he'd seen hadn't been a hallucination or a trick.

Silent Wolf is my brother...

'Would you do this for me?' he asked at length. 'Would you take the big buckskin mare that's tethered at our camp and return her to Manitou Wildman? Tell him – and anyone else you meet – that Tall Chief sent you back to camp the moment we saw the bodies of the Dutchman and his party, without ever letting you get close. And ask Wildman, would he come here to speak to me?'

The young woman nodded and started to turn away. Then she looked back and asked him softly, 'Is it true? Will I become sick, as Fingers Woman and the others became sick? Will I die as they died?'

'I haven't yet,' pointed out January. 'Nor has Frye. The sickness spirit has given us time, and time is always a gift that must not be wasted.'

When Morning Star had gone, January made his way down to the water's edge to gather up driftwood and deadfalls, then returned to the camp to brew coffee. By the time Frye woke, Pia had paddled over with a camp kettle full of bighorn sheep-ribs and the information – called across the quarantine barrier, after she'd set down the kettle for January to pick up – that Bridger and Carson had just returned to the camp with the news of Clarke's death and Shaw's disappearance...

And that Hannibal had located Klaus Bodenschatz's hat.

226

NINETEEN

'We camped near there the night,' reported Bridger, with the sun halfway to noon, when he, Carson and an assortment of traders and trappers gathered along the staked quarantine-line on what was rapidly coming to be known (to January's annoyance) as Plague Island. 'You'll understand we didn't want to get too near, 'specially after we found the Beauty.'

'Did you leave him unburied?' demanded the Reverend Grey, with the righteous horror of someone who wasn't confined behind a quarantine line ... and who hadn't seen the bodies in Groot's camp.

Carson looked like he was about to make a sharp reply, but Bridger answered, 'First light we dug a grave, and we rolled him into it with saplings. That's what's taken us so long gettin' back. It wasn't respectful,' he added grimly. 'But anyone here wants to take issue with it, I'll gladly take him out and show him the spot, so's they can rebury him more to their liking. We had a look around,' he went on, into Grey's total silence. 'The Beauty'd been took sick: that was clear as mule tracks. Whether Shaw was or not I don't know. I saw no sign of it. They was hit by Injuns – Blackfoot, I made 'em – and by all I could tell he was well enough to run for it, and to cover his trail when he reached timber. As for how far he got—' He shook his head. 'I read the tracks of twenty or more in the war party that killed Clarke, and more up the draw.'

'If you want to go in after him –' Carson looked across at January – 'I'll go with you. But I'm tellin' you, if that child has the brains I think he does, he'll have moved up east into the foothills to lose 'em. If he ain't took sick up there, he'll make his way back by an' by. An' if he is took sick, they'll find him 'fore you or I would. That's my call. But I'll go.'

'And I.' Stewart stepped forward, elegant in his white buckskins, Prideaux right behind him.

'Waugh! You can count this child in. You don't look all that perishin' sick to me.'

Moriamur et in media arma ruamus,' said Hannibal, and he moved up to Prideaux's side.

'No, Carson's right,' said January. 'Shaw'll be back or he won't. But if we go out there, one of us, maybe more, will be killed before we're anywhere near enough to help him.' He looked out across the swift-flowing green-brown silk of the main river, thinking about the trackless miles of foothills that rose beyond and the broken granite escarpments of the Wind River Range. Hearing again Manitou's screams in the night and what Morning Star – and every mountaineer he'd spoken to – had told him about the ways Indians of any tribe had of dealing with prisoners.

When the visitors had gone, trampling what was now a pale trace around the island's center

228

rise to where they could ford – or canoe – the thirty-some feet back to the point of land behind Morales's tent, January felt sick at heart.

'You owe me,' Tom had said. *'You can kill anything with one shot... 'Til you lost your nerve. You tellin' me you'll run away again?'*

And Manitou: *'You think twice about vengeance ... It never ends well.'*

For bloody deed, let bloody deed atone ... Who had written that? One of the Greeks, in some horrifying play about revenge and all that it led to.

Would Shaw leave his bones in the mountains, without ever having found his brother's killer? And who would that profit in the end?

Like Hamlet, he'd only leave a stage littered with corpses.

And then he saw that Hannibal, who had lingered, seemed to have acquired yet another girlfriend, and a new hat.

The girlfriend, at least, was familiar. She was Irish Mary, a doll-faced Aphrodite of seventeen. Her putative Celtic antecedents seemed most in evidence by the fact that her hair was curly, rather than of the Indian straightness more usual among Mexicans, and had in its natural blackness – trenchantly hinted at along her hairline – a reddish cast of which she took fullest advantage with the henna bottle. The youngest and the prettiest of the girls, she was consequently the most in demand and – by rendezvous standards – was the best-dressed, in a crimson skirt and a satin vest bedecked with ribbons and jingling with silver trinkets. These ornaments also

229

decorated Hannibal's new hat.

Which presumably, deduced January, was actually hers, on loan.

It never ceased to amaze him that in a camp consisting of five hundred mountaineers, three times that many engagés, and exactly six Mexican whores, two of those six kept regular company with Hannibal. Who had an Indian wife as well.

'May I show Benjamin your hat, my pearl of delight?' inquired Hannibal in Spanish.

Mary looked uncertain. 'Well, I don't want to get nuthin'—'

Considering her profession, January had to school his face carefully at the remark.

Hannibal reached into his coat pocket – like the traders, he kept to his New Orleans attire of old-fashioned cutaway coat and striped trousers – and produced a handful of credit-plews from every store in the camp, including Seaholly's liquor tent, mostly won at chess. 'I'll buy you a new one, *amor mia*,' he said. 'Better suited to your charms.'

It took her a few minutes to unpin all the ribbons and ornaments. Then she tossed it over.

Hannibal gave her another handful of plews – presumably in addition to what he was paying her for her time, since by the sound of it, Seaholly's tent was open for business again. 'Tell Benjamin where you acquired your hat – with the understanding that he is a gentleman and will guard your secret with his life.'

'Please, you got to.' Mary regarded January doubtfully. 'Mick'll skin me, if he knows I was meetin' anybody outside and not tellin' him.'

Who she had been meeting – four nights ago, the night after his fight with Manitou, with rain coming down and the moon two days old – had been Jed Blankenship.

'He come up to me behind the liquor tent all sore-assed after Mick threw him out.' She perched on a flat rock on her own side of the quarantine line, took tobacco and corn husk from the pouch around her neck, and pulled up her skirt to roll a cigarette on her knee. It was enough, reflected January admiringly, to make a man take up smoking.

'He could get liquor from Hudson's Bay or Morales or anyone, but he wanted *conejo*, and he'd pay real silver for it, he said.'

The assignation had been set for the woods on the south side of Horse Creek, where the pine tree had fallen across the water to form a fragile bridge. January remembered passing the spot.

'I told Mick I was sick an' couldn't work, and anyway with everybody out chasin' the Dutchman, it was a slow night. But I was late gettin' out of the camp, an' then the creek was high like you never seen. Then Jed didn't show up. So here I am, sittin' under some bushes in the rain, an' every now an' then I'll hear somebody rustlin' around in the woods, or sometimes horses goin' past. Now, I knowed it was probably just those *pendejos* out tryin' to catch the Dutchman ... but, you know, I was cold an' scared.'

And back in April, if somebody had offered me hard silver to go wait someplace in the rain with

231

Blackfeet running around in the woods behind me, reflected January, *I'd have taken it ...* To this girl, every piece of silver that she didn't have to divide with Mick was one step closer to getting out of Taos and liquor tents and ten or twelve trappers a day, provided that was what she wanted to do with it. Maybe it was just liquor money.

'So the rain quits, an' I think, Jed'll be along soon,' the girl went on. 'I had one of Mick's bottles of trade liquor with me, sippin' to stay warm, so I'm not real sure how long it was after the rain quit that I heard shots. Not real long. There was one shot, an' then sounds of fightin'. Somebody was bellerin' like a grizzly that sat on a porcupine, and then there was a second shot in the middle of that. Myself, I thought it was Manitou – you know how he gets when somethin' sets him off.'

She shrugged and took another drag of her cigarette. 'Not my business, anyway. They'd quieted down, and along comes Jed, and it started raining again. And after all that,' she added, those beautiful brown eyes turning ugly, 'the *carajo* didn't even pay me. Just said he'd tell Mick if I didn't keep quiet. Said he'd knock my front teeth out, too, and let me explain *that* to Mick...'

January's first thought was: *and you were surprised?* but he kept it to himself. From his experience in New Orleans, he guessed there was every chance that when the proposition had been put to Irish Mary to earn a little extra silver, she hadn't been completely sober.

232

'I swear to Christ, I wish somebody'd break that *coño*'s leg an' leave him where the Blackfeet'll find him. So after Jed takes off to see what he can see of Beauty and the Dutchman it started raining again, and I stayed smoking a little – he took my whiskey, too, the cheap *meado* – and I got to thinking. You've seen Manitou when he gets like he does, so I knew whoever he'd had an argument with probably wouldn't object to it if I sort of went through his pockets. And money's the last thing Manitou thinks about, when he goes off like that: last year here he got howlin' mad – mad-dog mad – at Jacques Chouinard and had to be dragged off him, and when he came back into camp three days later, I swear he didn't remember a thing about it. So I waited 'til it got good an' light – I wasn't gonna get myself lost again – and then headed up in the direction of where I'd heard the shoutin'.'

'You see anyone else in the woods?' January turned the hat over in his hands as he spoke, surprised and bemused by what he saw.

Irish Mary shook her head. 'While I was sittin' smokin' under the bush – which I tell you wasn't any kind of good as a roof in that last rainshower – I heard someone ride by further up the slope. It musta been the *hideputa* who got to the old boy 'fore I did, because when I got there, he'd been stripped of his coat, his boots, an' his weskit, poor old man ... I mean, yes, I was gonna go through his pockets, but I wasn't gonna steal the shirt off his back, for the love of Jesus!'

She piously crossed herself. 'He was layin' there with his back all over with blood from

233

bein' stabbed, an' blood soakin' into the ground under him, an' it looked like his leg broke – it was splinted up with a couple of saplings. An' I thought: *Daddy, if you was out here with a broke leg, pissin' off Manitou Wildman was probably one of the stupider things you coulda done.*'

'That's just it,' mused January. 'Why piss off Wildman? Why shoot at him? Those were pistol balls Shaw and I found in the trees near there – were there pistols by the body?'

She shook her head. 'Manitou musta taken them, or whoever got his coat an' boots, poor old *abuelo*.'

'But they didn't,' said January. At least, he thought, Frye, Groot and Clarke hadn't – and pistols were heavy to lug. If Manitou had had them on him, his 'brother' Silent Wolf could have taken them, before they tortured him ... 'Where'd you find his hat?'

'Downslope a little. There was enough light, I could see it, black against the bushes. It's a mighty pretty hat.'

'So it is,' agreed January, angling it so that the sunlight fell on the dark silk of the lining. 'And I hope, when you get back to Taos, you'll find one prettier. Hannibal,' he said, 'when you've walked Miss Mary back to Mr Seaholly's, I could do with a word.'

As the fiddler escorted Irish Mary – with tender courtesy that would have passed muster at a garden party – back toward the canoe tied at the northern point of the island, January returned to the shelter. 'That really the old boy's hat?' asked Frye, who had retreated after the initial conference with Bridger and Carson to practice knife-throwing at the slender trunk of a nearby sapling: competing right hand against left.

'I'm not sure.' January knelt in a corner of the shelter, opened the little satchel of medicines he'd brought from New Orleans. Beneath the packets of powdered willow bark and ipecac that his sister Olympe had made up for him, the so-called 'Indian tobacco' – which wasn't tobacco at all – to treat laryngitis and asthma, the little phials of tincture of opium and camphor, the rolled-up kit of his surgical implements, he found the other thing Rose had sent with him besides the little notebook: a powerful round-lensed magnifier.

From outside the tent he heard Morales call out as he came near the ring of stakes, was there anything you boys need, and what'd Mary want? January didn't hear what his young companion replied. He carried the hat back to the entrance of the shelter where the eastern light was strong and – against the sun-bleached canvas – examined again with the magnifying lens the hairs that he'd taken from its lining.

Two of them were obviously Mary's, thickly curling and springy, bright with henna for most of their length and the girl's native, mahogany-tinted black for the last half-inch.

And one was fine-textured, black for most of its three-inch length, and for that last inch or so, light brown, like the hair of the girl Mina in her silver locket.

TWENTY

'Boden came in with one of the tribes?' Hannibal pulled on his shirt, still damp from his swim downriver to the island, then quickly huddled back to the fire inside the 'plague tent'. Outside, Frye stood guard – or rather sat casually by the fire, ready to call out a greeting loud enough to be heard within the tent, should anyone come along the path from the rendezvous side of the island.

The discovery of the dyed hair within the hat had the effect on January of a sound in the night: a prickly watchfulness, a profound sense of nearby threat. He was more aware than ever that he was going to need friends within the camp who had freedom of action – neither kept within the quarantine line by their sworn word, nor expelled from the camp for breaking it.

'He *has* to have come in with one of the tribes,' said January. 'The hair in that hat – the hair that wasn't Irish Mary's – was brown that had been dyed black. So that hat wasn't old Klaus's. The only reason I can think of for anyone to dye his hair black would be to pass as an Indian or a Mexican, and no *blankitte* in this part of the world would do that voluntarily. It looks to me as if Boden was with his father at the shelter at some point in the night, and their hats got switched.'

'Then he would have been the one who splinted his father's leg –' Hannibal frowned as he tied his moccasins, mentally aligning the probable course of the night's events – 'and made the fire and the shelter. Which would mean that Manitou came later, beat him and killed him ... But why would Boden have left him alone there? If they were at the rendezvous at all, they'd have to have known Manitou was camped close by.'

'And why would Manitou have beaten him that way, if his leg was already broken?' Anger flared like a hot coal in January's chest: anger at himself, for he had liked the big trapper. 'I can see hurting him in a fight to get a gun away from him, but if he was hurt already, lying in the shelter helpless—'

'He was enraged,' pointed out Hannibal. 'Mad-dog mad. Mary heard him shouting.'

'And where was Boden during all this? And afterward, why didn't he return to the old man, knowing he was unable to help himself?'

'Could Manitou have killed *him*?'

'And not remember it?' January frowned. 'It's possible ... But no one in the camp is missing.'

'Except Shaw,' said Hannibal, rather grimly. 'And Asa Goodpastor. Unless letting himself be taken by the Blackfeet and tortured is some insane kind of penance.' The fiddler shook out his vest – a little damp, but the tight covering of waxed canvas in which he'd rolled his clothing for his downriver swim had worked well. 'One of my tutors when I was a lad was a little crazy that way. Not that he'd have beaten up an injured old man, but he'd sneak off into the village every couple of months, get well and truly hammered and roger himself speechless with the local commodity, a young lady named Peg Drowe ... Perfectly understandable behavior. But old Venables would lock himself up in his room afterwards and cut his arms and legs with a sharpened letter-opener, a fact we only learned one night when he tripped on the stairway – perfectly sober, I might add – and knocked himself senseless. When he was carried up to his bed and undressed, he was found to be covered with scars, all precisely spaced, as if he'd used a ruler as well as the letter opener.' Hannibal shook his head, as if after decades he was still puzzling it over.

'He could recite the whole of Hesiod's *Theogony* off the top of his head – Homer and the entire Bible as well. Astonishing. Poor Peg was mortified when she learned about it. Personally, I never found rogering her worth so much as a bitten hangnail.' He glanced sharply up at January, added, 'Well, we knew Boden had to be one of the traders, didn't we? It's not such an unusual style of hat – Edwin Titus wears one, and John McLeod, and others – but that narrows it to one of the new men.'

'Wynne, or Gonzales,' said January. 'Morales too – and what's the name of that fellow from Missouri?'

'Sharpless?'

January nodded. 'Do this for me, would you?'

238

he began, and broke off as the rear wall of the shelter rippled, lifted about six inches, and Morning Star slithered through.

'Manitou is gone,' she said softly and wrung the river water out of her braids. Her deerskin dress, like Hannibal's coat and weskit, was damp from being carried across rolled tight in a piece of oiled deer-hide. 'I reached his camp, and there was nothing there. Even the fire pit was filled in and hidden, as if he were in enemy country.'

January cursed in Arabic. 'Can your brothers track him?' he asked. 'I think he's the man Boden and his father were seeking, for killing Boden's sister. This wouldn't be any of our business, except for what Boden seems to think his vengeance entitles him to do: kill those who get in his way, or – it seems – kill some or all of the men in this camp in order to kill his man among them. Hannibal,' he added, 'can you get a description from Wallach of the horses Boden took from the fort last winter? He'll have known someone at the rendezvous might recognize them, so he couldn't bring them into the main camp. But I'm guessing that whichever Indian tribe he came most of the way with, you'll find the horses there.'

'Crazy Bear killed the daughter of the old man?' asked Morning Star worriedly. 'The girl whose picture Sun Mouse showed me in the locket?'

'We think so, yes.'

'And the old man as well, when he was crippled and helpless?'

'It looks that way. I want to speak with him

239

again,' January said, 'and ask him about Boden. Who he is, what he's capable of and what he might be up to. The laws of the United States can't touch Manitou here: he should have nothing to fear in talking to me. But the people he killed were innocent, as Tall Chief's brother was innocent when Boden killed him, only to hide what he's doing in his pursuit of Manitou.'

'If the laws of your country cannot punish him –' Morning Star's brow puckered – 'why would he lie and say he had not killed the old man? Crazy Bear has a thunder spirit that comes on him sometimes when he is angry, but he does not lie.' She shook her head. 'I will learn about the horses for you,' she went on. 'And I will ask Chased By Bears and Little Fish if they would seek him. But Manitou is not an easy man to find, if he does not wish it. And he can be dangerous to approach.'

'They don't have to approach him. Just let me know where he is.'

The young woman considered the matter for a time, sitting with her knees drawn up to her breast, her bare toes making small patterns in the dust of the shelter floor. 'I will ask,' she said again. 'But they may say, as I do, that these are other men's vengeances and have nothing to do with us. The more I hear of this, the less honorable it seems, for anyone who touches the matter. You should leave it.' She looked across at Hannibal. 'Both of you should leave it, husband. There will be no good in it for you.'

'A man doesn't leave his brother,' said January. 'And Tall Chief is my brother. And Boden killed his.'

Morning Star sighed and shook her head. 'I will ask,' she said. 'But this marrying of white men is more complicated than I thought.'

Because Charro Morales worked his store alone, without either a camp-setter or a clerk, once he'd waded across in the morning with a breakfast of corn mush and a couple of grouse – and asked if there was anything further he could get them – January and Frye saw nothing of the trader until early evening. Frye fretted about his traps and his horses – which Rob Prideaux had taken charge of – but in fact had sold up all his skins before setting forth on his ill-fated expedition to find the Secret Beaver Valley, and being of sober habits he had a considerable stock of credit to his name with the AFC.

To January's relief, Bo Frye proved to be a friendly and undemanding companion, although like many mountaineers he was unbelievably talkative when given a new listener. Another time January might have found the man's chatter irritating, but it served, in its way, to keep his mind off the gnawing worry about Shaw. More-over, in between tales of Frye's grandparents in Medfield, Massachusetts, his apprenticeship to a wheelwright uncle who had then moved to Ohio because of bad debts and a broken heart, and how he had answered the advertisement of the old Rocky Mountain Fur Company a few years back, to go into the mountains under Jim Bridger, the young trapper told stories of survival in the wilderness – Indians, sickness, and

241

all; and of men January had met in the camp: Tom Fitzpatrick, Jim Bridger, Robbie Prideaux – that were comforting in their way. Men had been lost before, and had returned.

Mid-morning Pia paddled across to the island again, bringing with her part of a haunch of venison she'd won at poker and the news that neither Abishag Shaw nor Stewart's hunting party had returned to the camp. Neither had there been any word from Tom Fitzpatrick in his search for the missing Indian Agent, and the bets were running two-to-one at Seaholly's that Frye would be down sick by morning.

'And which way are you betting?'

The girl looked offended, as if January had impugned her intelligence. 'Both ways,' she said. 'I got Mama to bet against, for noon, this evening, and tomorrow morning, and I'm betting for. Jed Blankenship said he'd fight any man who tried to put Poco in quarantine,' she added wisely, 'but I think that's because after this long, if Poco's quarantined, Jed'll be next.' She'd gotten someone – probably the motherly Moccasin Woman – to make her a trim little vest out of a red shirt, and had sewed on it silver trinkets and a couple of pierced coins, in imitation of her mother and the other Mexican girls. Around her waist she wore a couple of silk sashes that looked as if they'd been cut from worn-out shawls, which gave her the look of a hummingbird masquerading in peacock's hand-me-downs.

'And Jed would rather go off in the woods and die,' suggested January, 'than share a forty-foot circle and a shelter with a black man?'

'Jed's a jackass.' Pia tossed her head, making her braids flop. 'Nobody else in the camp is sick. I asked everybody who came by the bar. Hannibal said to tell you that he found out from Mr Wallach what the three horses looked like that Mr Boden stole from the fort, and Morning Star went off to look for them ... *and* he said it was a secret,' she added, when January put a finger to his lips. 'You don't need to worry about me, Ben. I'm true blue and will never stain.' She finger-marked an exaggerated cross on her flat chest. 'It's just that not having a clerk now except Hannibal, Mr Wallach is keeping him busy up there, so I'm minding the gambling tent. He'll be down tonight, he says, after it gets dark. Is there anything else I can get you, before I go back to the game?'

'Some whiskey for tonight would go good,' Frye put in. 'Morales come down on his prices any? Seaholly's, then,' he sighed, when the girl shook her head, and handed her a red-and-yellow AFC plew. 'There's a girl who's gonna make some man a fine wife,' he added, watching the thin little form dash away up the path, child-like for all her grown-up finery.

January grinned. 'Or break his heart.'

'Oh, they all do that,' said the young man, with an air of great wisdom. 'They all do that.'

Toward evening the northern skies began to cloud up, and Frye and January shifted tent and belongings up to the high ridge in the center of the island. Charro Morales came over to lend a hand, and though there was no evidence that the

243

river had ever risen that far, offered sanctuary in his own quarters onshore. 'I won't tell if you won't. Sounds like a bad one coming in.' And he paused to listen to the grumble of far-off thunder.

'I appreciate that.' January tried to recall if he'd ever seen Morales in a black beaver hat with a chimney-pot crown to it. The man was one of the traders new to the rendezvous, and like the other newcomers – Gonzales who claimed to be from Santa Fe, and a taciturn man named Wynne who didn't seem to have a great deal of business sense – was being soundly drubbed in the marketplace by the AFC, despite the quality of his whiskey.

'You gonna take him up?' asked Frye, once they'd got the new fire pit dug. It was surprising how much difference the ten-foot rise at the center of the island made, in terms of exposure to the wind. 'If this turns out to be the time that the river does come up more'n fifteen feet, I for sure don't want to be sittin' up here when we find out about it.' And he looked down from the modest height at the two arms of the river – deep and shallow – rippling in the fading light. Across the shallower western channel, the lights of campfires twinkled beyond the trees of the bottomland; with the restless tossing of the cottonwoods, January was conscious of how far off those lights were.

He shifted the logs on the fire, throwing up a brighter glare and a cascade of sparks. 'I don't know.'

'You mind if I do?'

January hesitated, wondering what it was that was ringing alarm bells in his mind, then shook his head. 'Worst comes to worst, I can climb a tree,' he added, to lighten the air. 'Can't be worse than sitting out a hurricane in bayou country. And I'd rather not be turned out of the camp, if someone were to drop in unexpectedly.'

While Frye made coffee, January settled on an outcropping of the island's rocky bones and gazed across the wider eastern arm of the river, over the bottomlands and up at the shouldering foothills, the dark fringe of trees on the east side of the river where the coulees ran up into the mountains proper. *I was raised in the mountains*, Shaw had said...

He's fast, January reminded himself. *He knows how to live off the land.* And he was very, very tough.

Would that be enough?

How long do we wait, hoping for word? In another week, January knew, the rendezvous camps would start breaking up. Most of the trappers had finished their business already. The traders would head back toward Mexico or Missouri, mules laden with furs, hastening their steps to avoid snows that could fall as early as September in these high valleys. The trappers and their engagés would begin the long trek toward new rivers to trap, new valleys to find where the beaver hadn't all been killed.

And if spring finds us in a war with England, thought January grimly, *the logical place for the British to land their army will be New Orleans. Again.*

245

'Well, you beat us there once,' remarked Hannibal, when he, Pia and Veinte-y-Cinco arrived – well after full dark – with a kettleful of supper and, as promised, a bottle of Seaholly's whiskey for Frye.

'Because General Pakenham was an idiot,' returned January. 'I can't imagine Parliament would appoint a general that stupid twice.'

'I have great faith in the rulers of my country.' The fiddler settled on a hunk of driftwood beside the fire while Pia and her mother got up a game of three-handed pinochle with Frye. 'I brought the letters.'

'Read them to me,' said January. 'Not just a summary – tell me what Bodenschatz actually tells his father, line by line.'

'Honored Father,' Hannibal read, and January bent his head and shut his eyes to listen. *This is the man himself speaking*, he thought. *There has to be an answer there.*

A description of Fort Ivy. Boden's contempt for the men among whom he found himself: trappers, muleteers, half-breed engagés. Card-games and drinking, the same stories told a thousand times: *I think I should burst into tears of joy, if a man came here who had read Shakespeare or Goethe, if I found one soul with whom I could speak even a broken fragment of what is in my heart...*

His admiration for the 'wild' tribes who passed the fort to trade, *whose honor is clean and who have not been corrupted by the Americans' obsessive greed and filthy ways.* His disgust at the 'fort Indians': *broken drunkards who will*

246

sell their wives and daughters for liquor...

Would that some great barrier, like the Wall of China, had been built the length of the frontier, to keep the Fur Companies, with their foul alcohol, their dirtiness and diseases, their corrupt and imbecilic 'Indian agents' and that great and filthy poison, Money, away from these savage, honest children of God, who know no Law but Rightness, as it is revealed to them in the magic of their dreams.

And from there, a long meditation upon his own dreams, and on the sacredness of Vengeance: *Law is the whore of the rich, but here beyond the frontier, a Man does what he Must...*

A doctrine that would appeal to a man in quest of vengeance. *Don't you give me no law and Constitution*, Tom Shaw had said. Evidently, Franz Boden agreed.

More prosaically, the second letter was filled with minute detail: put Gottsreich in charge of the greenhouses and the laboratory; sell your interest in the shop to Kleinsmark Apotheker-gesselleschaft; lay in a warm coat, some decent brandy (*of which there is none in the whole of the United States*), the green China tea and the African coffee. Take the diligence from Munich to Nuremberg, from Nuremberg to Weimar, complete with advice on which inns to put up at – clearly, January reflected, Franz Bodenschatz's own route – and then the steamer up the Elbe to Hamburg...

Purchase these things in New York – good boots, a pistol for your protection (*Purdey is the most reliable maker*) – then a steamer to New

247

Orleans. January wondered how, upon reaching New York originally, the younger man had traced his sister's fleeing murderer. And he must have been young, January thought, if poor Katerina had just borne their second child when her husband had deserted her in pursuit of vengeance. Steamboat to Independence – *lay in a good stock of liquor, fish hooks, trade-vermillion, mirrors. Join with one of the traders bound for Santa Fe – Merriwether has a reputation for honesty, as does Babbit, Becknell, McCoy...*

I will be in the vicinity of Fort Laramie, watching for you. Hepplewhite and his men will meet us there...

'Could Hepplewhite be an Indian?'

Hannibal looked up from the letter. 'I can't imagine where such an Indian would have been born, if the first thing his parents saw to name him after was a chair.'

January laughed. 'A mission Indian,' he said. 'Who took a white man's name, like Moccasin Woman – whom nobody ever calls Mrs Bryan...'

Hannibal was still considering this when Morning Star appeared from the moonless dark, still shrugging herself back into her deerskin dress. 'Will you stay in the camp?' She looked downslope, gauging the river and the wind. 'It will come close to you. Whether or no, my husband, you and these ladies had best be crossing back soon. Can you hear the anger of the river?'

'Can we stay in your lodge?' January glanced across the fire at Frye, who was recounting with extravagant gesture and wild exaggeration a 'sea battle' between himself and two other canoe-gliding trappers against a war party of Arapaho on the Bighorn. 'We'll slip out by morning. Morales has offered us tent space, but until I see some kind of proof that he isn't actually Franz Bodenschatz, I'd rather sleep near someone I know. Did you find the horses?'

'I did,' said Morning Star grimly. 'They're in Iron Heart's camp.'

'The Omahas?' Hannibal's brows shot up. 'Of course, Iron Heart is a mission Indian, by the sound of his English, but they're the last people I'd have thought would be helping a white man. He hates all white men alike—'

'Because his people died of smallpox,' said January softly, 'down on the Platte...'

There was silence, broken only by the pounding of the river, the growl of the thunder in the north.

'One of the lodges in Iron Heart's camp isn't being used as a dwelling, either,' continued Morning Star after a time. 'I lay in the grass and watched the camp until it grew too dark to see. No one went into it or came out—'

'What is it that Bodenschatz tells his father to bring from Munich?' asked January, and Hannibal turned over the thin yellowish sheets of the notepaper.

'A warm coat, two kegs of decent brandy (Hennessy or Rémy Martin), tea and coffee—'

'Exact words.'

'*The green China tea,*' read Hannibal, '*and the African coffee.*'

'Who is he selling the shop to?' Above them, the cottonwoods bent with the sudden onslaught

249

of wind; Frye got to his feet and walked a little ways toward the end of the island, listening too.

'We better be thinkin' about movin' if we're gonna. That river's comin' up fast.'

'Kleinsmark Apothekergeselleschaft...'

'Kleinsmark Apothecary Company,' translated January. 'And Klaus Bodenschatz needs to close up greenhouses and laboratories ... Remember how his hands were stained? He was a chemist.'

Hannibal's eyes widened as he understood. 'Oh, Christ.'

'African coffee isn't coffee. Any more than *Indian tobacco* is really tobacco, or fool's parsley is really parsley. It's *Ricinus communis* – castor-oil bean – and poisonous as the gates of Hell.'

'You mean those folks didn't die of sickness?' Frye came back to the fire, silhouetted gold against the rushing dark, the wind whipping now at his long hair. 'I told you they mighta been poisoned. How'd this Boden fella manage to—'

He gasped suddenly, his eyes flaring wide, and even as January started to his feet, Morning Star shouted *'Run!'*

Frye pitched forward on to the fire, an arrow in his back.

TWENTY-ONE

January dove instead for the fire, dragging Frye out by the arm, and even as he did it he knew it would cost him his escape. At the same moment Hannibal snatched up one of the buffalo-hide apishamores, flung it over the man's burning clothes, and January saw the young trapper's eyes roll back and the blood stream out of his mouth. By that time Indians were coming out of the darkness on the west side of the island from the camp, as well as the side toward the mountains. January swatted the first one with the burning buffalo-hide. A rifle crashed – *Veinte-y-Cinco?* – and in the instant that the attackers hesitated, Hannibal flung another saddle blanket over the fire and, in the sudden darkness, grabbed January's wrist, dragged him the length of the island and plunged into the river.

The skies let loose with rain.

Boaz Frye hadn't been wrong. The river was coming up like Noah's Flood. January fought to keep his head above water, felt the current grab him, snags of dead wood and broken trees ramming like live things stampeding. Hannibal's hand was still on his wrist, and January reversed the grip, catching the fiddler's thin arm and throwing his other arm over the first thing that

251

felt like a substantial log that slammed into him in the dark.

And it was dark, pitch-black, even when his head broke the surface. Rain hammered his face, and he could see nothing of either mountains or sky. He could feel the log he'd caught hold of was good-sized, and he half-hauled himself clear of the water, pulling Hannibal up beside him. The log promptly turned turtle, ducking him under and smiting him on the head with a branch. January clung, scrambled, gasping; he felt Hannibal drag himself up on to the thrashing mass of wood and then, still holding tight to January's arm, drop over the other side. January hauled himself up higher as something cracked at his legs underwater, grasping sinuously like sea serpents – *tree branches*? Then something that was definitely a rock gouged his calf.

He pressed his face to the wood, and tried not to feel the broken branch-stump that dug into his chest. *There better not be any snakes in this log.*

At least there aren't gators in the river.

Rose, he thought. *Rose, don't worry. I'll be home.* He saw her – brief and complete, as if he stood next to her wicker chair on the gallery, with a lamp beside her and mosquito-veiling hanging off her wide-brimmed hat – and folded the memory, with its thought and peace, down into a tiny fragment, and concentrated everything he had into hanging on.

Cold hammering water, and blindness. Chill gnawed his flesh, spread toward the core of his bones – he'd been in the Mississippi, and even the inexorable strength of its currents hadn't been like this awful cold. *It's July, how can it be this cold?* He couldn't breathe, wondered if Hannibal was dead, there on the end of the arm to which he clung, but there was nothing he could do about it one way or the other except hang on. A wall of water hit him over the head like falling bricks, throwing the whole log under – he clung desperately until another wave threw them up, choking, vomiting up half the river and still hanging on.

Virgin Mary, Mother of God, get me home safe.

Submerged snags tore his legs and feet, river-demon hands tried to drag him off. Two nearly succeeded, his own grip slithering and weak. The rain was like the sky mocking him. Another trough, tons of water pouring over his head like a building falling, no way to tell how long before they'd slam up again like a bucking horse into the air. The broken branch on the log itself seemed filled with a living malice, like the spirit of the tree trying to skewer him. Another current flung them sideways – blackness and water within blackness and water, and the only things real were the wet wood, the jabbing pain, the numb shock of the cold and the arm he held with so violent a desperation that he was surprised he didn't break the fiddler's bones.

Time lost meaning. Each breath was a battle, an event lasting years.

He wasn't even aware of it when the buffeting grew less. Just the gradual thought intruding: *it's not as bad as it was* ... His hands were nearly insensible in the cold, but rain no longer hammered his face. He tried to remember when the

253

rain had stopped, and couldn't, but at least he could breathe. Gleams of silver streaked the black water, though the river still carried them along like a runaway horse; the narrow moon broke the clouds. More snags tore his feet, sea serpents that rolled away when he kicked. Another kick struck gravel. January lowered his body as much as he dared, kicked again downward and felt his moccasin dig in sand, then cracked his knee on a rock. For a long time he struggled to push the log gradually in toward the eastern shore. The current thrust the log back into the main stream like a sullen stupid monster out to drown him.

Then two steps in succession; then three. The bed of the river shallowed underfoot, the log – branches or roots further back, for in the darkness January could see only a long unwieldy bulk behind him – snagged on the bottom. He called over the log, 'Can you make it to shore?' but was a little surprised to hear a reply.

'The wills above be done! – but I'd fain die a dry death.'

Only Hannibal would recall enough of *The Tempest* to quote it after being dragged through watery hell.

'Hold on. I'll come around for you.' January released his hold on the log, dragged himself around the front end on legs that shook so violently he feared he'd fall and be swept away. He'd meant to go back to help Hannibal ashore if he needed it, but found the fiddler had worked his way along to the front of the log as well, breast deep in the surging water. January had to

254

drag him to shore by the back of his coat.

Then they just lay on the bank among rocks and gravel, the river streaming over their feet, cold to the marrow and more exhausted than January could remember ever being in his life.

'I was distinctly led to believe,' complained Hannibal in a faint voice at last, 'we'd be carried across the Styx in a *boat*.'

'Charon's had to cut back on expenses because of the bank crash.'

Hannibal started to make some answer, then just lay on the bank and laughed 'til he cried.

'Come on,' said January after a time. 'Let's make a fire before we freeze to death.'

Another break in the cloud showed him the hills looming above them – God knew where they were – and the cottonwoods of the bottom-lands rising straight up out of the floodwater like a pitch-dark wall. January pulled Hannibal upright and limped through the belt of trees, the water retreating down his shins until the ground was solid underfoot.

'Was Frye dead?'

January nodded.

'You're sure?'

'I'm sure.' *Would I have stayed by him if he'd been still alive, unable to flee, unable to fight? With the Indians coming out of the darkness—?* January hoped he would have had the courage to do so, but didn't know. 'Did the ladies get away?'

'I don't know. I saw Pia run for the water ... Was that the Omahas?'

'Has to have been. Which means,' January

255

added, 'I'm guessing that Frank Boden alias Franz Bodenschatz is Charro Morales. He asked Frye about Irish Mary – he has to have known we wanted that hat. Then suddenly he's asking us to put up with him in his tent? *What they don't know won't hurt them?* After he was the one who demanded a quarantine? My guess is he was going to tell the camp a touching story about us being swept away when the river rose.'

Hannibal swore, thoughtfully, in classical Greek for a time, and collapsed on to a flat rock. 'So what do we do?' In the moonlight January could see he was shivering in his soaked clothing.

'Build a fire.'

'Shall you recite the magic spells to do that, or shall I?'

'You recite the magic spells to chase the bears away,' said January. 'I'll scrape bark.' He held out his hand, knowing they'd have better luck finding dry wood on higher ground. It was clear, even in the faint moonlight, that the flood had extended all throughout the bottomlands, leaving torn-up branches everywhere and everything soaked. He hauled Hannibal to his feet again.

'How far did we come down, do you think?'

'I'd say we were in the water for close to an hour.' January flexed his hands, felt his way from tree to tree toward the glimmers of light on the higher ground beyond. 'The moon was just past zenith when the clouds covered it over, and I don't think it was much more than an hour after that, that we were hit. Feel the grass,' he added as they came clear of the trees. 'It didn't rain down this far.'

'Thank God for small favors.' For a time there was silence as the two men collected the driest branches they could find, carried them to the edge of the trees. There was a clump of sagebrush large enough to make a sort of windbreak, and behind it, January scratched the wet layer of bark from a piece of dead wood with his knife and scraped a powder of the drier under-bark on to a split bough. Though he could barely walk, Hannibal brought handfuls of dry grass, his breath rasping like a rusty saw. Fingers made clumsy by cold, January struck the fire flint from his belt pouch with the steel. It took him seven or eight tries – laboriously re-scraping bark from time to time – while the night grew colder, but he told himself that if Jim Bridger could make a fire under these conditions, he, Benjamin January, certainly could...

'There,' he said at last as the whisper of smoke curled up. 'I owe God my first-born son.' Even as he made the jest he felt a strange shiver: *Rose will be close to her time, when I come home.*

The warmth that went through him had little to do with the new-flickering blaze.

I will have a first-born son. Or a beautiful daughter...

'Well,' remarked Hannibal a bit later, 'I understand now why the ancients worshipped fire.'

Longer silence. They arranged damp wood to dry, dragged the larger boughs to extend the crude shelter. The fire was small – a squaw fire, they'd call it in the camp. January gave thought to who might see it.

'There must have been a bottle of poisoned liquor in old Bodenschatz's coat pocket,' said Hannibal, when he'd warmed up a little. 'They'd all have drunk it – the Dutchman, Fingers Woman, the engagés. I expect Clarke found it among the bodies ... I can see him toasting their departing souls with the last gulp left. It's what I'd have done. If Frye thought it was the cholera,' he added quietly, 'castor bean – African coffee – must be bad, mustn't it?'

'It's bad,' January answered. 'It looks a great deal like cholera. Poison wouldn't bring on a fever, but if there were irritation or burning, that would account for their wanting water. You've heard how hard the smallpox struck the Indian villages south of the Platte,' he added. 'And, of course, when we were in Mexico City a few years ago, they all said – the *Indios* – that it wasn't so much the Spanish that destroyed the old kings and the old gods, as the smallpox. That there were not even enough of the living left to bury the dead...'

'*Et nous, les os, devenons cendre et pouldre* ... And Bodenschatz would need Indian allies, if he was planning on tracking a man through these mountains.' In the flickering orange light, his thin fingers seemed nearly translucent. '*Hath not a Jew hands, organs, dimensions, senses ... If you wrong us, shall we not revenge?* D'you think they'll be coming after us?'

'They have to be.' January huddled close to the flames, wishing he dared strip off his clothing to let it dry, for the clammy fabric chilled his flesh worse than the cold air would have. 'Right now, all anyone knows in the camp is what Veinte-y-Cinco and Pia have to tell: that we were set on by Indians. But if we come back – if even a whisper goes around the camp that Morales is Boden, and is in league with the Omahas to poison the camp...'

Hannibal sighed. 'I was afraid you were going to say that.'

Considering that not only the Omahas would be hunting them, but also that there were Blackfeet somewhere on the east side of the river, January half expected that he would be unable to sleep for as much as a minute between caution and cold. He was dead wrong about that and through the rest of the night, turn and turn about with Hannibal, had to fight not to drop off on guard duty, digging the sharpened end of a stick into the heel of his hand or the calf of his leg to remain awake. Even the gnawing hunger that swept him wasn't sufficient to keep him alert. Morning found him cramped, aching and weak from weariness. Even during the season of sugar harvest, old Michie Simon had fed his cane hands to keep them prime for work. He would have sold Hannibal to the Arabs for a bowl of rice and beans and thrown in Morning Star for lagniappe.

'Shall we cross the river?' asked the fiddler, when the first stains of dawn whitened the freezing air. By the roar of the current on the rocks it hadn't gone down much. 'What are you doing?' Hannibal protested a moment later as January scattered the fire, used the remainder of the dampish wood as a makeshift shovel to bury the coals.

'Trying to avoid sending up a smoke signal,' January returned – regretfully, since his clothes were still damp and the morning chill cut like a razor. 'It's light enough to see one now.'

Hannibal made a face and coughed. His body was racked with shivers, and he looked like a dying man. 'I suppose the next thing you're going to tell me is that you forgot to put a haunch of buffalo in your pocket before we fled.'

'Sorry.'

They made their way through the trees to the river, but as January had suspected, it had risen higher in the night.

'We were *in* that?' Hannibal stared, aghast, at the churning brown torrent, the white teeth of foam and the leaping snags of uprooted trees.

'He'll be hangéd yet; Though every drop of water swear against it.' January considered the flood, then the foothills behind them. 'It may be for the best,' he added. 'If the Omaha do come after us, they'll look along the river. There's less cover on that side. From here, we're not far from the foothills, where we can stay in the timber. All we need to do is follow the river north—'

'And not meet the Blackfeet. Or starve.'

'We're going to starve either way,' said January firmly. 'Let's do it on the move.'

According to everyone in the camp, from the youngest engagés on up to Jim Bridger, nobody – even set afoot without weapons – would starve in the mountains in summer. Any number of the mountaineers could tell of surviving such situations even if they were being chased by Indians. By noon, January had come to the conclusion that these men were either lying, or had arrived at some more favorable deal with God than he had despite years of going to confession. 'I think the trick is, that you have to not mind eating bugs and carrion,' offered Hannibal as they made a careful – and rather fruitless – search around the feet of every lodgepole pine at the timberline, when they reached it, and found no cone that had not been thoroughly looted of its minuscule nourishment by squirrels.

'As long as we don't end up carrion ourselves,' said January, 'I'll be happy.'

Where the trees began, high up the tumbled land around the feet of the true mountains, the river was visible for miles upstream. January could see no sign of habitation. A few miles to the north of them the river bent eastward around a knee of hills; water spread by last night's rise glistened in a wide bottomland where a multitude of streams came together.

'If the Omaha are following us down the river,' he said after a time, 'we've got a head start on them today, anyway. We should be able to get some fish, there where the river's spread.'

'At the moment,' sighed Hannibal as he climbed stiffly to his feet, 'bugs and carrion sound very good.'

During the course of the afternoon, January had cause to be grateful for his own interest in how other men made their livings, and for the loquacity of the mountaineers in sharing the tales of their survival. As they came down to the pools left by the flood, he recognized both cattails and camas, which had edible – if not particularly appetizing – roots, and, though it was early in the year, several varieties of berry. He cut a sapling and sharpened it to a spear, but when they reached the first of the shallow river-branches, he and Hannibal took the precaution of damming the moving water with rocks before going after the fish. They caught four, mostly by hitting them with sticks or simply scooping them up on to the bank, before a couple of bears ambled down out of the woods to investigate the new fishing-spot.

'Aren't you going to go after one of them with your bowie? Kit Carson would.'

'You go to hell.'

They bore their catch back up to the treeline. In the last of the daylight, January set as many snares as he could manufacture from the string in his pockets.

'Will this help?' Hannibal drew from his coat pocket a long, crumpled strip of black silk.

'What is it?'

'Pia was wearing it as a sash,' said the fiddler. 'She said Moccasin Woman gave it to her. After reading Bodenschatz *père's* letter to you – during which we were so rudely interrupted – I intended to visit the Delaware camp and ask her where she came by it, but I suspect it belonged to the old man. That it was one of the bindings used to tie the splint on to his leg.'

'That being the case,' said January, 'it must have been Moccasin Woman who got his shirt off him. Nice rolled hem,' he added, examining the silk. 'Tiny and strong.' With his knife he slit the narrow roll of the hem free of the rest of the cravat, fashioned three snares out of it – the delicate cord it yielded was about ten feet long, all around both sides of the cravat – and tried to recall everything Robbie Prideaux had said about where to set snares and how to make sure their intended victims – rabbits and ground squirrels – didn't catch human scent.

Only when the sun went behind the mountains did January light a fire, trusting the trees to disperse what smoke might be visible. He spitted the fish, emptied his pockets of the remaining cama bulbs and buried them in the coals.

On the higher hills, not far away, wolves howled.

Closer to, in the darkness among the thin-growing trees, gold eyes flashed – something small, a fox or a marten – then abruptly bolted away.

January realized that the night-chirping of the birds had silenced.

The thin woods were utterly still.

The fire was tiny – *they couldn't have seen it*...

Everything in him was shouting: *but they did*...

Don't we even get to eat our fish? But even as his soul cried out in protest, cold readiness jolted in his veins. He nudged Hannibal's foot with his own, touched his finger to his lips – saw the other man's eyes widen with an unspoken: *oh, Jesus*...

Too soon to be the Omaha, unless they'd ridden like the wind and known exactly where to

263

search for them. Which meant the Blackfeet.

His hand slipped down to his spear, and he tried to determine from which direction the attack would come.

'Best you douse that fire, Maestro,' said a soft voice from the darkness. 'Iron Heart an' his braves is less'n three miles away.'

TWENTY-TWO

'Dear God—'

Shaw stepped quickly into the firelight, January barely getting a glimpse of his thin face scruffy with sandy beard, his long hair tied back in a straggly braid, before he kicked out the flames and buried the coals. He had an impression of half-healed cuts and bruises, of a shirt torn open over corded muscle and too-prominent bone, of one rifle in hand and two others slung on his back. 'Get the fish an' let's pull foot,' Shaw whispered, ''fore they tracks you by the smoke. You all right?'

'I been better.'

The worst is not, so long as we can say, "This is the worst," quoted Hannibal, whom death itself probably would not have found without a poetic allusion. 'Yourself?'

'Breathin'.'

This was all any of them said for the next several hours. Shaw led them east through the

264

thin timber, where the waning moonlight glimmered between shadows like the abysses of Hell; along the granite backbone of a ridge; and down into a dry draw, where stones along what had once been a stream bed would obscure their tracks. They ate on the move. Twice Shaw signaled them to halt, and in the silence January heard the rustling movement of some animal ahead of them among the trees. Shaw passed him a rifle and powder horn – by the brass studs on the stock January knew it was Goshen Clarke's – but January knew better than to shoot it.

At the top of the draw they crossed sloped ground carpeted with thin bunch-grass, under a drift of starlight. He had only the dimmest sense of the country dropping away to the left – north, now, judging by the stars and the dark rim of mountains in the west. An owl hooted somewhere, and the men walked carefully, knowing that it was the hour when things besides vengeful Omahas did their killing.

Another draw, steeper-sided, one wall of it armored with an uneven rampart of granite escarpments. The flare of sparks as Shaw lit a makeshift twist of dry grass was almost blinding. Wordlessly, the Kentuckian took January's spear and swept it through a crevice in the rock face, checking for rattlesnakes, then crushed out the flare and carefully brushed away the ash. 'Lay up here.' He put a hand on Hannibal's shoulder and his voice was barely more than the scratching of fox claws on pebble. 'No sound, don't move, I don't care what walks acrost you.

265

Pretend you're back home with as much opium in you as you can hold. We'll get you when it's dark.'

'One thing—' Hannibal caught Shaw's sleeve as the taller man would have boosted him up into the cranny. 'Was there a liquor bottle among the dead at Groot's camp?'

'There was.' Shaw's voice was grim. 'Clarke drank to 'em – there wasn't but a swallow left—'

'What's here? A cup? Closed in my true love's hand...'

'Didn't hit him 'til we'd got everyone buried an' was startin' to head back. Then it took him hard. It was good an' dark, an' for an hour an' more I'd felt through my skin that we had to get movin'. He was pukin' an' purgin', but didn't have no fever – there was no keepin' him hid, but I couldn't leave the man. Any idea what it was?'

'Castor-oil bean, it's called,' whispered January. *'African coffee* is one of the names for it. Turns out old Bodenschatz was a chemist back in Ingolstadt.' Quickly, he outlined the discoveries deduced from the letters, and from Charro Morales's hat.

'Well, I knowed it was Iron Heart,' whispered Shaw. 'How it all fit together was only a guess, but when Iron Heart an' his braves come slippin' out of the woods, I put that together with the fact that old Bodenschatz was carryin' poison an' figured what Johnny stumbled into had to be his revenge on the white man, for the smallpox down by the Platte. We did have our eye on

Morales, him bein' new in the trade...'

'He was the one who suggested we use the island as a quarantine zone.'

'He said he'd look after them,' mused Hannibal softly. 'I must say, there he did not lie. According to Morning Star, it sounds like there's more poison hidden in one of the lodges in the Omaha camp—'

'Waiting for a time when Boden and his father were certain their own quarry would be in the camp,' said January. 'Which leads back to "Escher" being Manitou Wildman—'

'An' leads straight back to Iron Heart – an' Boden – havin' to get rid of us at all costs, 'fore we gets back to the camp. I had already figured out,' Shaw added drily, 'over these last three days, that they wasn't gonna let me get acrost the river. I come pretty close last night, enough to see you on the island.'

'Was that you who fired the shot?'

'That was me.'

'So what do we do?' asked January softly.

'Water'll be down by tomorrow evenin'. What we need to do today is lay low. It ain't just the Omahas; I come near to bein' took by the Blackfeet twice. You spoke to Wildman?'

'He's moved camp – gone.'

'Figures. Boden'll be off after him...' Shaw fell silent, standing in the starlight like one of the boulders around them, barely more than a shape – a part of this silent land where there was no law, only the strength of one's will to commit vengeance.

And you'll be off after Boden? wondered

267

January. *Following him into the mountain winter, like a wolf on a trail? Turning into a wolf yourself?*

For a time, all that he could hear was Shaw's breathing as Shaw himself pursued that thought – *and what then?* An intaken breath, long held, then released as if with conscious effort. Another the same, as if struggling to say words or not to say them. To frame thoughts or to thrust them underground in chains.

Would I follow a man who killed Rose? Or Minou, or Olympe? Would I leave all things behind me, like the hapless Baron Frankenstein? All my lesser loves – music and friendship and the peace of sleeping in a safe place each night – to kill the man who robbed me of my best love?

He realized he could see the thin features of the Kentuckian's face and understood that light was beginning to stir in the sky. In the pine trees, on the prairies below, in the grasses of the hillside and the tangles of barberry at the bottom of the draw, a million birds woke and sang.

He laid a hand briefly on Shaw's bony shoulder. 'Let's get through this day before we worry about what happens on the one after that.'

At some point about three-quarters of the way between noon and sunset, January – lying flat beneath the carcass of a deadfall pine-tree, with brush piled up before him so that he couldn't even see whether he was in danger or not – whiled away the time by envisioning a debate between the greatest orators he could think of, as to whether the worst part of this situation was hunger, thirst, not being able to piss, or not being able to move. The Roman Cicero, arguing for the last contention, eventually won, but the poet and preacher John Donne (sitting in the imaginary audience) pointed out that the advantage in January's situation lay that in being vexed with all four conditions, he must be considered blessed in part by having one discomfort displace the other three in the forefront of his consciousness, thus giving him three-quarters relief from complete misery. The fact that the tree under which January had squeezed his body had been dead for a considerable time, and had become a veritable apartment-house for grubs, wood beetles, centipedes, ants and spiders of all species did not improve either the situation or January's mood.

For fourteen long hours, the world consisted of the green light that came in through the heaped brush, the smell of dirt and rotting wood, the calls of birds in the trees around him – ravens, jays, wrens and thrushes – and the consciousness of how close he was to a lingering death by torture.

Those things, and his memories and thoughts. *I could be bounded in a nutshell, and count myself a king of infinite space...*

He ran through everything that he remembered of *Hamlet*, of Dante's *Inferno*, of *The Rape of the Lock*. He mentally played each piece of music he had mastered throughout his lifetime: Mozart, Beethoven, ballets, waltzes, operas. He turned over his memories of Rose: walking beside him with her gray cloak belling out in the moist, spooky winds of summer storms; sitting

269

on the gallery in the stillness of twilight; lying in his arms with her light-brown hair a silken river on the pillow. He tried to deduce the species and natures of everything that he could feel walking across the back of his neck of up and down his arms. He wondered if the patriarch Joshua had returned to the earth again and had made the sun stand still in the heavens, and if so, why?

Twice bears came close enough to the log for him to see their claws through the thin rim of space beneath one of the berry bushes that Shaw had thrust in over January to conceal him; close enough for him to smell the rank feral mustiness of their coats. Once – infinitely more terrifying – he heard the stealthy pad of moccasined feet, and the murmurs of voices speaking some Indian tongue.

Hunger, thirst and everything else had vanished, consumed in a white blaze of fear...

And returned within an hour, grinding and tortuous as ever.

Several times, he slept. From the last such nap he woke to find the light had faded, and the whole world breathed of pine and the river. As soon as he judged it dark enough, he moved the brush aside, with arms so stiff he could barely work them, and crawled out, used a broken branch to dig a hole to piss into, and was just covering the evidence when Shaw whispered from the gloom, 'Maestro?'

'Here.' Keeping his rifle within instant grabbing range, he slithered out of his shirt, shook out whatever it was that had been crawling around his skin for the past few hours – it was

270

too dark to see what they were – then moved toward Shaw's voice. Only then did he see him in the filtered moonlight. 'I never asked you: where are we? How close to the camp?'

''Bout twelve miles. We need to get ourselves acrost the New Fork River, then over the ridge to the Green again an across it. From there it'll be about eight miles 'til we get to the first of the camps. We can probably make it by morning if we're lucky. You tol'able, Sefton?' he added, for they had reached the rocks in which Hannibal had been cached, and January made out the pale shape of the fiddler's face against the shadows of the boulders.

January added – from Hamlet – *'Stand and unfold yourself,'* and Hannibal got to his feet, holding on to the rocks behind him for support.

'Very funny. *You come most pleasantly upon your hour* ... You just missed the rattlesnakes. Three of them crawled into my hiding place with me – to get out of the sun, I presume – and just left at sundown. I've spent better days.'

'If you'd struck at 'em, or made a noise,' remarked Shaw, 'you'd've spent a worse one.'

Hannibal started to reply, then broke off to cough, pressing one hand to his mouth and the other to his side in a vain attempt to still the sound. Even stifled, it sounded as if his lungs were being sawn in half. 'I'm all right,' he said, as soon as he could speak. 'A trifling indisposition only, as Aristotle put it. Nothing that food, rest and immoderate quantities of opiates would not instantly cure. The former two can be found in the camp and will suffice.'

271

With Shaw in the lead, they made their way through the scattered timber that cloaked the foot slopes of a tall butte, three shadows in the deeps of the night. In the hills to the east January could hear the howling of packs of wolves, fat with summertime and no great danger to men. Pallid moonlight sketched the shapes of deer in the open ground, trotting noiselessly down toward the valley below; of rabbits in such numbers that all the ground among the bunches of grass seemed alive. Water gleamed in the valley, and as they descended the side of the butte January could both hear and smell it, exquisite after a day of thirst and sharing sips from Shaw's water bottle at long intervals since sundown. From his own weariness he could only guess at Hannibal's, the fiddler lagging further and further behind and their progress slowed by frequent stops to let him catch up and rest. With these Shaw was infinitely patient, only sitting a little distance from the two of them and listening to the night with the wariness of a beast. Once January went over to him and whispered, 'Are we all right?' and the Kentuckian shook his head.

'We need to keep movin'.' He glanced back at Hannibal, sitting with his head between his knees. 'Let him rest now,' he added softly. 'He's gonna need his strength later.'

There was less moonlight beneath the trees. In addition to Clarke's rifle, January carried the sharpened spear he'd cut, and he used it as a probe and a walking stick, to test the ground before him and to balance as they descended toward the water. By the sound of it, the New Fork River was very high. The thought that they might get swept by the current back down to the Green again, and thence downstream and lose all the ground they had gained, brought him a sense of infinite weariness and futility.

'Ford's about a mile up,' Shaw whispered. 'They'll be watchin'. River goes over a rim of rocks a mile upstream of *that*, an' that's where we're makin' for. But it's no ford, so it's gonna be rough.'

It was. The river had gone down some, leaving the margin of the water – what in Louisiana was called a batture – strewn with flotsam, from small branches up to full-sized trees. Shaw and January found a young lodgepole pine about twenty feet long and as thick through as a man's doubled fists. It was all the three men could do to lug it to the river. Thrusting it ahead of them, they clung to the upstream side of the rocks, snow-melt water pouring over and around them, without the violence of the original rise but with terrifying strength. The longest gap between any two of the rocks was about twelve feet; with the force of the water holding the log against the rocks, it was possible to cross, but every second January was positive that one end or the other was going to slip and let him be swept away. Exhausted and famished, he knew his chances of getting out of the river again, even if he managed to cling to the log, would be nil.

The moon was low, when Hannibal and Shaw reached down from the bank to drag January – who was the last on the log crossings – up to

273

shore. 'I do not ever,' he whispered, shivering so much that he could barely get the words out, 'want to have to do something like that again.'

'Don't say that,' advised Shaw, ''til you knows what the alternative is.' He was already at work screwing the gun worm down the barrel of his Hawken to draw the bullet and charge, swiftly breaking down the lock to dry it and replace the soaked powder.

'And men do this, year in and year out, summer and winter,' said January, 'for a hundred and fifty dollars a year?' He reached for his gun to do the same, then let the weapon slip from his grip and sat heavily on one of the flat boulders on the bank, his hands momentarily too shaky to continue.

'Like I said –' Shaw dug ball and patch from his pouch, poured powder from the horn, which he'd carried wrapped in his shirt and tied around his head to keep it dry – 'all depends on what you'd be lookin' at instead. Blacksmithin' in some town in Missouri? Workin' a factory for thirty cents a week in Massachusetts? Or in your case—'

Shots cracked from the dark of the trees and January dropped behind the rock on which he'd been sitting. Hannibal scrambled down beside him – *God damn it wet powder!* – and the next second Indians broke from the trees, raced across the narrow band of riverside pebbles. January whipped his knife from his belt, made a dash for the river, and this time didn't make it.

Shaw had his bullet rammed home and got off one shot before the Omahas overwhelmed them.

TWENTY-THREE

It was a war camp, in a draw about two miles from the New Fork River and above the Green. There were no lodges.

January, at least, had managed to keep on his feet getting there behind the horses; he still wasn't sure how. After Hannibal had fallen and been dragged for a few hundred feet, the warrior in charge of the party – January thought he was Dark Antlers, one of the two who had come into the camp with Iron Heart when they'd viewed old Klaus Bodenschatz's body – had had him slung over one of the ponies like a dead deer and carried into the camp that way.

Iron Heart's orders, January guessed.

There were about fifteen warriors in the party that took them, not counting the four Shaw killed. They were tied, wrists and ankles, with rawhide thongs and left on the ground close enough to the fire that they could be seen. Only by the motion of Hannibal's sides could January tell that he was alive at all. The single woman at the war camp brought pemmican to all the warriors and led the ponies down to water further along the coulee, before – rather circumspectly – she approached the prisoners. The warriors watched her, but didn't interfere. It was Veinte-y-Cinco.

'They've sent for Boden,' she murmured, dropping to her knees beside January and filling her tin drinking-cup from the waterskin she carried. 'Iron Heart and the others are still out looking for you – there's about forty in the band. Dark Antlers –' she nodded at the warrior who had led the raid – 'speaks English; many of them do. There was a mission school near their village's hunting grounds on the Platte. A lot of them were baptized Christians – Protestants,' she added with a dismissive grimace, like the good Catholic she was, 'and have English names.'

'Is Iron Heart's name Hepplewhite?'

She looked startled, then nodded and brushed back the straggling tendrils of her hair. 'Matthew Hepplewhite. It was the name of one of his sponsors when he was baptized. He was called Eagle Heart by his parents. When they died, he said, his heart turned to iron in his breast. Some of them speak Spanish, too.' She rubbed – gingerly – a cut on her chin.

'Let me see that...' Even in the flicker of the small Indian fire, it was clear to him she'd been beaten. Probably, January guessed, raped as well.

Her mouth twisted in a sidelong expression as she read his thought in his voice and replied, 'Nothing I didn't get from my daddy and his drunk friends, a long time before I met Mick Seaholly. I'm not a little flower, Ben. Like a fool, I tried to get off a shot, and the powder didn't flash. I should have headed straight for the river like you did. By the time I ran for it they were coming in from both sides of the island. Pia got away.' Her voice wavered, ever so slightly, as she said it: hope that dared not speak its own name, lest it break what strength was left her. Briskly, she went on, 'They put me on a horse and came straight after you.'

January turned his head to look at where the others lay. He could see Shaw's eyes were open – the man must have a skull like granite – but Hannibal hadn't stirred. 'See the others are all right,' he said softly. 'Thank you for the water.' No sense asking her the intentions of their captors: those were clear enough, in Dark Antlers's eyes when he glanced their way. There was a chance they'd take Veinte-y-Cinco with them when they rode on, if the band was short of women. He'd heard how captive women were sometimes treated, and it seemed to depend on the personalities of the Indians involved, and how ready the woman was to settle in to become a drudge like the Indian women mostly were.

He watched her now, kneeling beside Hannibal with her dark hair hanging down over her face like a curtain, sponging his bloodied face with a corner of her torn skirt. Hannibal, who'd done nothing, sought neither profit nor vengeance, but had joined the party on the off-chance that he could be of some use to his friends.

Hooves in the darkness. Veinte-y-Cinco's long nose caught the firelight as she swiveled on her heels. A dozen riders came into camp, bareback on their painted horses. The woman rose at once and went to bring food to the warriors, to lead the horses away to where a fair-sized herd, by

277

the sound of it, was tethered among the trees upslope. She had clearly learned her duties in the camp and probably guessed that making herself useful was her only chance to avoid being kill-ed with the men. Iron Heart turned in their direction, said something to Dark Antlers. Dark Antlers clearly reported that five men had been killed in taking the prisoners, and the war chief's pock-marked face twisted with anger. He strode toward them; when Veinte-y-Cinco came out of the darkness and asked him something he simply struck her aside, with such force that she fell.

He kicked Shaw twice, full force in the ribs, dropped to his knees beside him, dragged him up into a seated position by his long hair and shook him, his knife in his hand. 'Who have you told about Boden?' he demanded. 'Who else knows?'

'I don't know,' replied Shaw quietly. 'Didn't take much work for us to guess. Likely, others did, too.'

'What others?'

'You gonna go after an' kill them, too?'

'Yes.' The chief's face was like a wooden mask, half eaten-away with acid. 'If I must.'

'But your plan was to kill everyone,' said January. 'Wasn't it?'

Iron Heart looked toward him, his knife blade still laid on Shaw's throat. 'Yes,' he said. Then he shoved Shaw away from him to the ground.

'Although most of the people in the camp weren't anywhere near the South Platte when your family died.'

'It is not vengeance only for my family, white man.' Iron Heart crossed to where January lay,

278

stood over him in the firelight, his bare chest, bare arms, silver knife-blade clothed in the low red light. 'Or only for my people, lying among their lodges with their bodies eaten up by birds and animals, dying so swiftly there was none to sing their death songs nor to remember their names as they died. Since I was a boy not old enough to gather firewood by myself, I have seen those whom the white man has pushed out of their homes: the Delaware who lived by the Eastern Sea, the Cherokee, the Houmas. They passed through our land, and they all said the same: the white man is too lazy to build fences, so his pigs and his cattle wander to eat the crops in our villages; the white man has ruined his land with growing cotton, so now he needs fresh land to ruin. And we must move, because we are not Christians. And even when we are Christians, we are not civilized. And even when we live in houses and print newspapers and go to school and read books ... Because we are enemies. And even when we have sworn friendship and had it sworn us in return by the men that the white men elect to represent them ... What does the white man want us to be?'

Passion twisted his voice for a moment, but his ruined face remained impassive, as if the scars went through the skin and flesh to the nerve and the bone. 'He wants us to be dead,' he finished, 'so that he can take our land, which is what he meant all along to do. Do you deny this, black white man?'

'No,' said January. 'I do not deny it.'

'If another man killed your wife and ate her

279

body for his dinner, would you seek revenge on him?'

'I don't know.'

'Then you are no man. If he came to you with her blood on his hands and stood before you and laughed in your face, would you strike him down?'

January sighed. 'Yes. Yes, I would.'

'And when he lay before you, would you kill him?'

'I would,' said January, knowing it to be true. 'But I would not kill his brother, who had been home sleeping in his own bed when his murder took place. Was it Boden who asked you to help him seek his revenge, or you who asked Boden?'

'It was Boden who came to me.' The warrior's dark eyes narrowed behind scar-thick lids. 'After the white man's sickness had burned itself out, I and what remained of my people came north. We meant to go on into the mountains. But the first snows found us still on the plains, taking buffalo. We wintered near Fort Ivy, and talk of the sickness was still on every man's lips. Counts Things – the chief of the fort—'

Had he not been in fear for his own life and those of his friends, January would have smiled at the name the Indians had given Tom Shaw.

'—asked me: would my people become trappers for Ivy and Wallach? I grew angry, and in my anger I spoke my heart: that I would sooner die than work for the white men. The deaths of my wife and my parents were new to me then. I said that I would have vengeance on the white men, whatever the cost, for the ruin they had brought to my people and my world.'

He was silent a moment, as if the remembering of it took him back to that smoke-stained blockhouse chamber, that isolated quadrangle of logs on the windswept hillside above Rawhide Creek. To bitter night and marble-hard snow and the comfortless moon that had watched his grief uncaring.

The last of the search parties had ridden into the camp while Iron Heart spoke, and the men were bedding down in their buffalo robes. A few, January noticed, knelt and folded their hands in Christian prayer.

'Boden came to our village that night. He said that the trapper called Manitou had murdered his sister, away in the country of the white men beyond the ocean. The white man's law had not hanged him for this crime, and so he, Boden, had been seeking him across half the world. You have seen Manitou and know that he is like a spirit bear, swift and hard to catch. The mountains are great and go on for many months' journeying to the desert, and to the sea beyond that. Boden knew that to trap one man in all this land, he must have Indians who knew the land and how to hunt.'

Softly, January said, 'And Boden knew Manitou would be coming to the rendezvous. It's the one time he knew where he would be.'

'To kill the deer, one does not lie out on a dry hillside,' returned Iron Heart. 'One goes to water and waits for the deer to come down.'

'And from saying you would sooner die than become a hunter for the white men,' said Janu-

281

ary, 'you became a hunter for a white man.' And when Iron Heart's face twisted with anger, January went on: 'What did he promise you for this? The deaths of other white men?'

'The deaths of them all. The trappers who strip our streams of the beaver people who have lived there in peace since the moon was young ... The traders who sell liquor to my people – not Omaha, not Sioux, not Shoshone, but *all* my people, all the people of this land! – and make them silly and drunk so that they give away not only the furs they have trapped, but also their wives and their horses and the clothes from off their backs ... The whites who bring in disease, whose touch rots the land. If I cannot kill all of them, I would see as many of them die as I can. This is what he promised.'

By the fire, Dark Antlers and the other men glanced at their chief and his prisoners; there was only one of them not visibly scarred by the smallpox. They were grouped around the bodies of the five warriors January and Shaw had knifed in the fight by the river: brothers and friends.

'His father was a medicine man, he said,' Iron Heart went on. 'He would bring a sickness medicine from across the ocean and would mix it with the white man's liquor on a night when Manitou was in the camp. For this reason he let it be known that he had the best liquor in the camp, so that when he gave it away free, all would drink it. This he planned to do after you fought Manitou, save that the man Blankenship angered Manitou and sent him from the camp in great rage. The old father had been staying

282

among us with his poison. He had said to me that day that he wished to poison only Manitou, and not the others. I told him that this was not our bargain, that all must die. Before Dark Antlers and I went to watch the fight, the old man and I had angry words. When I came back to the village later, I found he was gone.'

'And he met Manitou,' said January softly, with a sudden sense of having seen someone turn right, whom he had expected to turn left. Ridiculous, he thought, considering that he and his friends sat in the open mouth of the wolf ... 'Did his son go with him, then? He was at the fight—'

In his mind January saw Charro Morales in his crimson jacket, making his horse caracole and shouting: *'Free liquor tonight, if Wildman wins!'*

And every man in the camp had cheered.

'Boden remained in the camp. He never came to our tents while daylight was in the sky, or any man moved about awake.'

'Then—' January frowned, trying to fit times together: the start of the rain, the time of the shots. The dry inside of the roof wrought of boughs. 'Do you know what time the old man left your camp? At sunset? Before?'

'You speak like a fool,' snapped the warrior impatiently. 'You will die, and then you can seek out the old medicine man and ask him yourself. And I, I care not when the old man came to die, but only that my vengeance on those who killed my people be accomplished. It will be soon,' he added quietly, 'and I will walk through their camp as they are dying and ask them: *are you*

283

happy now, that you came into our lands?' He glanced toward the bound men, lying still as the dead in the shadows just beyond the small gem of the fire, and a bitter smile moved his lips. 'It will please me, to make a beginning tonight.'

He walked away. An owl passed close over the camp, wings silent as the wings of Death; somewhere in the darkness some small thing squeaked in pain.

I am a fool. January lay down again on his side. Only a fool would be troubled over that sense of a pattern broken, a detail disturbed, when the next hour would bring death in agony. Patiently, agonizingly, he began to work his wrists back and forth against the rawhide: *it's leather. It will stretch...*

He wondered if Shaw were doing the same.

We have to warn the camp...

Boden would find some other occasion to broach his kegs of very expensive liquor, to keep Iron Heart's good will. He would need it, for the long hunt ahead through the wilderness. With those deaths, Iron Heart would be obligated to fulfill his part of the bargain.

He twisted at the rawhide, until his fingers lost their feeling. On the mountainside the wolves howled, cold voices in the cold and empty darkness. *I have to succeed in this. I can't let Rose spend the next year wondering what became of me. I won't let her raise our child alone, as Bodenschatz made his poor Katerina raise hers...*

What had old Klaus Bodenschatz made of it, traveling all those thousands of miles at his son's

284

behest? Ship and packet boat and steamboat up the brown Missouri, the dirty clamor of Independence after the quiet cobblestones of Ingolstadt? He was a scientist. Had he missed his greenhouses and his laboratory, the quiet order of his days? Had he carried a notebook, full of observations and descriptions?

Had there been some friend waiting for him, whose voice he'd conjured for himself in those lonely miles? His son's deserted wife, his grandchildren? Or had he, like Franz, honed his life to a weapon of vengeance for that lovely daughter for whom he had never ceased to wear mourning?

He wished to poison only Manitou, Iron Heart had said. And when Iron Heart and Dark Antlers had gone to watch the fight, the old man had left the Omaha camp – for the first time since coming to the valley, January knew: probably for the first time since he had joined the village back on the high plains. Had crossed Horse Creek on that fallen tree and scrambled up the wooded ridge...

And now he lay in a shallow grave.

Beneath his cheek, January felt the distant tremor of hooves.

Boden.

And when I can't give them any specific information about who might or might not know about the scheme to poison every man at the rendezvous, they'll start by carving up Hannibal – who, like old Bodenschatz, had wanted only to do the office of friendship...

He turned to look toward his friend and saw, to his astonishment, that Hannibal was gone.

285

TWENTY-FOUR

In the same instant that January stared, rather stupidly, at the place where the fiddler had lain – how many minutes since last he'd looked? – he felt the blade of a knife slide between his bound wrists and part the rawhide like kitchen string. Beyond his feet he could glimpse Shaw lying suspiciously still...

The hoofbeats strengthened in the darkness – the fire's glow had sunk to a red flicker no bigger than a hat – and the camp guard all looked in the direction of the sound. The other warriors rose, waked by the sound, gathering to welcome Charro Morales – Frank Boden – as he rode into the camp...

And more silently than January could have imagined possible for a man of his own size, he rolled into the darkness where hands unseen were waiting to cut the thong that bound his ankles. A hand took his arm, guided him, stumbling, between trees of which he was barely conscious. He glanced back, saw that Shaw had disappeared from where he'd been an instant ago.

Someone pushed Goshen Clarke's brass-studded rifle into his hands.

The grip on his arm tightened – *stand...*

He saw ahead of them the moving shadow of a bear, ambling between trees where a feather of moonlight glimmered. Turning his head, he saw Shaw then – or Shaw's angular silhouette against the reflection of the war camp's fire. Since those first days of travel up the Platte, every man in the wagon-train – and later every trapper he'd ever spoken to – had cautioned him: *don't stand by the fire, you'll show yourself up...*

And there was Charro Morales – Frank Boden – in his bright Mexican jacket and his town boots, standing by his horse, next to the fire, lit up as Bo Frye had been lit, gesturing and arguing with Iron Heart with the red-gold gleam painting him against the night behind him. January was conscious that this was what Shaw was looking at too, small head turned like a raptor bird's, the slouched lines of his body clumsy-graceful as a very old tomcat's as he brought up his rifle, for a perfect shot that he couldn't miss...

And that would bring every warrior in the camp after them, afoot and within fifty feet of where they'd lain bound a few moments before.

You can kill anything with one shot, Tom had said.

You owe me, and you owe Johnny...

There wasn't even the chance to say: *Don't* ... because they were close enough yet to the Omahas that someone would have heard.

Shaw stood for all of three full seconds with his rifle raised. Then he lowered the barrel, turned away, touched January's arm with one hand to move them all on up the hill.

January could hear the sawing pain of Hannibal's laboring breath, and, in a moment's whisper of moonlight, he recognized that thin silhouette between the trees. He heard also the susurration of heavy fabric: Veinte-y-Cinco. In another blink of moonlight – they were following the trees, back east along the coulee – he made out the heavy shoulders and bear-like head of Manitou Wildman.

Manitou led them up the dry creek-bed at the bottom of the gully – pale boulders, jumbled stone that wouldn't hold tracks. January caught Hannibal's arm as the fiddler stumbled, the drag of his weight – even perceived through January's own aching exhaustion – telling him that his friend was at the end of his strength. 'Go,' the fiddler whispered, and staggered again. 'You'll never get away—'

January tightened his hold. 'Rose will kill me if I make her find another Greek tutor.'

'I'm not fooling.'

'Neither am I.'

'Please,' panted Hannibal, and he made an effort to plant his feet. 'I've never been anything but a waste of air and boot leather. Please don't make me die with my last thought being that I caused the deaths of the only people I care about—'

'If I have to carry you –' January doubled his fist in his friend's face – 'it's going to slow me down. But I'll do it.'

'I got horses up top of the draw,' rumbled Manitou. 'I'm guessin' Iron Heart's gonna head straight north after you into open country. He may not. Left Hand – brave that fetched Boden just now from the camp – brung him news that had him spittin' nails.'

'What news?'

'Somebody been an' burned one of the Omaha lodges at the rendezvous. Dunno what was in it—'

'I do.' Hannibal gasped for breath, hand pressed hard to his ribs. 'I think that was Morning Star, and the lodge she burned was the one where Iron Heart and Bodenschatz were keeping the poison.'

'*Poison*?'

'The poison Franz Bodenschatz and his father were going to put in all the liquor at the rendezvous to serve Iron Heart's vengeance on the white man,' replied January quietly. 'In exchange for Iron Heart's help in killing you.'

Manitou paused for a moment in his long stride, looked back at January, silent as his namesake, the great spirit-bear, in the starlight. It was too dark to see any expression on his face, but January heard him, very slightly, sigh. Then he turned and moved on.

After a long time he said, 'They say you're a doctor, Winter Moon.'

'A surgeon,' said January. 'I've studied medicines, but it's not my trade.'

'Ever done mad-doctorin'?'

'I've known mad-doctors.' January grimaced at the recollection of the asylums he'd visited, in France and in Mexico. Remembered the patients twisting and groaning in the so-called 'Utica crib', like a coffin wrought of bars; remembered the way the lunatics would cry and plead not to

289

be put into the 'swing', and the surreal 'water cure' that left the half-drowned victim temporarily incapable of any manifestation of their insanity, whatever voices might be screaming at them in their wandering brain. 'I never had the impression that any of them were doing anything more than guessing.'

They climbed in silence, following a ridge of rock up the side of the draw now, toward one of the outcroppings of granite that studded these arid hills among the trees.

'She could bring me back,' said Manitou at last, very softly, into the stillness. 'Mina could. Mina Bodenschatz. Only one who could, when I'd go blank.'

They moved across the boulders, moccasins soundless on the granite. Wind breathed down on them the smell of cloud; the air was clammy and cold.

'Silent Wolf says –' Manitou's slow voice fumbled at the words – 'when I was born, at the same time and same place a thunder spirit came into being and got trapped up in my flesh. Makes as much sense as anything else I've heard. Lot more than those mad-doctors in Munich.'

'You've been to mad-doctors, then?'

'Oh God, yes. My parents never would consult with 'em when I was little, when anger'd set me off an' I'd do things I didn't remember ... 'cept in dreams. I was six or seven, first time. Then not again 'til I was eleven. Air catches fire—' His big hand gestured, trying to find expression, and the movement flinched and caught, as it had by the ashes of the Blackfoot campfire, like he had a wound in his arm. 'I wake up, hours later, head hurtin' like I don't know there's human words to tell it. I'll sometimes dream about what I did, maybe not 'til years later...' He shook his head. 'I never have dreamed about Mina. Some nights it feels like I'm gonna. Those nights I get myself drunk.'

'Do you know what happened?'

'I know what they said at the trial. By the time I was fourteen I figured out I could use pain to bring myself out of it. I'd heat the top end of one of my mama's knitting needles in the fire, brand myself on the inside of my arm or on the thigh. If I caught it quick enough – 'tween the time somethin' would set me off, an' the fire closin' in around my vision – I could pull out of it. Pa was a doctor in Lucerne. We moved down to Nuremberg, I think so they wouldn't be around his family or Mama's – so they wouldn't know about me. But he said – Mama did, too – everyone would know there was somethin' goin' on, if I didn't be a doctor, too.'

'You're Swiss, then?'

'Yeah.' In the sing-song German of the south, he added, 'It's been ten years since I spoke German, but when I dream of the Alps – of the shepherds who worked for Mama's family – they all speak it, and I can still understand.' In the darkness, for an instant, January heard the smile in the mountaineer's voice.

'And your name is Escher? We read two of Franz's letters, that we found in his father's coat,' January added, when the big man glanced around at him with the sudden menace of a

291

startled bear.

'Escher. Ignatius Escher.' Manitou tilted his head as if trying to recall the name. 'I shoulda known they'd come after me.'

Manitou had hidden his gear in crevices high up in a shoulder of granite that thrust up through the trees, just below the backbone of the hills. Most of it he left cached, only saddling up his big cinder-gray mare for Hannibal and Veinte-y-Cinco to ride, while Shaw and January rode the two mules. The trapper himself walked, leading the way on what January guessed would be a wide swing north to lose the Omahas. He couldn't see that Manitou being afoot would hinder their speed much. The man was tireless – or else, reflected January, he himself was so exhausted from days of living rough, eating berries, fighting swollen rivers and being beaten into submission by infuriated Indians, that any exertion was enough to leave him unmanned. The only possessions the trapper removed from the cache were his waterskins and a couple of parfleches of pemmican, which January felt he could have devoured by himself without sharing, rawhide sacks and all.

The moon was down, the night jewel-clear. Even with his eyes accustomed to darkness and starlight, January could barely make out the shapes of the pine trunks as black columns in an indigo abyss. The first birds were waking.

After a long time of moving in silence, with Manitou scouting ahead, the trapper came back to the main party and January heard him say to Shaw, 'We got company?'

292

'Not as I can hear.'

Manitou grunted. Then: 'I gotta thank you for passin' up that shot at Franz. It woulda been a beaut.'

'It would,' agreed Shaw, as if they were speaking of shooting out a candle at two hundred and fifty yards. 'Tom woulda taken it. An' died.'

'He would.'

January thought about the hard, thin face and dark-gray eyes bitter as aloe in the firelight. *Not only died, but taken us all with him, without a thought.*

'I will have to tell him,' went on Shaw quietly. 'An' I fear that when I do, I'll have lost two brothers, 'stead of one.'

They rested shortly after sunup, Hannibal and Veinte-y-Cinco sliding off their single mule and falling asleep almost as their feet touched earth.

Manitou said to Shaw, 'You sleep, too—'

The Kentuckian nodded once, lay on the apishamore he'd pulled off his mule and slept, all without ever letting go of his rifle.

January staggered on stiffened legs to pull bunches of dried grass, as Manitou was doing, to rub the mules's backs. 'Tell me about old Bodenschatz.'

A week ago, January would have accepted that he wasn't going to get a reply, but he knew now that the trapper was just calling his memories together and trying to remember words. 'He had a shop in Ingolstadt,' said the trapper at last. 'All the professors at the University would go to him for chemicals. He'd been everywhere in the world and was always getting things – plants,

293

strange salts, poison mushrooms, dried bugs. Mina kept track of it. Mina was his treasure. Franz had got a job in Munich – accountant for the firm that imported the old man's chemicals – and married the daughter of one of the clerks there. I never met him. Mina seldom spoke of him, though he'd write her every day, twelve an' thirteen pages sometimes. Mina...'

The trapper slipped a rope around his brindled mare's neck, knotted the other end to a tree to let her graze. 'Mina wanted to study medicine. She'd have been a fine doctor. Maybe the first mad-doctor with brains and a soul. Her father hired me as a tutor for her, 'cause we all of us knew, to get into the medical classes she'd have to be half again better than the best of the men. Mina was the first – the only one – who could talk about this ... this whatever it is, that happens to me when I get angry ... when I get angry past a certain point. Not like it was something *I* could help if I'd just be a better person, or if I prayed, or if I tried harder ... She said, it was like the bad fairy had put a curse on me, an' we just needed to figure out a way to dodge around that curse when it came on. Like it wasn't somethin' *I* was doin' 'cause I was ornery or bad. It was just what it was.'

He rested his arms along his mare's back for a time, huge fists bunched together and his lips resting against them, looking out through the trees at the great sweep of the valley to the west, filled with the lilac of the mountains' shadow. Ten or twelve miles off, January could make out the isolated shape of Grindstone Butte, that he and Shaw had passed in their search for Clarke and Groot's party. The ford they'd taken must be almost due east.

'Did she use pain on you?'

'No.' Manitou shook his head, with an expression, even in retrospect, of mild surprise. 'No, not after the first. Well, she'd take my hand and take a little pinch of skin on the back of it, 'tween her nails, an' twist it – it was like bein' bit by a ant – an' say my name. An' I'd think: *that's Mina there ... I can't scare her, so I gotta hang on.* An' I'd look into her eyes an' it was like her sweet soul was a lantern for me to follow in the dark.

'An' it was a good thing she could do that,' he went on after a moment, settling on one of the smaller steps of the rocks behind which they'd camped. ''Cause in Ingolstadt, it seemed like these spells would come on me more an' more often. It was the people, I think. There was just too blame many people. In the town, at the University, gettin' underfoot, kickin' their dogs, beatin' their horses, bein' stupid ... In Lucerne, half the time we spent up with Mama's relations in the mountains, I could go for days without seein' more than the same two or three shepherds. In Ingolstadt...'

He shuddered, as if the old university town, with its moss-grown cobblestones and steep-roofed medieval houses, had been the place where he'd been tortured, and not some Indian camp in the Rockies. 'Like I told you before,' he said. 'I just ain't fit to be around humans. Maybe a bad fairy did put a curse on me, when I's too

295

little to notice. An' I suppose I was a fool – we were both fools, Mina an' me – to go thinkin' somethin' wouldn't happen.' He closed his eyes, seeking the blindness that he had sought, January guessed, every day for the past ten years.

'I don't even remember what it was. Just remember wakin' up in my lodgin's with my head hurtin' worse than I thought pain could go, an' blood crusted on my hands, an' the police comin' up the stair tellin' me...' His voice faltered. 'Tellin' me I'd...'

January put a hand on the big man's arm, and Manitou sat silent, eyes closed to the morning light that streamed up the valley, flashed gold now on the tips of the pine needles.

'They put me in a madhouse.' The trapper turned his face from the distant river, met January's eyes. 'They said I wasn't sane enough to be judged. I heard later, Franz an' his father both swore before the judges that I was as sane as the next man an' had never had no problem about gettin' angry before ... It was only my parents, an' two of the other students at the University, an' some of my grandpa's shepherds, tellin' of what I'd been like from childhood, that kept me off the gallows. Had I been better, to have hanged?'

He folded his hands again, pressed the heavy knuckles to his lips. 'I swear to you, I have no answer to that. I hope I killed no one when I escaped the place, but to be honest, I have no memory of that either, and every time I dream it, it's different. It's as if one day I was bein' walked to that "laboratory" of theirs to get more needles stuck through my neck, and then I was waking up in a goods yard in Regensburg, wearing clothes I didn't recognize.

'I thought about going back,' he went on quietly. 'But I'd been there two, maybe three months ... and I couldn't make myself do it. I thought about killing myself. I couldn't do that either. I was only twenty-two. I made my way to Marseilles, found a boat to New Orleans. I'm not happy,' he added simply. 'I don't think a man like me is ever happy. But to live in a world where it's only animals, and the rocks and the sky—'

He drew a deep breath, his face peaceful, like a man who comes from bitterest cold to a fire. 'I swear to you, it's the closest I can get. I should have known they'd follow me.'

'Do you remember killing Klaus Bodenschatz?'

Manitou had shut his eyes again; now they flared open, earnest and troubled and without a trace of anger in their gold-flecked brown depths. 'I didn't kill him.'

TWENTY-FIVE

January opened his mouth to make the obvious reply, then closed it again, recalling that sense of seeing some piece of a puzzle fall into place...
'Did you break his leg?' he asked.

Flecks of color came up under the mountaineer's heavy tan, and he looked away. 'He had pistols,' he said. 'I saw that fool lantern of his a mile away and thought it might have been you, or one of those numbskulls that were out all over the hills that night followin' Beauty and the Dutchman. Bodenschatz put a ball in my arm 'fore I ever saw him. He had a second pistol, and I knew I had to get it from him fast...' Some memory flickered for a moment like the reflection of that speck of lantern fire in his eyes.

'I was angry,' he added, more softly. 'At that pissant Blankenship. At you, as I thought, comin' after me. At all them damn cretins tramplin' all over the hills tryin' to find their way to the one best beaver stream in the mountains ... Doesn't matter.' He shook his head, like a bull in fly season, goaded beyond enduring by a thousand biting demons that he could not see. 'Anger comes over me ... I hurt him ... pretty bad, I think. His bones was like dry sticks.' For an instant his face convulsed: shame and pain and

298

grief at what he had done. 'But I never took a knife to him. I splinted up his leg and tore up his shirt to bind his ribs with, for I'd broke a number of 'em. Then I made a shelter for him, under that big deadfall, and made a fire, and give him my own shirt, for I could smell it was comin' to rain again.'

From the blanket beside him Manitou picked up his second parfleche, half-emptied, and handed it to January, who had to force himself to stop eating the pemmican lest he devour everything and leave nothing for the others. Their companions still lay like the dead on the apishamores spread on the ground: Shaw's bare arms and hands criss-crossed with makeshift bandages from his torn-up shirt; Hannibal and Veintey-Cinco clung together in sleep like some tattered Hansel and Gretel, adrift in a forest that neither could hope to survive. January wondered who was taking care of Pia back at the camp.

'Did he wake?' he asked at length.

'Nah.' The big man sighed. 'I thought of wakin' him, to ask his forgiveness. But I was riled from the fight an' could still feel the thunder spirit scratchin' to get out. I knew the old man had to be with someone. He musta come into the camp that day, maybe seen me when I fought you. I had to get away from him, where I couldn't see him: with the fire burnin' before him, he'd be safe enough. I thought I'd move on, soon as it got light. Him an' Franz – I figured it'd be Franz with him – would be easy enough to lose in the mountains.'

He sat for a time, looking out into the still blue

cold of the dawn woods. Then: 'I laid down, but the only thing in my mind – like a voice whisperin' stronger an' stronger – was that it'd be so easy to go back ... I got my horses an' went to where I knew Silent Wolf was camped. Silent Wolf is a medicine man, as well as the war chief.'

The trapper turned his arm, as if through the elk-hide war-shirt, the blanket capote, he could see the scars of a hundred slivers of fatwood, driven under the skin and lighted to bring his soul back from the frontiers of homicidal madness. 'I told him what I need to do, to keep that thunder spirit on its own side of the fence. He'd done it before. Blackfeet are good at it. The best.' His hand brushed his body, as if recalling every one of those shocking scars that covered him as if it were a blessing. 'Time we're movin',' he added and glanced at the gold sunlight as it washed across the rock escarpments behind them, the twilight below dissolving into color and brightness. 'You feel up to it?'

'As opposed to sitting here,' said January, rising, 'I could run all the way back.'

While January bridled the mules – stiffened muscles, knife cuts and bruises shrieking with every move – Manitou woke Shaw, Hannibal and Veinte-y-Cinco, who split the last of the pemmican among them. Day was growing bright and chill. Shaw looked out over the valley, toward the ford and the stumpy red-brown thumb of Grindstone Butte: 'What's our chance of makin' the camp by tonight?'

'God willin' an' the creek don't rise,' replied

the medical student from Ingolstadt.

Manitou led them down off the high mesa eastward, and into the rougher country along the New Fork, watching the western skyline for the point at which they could swing west again and come down near the site of William Bonneville's old fort. From there they could follow the Green River to the rendezvous camps from the north. They moved with a kind of swift deliberateness, Shaw and Manitou calling frequent halts, to rest the tired animals or so that their tracks could be covered. On these occasions January, Hannibal and Veinte-y-Cinco took turns foraging and resting, for even riding the mule, January found it was difficult to keep going for more than an hour at a time. He didn't like the way Hannibal and the woman sometimes clung to the saddle, as if it was only with the greatest effort that they kept from slipping off unconscious. Rough stretches of open grassland alternated with thin lodgepole timber; in the stillness the drone of a bee, or the far-off popping cry of a grouse, seemed loud as gunshots. Again and again he turned to scan the horizons and the sky for the telltale dust of horses.

As Iron Heart, he was sure, was watching for the dust they might raise.

'But now the poison is gone,' said Veinte-y-Cinco, at one of these halts, 'and Boden is of no more use to Iron Heart, will Iron Heart pursue us still?'

'Iron Heart's a man of honor,' said Manitou. 'If he's made a vow to help Boden with his vengeance, he'll do it ... An' there's no tellin' what

301

Boden'll feel obligated to do to help *him*, in return.'

The dryness of the hills was worsened by the thin dryness of the air, and though small game – rabbits, ground squirrels and grouse – seemed everywhere in the sagebrush, firing a gun was out of the question. In answer to Shaw's question, Manitou confirmed that the winter before – 1835–36 – Iron Heart and his Omahas had indeed camped near Fort Ivy, which was close enough to Manitou's own winter hunting-grounds that he preferred to come down to trade there, rather than going on to Laramie and dealing with the AFC.

'I trapped in Company brigades for two years,' said Manitou. 'Hundred dollars a year, and when time came to pay out, you found most of that hundred dollars, you owed 'em for the cost of your traps an' the liquor you'd drunk at the last rendezvous. Hudson's Bay gave me a better price, and after one good year I started trappin' on my own. Preferred it, anyway. Longer I stay out here, seems like the shorter fuse I got, when I come amongst my own kind.'

He only shook his head over the machinations of the Hudson's Bay Company and the AFC, though he agreed that it was probably Titus who'd set the AFC Crows on to January, Shaw and Gil Wallach after the feast. 'Part of the game,' he said. 'Red Arm don't really care who they scalp, long as Titus pays 'em in good knives an' gunpowder. It's all White Men's Business. But if it comes to war,' he added somberly, 'the tribes'll fight for the British, like they did back

302

in '12. The Brits keep their treaties. America'll back its settlers, an' there's more of them every year.'

His voice held an echo of sadness, as Sir William Stewart's had, back in the crowded banquet-tent, when he'd said wistfully: *it'll all be gone...*

The streets of Independence, January recalled, had been crowded not only with trappers and traders and bullwhackers and trail hands stocking up for the Santa Fe caravans, but also with farmers, farmers' wives and their children. Ordinary working-folk, who spoke with shining eyes of 'free land' in Oregon, as if the United States already held uncontested title to those untouched miles – and as if it were simply free for the taking.

'Will you go back to the rendezvous at all?' asked Hannibal, later in the afternoon as they sheltered among a few thin-trunked pines at the head of a draw.

'If you need me.' Manitou spoke without turning his head, scanning the jumble of gullies that fell away before them. 'Like I said, no tellin' what Boden'll get up to, to keep Iron Heart on his good side – an Iron Heart'll sure want somethin' from him, to go off chasin' me through the mountains. I'd as soon go on, but if you need bait, I'll stay.'

'It's good of you.'

Manitou shrugged. 'Every book, every play I ever read 'bout vengeance, I never read one of 'em that ends well ... Every man I talked to that's done it, they say the same. *A god implants in*

303

mortal guilt whenever he wants utterly to con-found a house ... Was that Aeschylus as said that? When he spoke of turnin' vengeance over to justice an' lettin' justice have its way? I'll do as I can, to make an end.'

January glanced back up to the top of the rocks behind them, where Shaw crouched, a tattered, feral scarecrow, watching the sky to the south-west. Easy enough to speak of making an end, when one had something to go back to. Without family to return to – without a life beyond vengeance – he saw, suddenly, that the quest itself became life. That Frankenstein needed his monster to chase, because without the chase he, too, would be swallowed up in his own inner darkness.

'And what do we do,' asked Hannibal, getting stiffly up – Veinte-y-Cinco had to help him – from the foot of the tree where he'd been sitting, 'if Iron Heart and his warriors have gone back to the rendezvous, to make sure Boden comes up with another plan of vengeance while we're out here?'

'Ain't much we can do.'

'An' it ain't a problem that's like to arise.' Shaw dropped lightly from the rocks, knocking bark and pine needles from his bandaged hands. 'Supposin' that's their dust we got, comin' up the draw from the east.'

'That wouldn't be Sir William's hunting party,' inquired Hannibal wistfully, even as he collected the last of the waterskins, 'heading back to the camp?'

'He'd be comin' due west.' Manitou shaded his eyes against the slant of the sun. 'Dust's in the south. Looks like, along our same route.'

'We split up?' Shaw checked the loads on Mary and Martha, his long Kentucky rifles. When they'd slipped away from the Omaha war camp, Veinte-y-Cinco had managed to retrieve three rifles, but the warriors who'd taken the captives' knives had kept them. Manitou was the only man who had powder and ball.

'Give 'em a horse trail to follow.' Manitou tossed one of his knives to Shaw; pulled a spare skinning-knife from his moccasin to hand to January. 'These poor beasts are so tired, I doubt they could outrun 'em.'

'I'll take 'em on north.' Shaw was already unwinding reins from trees. 'Those rocks we passed at the top of the ridge 'bout four miles back—'

'We should make it.'

'Once I turn the horses loose I'll head for the camp,' went on Shaw. 'Let 'em know we need help bad.' He held out one of his rifles to Manitou – January didn't even want to think about the Kentuckian's chances of making it the ten miles back to the Green River, after leading the Omahas several miles further along the ridge.

Hannibal – who had shown a surprisingly adept touch in such things – scratched the tracks from around their campsite with a branch.

Veinte-y-Cinco touched Shaw's arm as he started to move off: 'You make it back to camp, you tell Pia—'

She hesitated. *Tell her what?* thought January.

305

That she's on her own, at age thirteen, in the middle of the Rocky Mountains, with no home to go back to, dependent utterly on the likes of Edwin Titus and Mick Seaholly?

A slave cabin shared with twenty other people, and a drunken lunatic master thrown in for lagniappe, seemed like a sanctuary in comparison.

Veinte-y-Cinco's voice was almost a whisper. 'Tell her that her mama loves her.'

Shaw put his hand briefly to the woman's dirty cheek, then turned away. With the horse and the mules he headed off up the ridge, clumsily dusting at the tracks to make it look as if an effort at concealment had been made. Manitou led the way downslope to where a deadfall made a sort of road toward stonier ground that would hold no tracks. From there they doubled on their trail and moved back south toward the nearest cover, a distant tangle of huckleberry in a dip of ground. They went as swiftly as they could, but both Hannibal and Veinte-y-Cinco lagged, despite themselves, and it felt to January as if the hoofbeats of the Indians – still some miles off – hammered in his head. As if the sun was nailed to the sky above the ridge, never to go down again. As soon as they could, they went to ground – the thicket indefensible if they were discovered, but enough, January prayed, to shield them from enemy eyes until the Indians had ridden past.

After what felt like over an hour he heard the hooves, dim with distance as they swung on to Shaw's trail. Manitou lay with his ear on the

306

ground for a longer time yet, waiting until they were far off before he signaled them to move on. It was halfway to darkness by then, and Hannibal was falling further and further behind, the leg that he'd broken eighteen months before visibly weakening. They were in timber now, the rocks Shaw had spoken of still some distance off. January recalled they were a couple of boulders and a sort of granite elbow, close to twenty feet tall, thrusting up from the ground amid a tangle of sagebrush and laurel. He tried to picture where defenders could situate themselves to hold off a determined attack and failed.

And it didn't matter. Behind them he half-guessed, half-heard what might have been hooves, glanced back – Manitou grabbed Hannibal by the arm and dragged him along, though the rocks weren't even in sight in the slow-gathering twilight. Veinte-y-Cinco fell back beside January, hurrying her steps to his, looking back also...

Damn it, it's not my imagination, she hears it, too...

'I'll fire first,' Manitou said. 'You others, keep your rifles pointed but don't shoot 'til I say. Indians they mostly don't have enough powder or ball to waste it on a threat. You handle loading, Sun Mouse? Good. Winter Moon, you see anything big enough to get our backs against?'

Every tree – fallen or otherwise – in the dusky forest seemed uniformly less than a foot in diameter...

The hooves were definitely audible, and he could see movement behind them in the trees, on

307

both sides, too...

Christ, did they get Shaw? He'd heard no shots—

'There!'

It didn't look like much of a bastion – a dip in the ground formed when a lightning-struck tree had fallen, the trunk itself small, but a tangle of branches still relatively fresh. In the gloaming, it might be enough to confuse attackers' aim. They ran for it, skidding and stumbling on the slope of the ground, January thinking, in spite of himself: *Rose, I should never have left Rose by herself with a baby coming...*

The thought that he'd never see her again was almost worse than the thought that he was going to die.

Two painted horses flashed past them as they neared the fallen tree, wheeled to cut them off from it. Manitou raised his rifle and fired, one of the riders toppling and two others swinging in from the other side. They were still twenty yards from the log, and January knew that this was as good as they were going to get. He raised his rifle, put his back to Manitou's, covering the horses that whirled close, then veered away, ghostly shapes in the lowering dark. He recognized Iron Heart, and Dark Antlers, and other men who'd taken them before. Recognized, too, Franz Bodenschatz, in his bright Mexican coat and with his big American horse, riding at the back of the war party. Two riders charged in from either side, January shifting aim to cover them both—

A rifle crashed from somewhere in the dimness

of the woods behind them, and the Indian Manitou had called Left Hand fell somersaulting from his horse's bare back, struck the ground with the pinwheeling confusion of a man already dead.

Two more rifles spoke.

Shaw couldn't have gotten to camp that fast. Stewart?

And close to a hundred other Indians emerged howling from the twilight.

TWENTY-SIX

At least ten of the Omahas wheeled their horses and, shrieking war-cries, charged the newcomers. Two others wheeled from the melee and rode at the little group of fugitives by the fallen pine. There was just enough good light left for January to shoot one and Manitou – whose rifle Hannibal had reloaded with a swiftness Kit Carson himself would have commended – to shoot the other. Franz Bodenschatz spurred in through what looked, to January, like a Renaissance battle-painting of whirling horses and writhing half-naked bodies, brought up his pistol within yards of Manitou's head, and Veinte-y-Cinco fired, her bullet tearing the outside of Bodenschatz's left arm, but nearly knocking him out of the saddle with its force. An Indian warrior – one of the newcomers – launched himself from his own horse on to the trader, dragging him to the

309

ground. Bodenschatz screamed something – in the din, January didn't hear what – to Iron Heart, but the pockmarked war-chief and the remaining members of his band only bunched their milling horses tighter, spears and rifles pointing outward as they were surrounded.

Three of the newcomer riders – rifles held pointed at the fugitives – trotted in close, in what could have been either an encirclement or a protective ring. January noticed the sun design worked in quills on one man's leggings, the line of triangles painted on another's sleeve.

'They's Crows,' said Manitou softly.

Hannibal whispered, 'Is that good or bad?' He was loading both rifles with a speed born of desperation, chalk white and breathing like a broken steamboat-engine. The nearest Indian watched him, rifle leveled, but showed no signs of using it.

'Depends,' answered Manitou. 'You can talk to some Crows, the ones that ain't from a band that's at war with the white man. But they know my brother's Silent Wolf. An' just about every tribe in the mountains is at war with the Blackfeet.'

About half of the Omaha were down; the rest gathered in a group, Iron Heart talking furiously with the leader of the Crows. A Crow warrior rounded up the horses of the dead. Three others went systematically from one fallen warrior to the next, counting coup – striking them with hooked and decorated medicine-sticks – then scalping the bodies where they lay in the pine straw. The smell of blood was overwhelming.

Another warrior jerked Bodenschatz to his feet and thrust him into the group of white captives with such force that he stumbled. Manitou caught his arm to steady him, and Bodenschatz jerked free, lips skinned back from his teeth like an animal about to bite.

'Don't think you can get your savages to do your dirty work for you!' he snarled in German. 'I swear to you on the grave of my sister – my sister whom you murdered—'

'You're not one to talk,' broke in January, in the same language, 'about getting savages to do dirty work, Boden. That seems to be the way you play the game as well.'

Instead of answering, Bodenschatz – whom January still found it hard to think of as anything but the good-natured Charro Morales – whipped a knife from his belt and threw himself on Manitou, who caught his wrist easily – he was some eight inches taller and outweighed the man by a good fifty pounds. One of the Crows on guard over them shouted something, and January wrenched the knife from Bodenschatz's hand. The Crow rode over, and January immediately flung the weapon on the ground before him, then fished in the merchant's coat pocket and brought out a pistol, which he held out immediately by the barrel, so that the warrior could take it.

'Nigger dog!' Bodenschatz almost spit the words at him, clutching his bleeding arm. 'You think they'll let you go free?'

'Just making sure that if shooting starts, it'll be coming from in front of me, and not behind.'

311

The leader of the Crows rode over to them, a thickset, powerful warrior on a black horse painted with white hand-prints. Striking his chest, he said, 'Lost.' Dark eyes moved from January to Manitou, then on to Bodenschatz. 'Do you ride bound, do you ride free?'

Bodenschatz stabbed at Manitou with a finger. 'This man murdered my sister and murdered my father. Are the Crow women, to regard so little the right of a man to vengeance?'

As if his enemy had not spoken, Manitou answered, 'I will ride free.' He took his rifle from Hannibal – carefully handling it by the barrel – and held it out to the Crow warrior who came up with a horse on a lead rein.

In the end none of them were bound. Lost – the leader of the Crow war party – separated them along the line of warriors, and as the party filed through the darkness into the deeper mountains, January was well aware that the riders on either side of him had their rifles trained on him. Iron Heart – similarly guarded – rode next to Lost, and in the thin moonlight January saw the Omaha speaking in sign to the war chief as they rode, pointing back to Bodenschatz, to Manitou, to the west where the rendezvous lay, and sometimes back to the south, where the bones of his people rotted along the banks of the Platte.

Halfway up a steep coulee another party of Crow joined them, and by the time they reached the Crow village, strung out along a substantial creek between the hills, January guessed there were some two hundred warriors surrounding them. This was, he thought, the unknown band whose identity had caused so much speculation at the rendezvous. He knew there'd been a bet on it at Seaholly's. It was small comfort to know that he could now win it.

It was relatively early in the night, and little 'squaw fires' glowed in front of many of the lodges. In others, the blaze had been built inside, and a low, honey-gold radiance shone through the translucent skins. Camp dogs and camp children boiled out from among the tipis, the dogs noisy, the children pointing excitedly at the black white man.

In front of a lodge in the midst of the camp, Lost signed them to dismount. An older man – heavy-built like Lost, and with the same mouth and chin – emerged, his shirt flecked with row upon row of elk teeth, from which eagle feathers and ermine tails dangled. Lost said, 'Walks Before Sunrise,' and Manitou murmured:

'He's big medicine.'

A moment later two other men ducked through the low entry, one of them – hands bound behind him and looking considerably the worse for wear – Abishag Shaw. The other – a deeply tanned white man in a trader's well-cut frock-coat and riding boots – studied the captives appraisingly and said, 'You'll be Wildman – January – Bodenschatz – Sefton ... M'am,' he added, touching his hat brim to Veinte-y-Cinco. 'Iron Heart—' His glance shifted to the Omaha war chief. 'I'm Asa Goodpastor. And I've been hearin' some very strange things.'

'I am here on sufferance –' Goodpastor raised

313

his hand against Bodenschatz's angry tirade as they entered the lodge – 'like the rest of you. Walks Before got word that you –' he nodded to Iron Heart – 'and your men attacked white men just outside the rendezvous camp two nights ago.'

'We aided this man,' said Iron Heart, with a cold glance across at Bodenschatz, 'in his hunt for the man who killed his father and his sister. We promised to help him fulfill the vow of his vengeance, if he would help me fulfill the vow of mine. This promise he did not fulfill, nor will he, I think. Yet this is not through his own doing. These –' Iron Heart gestured to Shaw, January and their companions, who had seated themselves beside the small central fire-pit – 'followed him from the white man's country because, in the course of his pursuit, he killed the brother of Tall Chief. If he would accomplish his vengeance, they must be stopped in theirs.'

'Ain't you forgettin' one tiny detail,' put in Shaw, rubbing the weals on his wrists where January had untied the thongs that bound him, 'havin' to do with you plannin' to murder every man jack an' woman at the rendezvous with the poison this man's father was bringin' out for you?'

'They poison themselves,' sneered Iron Heart. 'I do not pour it down their throats.'

'And this is not your affair, Medicine Lynx,' spoke up Walks Before Sunrise, with a sharp look at Goodpastor. 'Many tribes hate the white men. If they choose to kill them without honor, either for themselves or for their enemies, this is nothing to me.'

'My people died without honor,' retorted the Omaha chief, stung by the imputation of cowardice. 'Why do I need any? Had this man –' he jerked his head toward Wildman, who had sat through the whole of the discussion beside the fire in silence, his head in his hands – 'not killed the old white father, I would have had my vengeance.'

'Did you kill them?' Goodpastor turned to Wildman. 'This man's father, an' his sister?'

'I killed his sister.' Manitou raised his face from his palms, looked across the fire with ravaged eyes. 'I got no memory of doing so, because of my madness—'

'Your madness that conveniently convinced your judges not to hang you!'

'So you were tried?'

'Judges heard my case, yes. And put me in a madhouse. I didn't kill his father.'

Bodenschatz opened his mouth to shout a refutation of this, but January cut him off quietly: 'No. You did that yourself, didn't you, Bodenschatz?'

Iron Heart's eyes widened in shocked rage. *'What?'*

'It's a lie,' shouted Bodenschatz. 'Can't you see he'll say anything? I never killed the Shaw boy. The Blackfeet did that—'

'The Blackfeet woulda kept his scalp, not thrown it away in the hollow of a tree,' retorted Shaw softly. 'You killed him 'cause he woulda kept you from your revenge—'

'The same way that you killed your own

315

father,' pointed out January quietly, 'because with a broken leg, he would have kept you from pursuing the man you sought. The man for whom you left your wife, and your children—'

'*He is a monster*!'

'*You* are a monster,' replied January. 'Manitou Wildman was born as he is. You made yourself – yourself.'

'That –' Bodenschatz's face worked with the effort to remain normal – 'is a damned lie.' His glance cut to Iron Heart. 'It is a lie.'

Iron Heart said softly, 'Prove it.' And there was something in the tilt of his head, the sudden flex of his nearly-hairless brows, that made January wonder if he had not suspected this before. 'Words are cheap, Winter Moon. White men's words most of all.'

January sighed. 'I wish everyone would stop calling me a white man. Send the woman back to the rendezvous camp.'

Veinte-y-Cinco looked up, dark eyes wide with shock and hope.

'Keep a guard on her, if you will,' he added as both Iron Heart and Walks Before Sunrise began to protest. 'Will you do this?'

He saw her hand close hard on Hannibal's, the two of them sitting side-by-side near Manitou on the other side of the fire, without speaking. She started to stammer something and stopped, the whole of her heart in her face, as if the marrow of her bones cried her daughter's name.

And though he spoke to Walks Before Sunrise, January's eyes held hers. 'Great Chief, have one of your men go into the camp and bring out to

316

her Moccasin Woman, the old mother of the Delawares. She knows Veinte-y-Cinco well, and Veinte-y-Cinco will speak for us. Promise Moccasin Woman safe passage here to this camp and safe passage back. Veinte-y-Cinco,' he added softly, 'we trust you with all of our lives. For if you cry out, or escape, or rouse the camp, or bring any attack against the Crow here, you know we will all of us be killed before we can be freed.'

The woman took a sip of breath, let it out, her eyes going to Hannibal, and then to Shaw, who had favored her, January knew, above the other girls at Seaholly's, despite the fact that at thirty-six she had half a decade over him in age, and despite her skinniness and two missing teeth. She looked at the doorway – the two Crow guards sitting outside in the firelight of the camp – and then at Bodenschatz.

'Did he really kill that poor old man?' she asked softly. 'His own papa?'

'*Schlampn* bitch, you'd believe any man who paid you—'

Her mouth twisted. Her gaze returned to January. 'I'll go,' she said quietly. 'And I'll return with Moccasin Woman, without rousing the camp.'

'Thank you. Tell Moccasin Woman that we know that she found the old man in the woods and took the last of his clothing, not only the shirt that he wore, but also the shirt that had been torn up to bind his ribs. Tell her to bring those things back here, if she would. Tell her that our lives hang on her doing this. Tell her also – or the

317

warrior who goes with you,' he added, with a glance at Walks Before Sunrise, 'to bring the camp chest from Bodenschatz's tent – Charro Morales's tent – unopened.'

The trader's face turned ghastly in the low firelight, brows standing out suddenly dark. 'Of all the impudent—'

'*Veritas odium parit,*' said Hannibal and added, to January, still in Latin, 'You're sure it's Moccasin Woman?'

'She's the one who gave Pia the old man's cravat. And who else in the camp,' he added, 'would have carried him back into his shelter and carved the sign of the cross above his head, to bless him as he lay? Of all the people in the camp,' he went on in English, 'I don't really think it could be anyone else.'

'Well, Maestro,' said Shaw, after Iron Heart and Bodenschatz had left the tent under guard, and Walks Before had likewise bid them good night, 'I purely hope you're right.' He got to his feet and limped heavily – a makeshift, bloodied bandage showed where an arrow had gone through his thigh – to lower the skin across the lodge entrance, against the growing chill of the night. ''Cause it seems to come down to: who is Walks Before gonna trust? An' if it ain't us, I do not see a good outcome for anyone in this tent.'

TWENTY-SEVEN

The Omaha Dark Antlers and two Crow warriors came into the tipi a few minutes later, to fetch Veinte-y-Cinco. The woman rose, kissed Hannibal and Shaw ('Don't I get one for luck?' inquired Goodpastor, and with a quick flicker of a grin she gave him one that would have been grounds for divorce in most states of the Union), and slipped out into the night.

'Now it lies upon the knees of the gods'.' quoted January softly.

Hannibal sighed. 'And we all know how trustworthy *they* are.'

Shortly after that, a couple of Crow women came in with food – chunks of roasted mountain-sheep, and a tin kettle of stew – and with them, Goodpastor's engagés, two young border-ruffians named Laurent and Tonio. They brought the news that the remaining Omaha warriors were setting up lodges of dead wood and sage-brush for the night, as if in a war camp, just beyond the tipis of the Crow, and that the Crow were keeping guard on them. 'That Mexican trader was with them,' added Tonio, the younger of the two – brothers, January guessed, by their looks, and by the way Tonio kept close to the elder as if for protection.

'As a guest, would you say?' Goodpastor poured out water from the skin hanging from one of the tent poles, into the pewter cup that the young men shared. 'Or a prisoner?'

'A guest, looked like. He sits with Iron Heart at his fire.'

'Well,' sighed Goodpastor, 'consarn.'

'And are *you* a guest here, sir?' inquired January as the two boys settled down with bowls of wild mutton and stew. 'Or a prisoner?'

'And *did* you drop out of the sky?' added Hannibal.

'Wish I had,' retorted the Indian Agent. 'I am entirely too old for that ride up the Platte in a wagon-train. No, I set out from Fort Laramie like a respectable representative of the United States Congress, with ten engagés, a secretary and a half-breed guide who couldn't find his way back from the outhouse. When we got to the Popo Agie we heard from a couple of Shoshone hunters that there was a band of Crow – eighty lodges – skulking around the mountains near the rendezvous without comin' into it, which sounded downright fishy to me. I had the boys make camp, took those two scoundrels with me, did some scouting on my own and here I am.'

'Here you are,' agreed January. 'But could you leave if you wanted to?'

'I could, yes. Or at least I think I'll be able to, once Walks Before has figured out what he wants to do with you and with Iron Heart. I'm on his territory. I'm no more than an envoy from the Congress to the Crow. And I wouldn't care to bet on it that he'd let me leave the camp tonight – or

320

that Iron Heart's boys wouldn't find a way of making sure I didn't get to the rendezvous if I *did* leave, sort of quiet like in the woods. We're a long ways from anywhere, here, and if they plan on killin' any white men they're not going to leave an Indian Agent to go tellin' the tale.'

'Ah,' said January. 'Then all we've done is make your position here worse.'

'Hell, I been in worse places. Though things could get damn sticky if that woman tries to make a break when she gets near the rendezvous, and there's an attack made on this camp. I ain't sayin' Titus wouldn't keep a lid on it if he could—'

'Titus?'

'That sourpuss Controller the AFC's got with their factory there this year. He's the one paid Walks Before thirty rifles and three barrels of gunpowder to come down here and not let a soul see 'em. There's talk all over this camp of them attackin' the smaller trains as they leave the rendezvous – an' of stagin' an attack on the AFC train, for show, so word can be took back to Congress that it was the Hudson's Bay Flatheads, an' that the military's needed to keep them pesky British an' their Indian allies in line, just like back in 1812. I been workin' on convincin' Walks Before that it ain't such a good plan.'

He pitched a clean-picked sheep-rib into the fire, wiped his fingers on his bandanna. 'Another reason I'm not tryin' to leave this camp just yet. So I would appreciate it,' he went on, 'if you boys would give me some idea of what's been happenin' at the rendezvous.'

The white-haired Indian Agent listened with interest to January's account of the trade in liquor with the Indians ('Lord, Bill Grey made it sound like Sodom and Gomorrah,') and the attempted scalping on the way back from the banquet ('That sounds like Titus, all right...'). He grinned at the effort to convince Congress that the dead man was himself, but his eyes narrowed sharply when January spoke of Bodenschatz's plan to give away poisoned liquor.

'That's no Indian plan,' he rumbled, and he stroked the milk-white stubble of his trail beard. 'Mission Indians, maybe – that have learned how civilized folks go about their business.'

'My brother stumbled on a half-wrote letter from Bodenschatz to Iron Heart.' Shaw spoke up from his side of the fire. 'I thought, myself, it mighta had somethin' to do with the AFC tryin' to push Congress into sendin' troops to take Oregon ... an' like the young fool he was, I think Johnny just up an' asked Bodenschatz about it, an' he was found dead not long later. Only when the Beauty up an' died, after drinkin' the last of the liquor they'd found in the old man's coat, did we start to put together that there was different game afoot. Worse game.'

'You still have those letters from Boden to his father?'

'They were in my hand when the Omahas attacked us on the quarantine island,' said Hannibal. 'Even had I had the chance to get my hand to my coat before running for our lives, they wouldn't have survived the river. And if they *had* survived, I'd have eaten them the following day.'

'An' you had no idea Frank Boden – or Franz Bodenschatz – would be posin' as a Mexican trader here?'

'We knew he'd be here,' said January. 'The only man who could have recognized him for sure – er – died the first day we were in camp...'

'And I'm not entirely certain,' added Hannibal, 'that I'd recognize Jim Bridger or Robbie Prideaux, if you scrubbed and clipped them. For that matter, Mr Goodpastor – and I hope you'll forgive my making the inevitable inferences – it sounds as if there are men at the rendezvous who should have known the body we found wasn't you.'

'Make all the inevitable inferences you please.' Goodpastor plucked another rib from the fire, tore the meat from it with strong white teeth. 'They'd have known quick enough the old man you found wasn't Medicine Lynx – which was the name I went by when I was living with the Mandans in '09. When I was trapping down around Taos later on, I still went by El Lince. Carson and Bridger and a dozen of those boys *would* have known me, if they'd seen me face to face. I only started using my right name again when I went back to Missouri and met Mrs Goodpastor – Miss Milliken that was – and got into politics. But Grey sure as hell knows me. How bad was the old man tore up when he was found?'

'Bad enough,' said January, and Manitou – silent on the other side of the fire – looked away.

323

'But obviously Bodenschatz knew *you.*' Hannibal turned to the trapper.

'I'm hard to miss.'

Particularly, reflected January, surveying that bear-like hulk, if a man of such massive size had a reputation for ungovernable, murderous rage. Once Franz Bodenschatz had reached the frontier, rumor of his quarry would not have been hard to find.

Manitou frowned into the fire. 'And he'd seen me in the court. I musta seen him when he spoke to the judges against me, but them weeks gets confused in my mind. An' he was bearded at Fort Ivy. Nobody ever called him nuthin' but Frank in my hearin' – an' now I think on it, I'm not sure I ever saw him in full daylight.'

His heavy eyebrows drew down, trying to call back recollections of chance meetings, years ago, in that dark little store. 'Give me a hell of a turn, to see old Herr Bodenschatz's face in the lantern light. Near to cost me my life, too, for I slacked my grip on him and he got his second pistol out. I figured he'd come up with Franz, but it wasn't 'til you told me, Frank at Fort Ivy's name was Boden, that I knew how they'd found me.'

Outside, the camp had grown quiet. Somewhere, a woman sang to her children; elsewhere, a dog barked, the irritable yip of confrontation with some insignificant beast. January wondered if he'd be able to call all of this back to mind, to write it down for Rose – smiled at the thought of her envious lamentations: *you actually stayed in an Indian encampment...!*

And thought of Veinte-y-Cinco, close enough to the rendezvous to deceive herself that she could escape from her guards, swim the river, find her daughter...

And who could blame her? January closed his eyes: *Mary, Mother of God, watch over her, who is trying to be the best mother she can be...*

Much later in the night, he was waked from a light sleep by the sound of scuffling and whispering, close to the wall of the tipi. He thrust up the lower edge of the lodge skins and in the starlight he saw, a few yards away, Franz Bodenschatz struggling silently in the grip of two warriors, a knife in his hand. 'Is this how you treat your brother,' the German whispered furiously, 'who did all he could to help you avenge your people?'

The Indian – a young Omaha warrior whom January did not recognize – replied, 'My people are not avenged, and a man who seeks to do that which will cause the Crow to kill us all is not my brother. Come back and sleep. If the lies of the white men trap them tomorrow, the Crow will kill them, and you will be avenged.'

'Their lies will poison the minds of the Crow, as they have begun to poison *your* mind, Kills With A Rock. Else you would let me do what I have sought now for ten years to do. And as for sleeping, there is no sleep, when my goal lies so near to my hand.'

Not long after noon on the following day January heard the camp-dogs barking, and he emerged from the lodge to see everyone hurrying

325

toward the ford. He and his fellow prisoners followed the Crow to the river's edge, in time to see the five horses come down to the opposite bank, with the sharp sun dappling them through the pine boughs as they crossed. With Dark Antlers and the two Crow rode Veinte-y-Cinco, in her torn and ragged red-and-green finery, and beside her, in matronly calico and a sunbonnet, Moccasin Woman, with a battered leather camp-chest lashed to the back of her saddle.

January whispered a prayer of thanks, and another one requesting that he'd be able to convince Walks Before – and Iron Heart – that what he suspected was true.

Warriors, women, children surrounded the five horses, so closely that none of the prisoners could push their way close, but over the dark heads of the crowd, January saw Veinte-y-Cinco's eyes seek him, then Hannibal, then Shaw. He smiled at her and raised his hand.

Walks Before Sunrise and his son, the warrior Lost, were sitting on a blanket before the old shaman's lodge when the little cavalcade approached. He got to his feet, and the Indians made way for him to approach the horses. In the crowd January picked out Iron Heart, and Bodenschatz, in the center of the Omaha warriors. Bodenschatz saw him, and for a moment their eyes met, a look of such hatred and spite in the other man's that January was taken aback.

I'm only here as Shaw's henchman...

To Bodenschatz, he realized, it was all the same. *He who is not for me is against me...*

He saw the German's face when Bodenschatz

saw the luggage tied on Moccasin Woman's saddle and felt his own twinge of spite at Bodenschatz's horror. Spite and triumph.

It's in there...

He suddenly felt much better.

Walks Before held out his hands. 'You are Moccasin Woman?'

'I am.' She kicked her feet free of the stirrups, slid to the ground and shook out her faded skirts.

'And have you brought the clothing of the old white man whom you found dead in the woods, two nights after the new moon?'

'I have.' She touched the quillwork bag that hung at her side. Her broad, brown face was sad but peaceful. 'I asked his forgiveness of him, for taking it away, and did what I could to honor him. Yet I am a poor woman, and even the smallest pieces of cloth can be turned to good account, in repairing clothing.'

Walks Before Sunrise turned to January, motioned for him to step forward and speak.

Bridger and Prideaux, and every trapper to whom January had spoken, had said the same thing of the peoples of the plains and the mountains: that they valued speech-making as a form of honor and would follow explanations and tales with avid interest, the length of them and the shape of them a compliment to the listeners. He took a deep breath, and turned to Iron Heart.

'When your warriors surprised Tall Chief and the Beauty, at the place where they were burying the dead in Dry Grass Coulee, did one of them take the black coat that lay in that place?' He knew the answer was yes because he'd already

327

seen the coat on one of the Omaha warriors, a bizarre sartorial effect in combination with the young man's leggings and breech cloth. Iron Heart signed the warrior forward, and January motioned for him to turn around before the Crow shaman, to show the knife hole in the back of the coat.

'And when you attacked us on the island near the camp,' January went on, 'and killed the young trapper who was with us, did you also take his clothing?' This question also was rhetorical. No Indian in creation would pass up a black silk waistcoat, and in fact he'd seen Boaz Frye's yellow calico shirt on one of the warriors, and thought he'd glimpsed the black satin vest on someone else ... Which indeed proved to be the case.

But the question was asked in the proper form, and there was a murmur of approval from the assembled tribe.

'Listen, now.' He turned again to Walks Before Sunrise and raised his voice to carry, his gestures taking in all the tribe gathered around, as if he were telling a story to Olympe's children. 'And I will tell you all that took place beside Horse Creek, on the night of the rain just after the moon was new.'

'He lies!' shouted Bodenschatz. 'He is lying to save his own skin, and that of his murdering friend!'

Iron Heart glanced sidelong at him, expressionless. 'Let the black white man speak.'

'Is it true what you told me, Iron Heart,' said January, 'that the old medicine-man, Boden's father, left the lodges of the Omaha on the day that I fought with Manitou, with a bottle of poisoned liquor in his pocket? That he sought to poison Manitou the Spirit Bear in his own camp, because he had decided he did not wish to kill all the men at the rendezvous?'

'It was because he saw the child,' replied Iron Heart. 'The little Mexican girl who played cards at the liquor tent. She was out in the meadows near our camp that day, looking for feathers in the long grass. The old man said that he accepted that the women would die, who were harlots and had come here of their own accord to lie with men for money. But the child was innocent, he said.'

January reflected that Klaus Bodenschatz had obviously never seen Pia dealing faro, but let that pass. Across the open ground, he saw Veinte-y-Cinco silently take Hannibal's hand.

'He and I quarreled over this,' Iron Heart went on. 'It had been agreed that Boden would poison the liquor and give it away after the fight, but there was no victory. Men came back to the camp and told the old man of this, and also that Manitou had returned in anger to his own camp. When I came back to the tents of my people, the old man was already gone.'

'And you, Manitou.' January turned to the trapper, standing huge and silent among the warriors of the Crow. 'Did you meet the old man in the woods near your camp?'

'I saw the light of his lantern.' Manitou, also, had learned what the nations of the plains considered the honorable way of speaking. 'I had

329

not known the man Boden in the camp, but his father I knew. The old man was the father of a woman that I loved, a woman I killed in a fit of madness, many years ago. He fired a pistol at me from hiding. I had my rifle, but I did not want to kill him. He had a second pistol, and in the struggle to get it from him I hurt him – broke his ribs, and broke his leg. I was angry already from fighting Winter Moon –' he nodded toward January – 'and I could see the fire of my madness beginning to flicker at the sides of my eyes. Still I remained long enough to tie up the old man's wounds. I tore up the shirt he wore, to brace his ribs and to bandage my own arm where his first bullet had struck me. I used his neck cloth, and strips torn from my own shirt, to put a splint on his broken leg. Then I made a shelter for him, knowing it would rain again, and built a fire to keep him safe from animals. I knew his son must be nearby and would search for him before long. I put my own shirt on him to keep him warm, and over it his waistcoat and coat again. Then I went to the camp of the Blackfeet. My brother Silent Wolf knows the ways to take the thunder spirit out of my brain, before I harm those around me. I was in their camp—' He frowned, trying to remember.

'Two nights. Then Tall Chief and Winter Moon came – Bo Frye, too, and the Beauty. They told me that old Bodenschatz had been found dead. I returned to my own camp and left the rendez-vous.'

'So when you left the old man,' reiterated January, 'he was wearing your shirt – was this

330

the shirt you had bought from Ivy and Wallach the day before?'

'It was. Black and yellow checks, cotton. Of good quality.'

'And his own shirt was torn up for bandages around his ribs?'

Manitou nodded.

'What was that shirt made of? What color was it?'

'White,' said the trapper immediately. 'Linen—'

'Like the one his son now wears?'

All eyes went to Boden, who snapped, 'This is all lies!' He turned to Iron Heart, caught him by the arm. 'This man talks nonsense, about what color our shirts are and who wears what. What does it matter? He will say anything—'

'And I will listen to anything,' replied the Omaha chief, his voice deadly quiet. 'The truth leaves its tracks, like a fox in the snow, for a wise man to follow. Be silent.'

Boden started to reply, then looked around him, at the warriors who had moved in closer.

'Moccasin Woman?'

Still with her air of serene sadness, the matriarch opened her quillwork pouch and brought out a bundle of cloth. The garments had been washed of their bloodstains, leaving only pale brown ghosts, and the hole in the back of the checked shirt had been neatly mended. Its torn-off hems had been sewn back as well – she must have found those in the bushes around the camp, where Poco had thrown them and the black silk cravat when he'd untied the splints. There

331

wasn't a man among the warriors – hunters and trackers from birth – who hadn't been brought up making inferences from such details, putting together evidence in order to survive.

January summoned back the two Omaha warriors who wore the old-fashioned black coat and the satin vest with its outdated collar, and he held the black-and-yellow shirt up first to one, and then the other. Walks Before rose from his blanket and studied the holes, which matched one another exactly. Then January handed him the last garment, the torn-up sections of the white linen shirt.

The seams had been ripped apart, and one sleeve was missing—

'I got that here.' Manitou slipped his left arm free of his deer-hide hunting-shirt, to show the filthy, bloodied white linen that bound the bullet wound in his own arm. 'You can see the cloth's the same.'

The back of old Klaus Bodenschatz's white linen shirt was intact.

'He was stabbed, then, *after* Manitou's black-and-yellow shirt was put on him,' said Walks Before Sunrise, holding the two garments in his hands. 'There was a great bleeding here, more than he would have bled had his throat been cut earlier ... And indeed, if his throat had been cut first, what need to stab him in the back? What have you to say to this, Boden?'

'That he's lying,' argued Boden frantically. 'That that lying monster came back and stabbed him later—'

'Why would he have done that?' asked Walks

Before reasonably. 'The old man's leg was broken. He was no danger to Manitou then. Why not kill him the first time, rather than build a shelter for him and bind his wounds?'

January folded his arms, looked steadily at Bodenschatz where he stood among the Omahas. 'But that broken leg meant that your father was now a liability to *you*,' he said softly. 'You knew where your enemy was – and you knew that, having seen your father, he would flee. Yet you couldn't pursue him as long as you had to care for the old man. You'd have to take your father back to the settlements. Certainly, your Omaha brothers weren't going to do it—'

'I – I knew nothing of it,' Bodenschatz stammered. 'I didn't know he was dead until they brought him into the camp—'

'But it was your hat that one of the camp whores found beside the body later that morning,' said January. 'With your hair in it, dyed black except for the brown at the roots—'

Sharply, the young Omaha Kills With A Rock put in, 'He renewed the false color on his hair the day he left our lodges, to ride into the white men's camp as a trader! It was, as you say, brown as a raccoon's fur where it grew from his head, to the length of a child's knuckle.'

'And the old man's pistols were in your pockets yesterday. None were found on the body by the men who took his coat. Yet he'd shot Manitou with one of them, and the other had fired, putting a bullet into a tree, so he had them that night. And as well as all that, Boden,' added January grimly, *'no one else had any reason to kill him*. He was harmless, he was crippled, he was in a foreign land. He needed help, that only his son could give him—'

'He would never have asked me to give up my revenge!' shouted Boden. 'He was as vowed to it as I!'

'Maybe he mighta changed his mind,' put in Shaw softly, 'whilst lyin' there listenin' to the rain? Let's see what's in that camp chest, Maestro—'

Boden moved like a snake striking, snatched the knife from the warrior nearest him and slashed the man, plunged for the momentary gap in the group around him. There was a vicious struggle that ended with the trader being thrust back into the open space before the lodges, two Omaha warriors now holding grimly on to his arms. Boden gasped for breath, his face terrible to see as January unbuckled the straps on the luggage, took out the trapper's spare shirts and trousers, socks and drawers – and from beneath them, folded into a tight bundle, a short jacket of cinnabar-colored rawhide, like a vaquero's, of the sort that many of the Mexican traders wore for rough work on the trail. Then another shirt – like all of them, white linen and much worn. Jacket and shirt, front and sleeves, were stained and crusted with dried blood.

'You couldn't throw them away,' went on January, 'because they'd be found. Nor could you wash them without causing comment – not in the middle of the rendezvous camp. Nor have them washed, because someone would talk. You killed him, and you left him—'

'What's the matter with you?' Boden's voice was almost a scream. 'Don't you understand what that monster *did*? Are you actually going to let him *go*? We vowed, my father and I, that neither of us would rest until that man was dead. Before ever we started, he said that I must not permit *anything* to stop me—'

'Then why did you need to stab him in the back,' asked January quietly, 'before you cut his throat?'

Iron Heart stepped from among his warriors, stood before Boden in the open ground before the tipis. 'You disgust me,' he said in a level voice, and his pockmarked face was as cold as his words. 'At Fort Ivy you said that you were one of us in your heart, that you were our brother. In my own hunger for vengeance I listened. Yet I see that you are a white man after all, who will let nothing stand in the way of what he craves. To avenge yourself is the act of a man. To bring your father far from his home to help you – and he came, willingly, because it was his son who called, leaving all that he knew – and then to kill him rather than burden yourself with his care ... This is dishonor. Such a person is not my brother.'

He turned to Shaw, and taking his scalping knife from his belt, held it out to him. 'And for this dishonor, twenty of my friends have died, killed by the Crow, or by you, Tall Chief. They thought they were fighting for a brother, whose honor equaled theirs. He has shamed them and dirtied even their deaths. He is yours.'

With an incoherent shriek, Bodenschatz flung

335

himself against the grip of his captors, kicking and thrashing like a horse at the breaker's. Iron Heart stood aside as the men dragged Bodenschatz to Shaw and pushed him to his knees.

'You have won.' The Omaha chief stood facing Shaw, with the prisoner between them. 'Even our vengeance is denied to us, that this man and his father promised us on the banks of the Rawhide Creek. We will have our vengeance,' he went on, 'those of us that are left. Yet we will have it without the help of those against whom we would take it. My friends died, because I believed a white man would help me against white enemies. You do not keep warm at night by sharing your blanket with a wolf. Take your vengeance on him, Tall Chief. He is not my brother.'

Shaw stood for a time, like an Indian himself, the scalping knife in his hand. *Seeing his brother*? January wondered. Seeing the twelve-year-old boy, wild to go downriver on a flatboat and see New Orleans...? Seeing the child who had learned, with horror and shock, that he had no home to go back to? That the only people he could rely on in the world were his brothers?

Seeing Tom in the firelight of Fort Ivy, long fingers stroking the pale silky scalp that he held in his hand?

Or seeing the hills that had been his home, where you had to bar the doors of your cabin at night, because your cousins had killed the son of the clan in the next holler, and if they couldn't catch your cousins they might just come after you or your wife? The world he didn't want to

336

bring up his children in?

I walked away...

With a sigh, the Kentuckian flung the knife down, so that its blade stuck in the dirt between Bodenschatz's knees. To Asa Goodpastor he said, 'You stayin' in the mountains when the rendezvous breaks? Or headin' back to the settlements? Can you notarize affidavits, so's Boden here can be tried for what he done, an' hanged in form of law for murder by poison an' by knife? I'd say we got evidence enough.'

'That you do,' agreed Goodpastor, and he stroked his white mustache. 'An' yes, I'm ridin' back to Missouri. An' I'll make your case for you, if you manage to get this weasel back there. But you'll have your work cut out for you, keepin' guard over him—'

'He'll come,' rumbled Manitou. 'For I'll ride with you and stand my trial as well. That's what you want, isn't it, Franz? You won't pass up the chance to take the witness stand against me a second time, will you?'

'For that pleasure, monster,' whispered Boden, 'I will happily face the gallows myself.'

TWENTY-EIGHT

In the Ivy and Wallach camp on the banks of the Green late that night – after a ride of some twelve miles over the hills back to the rendezvous – Shaw, Hannibal and January unpacked the rest of Franz Bodenschatz's camp chest.

The rendezvous was breaking up. Some of the men would continue to camp along the Green for another week or two, but the high summer was passing. The weather would be bitter by the time McLeod and his traders got back to the headwaters of the Columbia, and snow would fly before some of the independents found the high valleys where there were sufficient beaver to justify a winter camp.

The Indians were leaving, too. 'It is time for the Fall buffalo-hunt,' Morning Star said, when she'd embraced Hannibal, Shaw and January in turn as they'd dismounted before her lodge in the twilight. 'I'm so glad you returned before our departure.' She kissed Hannibal again, with the warm affection of a wife of years' standing, and added, 'And that you were not killed, of course. Will you hold one more feast for my brothers, Sun Mouse, before we leave?'

'With all the pleasure in the world, beautiful lady.'

Even Gil Wallach, who came from his own tent with exclamations of joy and relief at the travelers' return, didn't object.

When they went into the lodge, January could see that Morning Star was already packed to go. Her small cooking gear was bundled up, her drying racks disassembled and tied together. She had, to January's great astonishment, thought to steal one of the packets stored in Klaus Bodenschatz's lodge in the Omaha camp before she'd burned it, which made things a great deal easier when the camp's chief citizens came calling. Even as Morning Star and Pia were making supper – the girl had run all the way from Seaholly's, but had not, January was later informed, neglected to set a guard on her faro table – Titus, McLeod, Stewart, Bridger and Tom Fitzpatrick came up the trail.

They listened unmoved to Franz Bodenschatz's furious counter-accusations against Manitou and Shaw, then viewed the dead man's assembled garments with the watchful intelligence of men – like the Crow warriors – whose lives depended on inference from small details. Bridger and Fitzpatrick were in favor of rough justice then and there, and it took all of Shaw's arguments to convince them to let the man be taken back to Missouri for trial. In this, Stewart, McLeod and Titus seconded him: the former two out of an innate sense of law, the latter because Shaw took him quietly behind the tipi and threatened to reveal who had hired Walks Before Sunrise and his band of Crow to ambush stragglers on their way back to the mountains.

'Can you prove it?' Titus asked narrowly. 'About Morales – Bodenschatz, I mean.' He glowered at Shaw in the distant light of the supper fire. 'That nonsense about the Company paying the Crow to cause trouble is pure fantasy.'

'Well, I thought as much,' assented Shaw mildly. 'So'd Mr Goodpastor – who's ridin' the first day or two back to the Yellowstone country with 'em.'

January – who'd followed the Lieutenant and Titus back behind the lodge for this conversation – wondered if the words that Edwin Titus so violently bit back at that point had anything to do with the barrels of AFC gunpowder and the thirty AFC rifles for which he would now receive nothing. But Titus hadn't risen to his present position with the Company by saying what was in his mind.

'I think we have more than enough evidence to hang Bodenschatz when we get to Missouri,' January interpolated comfortably. 'Was anything taken from his tent, sir, while he was away?'

The end of Titus's cigar glowed momentarily, a gold eye in the darkness. 'When he headed out of here two nights ago – that'd be, I guess, when he got word you and Sefton had been took by the Omahas – he paid a couple of my boys to keep an eye on his stores. Doesn't look like that stopped Moccasin Woman from walking into his tent, though. You can have a look through the place tomorrow. I'll square Bridger and Fitz, to keep this quiet.'

When supper was done, and Robbie Prideaux

set to guard Bodenschatz, the three companions retreated to the lodge to go through the camp chest for whatever else of interest it might contain.

'This should probably do it.' Hannibal thumbed through the thin packet of letters he'd taken from the back of one of Bodenschatz's ledgers. 'I'll need to go over them more carefully–Manitou,' he added, as the big trapper ducked in through the doorway of the lodge, '–can you still read enough Bavarian to translate? But it looks like old Klaus wasn't any too happy with Franz's scheme even before he saw little Pia playing in the meadow with flowers in her hair. *Is there no other bargain which can be struck?* he asks here – dated December of last year, just before he leaves Ingolstadt. And here: *my heart goes out to these unfortunate savages, yet their vengeance is no affair of ours*. But in the next sentence he says he can bring about thirty pounds of powdered castor-bean – I suppose that's why Franz kept this particular letter – and that it should be enough to poison everyone in the camp ten times over. *It is the price that must be paid.*'

'*It is the price that must be paid*,' echoed January wonderingly. 'Just like that. Hand over poison to kill six or seven hundred men...'

Manitou settled cross-legged by the fire, turned the papers over in his huge hands. 'He was a good man,' he said softly. 'He hired me, that Mina might become a doctor ... There wasn't a malicious bone in the whole of his body. Don't know how many times I played

341

cards with him...' He shook his head, rubbed his forehead as if trying to clear away some shadow from his eyes. 'I thought he'd be my father-in-law.' And his hand went, almost without the appearance of conscious thought, to knead his left arm, where the old man's bullet had plowed through the flesh. 'Thing is ... I don't feel this evil in me. I don't think that I ever *would* do such a thing ... except that I know I *did*.'

Hannibal said, *'But yet I could accuse me of such things that it were better that my mother had not borne me* ... I don't suppose he thought he'd turn poisoner, either, if you'd asked him fifteen years ago.'

'If I could do that,' the trapper went on. 'Could turn him from the man he was into someone who'd make a bargain like that – maybe it's just as well that I *do* hang.'

'You already had one trial.' Shaw folded his long arms around his knees. 'Or, at least, one set of judges declared it weren't your fault.'

'An' sent me to a madhouse,' replied Manitou. 'I think I'd rather hang than go to another.'

'What was Franz like in those days?' January lifted from the bottom of the chest an octavo volume of Shakespeare in translation – *Hamlet, Lear, Othello* and *Macbeth* – and another of *The Sorrows of Young Werther*. 'His sister must have spoken of him.'

'She didn't, much.' Manitou's single bar of brow furrowed at old memories. 'She'd laugh at the letters he'd write her every day – joked that his wife Katerina would get jealous. Their pa said he once beat up a local boy that courted her—'

He broke off as January lifted from the very bottom of the box, where they'd been beneath the books, a pair of women's gloves – faded pink – and, creased and folded, a batiste chemise embroidered with lilies, white upon white. 'Them was Mina's,' he whispered.

'Were they, indeed?' With them was a locket, such as old Klaus had worn in his waistcoat pocket. The picture inside wasn't as accurate, but idealized and ethereal. January guessed it had been done after her death. It also contained a lock of her hair.

'She said he was jealous,' murmured Manitou after a time, and he turned the glove over in clumsy fingers hardened by pack ropes and trap springs. 'Jealous of me. Jealous of her love.' He looked aside. ''Bout time I went back, I guess. Let him have his say in a court of law. 'Cause I sure can't say the right an' the wrong of it.'

'No.' Shaw shook his head and sat considering the face of the girl in the locket and the chemise that her brother had saved. Had brought to the New World with him, when he had carried pictures of neither his children nor his wife. The Kentuckian's thin, ugly face looked tired, with a haggardness it hadn't shown during pursuit through the wilderness, or wading icy torrents, or as a prisoner in the camp of vengeful savages, and there was a sadness in his eyes. As if, January thought, this whole thing were just one of the cases he solved in New Orleans, the fox tracks of grief and sin and rage that he'd only stumbled across in pursuit of his calling. 'No, I ain't sure as how anyone can.'

In the afternoon, as January was helping Morning Star butcher out an elk for that night's feast, Veinte-y-Cinco came to the camp to bid the Indian woman goodby. 'You go back Taos?' Morning Star asked, in the rather shaky English that Hannibal had been teaching her, and Veinte-y-Cinco nodded.

'Hell, Mick and I know one another,' she sighed. 'I don't give him trouble when he drinks, and he don't give me trouble when I don't.' She held out to the younger woman a necklace strung with silver coins and a silver cross. 'I want you to have this, *corazón*.'

'You can come to New Orleans with us,' offered Hannibal as his bride joyfully put on the new ornament and kissed everyone in sight. January suspected, by the wistful note in his voice, that the fiddler would miss his Sioux wife very much, despite the fact that both knew that neither could survive in the other's world. 'I don't think Shaw would mind an extra rider.'

Veinte-y-Cinco smiled and laid her thin palm to his cheek. 'That's sweet of you, Sun Mouse. But I know Taos. And what would an old whore like me do in New Orleans, up against so many that're pretty and young? But if it's true Mr Shaw wouldn't mind another rider—' She glanced, a little shyly, toward the store tent, where Shaw was helping Gil Wallach pack and count the unsold goods, and then back at January. 'Would you take Pia? She's got nothing waiting

344

for her in Taos but what I've got. Last year I almost sent her off with those missionaries that came through here, but she was so young then ... I thought I could keep her another few years. But after what happened with that bastard skunk Titus ... Would you take her? Take her and see to it she gets work with a good family, who'll look after her? The world is hard,' she finished softly.

'My wife'll look after her,' promised January. 'After you fetched Moccasin Woman to the Crow camp – when you very well might have run off and left us – we owe you that and as much more as you care to ask.'

That night the whole of the Ogallala village came to the feast – joined by large numbers of Delaware, Crow, Shoshone, and also by Asa Goodpastor, who'd ridden into camp that afternoon. 'First time I've had a banquet to celebrate a divorce,' Hannibal remarked, incongruous in his much-battered frock-coat with feathers braided into his long hair. 'Something I should do more often.' But January guessed, as the liquor went around, that the fiddler would have liked to get drunk, to forget that he was leaving her. He played instead, as stories said Compair Lapin had played, calling the stars down out of the sky and the Devil up from Hell: Irish airs and Mozart dances, sweet wild tunes that seemed to flow upward into the Milky Way, all that he could give this girl in farewell.

In the morning, before the mist was off the river, the tribes were gone.

Hannibal spoke little through the day as the Ivy and Wallach men broke their camp. He

345

seemed anxious and nervous, as he had when first he'd ceased taking opium, but the mundane work of packing seemed to steady him. Robbie Prideaux and his partners brought Franz Bodenschatz with them and left him tied to a tree while they assisted. 'You're taking a chance with that one,' warned Goodpastor quietly as he took January aside.

The German sat on the ground by his tree reading Goethe – silent and as contemptuous of the men around him, as Tom Shaw said he had been at Fort Ivy ... but every time January looked at him, he felt the hair lift on his nape.

Although Shaw was helping Gil Wallach pack furs, January noticed that the Kentuckian never got where he couldn't see his prisoner, and never let his rifle out of instant reach of his hand. He had stayed awake guarding Bodenschatz for two nights now. January guessed he was expecting something, too.

'Any suggestions?'

'Hell.' Goodpastor grinned crookedly. 'If I knew what he was planning to try I wouldn't be twitchy.' His bright-blue eyes went from Shaw back to Bodenschatz, who after his bitter imprecations and curses thrown at Titus and McLeod that first night, had said little to anyone. 'It's six weeks back to the settlements. Tall Chief's gotta sleep sometime.'

'I'll do what I can.' Though January guessed that writing was something of a labor to Shaw, he knew that the man had patiently prepared a stack of affidavits – from Poco, Moccasin Woman (under her English name, with no mention of her race), Morning Star, Hannibal and everyone else he could find – as to the circumstances of the deaths of Klaus Bodenschatz, Clemantius Groot, Goshen Clarke and the Dutchman's three camp-setters, and had gotten Goodpastor to sign and notarize them.

He hoped this would be enough for Tom Shaw.

'And you watch out, especially for that little girl.' Pia and her mother waved to them as they came up the path from the AFC camp, where tents were being struck also: furs weighed, plewsticks tallied. Pia, too, had been quiet all day, and it crossed January's mind to wonder if Johnny Shaw was the only child to dream about running away with the Indians. Today she looked very grown-up, in her red vest and a new skirt, with one of Morning Star's beaded necklaces around her throat.

'Don't you let her get anywheres near him,' said Goodpastor quietly.

'I won't.' January's instincts told him that whoever else Shaw might sacrifice, to bring his brother's killer to justice, a threat to the child would render him helpless.

Bodenschatz would know that, too.

But on the following morning, when the Ivy and Wallach train was preparing to leave, Pia couldn't be found. Shaw had sat awake a third night guarding Bodenschatz, and he attested that the girl had had no contact with the prisoner. She'd come back to the camp past midnight with Hannibal, after doing a land-office business on her final evening dealing faro in front of Seaholly's.

347

'Scarcely surprising, considering the number of eleventh-hour customers waiting in line,' added the fiddler, who had spent the evening alternately playing chess with Sir William Stewart and making music for men who would hear nothing for the next eleven months but wolves howling and the chants of Indians. 'I understand she and Jed Blankenship, working in concert, took three hundred dollars off John McLeod at vingt-et-un.'

The child had slept close to the fire, near Hannibal and Manitou. Her blankets, folded neatly, had been there when Manitou had woken at the first whisper of light.

'What do you expect?' said Bodenschatz, when he heard of the matter. 'The girl is a whore.'

Hannibal and Prideaux went out to search the camp, while the rest of the party loaded the mules. 'We can't wait long, if she ain't found,' warned Goodpastor. 'I'd search that skunk Titus's tent, myself—'

'Given that McLeod's watchin' like a hawk for somethin' to cause the Company grief,' Shaw said, returning from a careful inspection of the ground all around the campsite, 'I *think* he'd be too smart to try anythin', though there's no sayin'. Anyways,' he added grimly, 'by the sign it looks like she walked away from the camp alone.'

It was Hannibal who brought the news, hastening back down the path from the Hudson's Bay compound. 'A couple of McLeod's engagés saw her leaving camp at first light,' he said, pressing his hand to his side. 'With Jed Blanken-ship.'

Into the stunned silence which followed, January said, *Blankenship?*'

And tied to his tree, the prisoner sat down and laughed uproariously at the consternation in his jailer's voice.

'She kept company with him, Prideaux says, while her mother was away.' Hannibal sat on one of the rocks that surrounded what was left of the fire pit. 'And with Edwin Titus, evidently. The men who saw her leave say she was laughing with Blankenship; riding one of his horses, and making jokes with his engagés. It doesn't sound as if she was forced.'

'She's thirteen—'

Hannibal only looked up at him with weary eyes. They both knew whores in New Orleans younger than that.

'Hell, I was thirteen when I left the settle-ments,' said Prideaux, with a trace of sadness in his voice. 'I joined Fitzpatrick's brigade to go trap on the Popo Agie. An' for the same reason. There wasn't nobody much lookin' after me. An' it looked like a whale of a lot of fun.'

Nevertheless, Gil Wallach and – to his enormous and unexpected credit – Mick Seaholly delayed their departures from the much-trampled valley of the Green River for another forty-eight hours, while Prideaux, Manitou, Shaw and Asa Good-pastor scoured the hills, trying to pick Blanken-ship's trail out of the mazes of departing hoof-prints of independents, the early-leaving Hud-

349

son's Bay trappers and the numerous Indian villages heading north and east and south on the autumn hunts. January and Hannibal spent most of the two days either guarding Franz Bodenschatz – who seemed glumly disinterested in anything other than how badly the world had treated him – or comforting Veinte-y-Cinco.

'The girl was a whore,' was all Bodenschatz would say. 'You could see it in her eyes. Why all the world weeps over a brat like that and lets the murderer of my beautiful sister go free...'

All he had asked for was his books – which he read and reread – and Mina's gloves, portrait and chemise. These he kept inside his clothing, next to his skin, and turned in smouldering disgust from January's attempts to draw him into speech.

Through most of the first day, Veinte-y-Cinco cried, on and off, and talked incessantly of her daughter. Again, to January's surprise, Mick Seaholly proved to be a patient listener – in-between working the bar – and doled out to her the hard comfort that: 'It ain't like she's turnin' her back on finishing school and engagement to some nice boy from Philadelphia, *acushla*.'

'I wanted something better for her,' the woman whispered, huddled against January's side in one of the makeshift crib-tents that had been temporarily reset, this one apart from the others. Even the most loutish of the trappers kept their distance.

January met the barkeep's wide, heaven-blue glance over her head.

'We all want somethin' better for other people,'

350

said Seaholly dispassionately. 'But they go right on ahead and make their own mistakes, just like we do.'

By the second night, when the searchers returned with word that they hadn't been able to pick out Blankenship's tracks from the hundreds in all directions that they were mixed with, Luz Veinte-y-Cinco was able to thank them, and to let her daughter go.

It was four weeks down from the mountains, through the gap in the ranges called the South Pass, and across mile upon mile, day upon day, of arid scrubland to Fort Ivy. All the way, January was oppressed by a vague sense of failure and defeat. 'What would have given you a sense of success?' inquired Hannibal, when he spoke of it one night when they both had guard duty. 'Shooting Bodenschatz from behind a tree? Your success is that you'll come home.'

'With another two hundred dollars,' added January, trying to speak lightly. Trying not to think of what he'd seen daily in his heart: the house on Rue Esplanade closed up when he reached it, the frantic canvassing of neighbors. Seeing in his fears how their eyes would avoid meeting his: *shall you tell him or shall I?* *Rose...*

Even on better days, he knew that Hannibal was absolutely right. The two hundred dollars barely mattered.

His success was that he'd come home.

And Rose would be ripe with their unborn child.

Virgin Mary Mother of God, he prayed to the desert stars, *let it be so*. It had been five months since he'd seen either her or a single line of her handwriting ... *Let it be so.*

The desert stars made no reply.

Sitting on guard at the edge of the camp, his rifle in his hand, looking out across the silvery darkness of sagebrush and bunch grass for some break in the patterns of what he knew to be safe – jackrabbits, foxes, prairie dogs, kangaroo rats – he realized he would miss this open silence, this thin, free air. Far off he could still see the white peaks of the Wind River Mountains, glittering in the starlight: the Green River in which he'd almost drowned, the dry coulees where he'd almost starved, where he'd fought for his life against the Omaha and the Crow...

He'd miss those, too. No wonder the mountain trappers stayed in the mountains.

It wasn't only beaver that they sought in those valleys that whispered with the voices of the pines.

Beside the fire, Manitou slept – *and dreamed of what*? The medieval streets of a German University town? Or the empty world where he was safe from the danger that the thunder spirit in him would awake?

By daylight the big trapper kept close to the train, as if to reassure – or remind – Bodenschatz that he, too, was going back to the United States to face justice for what he had done. But as they moved east and the endless pale-yellow miles stretched on, he became more and more uneasy. 'We should be seein' Indians by this time,' he said one evening, as the engagés were setting camp. 'This's the time of their Fall hunt. Plain should be crawlin' with 'em. I ain't even seen sign, have you?'

Both Shaw and Goodpastor shook their heads.

Shaw was quieter also as they put the miles behind them. He took his turn at scouting, but January could tell it bothered him to let Bodenschatz out of his sight, and most nights he would stay awake, watching him. Having risked his brother's anger for the sake of doing justice, January guessed, he lived with the dread that something would go wrong and leave him bereft of both justice and revenge. And if that happened – as he had once said to Manitou – he stood to lose not one brother, but two: all the family that remained to him in the world.

For his part, the prisoner had little to say for himself, and what little he did was mostly sarcasm: 'If to destroy me, I have made that beast take himself back to justice,' he remarked on one occasion, 'then I have accomplished my aim.' When he wasn't reading – and he scorned Hannibal's small volume of Shakespeare's comedies – he watched Manitou with glittering eyes. 'I will confess whatever you ask me to,' he said on another evening to Goodpastor. 'Just so that you bring him also to the scaffold and let me tell in open court the things that man has done.'

But January thought that as they went east, Shaw was bracing himself.

Tom Shaw met them at the gate of Fort Ivy, his narrow face dark with shock, anger and disbelief as he saw who rode in their train. 'What the *hell* you think you're doin', bringin' that piece of pig snot back with you?' he demanded, when Shaw dismounted and helped Bodenschatz from the saddle. He turned and struck Shaw open-handed across the face. 'Where the *hell* you think you are, brother? New Orleans? Goddam Philadelphia? You think *any* jury back in the States is gonna convict a man for shootin' another way the hell and gone out past the frontier?'

'I do, yes,' replied Shaw in his mild voice. 'I said I'd bring him to justice—'

'There ain't gonna be no justice for what he done to Johnny!' retorted Tom. 'You think twelve "good citizens" is gonna *care* about somethin' that happened out here? Like God Himself could even *find* twelve good men in Independence—'

'Been awhile since you been to Independence, sir,' Goodpastor broke in. 'It's settled some, and there's enough men there who'll convict a man, if not of killin' your brother, then of killin' his own father – which is what we got plenty of evidence for, an' affidavits, too. Not to speak of plottin' with the savages to murder every man in the rendezvous. Believe me, he'll hang.'

'You stay outta this.' Tom Shaw barely glanced at the older man. 'I don't give spit in a whirlwind about what-all else he done. This's blood. An' we was brought up – *I* was brought up – that blood wins out, over what twelve "good citizens" or the whole damn Constitution of the United States *might* say ... or might not. I was brought up not to take chances with your blood.'

He took the pistol from his belt, and Shaw

stepped between its barrel and Bodenschatz. Tom reached to thrust him out of the way, and Shaw, his face a careful blank, thrust back. 'We had enough murder here,' he said. 'Seven white men an' a woman, killed 'cause of another man's revenge, not to speak of a score of Indians who got dragged into it just through bein' there. It needs to stop.'

'No, brother,' said Tom quietly and lowered the pistol to his side. 'We's one death short.'

They camped outside Fort Ivy for two nights. Shaw and January divided their time in guarding Bodenschatz while Goodpastor and Hannibal negotiated for supplies. The engagés who'd traveled to the rendezvous with them were clearly troubled by the whole affair: *'En effet,'* said Clopard to Shaw, when he helped Manitou carry out sacks of flour and cornmeal to be loaded on to the mules, 'what does it matter, eh? It isn't like anybody will know, or come after you.'

'Nope,' agreed Shaw, and he shifted his rifle across his knees. 'It ain't.'

Tom Shaw never crossed the twenty yards of open ground that lay between the fort's gates and the camp, or as far as January could tell, even came as far as the gate. Gil Wallach spoke to each of the brothers once, about settling their affairs with one another: 'You think how long it is, from New Orleans out to here, Abe. You think of all that happens out here. You really want to risk never seein' your brother again, for the sake of justice to a stranger who so far as I can tell is

355

pretty much a murderin' weasel?'

Shaw leaned his head back against the thin trunk of the lodgepole pine by which he sat – one of the small clump of trees near the fort, where in other years the local Indians would have been camped by this time – and repeated: 'For the sake of justice. I have lived where there's no justice, Gil.' For a time he sat in silence, then added, 'An' I have lived where I had no brother. I'll think on what you say.'

But January guessed he wouldn't.

It was from Wallach, too, that January learned why they'd seen no hunting parties as they'd crossed the high plains back to the Fort: 'There's smallpox in the tribes, all up and down the river. It started among the Mandans at Fort Clark – there was a couple cases in the deck passengers on a steamboat that come through. Now there's ten, twenty a day dyin'. Blackfeet, Minnetarees, Arikara, Assiniboin ... they've all got it now. Whole villages wiped out, wolves an' rats eatin' the dead among the lodges.'

'Looks like our friend Iron Heart was a little ahead on his revenge,' said Manitou quietly.

Wallach bristled like a miffed porcupine. 'Well, it wasn't us that did it. Not the folks at the rendezvous, I mean, nor the trappers—'

'No,' sighed Manitou. 'It never is. Didn't mean to say it was.' He turned and walked away from the camp then, out on to the prairie: silent, open grassland that would never thereafter be the same. The tribes were dying. There weren't even buffalo to be seen. Only dry wind, and heat.

Bodenschatz called out angrily to January,

'You gonna let him just run off like that? You gonna let him get away, just 'cause he's a friend?'

'Oh, shut up,' said January, weary to his back teeth of vengeance and anger, hate and death. 'He isn't going anywhere.' He wondered if Morning Star and her family were still alive, or Silent Wolf and his Blackfeet, or Walks Before Sunrise...

And knew that there was not the slightest likelihood that he would ever find out.

Manitou was silent when the train moved out the next morning, on the worn trail down toward the distant Platte. The beaten trace snaked like a blonde ribbon, visible for miles in the brown distance and rutted now with the wheels of the big immigrant wagons. January was conscious that among the debris of the trading caravans along the ruts, there were objects that could only have been thrown out by those seeking Oregon land. A broken spinning-wheel, like the echoes of a woman's voice. A small trunk of books. Anything to lighten the load as the dry air shrank the wood of axles never designed for these high plains and the ox teams broke their sinews at labor...

'More of 'em this year,' remarked Goodpastor. 'Fleein' the bank crash, probably. Headin' for free land in Oregon.'

'And they took their journey from Elim,' quoted Hannibal, *'and all the congregation of the children of Israel came unto the wilderness* ... where God obligingly slaughtered everyone

357

they met for them.' It was the closest he came, in all that journey, to speaking of Morning Star.

'That's gonna sit well with the British.' Shaw edged his horse over beside the Indian Agent's, his pale eyes in their worn dark circles never leaving the sharply rolling land, the dry watercourses and the empty skylines. 'Get enough settlers in that territory, we ain't gonna need the American Fur Company startin' schemes with the Crow to get us into another war with England. Settlers'll do it every time.'

'An' now their king's dead –' this news had also been waiting for them at Fort Ivy – 'I doubt that little niece of his – what's her name?'

'Victoria.'

'I doubt that little gal's gonna go startin' any wars over fur.' Goodpastor shook his head. 'Independence'll be crawlin' with 'em.'

'Good.' On his led horse, his hands still tied to the saddle tree, Bodenschatz turned cold eyes on Manitou. 'That way it will need no testimony of mine to prove that the judgement against him in Germany was unjust, a fraud by the rich. You had best watch him, when he gets among civilized men. You who keep *me* bound, who keep watch on *me* with a rifle, as if I were some kind of dangerous criminal – you will see your mistake. He is the one who—'

The crack of the rifle seemed very small in the dry hugeness of the scrubland; like a firecracker, January thought, even as the prisoner's body arched backward with the impact, mouth popping open, eyes staring in shock at the sky. Shaw wheeled his horse at once, scanning the horizon

358

for dust while January flung himself from his saddle, caught Bodenschatz as he sagged sideways. The prisoner's wrists were still tied to the saddle, and by the time January had got them cut free Bodenschatz was dead. He heard Shaw say: 'That draw we passed—'

Hooves thundered away. An engagé brought a blanket. January laid Bodenschatz on it and opened his shirt. The bullet had struck him just behind the right armpit and gone through both lungs and the heart. The worn batiste chemise, the pink kid gloves, folded small into a packet beneath his shirt, against his skin, were soaked through with blood.

They came back to the camp at fall of night, having found no tracks. January could have told them they wouldn't. He guessed, from the angle of entry of the bullet, that in fact the killer had been elsewhere than the cover they'd suspected. 'Don't matter,' said Shaw quietly, when he helped January dig the trail-side grave. 'I know who done it.'

'You want to go back for him?' asked Manitou. Stripped for the work, his chest and arms showed in the firelight the horrific mazes of scars left by repeated torture, tracks of a pain that was his only salvation.

'An' do what?' Shaw's face was covered with dust, the straggly beard he'd grown on the trail thick with it, his eyes strange and light in the dark grime, like a bobcat's, except for the pain in them. 'Arrest him by an authority I ain't got, for a murder I can't prove, that no jury in the State of Missouri's gonna convict him of? They's only so much I can do,' he said, driving his shovel to break the hard knots of interlaced grass roots, 'an' I done it. Now let's put this sorry bastard to bed an' go home.'

Manitou Wildman rode with them for three more days, then disappeared one night, leaving not even tracks behind. January guessed he'd go back to seek out his brothers the Blackfeet, if any of them had survived the epidemic.

'Did it ever occur to you,' January asked Shaw on the following night, 'that it might have been Franz who killed Mina, and not Manitou at all?' He'd left the chemise and gloves inside Bodenschatz's shirt when they'd laid him in his shallow grave. The locket as well, which they'd offered to Manitou and which he had refused to touch. 'He loved his sister – passionately, it sounds like. Jealous men have done worse. And guilty men have gone to greater lengths, to absolve themselves of what they feel is another's fault.'

'That crossed my mind from the first.' Shaw stirred at the fire with a stick. January had shot a buffalo that afternoon: probably the last time he would do so, he guessed, before they reached Independence. They'd begun to find the droppings of corn-fed horses, and to see the signs of white hunters, with their large fires and boot prints in the earth.

His journal to Rose – which he'd kept every evening of the return journey – was overflowing with these observations, and with the remembrances of the men who'd taught him. *Please, Mother of God, let me put it into her living hand...*

'They's no way of provin' it,' Shaw went on. 'An' no point doin' so. We can only know so much, Maestro. Then we got to let it go. Like that old play Manitou spoke of: it's why we got to get twelve strangers to sit down an' say, *"This is how we settle it: it's done."* It's got to be taken out of our hands. If it ain't, it eats us alive.'

TWENTY-NINE

They reached New Orleans on the eighth of October, on a low river, well ahead of the winter rise. They traveled deck-passage from Independence, Shaw and Hannibal sleeping forward among the white ruffians and river rats surrounded by an assorted cargo of St Louis furs, travelers' trunks and sacks of corn from the Missouri farms. January bedded down among the few slaves and such free blacks as were on the river at that time of the year, on the narrow stern-deck near the paddle wheel. Every few hours he would wake and warily touch the money belt strapped around his waist beneath his clothes: Gil Wallach's payment of the final two hundred dollars in silver, which would be, January guessed, the salvation not only of himself and Rose, but also of his sister Olympe's

361

family too. As the *Deborah T.* began to pass familiar landmarks – the sharp bend at Bonnet Carré Point, the marshy pastures above the hamlet of Kennerville, the old oak on the levee at Twelve-Mile Point – January's frantic restlessness redoubled, the longing to hold Rose in his arms again battered by the conviction that he would return to find Rose dead of summer fever – of the smallpox – of the cholera. Three letters from her had waited for him at General Delivery in Independence, the most recent dated mid-August: she had said that there was fever in the city.

'Benjamin, there's *always* fever in the city in August,' Hannibal pointed out.

January took little comfort in the words.

Shaw said nothing, his elbows on the rail, his eyes on the low white American houses of Carrollton and the dark-green fields of sugar cane just visible beyond the levee. He had been nearly as silent on the return journey as he had been outbound, though his quiet had a different quality to it: weariness beyond speech. But as they'd come into the sticky green monotony of sugar country, the endless fields of cane readying for the harvest, the matte walls of cypress bearded with Spanish moss, he had begun to speak again about the city that had been his home for eight years: were the French creoles and the Americans blaming one another for the panic? (*Probably*). Had any of its gambling parlors been put out of business by the bank crash? (*I wouldn't bet on it*, January had replied.) The gluey heat of the summer still smothered the

362

lowlands, and as the small sternwheeler came in sight of the pastel houses of the French town, the gray gravely slope below the levee where other small steamboats were pulled up at the wharves, January found himself remembering that before leaving the town in April, Shaw had given up his boarding-house room on Girod Street, and so had nowhere to go when he stepped ashore.

With his long hair lank on his shoulders and his two rifles slung on his back, he must look very like he had in 1829, when he'd come down-river with his two brothers and a load of hogs, fleeing the hills that were called by all the Dark and Bloody Ground. Seeking justice and a different life.

The *Deborah T.* was poled and hauled to the docks, which would have seemed fairly lively to any who didn't know the city as January did. As they came down the gangway in the hot twilight that whined with mosquitoes, January said, 'Come for supper,' something he had never offered to the policeman before. Hannibal, though undoubtedly welcome at Kentucky Williams's saloon and bawdy house in the Swamp, would – January reflected – probably do better not to try to cadge sleeping room in its attic at this time of the evening. So the three of them walked up Rue Esplanade together, January's heart pounding faster and harder as he calculated and recalculated how close to her time Rose was, and the dangers a woman faced bearing children.

How could I have left her? How could I have done this to her—?

363

The money belt around his waist felt like a penitential cincture of spikes. Pictures flashed through his mind as if he hadn't seen them, dreamed them, for months: the house shut up and dark, the horrible race to Olympe's house for news of her ... if Olympe was even alive, after the fever seasons of the summer... (She had been in August, Rose had written, and her daughter Zizi-Marie was being courted by a tailor...)

In the worst of his dreams, Olympe's house, too, was closed up, or already sold to strangers...

Quiet as the town was, in the brazen heat, it felt strange to see so many people. Crowded. The houses seemed close together after the wind-combed distances of the Plains. They seemed small, too, as if like Gulliver he could knock them over accidentally with a careless elbow. After the mountains, all the world seemed achingly flat, and the reek of mildew, sewage and smoke felt new and harsh in his nostrils. Lights glowed in French windows through the blue twilight. Behind shut jalousies, shadows moved, and he heard friends' laughter and some-one playing the piano, music he had not heard in half a year. He was aware of Shaw and Hannibal talking behind him, and it was as if they spoke Chinese; not a word they said penetrated his mind through the pain of anxiety, of hope, of fear.

Lights in the big Spanish house, golden striped rectangles in the indigo dark.

To hell with them, January thought and broke into a run.

'I'm sorry,' said Olympe, who was standing on the porch to catch the night breeze, 'Rose decided you weren't coming back and has married a plumber.'

'Olympe—!' Dominique – January's youngest sister, beautiful as ever in lacy white – tapped Olympe's arm sharply with her fan.

The world remade itself, fell back into place with a sense of almost physical jolt. Then from inside the house, January heard the cry of a child. And his heart turned to light within him, like the exploding of a star.

He thrust his way past his sisters, through the French doors into Rose's bedroom. She was propped on the bed in the lamplight with her silky walnut-brown braids spread around her and the most perfect, the most beautiful, the strongest and rosiest and most magical baby ever born at her breast.

January's mother sat in the chair at her bedside. Dominique's maid Thérése was preparing a little bed in a basket. The room still held the faint echoes of birth smells, of blood and sweat, and as January dropped to his knees beside the bed Rose smiled at him, with a kind of sleepy acceptance that *of course* he would walk through the door at this hour. His mother said, 'Hmnph. It's about time you showed up, Benjamin.'

January put his arms around Rose and the infant and laid his face beside hers on the pillow. *Thank you, God; thank you God thank you God thankyouthankyouGodthankyouGod* ... He felt both as if he couldn't breathe, and as if all he could do was breathe the scent of them, the

365

peace of this room, forever. *I didn't die and they didn't die and I have two hundred dollars here around my waist...*

He felt her stroke his hair. 'Journeys end in lover's meetings,' she said and kissed his forehead. And then, as her fingers touched the new-healing scar above his hairline, 'Benjamin, did you get scalped?'

'Yes,' he said. 'Well, almost.'

'Show-off. You came back just in time.' She smiled at him as he brought his head up to kiss her hand, her lips, the baby's downy head. 'I was going to name him Polycrates Ishbosheth, but now you're here, you can think of something.'

'You were going to call him nothing of the kind!' protested Dominique, coming through the French door. The room was suddenly filled with people: Hannibal and Therese and Rose's friend Cora and Olympe – astounding to see Olympe in the same room with their mother – and Olympe's husband Paul, all beaming, as if the world had been suddenly healed and made well. Even Shaw, standing with one bony shoulder leaned on the French door out on to the gallery, seemed for the first time in half a year to relax, looking on this gathering of family and friends not his own, this quiet place of lamplight and new life and love. Rose drew her shawl over her breast and the baby's tiny face. January had seen, and had in fact delivered, hundreds of babies, but this child was different.

My child. Rose's child.

My son.

He wanted to shout or laugh or burst into tears.

366

The world would be different from now on.

'I thought Tiberius sounded strong,' went on Dominique, 'but Olympe says it's too fancy; Maman says it should be Denis, for M'sieu Janvier—' Dominique's father, who for many years had been their mother's protector.

'Of course it should be Denis,' snapped their mother, as if the matter were self-evident.

Olympe rolled her eyes. Unusually for Olympe, she didn't make her usual sarcastic comment. So great was the joy of the hour that it would mellow even her.

'What's wrong with calling him Benjamin?' asked Olympe's husband Paul.

'If you don't mind –' through the gathering of friends and family, of the people who'd made it possible for him to live again after Ayasha's death, January looked across at Shaw, alone between lamplight and darkness – 'and with your permission, sir, I'd like to name him John.'

'Maestro,' said Shaw, after a moment's startled silence, 'thank you. I – an' my brother – would be most honored.'